He's
Cancelled

BOOKS BY SOPHIE RANALD

Out with the Ex, In with the New
Sorry Not Sorry
It's Not You, It's Him
No, We Can't Be Friends
Just Saying
Thank You, Next

SOPHIE RANALD

He's Cancelled

Bookouture

Published by Bookouture in 2021

An imprint of Storyfire Ltd.
Carmelite House
50 Victoria Embankment
London EC4Y 0DZ

www.bookouture.com

ISBN: 978-1-80019-653-7
eBook ISBN: 978-1-80019-652-0

For Lizzie and Charlie – good neighbours even before we got a good fence.

Chapter One

Archie had been my boyfriend for just over a year, which was more than long enough for me to have learned that – although he was a wonderful person and my ideal man in almost all ways – romance was not his strong point.

I got my first hint of this the first time I slept over at his. I'm no diva and it's not like I was expecting him to serve me breakfast in bed, featuring smoked salmon and vintage champagne with freshly squeezed orange juice served on a silver tray, rosebud in a vase optional. But he woke me up by bringing me a cup of tea, brewed for so long the spoon was practically standing up in it, and a bowl of soggy cornflakes – which I wouldn't have minded a bit, except he tripped over my shoes and sent a tidal wave of cold cereal all over the duvet, the pillows and me.

Our first anniversary – well, technically the anniversary of our first date – passed unmarked because Archie's sister Poppy had just announced that she was having a baby and I was working late. A couple of days later, Archie said, 'Blimey, Nat, you know we've been together more than a year?' and I said, 'You'd better watch your step or this is going to start getting serious.'

And when it did get serious – serious enough for me to move into Archie's flat, anyway, which in today's world is about as much of a commitment as signing your names in your commingled blood on the front page of the family bible – Archie marked the occasion by giving me a cordless battery-powered screwdriver. And when I suggested opening a bottle of fizz to celebrate, he said he'd be right there just as soon as he'd finished assembling our Ikea chest of drawers with said screwdriver, which had clearly been a gift for himself more than for me.

So, one Saturday in early November, a bleak, drizzly day with a cutting wind blowing hard enough to take the skin off your face, Archie's suggestion for how we might spend the afternoon took me entirely by surprise.

'Fancy watching some telly, Nat?' he asked.

I looked up from my phone, to which I'd been glued following the latest developments in the high-profile spat between the wives of two footballers, and said, 'Sure. Do you want to want to watch the *MasterChef* final?'

'Nah,' Archie said. 'I thought we might watch *Love Actually*.'

'Really?' I heard my voice rise incredulously and managed not to ask who the hell he was and what he'd done with my boyfriend.

'Yeah, why not?' he said. 'And I could make some hot chocolate with Baileys in it.'

'Hot…? Okay. Sure. Sounds great.'

I flicked the button on the remote control and shifted up on the sofa, but I wasn't looking at the screen. I was watching Archie as he frothed milk in a pan, grated actual chocolate into it, warmed two tall glass mugs in the microwave, added generous glugs of cream liqueur and arranged some posh shortbread – which I couldn't recall either of us buying – on a plate.

I was thinking, *This is the kind of shit guys do when they're softening you up to break bad news.* Had Archie shrunk yet another of my jumpers by putting it on a boil wash, and was he about to fess up and beg forgiveness? Was Craft Fever, the artisan beer shop Archie had opened on the high street a year before, about to go bust, bringing his life's dream crashing to the ground, sending a hefty loan from the local council and an even heftier one from his mum and dad down the tubes, and leaving us in debt we'd have to sell the flat to repay? Had he invited his family to spend Christmas at ours?

But Archie carried the tray over to the coffee table quite calmly, put it down and handed me my drink.

'Here,' he said, 'put your feet on my lap and I'll tickle your ankles.'

I'm a physiotherapist and I give a killer massage, but nothing in the whole world was as relaxing as Archie's ankle tickles. He had me right there. I kicked off my trainers and put my feet up, not caring that I was wearing silly socks with purple dinosaurs on them. I leaned my head back against the sofa cushions and sipped my creamy, boozy hot chocolate, half-focusing on the television as Archie flicked through the menus until he found *Love Actually*, and half-listening to the rain swishing against the windows.

It was already almost dark outside, and the flicker of the telly and the glow of the lamp over our heads, as well as the feel of Archie's warm hands and the warmth spreading inside me from the sweet, mildly alcoholic drink, made me feel pleasantly drowsy.

'Just as well we don't have to go outside,' I said. 'It's grim out there.'

'But it's the fireworks display in the park tonight.' Archie sounded almost alarmed. 'We said we'd go, remember? And then chilli at the Ginger Cat after.'

'Yeah, but…' I weighed up the options in my mind. Standing outside, being battered by wind and rain, mud soaking into my socks, versus staying warm and dry in our living room? A fireworks display, however spectacular, versus the fireworks there'd be on screen in the five episodes of *First Dates* we still had left to watch?

'You could wear your new coat,' Archie said.

'True.' The balance in my mind shifted a bit. The coat had been a gift from Archie a few days before – he'd clearly noticed me eyeing it longingly every time we walked past the new boutique on the high street and surprised me with it. It was bright yellow with a silvery-grey faux-fur collar and cuffs, and although it hadn't really been cold enough to wear it yet, it certainly was tonight.

'And I'll run you a hot bath, with that geranium oil stuff in.'

'Okay,' I said, slightly amazed that Archie even knew essential oils existed, never mind that I had a bottle of the stuff in our bathroom cabinet. 'We'll go. So long as you promise not to interrupt my bath to cut your toenails over the loo, like you did last time.'

And so, three hours later, Archie and I joined the throng of people snaking steadily up the hill towards the park, the sparkling lights of London gradually appearing over the horizon, shrouded in misty drizzle. In spite of the mud sucking at my shoes, my reluctance was forgotten, and I felt almost as eager as the little kids in front of me, who were waving sparklers and dashing ahead of their parents in their welly boots. Progress was slow in the crowd, but at last we made it through the gates and followed the path upwards.

'Shall we stop here?' I asked.

'Let's go a bit further.' Archie's hand was clasped around mine, and I could feel the warmth of his fingers through my woollen mittens. He led me further up the hill. 'We'll get a better view from here.'

His enthusiasm was infectious, and I was beginning to feel excited too, surrounded by the eager crowd and cosy in my jeans, jumper and new coat.

Archie took his hip flask out of his coat pocket. The flask was pewter and had his initials stamped on it. It had been a twenty-first birthday present from his uncle Ray, and Archie basically lived for occasions when he could use it, which were few and far between. The coat was a vintage tweed thing he'd found in a charity shop and put on whenever he wanted to look like the kind of person who wore tweed coats, which was a bit more frequently. He offered it to me.

'Rum?'

'Sloe gin. I know it's your favourite so I got some in especially.'

I took a sip and felt the fiery liquid make its way from my mouth to my stomach and then up to my cheeks. With it came another little tingle of alarm. Archie was lovely – more than lovely; I wouldn't have been with him otherwise – but this level of attentiveness, on a day that wasn't even my birthday or anything, was unheard of.

Live in the moment, Nat, I told myself. *Enjoy it.*

But my introspection was cut short by a bang and a fusillade of crackling pops as the first firework lit up the sky. Everyone around me gasped, and I heard Archie's gasp and my own along with them.

His hand squeezed mine, and when I turned to smile at him I could see his face illuminated by the violet sparks, his ginger beard and brown eyes and infectious grin transformed from familiarity into a handsomeness that almost took my breath away.

Then another firework filled the black sky and I looked away from Archie and lost myself in the display, watching as fountains of red, green, gold and silver light shot up into the night and then showered back down again, disappearing into nothing before the next bang and explosion of light.

There were fireworks that looked like ferns, fireworks that looked like smiley faces, fireworks that looked like love hearts, and one that looked vaguely like the logo of our local council, which made everyone laugh as well as gasp. But mostly there were just cascades of brilliant colour, each more spectacular than the last, filling the sky and filling my eyes until I lost track of everything except the spectacle and the feel of Archie's hand in mine.

I lost track of time too. I suppose the display must have gone on for half an hour or so, but it felt both like an eternity and only a few seconds. At last, an extra-big, extra-high burst of brilliance, like opening a magnum of champagne made of light, shot upwards and then drifted down into sudden silence, which lasted a few seconds until everyone broke into applause, laughter and chat.

Archie and I met each other's eyes, smiling, and then he bent his head and kissed me, his warm lips on my cold, damp skin sending a thrill of happiness and pleasure right through my body. When the kiss ended, he looked at me for a long moment, his face serious and questioning, as if there was something important he wanted to ask.

But he only said, 'Come on. We'd best get our skates on if we're going to be able to nab a table at the Ginger Cat. It's always rammed on Bonfire Night.'

I thought of the Ginger Cat's hot, crisp-skinned jacket potato, cooked over the coals on the barbecue and served with the pub's secret-recipe chilli con carne, deep brick-red and spicy enough to leave your lips stinging, and suddenly I realised the posh shortbread had been a long time ago. But the throng of people was moving slowly, the little children tired and cranky or super-hyped and uncooperative now that the excitement was over. Groups of teenagers were cracking open cans of cider and showing each other the videos they'd made of the display as they meandered back down the hill.

'We can only go as fast as the slowest people,' I pointed out. 'We'll have to take our chances.'

'No we won't,' Archie objected. 'We've got inside knowledge. Come on.'

And, still clasping my hand, he veered off the path and headed down the grassy slope towards the side gate to the park. The ground was uneven under my feet, muddy and slippery from the heavy rain, but I was wearing lace-up boots with grippy rubber soles and had spent enough time hillwalking when I was a student not to care.

'All right,' I said. 'Race you to the bottom.'

'Seriously?' Archie's face lit up in a grin.

'Nah,' I said. 'I'd win for sure. We'll go together.'

I gripped his hand more firmly and set off down the hill, at a gentle jog at first. But gravity and hunger spurred me on, and soon I was running, my strides growing longer and longer as my feet found their natural holds on the uneven ground. I glanced around at Archie and he flashed a grin at me, then turned away.

He's not looking where he's going, I thought, but then my attention returned to where I was putting my feet. The wind was icy against my face and the sky, empty now of flashes and sparks, whizzed above me in dizzying blackness. The grass was impossibly bright green in the darkness, and I could see the glimmering lights of the street growing closer and closer.

Then I heard Archie cry out, 'Woah!' and his hand slipped out of mine.

I skidded to a halt and turned around. He was on his bum on the grass, his coat rucked up around his chest, his arms and legs splayed out, divots of muddy grass pushed out around his boots.

'Shit. Are you okay?'

I could see what looked like tears on his face, but might only have been rain. Then I realised he was laughing.

'Oh my God. What a dick. I'm fine, just got half the park on my arse.'

I stretched out a hand and helped him to his feet. He took it and I tried to pull him up, only my feet slipped out from under me and I ended up on my bum on the soaking grass next to him, both of us laughing helplessly.

'Sure you're okay?' I asked, once I was able to speak again. 'Can you move your ankles? Any pain in your spine?'

'Chill with the *Rescue 911* stuff. I'm definitely expected to live.'

'Oh God, look, your hip flask fell out of your pocket. Have you got your keys?'

'Yeah, they're in my jeans pocket. But my phone…'

I took out my own phone and switched on the torch, getting up onto my now-muddy knees and swinging its light over the expanse of sodden grass.

'Got it. But wait – what's this?'

The brilliant beam from my mobile caught a glimmer of brightness deep in the mud, and I reached for it, feeling the wet ground soaking through my jeans.

'Here, give that to me,' Archie said.

'No, hold on. It's a ring. Someone must have dropped it. We'll have to take it to the police or something.'

'Nat, shut up for just a second.'

Archie crawled over to me and our hands met, sharing the circle of bright metal. I could see a diamond sparkling against my grubby glove, its brilliance undimmed by the darkness and mud.

'It's lovely,' I breathed. 'Someone will be really glad we found this.'

'Oh, for fuck's…' Archie began, and then he stopped and said, 'Nat. It's yours, if you want it. I bought it for you. I was going to ask you to marry me tonight. I was working myself up for a proper proposal when the fireworks were going off, but I bottled it. But since I'm on my knees anyway… Nat, I love you. You're the most incredible woman I've ever met and – well, will you?'

Like I said, Archie wasn't the most romantic of men. It didn't bother me, same as having soggy cornflakes chucked all over me hadn't. But in that second, with both of us on all fours in the mud, it was like the fireworks that had danced in the sky that night like a billion stars were all going off again in my heart.

'I'd better say yes before you change your mind,' I said.

*

Of course I was absolutely itching to tell someone about Archie's proposal. But I didn't ring my mum, because I was meeting her in a couple of days' time, as I did every Tuesday, and I wanted to see her face when she heard the news.

I didn't ring Lara, who was my best mate from university and now worked with me in the physiotherapy team at Queen Charlotte's, because she was on a Tinder date: if it was going badly, I'd feel like I was rubbing her nose in it, and if it was going well I might interrupt the flow. I couldn't text Precious, my other friend at work, because Lara would be hurt if Precious found out first.

So, in the end, the first person I broke the news to was my hairdresser. To be fair, my relationship with Tilly was pretty close, given we'd seen each other once a month for the past three years. I wasn't at all high-maintenance in most ways – I rarely painted my nails and hardly ever bothered with more than five minutes' worth of make-up – but my hair had become a Thing.

When I first moved to south-east London after getting the job at the hospital, I'd booked an appointment for a cut and blow-dry and, totally on a whim, had said the fateful words, *Actually, I fancy something different.* Tilly had got a glint in her eye, flexed her scissors and started cutting. The result was a haircut that – for the first time in my life – actually suited me: a blunt, choppy bob with a heavy fringe, tinted the colour of black coffee. It was a bit 1920s flapper and a bit Demi Lovato, and totally fabulous. The only problem was, its window of fabulousness was a short one. Any more than a few weeks and my natural mousy-brown roots would begin to emerge, the fringe would go straggly and the ends start to stick out sideways no matter how much I rolled a hot brush round them, and Demi Lovato would morph into Sideshow Bob.

So I spent a huge amount of time and money sitting at Tilly's station in It's a Snip, and although my mind sometimes boggled a bit at the excessiveness of it, it was worth it to have really great hair. And, over the course of our client–stylist relationship, I'd come to quite look forward to those ninety minutes on a Sunday morning when all I had to do was sit there, listening to Tilly chat away about her nan's colostomy and her boyfriend's unsuccessful DIY projects and the ongoing feud between her two cats, occasionally contributing a snippet of news of my own.

And this Sunday, as soon as I'd walked through the glass door, had a gown draped round my shoulders and been shown to a chair, I heard myself blurting out that I'd just got engaged.

'No way! Nat, that's amazing! Best news ever. You can tell me all about it while I put your colour on. And look at your ring! That's a proper rock, that is.'

I turned my hand so the diamond caught the light, throwing rainbows onto the ceiling of the salon and bouncing it off the mirror. The stone was big – maybe bigger than I'd have chosen myself, standing proud of the slender platinum band that embraced my finger. I wondered whether Archie's father had been involved in its purchase and realised that, of course, he must have been – Archie could never have afforded such a thing on his own.

But I pushed aside the flicker of unease that realisation brought and related the events of the night before, bigging up our headlong dash down the hill and Archie's tobogganing on the seat of his jeans for comic effect while she carefully brushed colour onto the roots of my hair.

When she was done, Tilly didn't ask me as she normally did whether I wanted a magazine to read ('Fashion or gossip today, Nat?'), but instead returned, unprompted, with a pile of wedding magazines.

'You'll want to have a flip through these then,' she said, and I discovered that, actually, I did.

I'd never given weddings much thought before. Of course I'd assumed that eventually, at some point quite far off in the future, marriage would be the logical next step. But Archie and I hadn't even been together that long, and although for almost all that time I'd lived with him in the flat his parents had helped him to buy, in my head it was still a newish relationship – still in the honeymoon phase, which surely meant it was way too soon to think about actual honeymoons.

But now I found myself irresistibly drawn to the glossy covers of the magazines. Each of them had a beautiful girl in a white dress on the cover. Each one enticed the reader to pick it up and discover the latest trends in veils, canapés, classic cars and pageboys' suits. I fanned them out on my lap, wondering which one to open first.

And then a cover line caught my eye.

All set to settle down? How to know if you're ready to level up your relationship.

Almost without thinking, I put the other magazines aside and opened that one. *Inspired Bride*, it was called. The first few pages were all adverts – double-page spreads, many in arty black and white, showing radiant women in designer dresses and handsome men in what I supposed must be cravats. There were ads for perfume and jewellery – extravagant circles of diamonds and simple solitaires, none of which, I thought smugly, were as pretty as the ring sparkling on the third finger of my own left hand.

But I flicked quickly through until I found the contents page, which told me the article I was looking for was on page 111.

Except it wasn't an article – it was a quiz.

He's gone down on one knee – and he makes you go weak at the knees. But are you truly ready to say I do? I read.

'Right, that's you cooked,' Tilly said. 'Come over to the basin and we'll take your colour off and give you a nice head massage, then do your cut.'

'Great, thanks.' Reluctantly, I set the magazine aside, then put my handbag down on top of it, just to stake a claim. What if some other newly engaged girl nabbed it and I never got to find out my score? It would, obviously, be high – I'd always been pretty good at passing tests – but still. For some reason I wanted quite badly to know.

After all, a year wasn't that long a time. Not at all. Archie's and my relationship had pretty much gone from nought to a hundred in just a few weeks, and now the pace of it was accelerating even further. But what if it was too fast, too soon? I knew I loved Archie and he loved me – I had no doubt about that at all. But what if I'd said yes to his proposal just because I'd been caught up in the excitement and surprise of the moment? What if I wasn't ready for marriage after all? I knew it was just a stupid quiz in a stupid magazine, but still I craved its reassurance.

I barely registered Tilly's questions as she washed my hair. Had we decided on a venue yet? Had we a date in mind? Was I going to have a hen do? The answer to all of them was that I really didn't have a clue, because it was too early to have thought about any of that stuff.

'We're having lunch with Archie's sister and her wife right after this,' I said. 'I expect she'll have lots of ideas.'

'Ah, lovely,' Tilly said. 'So nice to get both families involved in all the planning.'

Is it? Uninvited, a picture of Archie's mother giving me one of the sideways glances she specialised in, which always made me wonder if I had spinach stuck in my teeth or was wearing odd socks, appeared in my mind. *Is it really?*

Tilly swathed my head in a towel and led me back to my seat, and I was relieved to see the magazine was still there. Peeping out from underneath my bag, I could just read the words 'his family'.

There was no way I could start the quiz now, not while Tilly was snipping away at my fringe and telling me the story of her cousin's wedding, which had ended in a massive punch-up between the best man and the photographer. Apparently, when the father of the bride tried to intervene, he'd tripped over a tripod and landed face first in the cake. But there was no way I couldn't have just a little look, either.

I slid the magazine out from under my bag and glanced down at the page. There were well over a dozen questions, all with four options for answers. Standard stuff – and absolute rubbish of course, probably written by the work-experience girl in between checking her TikTok. But still…

You're dreaming of your big day, certain that you've found The One, and preparing to make a life-long commitment. But first, test your wedding-readiness with our quiz.

A drop of water from my hair fell onto the page, wrinkling the paper and smudging the print.

'Just tip your head back for me, please,' Tilly said, 'and uncross your legs. That's lovely. Yes, so it all ended with Jason going off to A&E in an ambulance and Tommy being carted off by the peelers. Talk about a day to remember! That won't happen to you, of course.'

'I really hope not. I expect we'll only have a small wedding anyway. We don't have much money and all these things...' I gestured down at the glossy magazine covers, with their promises of fairy tales come to life, 'look super-expensive.'

'Oh my word, you won't believe it. One of my other clients – I won't name any names, but she comes in here regular, same as you – she told me her wedding cost forty thousand pounds. Forty thousand!'

'That's a deposit on a house!' I squeaked.

'It did include the honeymoon, which was two weeks in a five-star resort in the Maldives. But still. Just look straight ahead for me.'

Tilly moved in front of me and pulled the ends of my hair down, checking that the left and right sides matched. Evidently they did, because she nodded in satisfaction and unhooked her hairdryer from under the counter. There was no talking after that, the roar of its motor drowning out the possibility of conversation. Soon she was done, whisking a big brush over my neck to get rid of stray hairs, smoothing serum over my hair and snipping off the odd strand that had escaped her scissors first time round.

'Fabulous,' I said, smiling at my reflection. 'It looks great, as always. Thank you so much.'

'Don't mention it. Chloe at the front desk will book you in for next time, and I'll see you in a few weeks.'

She bustled off and I stood up slowly, putting on my coat and tucking my phone back into my handbag. Then, surreptitiously, I tore pages 111 and 112 out of the magazine, folded the sheet of paper into quarters and put it in my bag too.

Tilly might have let me have the whole magazine if I'd asked, but I couldn't have been sure. I was fairly confident no one would miss the page I'd ripped out, and if they did Tilly wouldn't be blamed for it – but I tipped her an extra tenner, just in case.

Chapter Two

You're starting to share your big news with friends and family. What's their reaction?

A. No one's even slightly surprised – it would be quite nice if they were, actually! But I guess it's obvious we were meant to be together.

B. It's not news, exactly, because we've been talking about it for a while now; the engagement is just a formality.

C. They're happy for us, of course. But I do sometimes wonder if they think we could be rushing it a bit.

D. Um… there may have been some raised eyebrows. But haters gonna hate, and I've got a ring on my finger, so…!

'Honestly, I couldn't be happier for you two,' Archie's sister Poppy said, digging her fork into a Yorkshire pudding almost as big as her head. 'God, this place is such a gem, you are lucky to have it right on your doorstep. Our local's dead depressing, isn't it, Freya?'

'Grim,' her wife agreed, carefully removing a pea that had dropped onto their son Linus's head. 'It's all beige food that comes in catering packs and gets shoved in the deep-fat fryer until it's basically a heart attack on a plate.'

'Like the Ginger Cat used to be, before Alice took over,' Archie said. 'But you're right, it's great now. We could even have our wedding reception here, you know, Nat. They do private parties now.'

'And we could have the ceremony at the town hall,' I agreed. 'You know, keep it all really low-key and local. That would be amazing.'

'You'll be lucky, knowing our family,' Poppy said. 'If I were you, I'd get on a plane to Vegas, get married there and not tell anyone, like we did.'

'I still haven't forgiven you for that,' Archie teased. 'Seriously, my own sister, depriving me of the opportunity to see Elvis conducting a wedding ceremony.'

'You saw the video, though,' Freya argued.

'Not. The. Same.'

'Yeah, I know,' said Poppy. 'I do feel kind of bad about it, although it was totally amazing. But we knew that if we let Mum and Dad get involved, we'd have been up to our eyeballs in floral centrepieces and favours and crap like that before the ink was dry on the invitations.'

'And we'd have had to invite about a million of your parents' friends,' agreed Freya. 'I mean, I'm sure they're perfectly nice and everything, but…'

'But I had absolutely zero interest in sharing my special day with Trevor and Karen from the golf club.'

'Poor Trevor and Karen,' Archie said. 'You know how they love a good knees-up.'

'You're not serious, are you?' I asked. 'I know Archie's parents will be excited for us and everything, but they won't really want to invite their friends and stuff. Will they?'

'Just you wait,' Poppy said, pouring more gravy over her roast beef and taking a gulp of red wine. 'I love Mum and Dad to pieces, and Daisy too obviously, but when you get to know our family a bit better, Nat, you'll realise that they do like to get their own way.'

'I've known Archie long enough to have spotted that family trait,' I said.

'Oi! I won't have any of that kind of cheek from my missus.' Archie poked my shoulder with the handle of his fork, but I barely felt it; I was too busy enjoying the little glow of happiness I got when I heard him say 'my missus'.

'Of course, you could do what I did and get pregnant,' Freya said. 'Then you'd have the perfect excuse for getting the wedding over quickly.'

'Linus is adorable, obviously,' I said. 'But I think that's probably a bit extreme.'

'At least you and Archie could do it the easy way,' Poppy said. 'Not like us. Our mate Miguel had to… uh… deposit his semen—'

'Into a champagne flute,' cut in Freya, 'because, you know, you may as well do these things in style.'

'And then I had to use a syringe to—' Poppy went on.

'Stop!' Archie said. 'Seriously, there are some things I really don't want to picture my sister doing.'

I boggled at them all – I'd known that Linus must have been conceived using donor sperm, but no one had ever shared the details with me before. The semen was a given, of course, but the champagne flute was kind of extra, even by the McCoys' standards.

'Back to weddings,' I said hastily. 'We won't have to have a massive do, will we?'

'Don't say I didn't warn you,' said Freya. 'When you're doing the quickstep with Trevor in a massive meringue of a dress after months of stress—'

'And the whole thing's cost thousands of pounds,' cut in Poppy.

'And you've seen more of the florist over the past few weeks than you have of Archie—'

'Which is just as well, to be fair, because the two of you aren't talking since the disagreement you had over the colour of the best man's cravat—'

'And you've given up hours of your life you'll never get back working on the seating plan—'

'And when you type "wedding" into your phone it autocompletes with "regret"—'

'Oh, stop it, you two!' Archie interrupted. 'I know you're joking, but look at Nat's face. You're meant to be encouraging, not putting a massive downer on the whole thing before we've even started. There's sticky toffee pudding on the menu. Who's in?'

Kelly, the waitress, cleared our table and brought massive plates of steaming dessert, a jug of salted caramel sauce and a bowl of clotted cream, and we all dug in.

'Seriously, though,' Poppy said after a bit. 'Have you thought about how you're going to break the news to Daisy? Because she'll be made up for you, but at the same time...'

'Daisy is Daisy,' Archie said.

I watched as the two of them looked at each other and gave an almost imperceptible eye-roll. I knew Archie loved his younger sister just as much as his elder one, but I wished I had the same easy friendship with Daisy as I did with Poppy. Especially now, with Archie's family about to become my family, and his sisters my sisters – a prospect that was as daunting as it was exciting, given I'd never had a sibling of my own.

'Why do you think she might mind?' I asked. 'I mean, I know she's been single for a while and everything, but that's kind of her choice, isn't it? She's so pretty, she could easily have a different boyfriend every week if she wanted to.'

'You mean you don't know?' Freya asked. Linus had woken up and was bleating softly, and she eased her top open so he could attach himself to her breast. 'Come on, little chap, time for you to have some lunch too.'

'I was kind of waiting for Nat and me to be married before I revealed all the skeletons in the family closet,' said Archie.

'Don't scare the poor girl,' said Poppy. 'It's not that big a deal.'

'It is for Daisy,' said Freya.

'What is?' I asked. 'What happened?'

'Daisy was engaged,' Archie began. 'Before I met you, Nat.'

'To a boy called Donovan,' Poppy went on. 'They'd only been together about five minutes.'

'Five months,' Freya corrected.

'Yes, because Daisy was kind of on the rebound,' Archie said. 'After her childhood sweetheart, Jamie, decided to go and work on an oil rig in Alaska and broke her heart. They'd been together since they were, like, fourteen or something.'

'Wasn't there another bloke in between as well?' Freya asked.

Poppy stared hard into the distance, like she was thinking. 'Fidel! He was some sort of celebrity nutritionist. They got engaged too, but I think it was mostly for the Insta likes.'

'And he ended it after a few weeks,' said Archie. 'Or maybe she did, I'm not sure.'

'And then she met this Donovan and got engaged to him?' My head was spinning trying to keep track of it all.

'They were both way too young, if you ask me,' said Freya.

'Well, yes,' agreed Poppy. 'But you try telling Daisy that. Or any twenty-three-year-old, for that matter.'

'Or Mum,' Archie said, rolling his eyes again.

'God, yes,' Poppy said. 'If it had just been up to Daisy, she might have seen sense when Donovan proposed to her and waited a few more years, or suggested they try living together first or whatever. But no one had the chance to try and persuade her, because Donovan did the full "asking the parents for their daughter's hand in marriage" thing before he even popped the question.'

'And Mum went full mental right from the get-go, didn't she, Poppy?'

'She did. Right away, she decided Daisy was going to have the wedding to end all weddings, and Daisy got on board with it, and the two of them just egged each other on.'

'Remember when Jordan and Peter Andre got married? And she had that glass coach shaped like a pumpkin drawn by four white horses and her dress was so big he could hardly get near her?' Freya asked.

'Oh my God, of course,' I said. 'It was in *Hello!* magazine for months. I had a Saturday job in a hairdressing salon back then, sweeping up hair and washing coffee cups and stuff, and I used to spend my breaks looking at the pictures and thinking that was what my wedding was going to be like. I was sixteen, don't judge me.'

'Which,' Freya said, 'is why people shouldn't get married too young. You've got to grow up a bit and get that All Hail the Veil bollocks out of your system before you're allowed anywhere near an engagement ring.'

'Although to be fair, Mum's almost seventy and she hasn't got it out of her system yet,' said Archie.

'Especially given what happened with Daisy and Donovan,' said Poppy.

'What did happen?' I asked.

'Oh yeah, sorry, we went off topic. Like I said, Daisy and Mum made all these plans that seriously made Jordan's wedding look low-key.'

'The carriage wasn't glass, admittedly.'

'But there were four white horses. Daisy wanted palomino ones – you know, the ones that are kind of gold-coloured with white manes and tails – but they couldn't get any.'

'So she suggested dyeing some white ones.'

'But that idea got shelved, thankfully.'

'None of the other ideas did, though. Honestly, it was mental. She was going to have a second dress to change into for the evening do, like Kate Middleton, and everything had to be lilac and silver.'

'Mum even made the florist cut the stamens out of the flowers because they didn't match.'

'And she made poor Dad do the Dukan diet because his cummerbund wouldn't fit.'

'Dad said he was basically living on ham omelettes for weeks. And it would've been worth waiting for: there was going to be a cake made out of pork pies for the evening do and everything,' Archie said wistfully.

'But what happened?' I demanded, having watched the rapid-fire exchange between Archie and his sister like a spectator at a Wimbledon final.

'Bloody Donovan happened,' said Poppy. 'Or, to be more accurate, Donovan's bloody stag night happened.'

'They went to Prague,' Archie said. 'I mean, you can imagine. Five young lads, it was always going to get messy.'

'Young or not, lads or not,' Freya snapped, 'there's no excuse for that kind of behaviour. None.'

But what did he do? my mind screamed, but I was familiar enough with Archie's family by now to know they'd get to the point eventually. And besides, I was already aware that whatever end the story had, it wasn't going to be a happy one for poor Daisy.

'You're right, of course, babe, there isn't. None of us would have expected it from him, though. He'd always been so lovely and he did really seem to love Daisy.'

'But a guy who cheats on his stag do is going to cheat again, right?' Freya said. 'Especially one who's so indiscreet about it he gets caught bollocks-deep in a hen from Hartlepool in a nightclub toilet.'

'He said it was just a kind of final fling,' Archie said. 'And I think Daisy wanted to believe him.'

'But I set her straight,' said Poppy. 'If you're going into marriage with an attitude like that, you're not ready for it. End of.'

'So the wedding got called off?' I asked.

'That's right,' said Archie. 'All that money and effort and planning, and of course the wedding insurance wouldn't pay out because Daisy had changed her mind. Not that any of that mattered that much, in the grand scheme of things.'

'Poor Daisy. She must have been devastated.'

Poppy shook her head sadly at the memory. 'She was in pieces, bless her. Of course she was. I mean, with hindsight you could tell she'd had a lucky escape, and like I said they were both way too young to get married. But at the time she couldn't see that, at all.'

'I sometimes wonder if she can, even now,' said Freya.

'Is that why she's still single?' I asked.

'Pretty much. She swore off men at the time and she's never really dated since,' said Archie.

I thought of my sister-in-law-to-be, three years younger than me, stunning and bubbly and funny, if a bit high-maintenance. Okay, a lot high-maintenance – the woman had hair extensions, eyelash extensions, nail extensions and, for all I knew, deadline extensions. If those were a thing for minor Instagram influencers. But now I knew the whole story, I couldn't really blame her for feeling a bit insecure about herself. Who wouldn't, after going through so much heartbreak in just a few years?

'Well, at least if Archie cheats on me on his stag, there won't be all the hassle of calling off the wedding,' I said.

'What, you mean you'd marry me anyway?'

'Not a hovering bat-fuck,' I said. 'You'd be dumped so fast you wouldn't know what had hit you. But we're not going to have a massive wedding, so it would just be a question of cancelling the party here and telling you to pack your bags and not let the door hit your arse on the way out.'

Archie laughed and reached his hand over the table to me, and I took it, feeling the familiar warmth of his fingers and the still-unfamiliar pressure of the ring pressing into mine. A shaft of sunlight came through the window and lit up his face, making his red hair shine like burnished copper and his brown eyes glow like conkers.

'I'm not going to cheat on you,' he said.

'I know you're not,' I replied.

Shortly after that, Poppy and Freya left to take Linus home for his nap. Archie went up to the bar to settle the bill, and I took the sheet of paper I'd liberated from the hairdresser out of my handbag and unfolded it on the table.

You've started to share your news…

I scanned the four possible answers. It was kind of hard to say. What was puzzling was that, almost as soon as Archie had told Poppy he'd proposed to me, the conversation had moved away from us and on to his younger sister. That was fine with me – I'd never liked being the centre of attention. But it had been almost as if it wasn't about us at all.

Chapter Three

Cast your mind back to when you first met. Was it...

A. Love at first sight. We gazed into each other's eyes and a violin started playing somewhere (in my head?) and that was that.

B. Let's be honest, I just fancied the pants off him. All the love stuff came later.

C. A slow burn. I think it takes time to build mutual trust and respect, and you can't have love without those.

D. We couldn't stand each other! And the sparks are still flying but, you know, in a good way as well, mostly.

There were about a million things I loved about my job. Being a physiotherapist was all about helping people to get – literally – back on their feet, and I loved that. Seeing someone who just a few days before hadn't been able to stand, lying in bed in a haze of pain medication or, worse, in actual pain, walk off the ward wearing their own clothes and even make-up, ready to go home, gave me a massive thrill that hadn't diminished even after six years of doing the job.

I loved the frenetic bustle of the hospital ward, the sense of having to keep a whole bunch of balls in the air at once and make sure whoever needed to be helped to learn to use crutches or a walking frame or the stairs again was in the right place with the right person and the right equipment to do so. I loved the camaraderie with my colleagues: the drinks in the pub on Fridays and the cake in our office on Wednesdays.

But it wasn't all roses. I didn't love waiting for a bus in the rain at seven thirty in the morning, standing shivering under the inadequate shelter, my fellow commuters as pinched and glum as me. I didn't love when two buses came along at once and, jostled out of the way by a gaggle of queue-jumping schoolkids, I ended up on the one on which someone was eating fried chicken for breakfast. I didn't love Nisha, the nursing sister in charge of the orthopaedics ward, whose territorial attitude towards the patients she saw as hers made me think of a dragon guarding treasure. I didn't love my polyester uniform, which, since all hospitals are heated to approximately the temperature of the surface of the sun, made me sweat as soon as I put it on.

And, I realised on Monday morning as I peeled off my normal clothes in front of my locker and prepared to pull the hated blue uniform top on over my head, I was going to not love taking off my precious sparkly engagement ring every day before starting work.

I slid it off my finger and looked at it for a second. The diamond flashed in the harsh fluorescent light; the platinum band gleamed.

Although it was a perfect fit, there was already a slightly paler indentation on my finger where it sat.

What if I lose it somehow? I fretted. *What if I forget to put it back on this evening and it slips to the bottom of my locker and onto the floor and it's gone forever?*

Reluctantly, I tucked the ring into the change compartment of my purse – *What if I buy a Coke from the vending machine at lunchtime and put the ring into the slot instead of a pound coin?* – and slipped the purse into my backpack.

It would be okay, I told myself firmly. Rings didn't suddenly learn to walk – not even when surrounded by professionals whose job it was to help people do just that. I'd be able to put it back on at the end of the day, and soon I'd get used to this; it would become just another thing I did every day, like filling in patients' notes in the sacred Ward Book and eating last night's leftovers at my desk out of a plastic box while flicking through my Instagram and answering emails.

And anyway, there was no time to brood. I could hear feet hurrying past me along the corridor outside, laughter and snatches of conversation, and I knew the morning meeting was about to start. I tied my shoelaces, stuffed my bag into my locker and slammed it shut, then opened it again, took out my bag, checked that my ring was safe in my purse, and repeated the process again in reverse.

Then I turned away, and my own feet joined the hurrying throng, the rubber soles of my shoes squeaking on the non-slip flooring along with everyone else's.

'Good weekend?' Lara asked. 'Anything to report?'

'It was great,' I replied. 'Busy. We had lunch with Archie's sister yesterday.'

And Archie asked me to marry him. The words were crowding to burst out of my mouth, but I wanted to relish the moment – to have the chance to hug and squeal and show off my ring, not to blurt out my news in a rush as we hurried along a corridor before Nisha could tell us off for dawdling.

'How was your date?' I asked instead.

'Oh, you know.' Lara rolled her eyes. 'Okay, but zero chemistry. Meh. Your hair looks fab, by the way. I keep thinking I'm ready for a change but then I always bottle it and ask them to just trim a bit off the ends. Come on, we'll be late for the meeting if we don't get a wiggle on.'

I spent the next half hour perched on a plastic chair, a notebook in my lap, while the rhythm of the day took shape. Mrs Flint was going in for her hip replacement and would need to be seen by one of the physio team afterwards. Mr Patel would need to be coaxed into using his crutches. Mr Keating was due to be discharged, right after he'd completed his stairs assessment.

'And we have the complex repair of Mr Dawson's Saw fracture,' said Precious.

There was a collective intake of breath from the team. One of the first things I'd learned as a student was that orthopaedic surgeons regarded it as a badge of honour to be able to name an injury after themselves, and Mr Saw, the consultant in charge of our ward, was no exception. I'd also learned, in pretty short order, that consultants were the gods of the ward, and Mr Saw was no exception to that, either.

From my position at the rear of the room, I could only see the back of his head, his silvery hair framing a bald patch of dark skin. As a surgeon, he was one of the best in the country. As a doctor, he was endlessly empathetic, listening to his patients and reassuring them they were in the best possible hands. As a boss, he was downright terrifying.

I'd learned, though, that the best – indeed the only – way to avoid Mr Saw's laser gaze of disapproval (even though, at about five foot four, he had to direct it upwards at me, he still managed to be intimidating as hell) was to get on with my work as efficiently as possible. So I joined the stream of my colleagues as we made our way out of the room and on to the ward, and began my morning's work.

As always, managing to see the patients I needed to was a total juggling act. There was no point in trying to get Mr Patel on his feet, crutches or no crutches, until he'd had his pain medication. All the patients were cranky and uncooperative until the junior nurses had been round with the morning tea. Mrs Flint's operation was delayed and she wouldn't be back on the ward until after lunch.

So I spent the morning dashing around, negotiating with the nurses, trying to keep my notes up to date and snatching a coffee whenever there was a brief lull. Lara was a similar blur of activity, but my friend Precious, one of the senior nurses, seemed to glide around the ward like a swan, competent and unruffled, yet getting through a phenomenal amount of work.

The time seemed to slip by with alarming speed, as it always did, and it was the rumbling of my stomach rather than my watch that told me it was past midday and almost time for lunch. Also, I'd been bursting for a pee for the past hour but hadn't had time to stop what I was doing and dash to the loo. However, I wasn't going to get away that easily.

'Mr Keating's stairs assessment, Natalie.' Nisha had an unerring ability to remind you of something vital that needed to be done just when you were on your way to do something equally vital.

'I was just—' I began.

'We need the bed,' she said. 'Mr Saw wants him discharged this afternoon, and as you know perfectly well…'

'The stairs assessment has to be done first.' Reluctantly, I turned back. She was quite right, of course – after surgery, no patient could be allowed home until we knew that they could manage to get around safely. Sometimes this meant a complex multidisciplinary approach involving the installation of stair lifts and the combined efforts of the occupational therapy, outpatients and community nursing teams. But in the case of Mr Keating, it was more straight-forward. He'd bashed up his knee in a cycling accident, the surgery to repair it had gone smoothly, he'd done his exercises diligently, and all that remained was to ensure that he'd be able to get up and down the three flights of stairs to his flat on his crutches without tumbling to the bottom and breaking something else.

I thought of the lengthy form I'd have to complete detailing whether I'd observed Mr Keating on steps outside, inside or both; whether he needed one handrail or two; whether he led with his left or right foot and went forwards or backwards. It had to be done and I had to do it.

'Mr Keating?' Normally, I'd revert to calling patients by their first names after seeing them once or twice, but there was something about this particular patient that made me cling to formality. I approached my patient, who was sitting up in bed, a laptop perched on his plaster-encased leg. He was a good ten years older than me – more, probably – but strikingly attractive, with a kind of burning energy that had made his time in hospital particularly frustrating for him, but made him extra motivated to get out and back on the racing bicycle that had landed him in here in the first place.

'All right, Natalie? I've been looking forward to seeing you all morning.'

'I'm sure you have. I'm your ticket out of here, aren't I?'

'That and I like looking at your legs.'

Once again, I was reminded why I'd carried on calling him Mr Keating.

'Come along, let's get you on your feet and up and down some stairs,' I said briskly, ignoring his inappropriate comment.

Despite my bursting bladder and rumbling stomach, I conducted the assessment thoroughly, ticking all the boxes on the form and keeping up my best professional demeanour, despite his attempts to flirt with me.

'All done then?' he said at last.

'All done,' I confirmed. 'I'll let Sister know you're free to leave.'

'Thank you. Really, I appreciate everything you've done.' There was a new sincerity in his voice, and I felt a familiar glow of pride and satisfaction.

'Don't mention it.' I smiled – too warmly, I realised instantly, because my smile was returned with a leer and a wink.

'Any chance I could buy you a drink? You know, as a way of expressing my gratitude?'

No matter how often this happened to me, it never got any less awkward.

Except the one time. The time last autumn, when I'd been hurrying back from my break, my mouth still burning from the too-hot cup of tea I'd gulped down, and a voice behind me said, 'Excuse me?'

I'd spun around impatiently, because random members of the public oughtn't to have been wandering around the ward; if there was no one at the reception desk, they were to take a seat and wait, as the large, laminated sign quite clearly said.

Standing there in front of me was a man about my age, tallish and red-haired. His jeans had worn through on one knee and he was wearing brown lace-up canvas boots. A battered leather jacket was slung over the shoulders of his faded black T-shirt. All that was quite ordinary – and then he smiled.

It was the warmest, kindest smile I'd ever seen, and I'd felt my annoyance melt away instantly and my own lips and eyes smiling straight back.

'I've got an appointment for my rotator cuff tendonitis.' The man flexed his right shoulder, winced, and then his amazing smile was back in place.

'Nasty,' I sympathised. 'You're a plasterer, right?'

'And you're a psychic. I'm not actually, but I've just taken on a lease on a shop and I've been doing a load of the refurb work myself. I've been decorating the ceiling for the past few days, and...' He winced again.

It was none of my business; I had work to do, but I found myself asking, 'What kind of shop?'

'Craft beer and artisan gin.' He grinned. 'It's just on the high street, next to the Nag's Head pub.'

'Nice. I love gin. Gin and tonic's my fave but it's all good – gin gimlet, mulled gin, dry gin martini… Mmmm.'

'I'll make you one, as soon as my shoulder's up to shaking cocktails again.'

This reminder of what he was actually doing in the hospital made me gather my professional demeanour again, rather than banging on about gin like I had a substance abuse problem.

'Anyway, this is the orthopaedics ward. You'll be wanting outpatients, two floors down.'

'Outpatients. Gotcha. Sorry to bother you.'

'It's no bother.' I hesitated. I'd probably never see this man again, but I did want to see that smile, one last time. 'My name's Nat.'

'Archie.' There it was – like a blaze of sunshine.

'Come on,' I said. 'Hospitals are like the Crystal bloody Maze. I'll show you where to go.'

By the time we reached the second floor, we were chattering away like old friends, and I'd given him my number – slightly guiltily, even though I knew Nisha was safely occupied two floors away and would never find out.

I tugged my attention away from the memory, and away from the quiz question that I guess had partly awoken it, and back to Mr Keating. Arranging to see Archie again had been one thing – he wasn't my patient and never had been (and, let's face it, it had been lust at first sight, like option B in the quiz said). But this was something entirely different.

'That's very kind of you,' I said firmly, 'but I'm going to have to say no.'

'Why? Got a boyfriend, have you?'

'Actually a fiancé.'

'Ah, fair dos. Can't blame me for trying.'

I returned him to his bed and headed off the ward, relieved. But I heard hurrying feet behind me and Lara rushed to join me.

'Did I hear you say fiancé?' she demanded. 'Don't tell me Archie proposed?'

'He did. I was going to tell you but it's been so hectic all morning.'

'That's amazing!' she squeaked. 'Oh my God, I can't believe it!'

'I couldn't quite believe it either. It's not like we've even been together that long. You'll be my bridesmaid, won't you? You and Precious?'

'Did you say Precious? And bridesmaid?' On her rubber-soled Crocs, Precious's approach had been entirely silent, but her voice was raised in excitement.

'You heard right.' We pulled one another into a group hug.

'Oh my God,' Precious said. 'I'm so glad I don't have to worry any more about being boring about my wedding. I see my mates' eyes glaze over when I talk about it and there's still six months to go. We can be boring together, can't we, Nat?'

Chatting and giggling, we made our way to the break room. I looked at my friends' faces, lit up with happiness for me and Archie, and I said the word again to myself: *Bridesmaids*.

For the first time, it felt like planning a wedding was going to be a whole lot of fun.

*

'Oh sweetie!' Mum brushed a smudge of mascara from under her eye. 'I can't believe it. I can't. My baby girl. And Archie – you know how much I've always liked him. I couldn't have wished for a nicer son-in-law. Let's open the emergency prosecco, right away.'

I watched as she wafted over to the fridge, pulled it open and produced a bottle of sparkling wine. Mum's emergency prosecco had been a thing for as long as I could remember – to be honest, I suspected that her life with me had been pretty tough for a really long time, and the knowledge that she could have that one indulgence – if something wonderful were to happen or just to stop her life feeling so relentlessly un-wonderful – must have kept her going at times.

When I brought home a praise-filled school report or Mum got a pay increase at work; when the washing machine repair guy pointed out that the appliance had come unplugged at the wall and was otherwise in perfect working order; when the downstairs neighbours who smoked weed at all hours and blasted Mariah Carey power ballads on their stereo finally moved: out came the emergency prosecco.

Equally, the arrival of a higher-than-usual council tax bill, my sixth-form boyfriend dumping me the day before I left for university, and Mum discovering her first grey hairs were all marked by the pop of a cork and the hiss of bubbles hitting a glass. Sometimes the bottle would stay unopened in the fridge for months as our lives ticked uneventfully on; sometimes two fresh bottles were needed in the space of a week.

'He sends his love,' I said. 'He's sorry he couldn't come this evening, but, you know, the shop…'

'It's still going well, then?' Mum asked.

'It is. It's taken a year but it's starting to make a profit, and apparently that's a real achievement for a new business.'

'He's got a good head on his shoulders,' Mum said approvingly. 'Even if he does tend to stick it in the clouds.'

I laughed. 'He does, I know. But he said this would be a success and he was right. He works really hard at it and it really seems to make him happy. And… well, that's even more important to me now, I guess.'

'Of course it is.' Mum eased the cork out of the bottle and splashed fizzy wine into two glasses, then handed one to me, plonked a bowl of Twiglets on the coffee table and sat down on the sofa, cross-legged so she was facing me.

'Now,' she said, 'tell me all about it. How did he pop the question? What did you say? Have you started thinking what sort of wedding you want? Because you do know, don't you, sweetie—'

A shadow of worry had crossed her face.

'Mum,' I interrupted her, 'whatever happens, no one's going to expect you to pay anything at all towards our wedding. Don't even think about it. Archie and I are still basically skint because of the mortgage payments on the flat and all the stuff with the shop – and we wouldn't ever have been able to afford the flat if Archie's parents hadn't helped him with the deposit. So we're going to have to cut our coats to suit our cloth, as you always used to tell me.'

'When we were having boiled eggs and soldiers for dinner for the fourth night in a row.' Mum sighed. 'Happy days! But we got through it all right, didn't we? And now look at you.'

'I know, right? Marrying the son and heir of McCoy Construction, only Archie didn't want to be the heir.'

'And just as well, otherwise he'd never have opened that lovely shop that makes him so happy.'

'And so broke. So honestly, Mum, we won't have a massive wedding. I don't even want one. A quick registry office ceremony and a reception at the Ginger Cat will be absolutely perfect. I even saw on Instagram – there's a wedding inspiration account I've started following – one bride wore a dress that cost fifteen pounds from Primark and she looked amazing.'

Alarm flashed across Mum's face. 'Primark? Isn't that going a bit far?'

'Maybe.' I tried to imagine Archie's mum's reaction to me marrying her son in a Primark dress, but fortunately failed. 'But it's all a long way off, anyway. There's no rush for us to get married. Lots of people spend absolutely ages planning it, like two years or more.'

'Of course there isn't. But there is one thing, Natalie.'

Again, that cloud of worry had drifted across her face.

'What's that?'

'Your grandpa. I don't want to worry you – and there really isn't anything to worry about – but he is eighty-three and he's not as strong as he was. Since Mum's death he hasn't been the same, you know, and I do sometimes wonder how long he'll be able to live independently for. And since you're his only granddaughter, I know he'd want…'

Her words petered out and she took a gulp of prosecco and a handful of Twiglets.

'Is he okay?' I felt a sudden hollowness inside me, a lurch of fear. 'He hasn't been diagnosed with anything serious, has he?'

Mum shook her head. 'Sweetie, he's just old. You know better than anyone what it's like, working in a hospital. People get frail and they need more support. And health can decline quickly at that age. I'd hate him to not be able to enjoy your big day, that's all. You know how he loves a party.'

I remembered Grandpa hovering over me with a camera while I blew out candles on cakes, him hitting the snowball cocktails at eleven sharp on Christmas morning, him trying to do the moonwalk at my eighteenth birthday party. It was unthinkable that I could get married without him there.

'Well,' I said. 'That's that settled then, right? We'll have to get our skates on. What do you reckon, April next year? That would give us almost six months to plan it and that's got to be enough, surely? I mean, Prince Harry took less time than that.'

'Especially if you don't want anything elaborate,' Mum said. 'I don't want to push you into something that's not right for you.'

'You're not. Remember, quick civil ceremony, sausage rolls down the pub, off-the-peg dress? That's all I want. You hear about people going into tens of thousands of pounds of debt for these massive flash weddings and that makes me feel a bit sick, to be honest. We'll keep it simple. I'll talk to Archie.'

'And Archie will talk to his parents, if he hasn't already.'

'We're going round there for lunch on Sunday.'

Mum met my eyes for a second, then she got up and topped up our glasses.

'I've made that lentil stew you like for tea. Shall I set the table or shall we eat on our laps?'

I kept a careful smile on my face. Cooking had never been Mum's strongest point and the addition of ketchup to her lentil stew made it taste of not much else, even though she claimed to vary the recipe depending on what vegetables were in season. But she was my mum and I loved her and I'd never, ever let her know that.

'Laps,' I said, 'and we can watch the *Great British Bake Off*.'

And I could imagine I was eating a showstopper cake, feather-light and heaped with buttercream, and maybe the sheer power of my thoughts would make the lentils taste less like something you'd use to spackle a wall, if you worked for Archie's dad's construction company.

'I suppose Yvonne McCoy will want to wear a hat,' Mum mused a few minutes later, as we forked up our dinner.

'To the wedding, you mean?'

Mum laughed. 'No, sweetie, to weed her garden. Of course to the wedding.'

'I expect she will,' I said. In fact, I'd have laid money on it. Archie's mum was a woman who didn't believe in doing things by halves, and I suspected persuading her to go along with my idea of a low-key wedding would be challenging enough without trying to rein in her sartorial choices.

'And I suppose that means I'll have to, too.'

'Honestly, Mum, you'll look amazing whatever you wear.'

It was true. My teenage years had been blighted by having a mother who was so much younger and prettier than all my friends', by us being mistaken for sisters on more than one occasion, and by overhearing a group of the sixth-form lads referring to her as 'that MILF in the ripped jeans', which was just the most cringe thing ever. Fortunately, I was old enough to be over all that now.

'God, look at the piping on that cake,' Mum said. 'Seriously, where do people get the time to practise that stuff? I suppose we'll have to think about a cake for you, Nattie. And flowers and everything.'

'Mum! Please please believe me, I don't want a massive fuss. We can buy a cake at M&S and the florist across the road from Archie's shop will do me a bunch of roses or something. Whatever's in season in April. I haven't got a clue.'

'Tulips?' Mum suggested. 'I haven't got a clue either. Never having done this wedding malarkey before.'

'We'll work it out,' I assured her, although I couldn't help feeling a stab of guilt.

Because, although she'd never, ever say as much to me, over the years I'd managed to figure out that the reason for Mum never having done this wedding malarkey – for herself, that is – was me.

She'd been just twenty-two when she had me, and I'd been what she described as a 'surprise', but in my darker moments I wondered if the word 'mistake' might have been more fitting. Because the years of my childhood had been tough for Mum – tough and, I imagined, lonely, since my father had been out of the picture since I was small. She'd scraped by, working her arse off in low-paid jobs to try and make sure I could have the nice things my friends had – new clothes, holidays sometimes (even if they were spent camping in a tent that leaked), even a couple of terms of ballet lessons before we both admitted with relief that I was too shit at it for it to be worth carrying on.

And she'd stayed single, for almost all the time, in spite of being young and pretty and a total catch, because of me.

As if she'd read my mind, Mum said, 'It'll be a bit strange, I suppose, there being no father of the bride.'

'No one will care,' I said. 'I promise. I certainly don't – I've got you.'

She reached over and patted my knee. 'Thank you, sweetie. But maybe…'

'Maybe what?'

'Nothing. Just a daft thought I had.'

'Go on.'

Mum poked her food with her fork but didn't raise it to her lips. 'Maybe it is time I started thinking about… you know… putting myself out there a bit.'

'Are you saying you think you want to meet someone? To be your plus-one at my wedding?'

'Of course not. Well, maybe. But it'll be your day – it's not about me. Just, you know, wouldn't it be weird if someone were to come along, between now and then?'

'If six months is long enough for me to plan a wedding, it's definitely long enough for you to find a date for it.'

'Ah, no. I'm not going to go looking. I'm too old and bitter and cynical to do online dating or any of that stuff. And I'm too set in my ways for anyone to want to date me, anyway. Imagine some poor bloke loading the dishwasher wrong or clicking his fingers at a waiter or whatever, perfectly innocently, and I'd have to dump him. I just wouldn't be able to handle it.'

I laughed. 'Fair enough. But you should keep an open mind, because you never know – Mr Perfect could be anywhere.'

And then I thought of the quiz. Mum was almost fifty and she knew she wasn't ready to settle down with a man. And I, at twenty-seven, was planning to make promises to Archie, who I'd known for only a bit more than a year, that were meant to last forever.

'What are you looking so serious about, Nattie?' Mum asked.

'It's just… Six months isn't very long, is it?' I could hear the uncertainty in my voice. 'And Archie and I haven't been together that long. It all feels quite quick and a bit… you know. A bit scary.'

It was Mum's turn to look serious. 'I don't want you to feel rushed into anything, not by me or by Archie or anyone else. If you don't think you're ready for this, you need to press pause, Grandpa or no Grandpa.'

'I think I am ready. Honestly, I do. But I don't one hundred per cent know. How do people know? Or do they?'

'Oh, sweetie.' Mum pulled me across the sofa into a hug, sending the discarded bowl of Twiglets flying. 'I wish I could answer that, but I can't. Only you can.'

Chapter Four

All relationships involve compromise. How does that work for you two?

A. That's not something we've ever really had to do. We just agree on everything – it's like we're the same person!

B. We don't always agree on things, obviously. But we talk through it and find a solution we're both happy with.

C. Um… To be completely honest, I sometimes feel like it's always me who gives ground. But it's worth it – isn't it?

D. Compromise? As if. I know my own mind and if he doesn't agree, he knows better than to argue.

'The Gables, mate.'

The taxi swept up the gravel drive leading to my future in-laws' home. As always, I felt like we ought to be arriving in an Aston Martin, or possibly a horse-drawn carriage. The house was huge, with cream-coloured columns on either side of the scarlet front door and a perfect circle of manicured lawn around which the driveway curved.

'Thanks a lot,' Archie said. 'We'll be sure to give you the five-star rating.'

He felt guilty, I knew, about the half-hour drive from the station and the fact the driver had no chance of getting a fare back. I would have felt guilty too, only I was too nervous.

We scrambled out of the car, our shoes crunching on the gravel, and I checked for the hundredth time that the shining circle of platinum on my finger was hidden by my fluffy wristwarmers. Breaking the news to his parents was a task I'd delegated to Archie, and there was no way I was going to let the ring reveal our engagement before he did.

Archie pressed the button next to the door and I heard electronic chimes sounding throughout the house. There was a long wait – there usually was, because the size of the place meant it took ages to get from anywhere to anywhere else – but at last I heard the click of heels and the door swung open.

'Here you are, loves.' Yvonne swept first Archie and then me into an Opium-scented embrace. She was wearing snake-effect leather jeans, a cream silk blouse and pointy gold ankle boots. Her ash-blonde hair was sleekly blow-dried and diamond studs sparkled in her earlobes. Although she was nearer seventy than sixty, she looked way younger. I'd never seen her without a full face of make-up and I knew without having to check that her lipstick would have left a perfect imprint on my cheek, twin to the one on Archie's.

The only difference was she'd kissed her son with genuine warmth, whereas I couldn't help feeling as if the scarlet mark left by her lips on my own cheek was icy cold.

'Come in! You must be freezing, you poor things. We're all in the lounge.'

At least the cold gave me an excuse not to take off my gloves just yet, although the house was toasty warm as always. We followed Yvonne down the long marble-floored hallway, which was lit by a chandelier and had a round table at its centre, on which a huge arrangement of lilies stood, filling the air with fragrance.

'Daisy and Poppy are here already,' Yvonne chattered on. 'Poppy's just been out for a run but she promised she wouldn't be long. Would you like to freshen up after your journey?'

I thought of the wonderfully luxurious guest loo, with its Molton Brown handwash, piles of fluffy white towels and heated toilet seat, where I could quite happily spend the entire afternoon. But then I realised that emerging from the washroom with gloves on would look incredibly weird.

'I'm fine, thanks,' I said, and kept hold of Archie's hand, feeling the still-unfamiliar pressure of the ring on my finger.

'We'll go through to the lounge then,' Yvonne said, and led the way through a white-painted panelled door into the vast sitting room. My boots sank into the carpet and I hoped there wasn't any mud on them. 'Would you like tea or coffee before dinner?'

I'd have liked something a bit stronger to brace myself for breaking our news, but I didn't want to ask.

'Just a glass of water, please,' I said.

'I'd love a tea, thanks Mum,' said Archie. 'All right, Daise?'

Daisy unfolded herself off the white leather sofa, where she'd been engrossed in a copy of *Tatler*, and came over to hug us both. Archie's sister was the spit of her mother: spray-tanned and highlight-and-contoured and lip-fillered; the kind of slim that stays that way through rigid self-denial and a personal trainer. She was wearing a white jumper dress with fur (or, I hoped, faux-fur) trim around the cuffs and hem, and caramel-coloured, thigh-high suede boots.

'How's my favourite brother? You're looking well, Nat – love your hair.'

We sat down and chatted a bit about how our weeks had been. I could see Archie casting hopeful glances towards the door, wishing that his father and older sister would make an appearance soon so he could get on with breaking the news to his family. Surreptitiously, I eased off my gloves and hid my left hand under my right thigh.

'And here's Poppy,' Yvonne said.

Unlike her mother and sister, Poppy hadn't dressed up for Sunday lunch with the family. She was still in her gym kit, strands of damp hair escaping from her ponytail, a grey hoodie open over her vest top.

'Hello! Freya and Linus are up in Yorkshire with her parents. She sends love.' She bounded over to us, eager as if we were long-lost friends, even though we'd had a drink together in the Ginger Cat just a week before. I jumped up to greet her.

'Don't hug me – I'm all sweaty,' she protested, taking hold of my wrists.

'Natalie! What is that on your finger?' Yvonne demanded.

Suddenly all their eyes were on me and I felt myself blushing. Archie loved me; he wanted to marry me. Surely his family would be happy for him? But, however kind they were to me, I always had the sense I wasn't quite what they'd expected for their precious only son.

'I…' I began, and then tried again. 'Archie…'

'I asked Nat to marry me,' Archie said. 'And, believe it or not, she said yes.'

'What's that?' Archie's dad burst into the room. 'Did I hear right? You going to make an honest man of him then, Natalie?'

'Awww, you two!' Poppy exclaimed. 'That is just the best news ever. I'm so made up for you.'

'Well,' Yvonne said. Was it my imagination or could I see a muscle twitching in her jaw, as if she was grinding her teeth? 'This is certainly a surprise.'

Daisy was staring at us, wide-eyed. 'Congratulations,' she said at last, so quietly I could barely hear it.

'Now,' Yvonne said, 'if everyone would like to take their places in the orangery, I'll plate up, and we can talk about plans while we eat.'

We all trooped back out into the hallway and through to the conservatory. Archie's dad was slapping him on the back, full of pride. Poppy was chattering away, making me retell every detail of Archie's proposal, especially the bit when he fell over in the mud. Yvonne whisked off into the kitchen, and I could hear the clink of plates.

Daisy hesitated, glanced at me and then followed her mother.

For once, I was glad of Yvonne's portioning habits. The first time I'd been introduced to Archie's parents, it had been his birthday dinner and Yvonne had cooked a beef stew with buttery mashed potato – one of my favourite meals in the world. But when she brought the plates to the table, I noticed there was something strange going on. Archie's plate and Keith's were piled high with food, mostly meat and potatoes, with a few broccoli florets squeezed onto the side of the plate.

In contrast, Yvonne's own plate, Poppy's, Daisy's and mine were reasonably heavy on the green veg and light on everything else. There was a neat little quenelle of mash on each of them topped with a puddle of sauce containing a homeopathic amount of meat.

'Oh, for God's sake, Mother,' Poppy had complained. 'Will you ever stop with your penis portions? I'm starving. How come Archie gets loads and I get nothing?'

Yvonne had bridled. 'Well, some of us are watching our figures. Aren't we, Natalie?'

And I'd been too shy to say that actually I was starving too and mashed spuds were a lot higher up my priority list than fitting into size-eight jeans, so I'd smiled politely, said it looked delicious and tried to eat slowly enough not to be the first to finish. Ever since then, Yvonne had assumed I had an appetite like a bird and given me tiny plates of food, and often it was touch and go whether I'd get any pudding.

But today I was grateful for the meagre slice of beef, small roast potato, miniature Yorkshire pudding – it must take real skill to make them so tiny, I thought; mine always exploded into monster batter balloons – three Brussels sprouts and four sticks of carrot. I didn't feel hungry at all, because I kept looking across the table at Daisy, who was picking at her food with even less enthusiasm than me, and then glancing away again and trying not to meet Yvonne's eye at the opposite end of the table.

Even though I knew that what had happened to Daisy wasn't my fault, and it had been a long time ago, and she was well out of it, I felt a horrible weight of guilt. Here was I, getting married when she'd had her special day practically torn from her grasp. I was going to be the centre of attention, the bride being fussed over and photographed by everyone, while she was only a bridesmaid.

Then I thought, *Shit, do I ask her to be a bridesmaid or not?* Wouldn't that just be rubbing salt into the wound, adding insult to injury?

But I had no idea, I realised, what the etiquette of all this stuff was. I thought of the page from *Inspired Bride* with its series of questions, lying folded in my handbag. I'd return to them soon, I promised myself, but there would be other wedding magazines in my future too, and probably websites as well, that would guide me through everything I needed to do. I hoped so, anyway, because already the complexity of it all was making me feel like my head might explode.

'Of course we're all absolutely delighted for you and Archie,' Keith was saying, and I realised I had almost totally tuned out the happy chat around the table. 'We can't wait to have you as part of the family. Although to be honest, we feel you already are, don't we, love?'

'Of course we do,' agreed Yvonne, reaching across the table and giving my hand the world's fastest squeeze with her cool fingers. Her smile, I couldn't help noticing, was no warmer than her skin. 'But when were you thinking of having the wedding? You see, we know from experience that these things can take time to arrange and it's as well to get cracking as soon as possible. Booking a venue, for instance. The really magical places get reserved months – even years – in advance.'

'Unless you do a runner to Vegas,' Poppy said, aiming a sassy grin at her mum. 'It doesn't always have to be the swanky golf club or a five-star hotel, you know, Mother.'

'I have no idea why you and Freya had to sneak off like that,' Yvonne scolded. 'It was almost as if you—'

'Didn't want a massive, over-the-top wedding? We didn't.'

'But you want to do it properly, don't you, my boy?' Keith said. 'A real celebration, and a proper get-together. What do you reckon?'

There was a clatter of cutlery falling onto a plate and a choking sob, and Daisy pushed back her chair so hard it fell to the floor with a thud and hurried out of the room, her dramatic exit only slightly slowed by her heels sinking into the deep pile of the carpet. The conservatory door slammed behind her.

'Oh, poor love,' Yvonne said. 'She still isn't properly over what happened. I'll just—'

'Stay here, Mum,' Poppy said. 'Finish your lunch. I'll go and give her a cuddle.' Then her phone began to trill insistently in her handbag, and Poppy added, 'Just as soon as I've got that – it'll be Freya.'

I put my knife and fork together on my now empty plate. Somehow, in spite of the awkwardness, I'd managed to finish what little there was of my lunch.

'Let me go and talk to Daisy,' I suggested, and before anyone could tell me it was a bad idea, I'd jumped up and hurried out of the room in the direction I'd seen her go.

When I cry, I properly ugly cry. My nose streams, my eyes go red and puffy, and my face looks like I've put one of those vicious acid peels on it, and stays that way for hours. But Daisy, sitting on the stairs with her face in her hands, was weeping like a princess in a fairy tale, or a wilting snowdrop or something. Nonetheless, my heart went out to her. I've never been able to see another person crying without wanting to cry myself, and I could feel a lump in my throat as I squeezed onto the step below her and put a hand on her knee.

'I'm so sorry you're upset. It must have been hard to hear and brought back so many difficult memories.'

She raised her head and sniffed. 'So you know, then? About Donovan?'

I nodded.

'And Jamie? And Fidel?'

I nodded again.

'Did Archie tell you?'

I opened my mouth to say that, actually, it had been a team effort by Archie, Poppy and Freya, but thought better of it. It would mean revealing that we'd told one sister about our engagement before telling the other, and that we'd been talking among ourselves about Daisy's misfortune, which I suspected wouldn't go down well. So I just nodded again.

'It was awful,' Daisy said. 'The worst thing that's ever happened to me. I was so humiliated. Especially since I'd been engaged twice before. Having to cancel everything, and everyone knowing why. Everyone thinking there must be something wrong with me, to send three men in a row running for the hills. Everyone knowing Donovan had chosen a shag with some slapper abroad instead of marrying me.'

'He thought he'd get away with it, I suppose. Some men are like that. But you didn't let him – it was incredibly brave, actually.'

'You think?' Daisy mopped her eyes with the cuff of her dress, leaving a black smear on the fur.

'Of course. It would have been much easier to go through with it, in the short term, but much worse in the end.'

'Especially as he's shagging his way through half of Essex right now,' Daisy said, with a bitterness that seemed almost pleasurable. 'The female half.'

'Ugh, you're well rid of him. Seriously, he'd only have made you miserable.'

She looked at me, her blue eyes wide and damp with tears. 'Oh, Nat. I'm such a bitch. This should have been your and Archie's celebration, and I made it all about me.'

'You couldn't help it. You were upset, and we were all clumsy about announcing it.'

'You weren't. I was being silly. Come on, let's go back. Mum's made trifle, I happen to know.'

We stood up together, awkwardly bumping our hips together as we did so, and suddenly Daisy folded me into a hug.

'You're so nice, Nat. I'm really pleased Archie's marrying you, not someone else.'

I hugged her back, breathing in the jasmine scent of her perfume and something biscuity that must have been her fake tan, and whatever she'd put on her hair that made it so silky it was more like water than strands of keratin.

And I don't know whether it was relief that she didn't hate me, or pity for what she'd been through, but whatever it was, I heard myself say, 'You'll be my bridesmaid, won't you? And help with all the planning? If it's not too upsetting?'

Daisy chewed a long, lemon-yellow nail thoughtfully for a second. 'I've only been a bridesmaid once before, so I've got one more go. You know – "Three times a bridesmaid, never a bride." I won't be able to be one again until I get married myself, but that's okay. Maybe being yours will make it happen. I'd love to.'

'That's settled then,' I said. 'Thank you for saying yes.'

Visibly cheered, Daisy took out her phone. 'One thing about having been engaged loads of times is you get shit-hot at wedding planning. I can help with so many ideas and contacts and stuff. I've still got the number of this woman who has horses and a carriage. I can call her if you like?'

I bit back a horrified refusal and said diplomatically that it was still early days and there was loads to think about, but of course I'd be really grateful for her help.

'There's this vineyard we looked at where they'll actually bottle a vintage of wine named after you, only it was already fully booked,' she prattled on. 'And have you thought about a monochrome colour palette for your theme? I read the other day that's totally on trend right now. We can do our pre-wedding diet together and spend a weekend at a spa doing a juice cleanse – it'll be so fun!'

Really? I thought. *A juice cleanse?* But I smiled and nodded and let her carry on.

Looking back, that was probably my first mistake.

The ordeal of breaking our news to Archie's family over and done with, I felt like I could breathe a massive sigh of relief. All things considered, they'd taken it better than I'd expected. Yvonne hadn't actually had a fit of the vapours and hissed, 'Over my dead body!' as I'd feared she might. Even Daisy had seemed almost happy for us, once she'd been mollified by the offer of a bridesmaid role.

But I'd reckoned without Yvonne's ability to descend on me when I was least expecting it. I should have known better – after all, she had form for that sort of thing. It was how I'd met her and Keith for the first time, and it had more or less set the tone for our entire relationship since then.

It wasn't my fault. Honestly, if I'd known I was going to be introduced to them for the first time, I'd have made sure to have had my girlfriend A game securely in place. I'd have thought for ages about what to wear and tried on different outfits in front of the mirror, consulting Archie on each. I'd have got him to tell me all about his family, so I knew the right questions to ask. I'd have bought flowers, or wine, or chocolates, whichever Archie deemed most appropriate. Or maybe even all three.

But I hadn't had any warning at all.

It was shortly after Archie had moved into his flat. The place was still a shell, with bare, unsanded floors and the kitchen cabinets hanging lopsided on the walls. But we didn't care – I spent most weekends there, helping him with random bits of DIY when we weren't having endless, wonderful sex on a mattress on the floor, because the bed he'd ordered hadn't turned up yet. It had been a while since we last had that sort of sex, now I came to think about it.

But on this particular Saturday, I'd had to tear myself out of his warm arms and head off to play football, because by some miracle our five-a-side team had landed in the league semi-final and I couldn't possibly let the others down, new boyfriend or no new boyfriend. I'd promised not only to bring us falafel flatbreads from the Lebanese takeaway down the road, but also to swing by the plumbers' merchant to pick up a vital piece of tubing Archie needed for his uncle Ray to connect the washing machine.

I got back to Archie's – via a beer garden, where we'd sank a couple of pints to celebrate our victory, still in our football kit – looking quite the worse for wear. Actually *a lot* the worse for wear. It had rained during the match and my legs were plastered in mud, apart from one of my knees, where I'd fallen and taken all the skin off, which was plastered in blood. My hair was sticking out like I'd put my finger in a plug socket. I badly, badly needed a shower.

But I didn't care about any of those things: the few hours I'd spent away from Archie had felt like an eternity and I was itching to see him again and – as soon as I'd cleaned myself up and we'd had something to eat – tumble into bed for a repeat performance of the mind-blowing shag we'd enjoyed that morning.

I fitted the key Archie had lent me into the lock and pushed open the door.

'Hey you!' I said. 'I'm back! I scored! I've got wraps, and your pipe!'

Instead of Archie's voice calling out a reply, I heard only silence. A long silence, followed by the click of heels on the floor and a woman's voice saying tentatively, 'Hello?'

Yvonne appeared in the doorway to the kitchen. I had no idea who she was, this immaculate woman in her skinny jeans and her pointy kitten heels and her little Chanel blazer. And she had no idea who I was either: this dishevelled girl announcing that she'd come bearing hard drugs.

'I'm Nat,' I said lamely, feeling a massive blush working its way up seemingly from my toes to my hairline. 'And this really isn't what you think.'

Archie and his father got home a few minutes later, and Archie explained that his parents had been passing by and popped in to measure up the kitchen, and he and Keith had gone out to buy paint. Archie introduced us, and I made coffee, and we spent a few toe-curlingly awkward minutes making conversation before Keith and Yvonne left.

As starts go, it wasn't the most auspicious. Ever since then, I'd been unable to shake the feeling that Yvonne tolerated rather than liked me, and that I most certainly was not the kind of woman she'd have chosen for her precious only son. Especially when I heard her nostalgically ask Archie whether he'd heard from his ex-girlfriend Marina recently, at all, and wasn't she a lovely girl.

No matter how hard I tried, I never seemed to get it right. When Yvonne asked what my father did, I'd had to explain that he'd never been part of my life, leaving when I was still a baby. She'd given me a look so pointed she might as well have said, 'That explains a lot.'

When we'd had them round for dinner, the new oven had malfunctioned and the roast lamb had come out looking like a burned offering to some pagan god, and Yvonne had said, 'I suppose you've been eating a lot of takeaways, in spite of that brand-new kitchen.'

When we went round to theirs for Keith's birthday, I'd turned up in jeans only to find Yvonne, Daisy and a load of Yvonne and Keith's friends dressed up in cocktail frocks and dinner jackets, and Yvonne introduced me to people as 'Archie's latest girlfriend Natalie, who's ever so *sporty*'.

When we attended their annual summer tennis party, my competitive side had come out and I'd smashed an ace into Keith's business partner's face and bloodied his nose.

Sometimes I caught Yvonne looking at me with a mixture of bemusement and horror, like *Who is this person? What was my son thinking? Has she got him under some kind of spell?*

I knew that, deep down, she would have preferred Archie to be going out with someone – practically anyone – else.

Now, arriving home after work on a normal Tuesday evening, I found my thoughts returning dolefully to my future mother-in-law, and whether, over time, I'd be able to forge a good relationship with her. We'd never be as close as Mum and me but we could be… I didn't know. Not friends, exactly. That would be weird. But we could have a relationship based on mutual affection and respect, cemented by the fact we both loved Archie.

I turned the corner into our road, deep in thought, walking slowly although there was an icy wind cutting through my woolly hat and scarf. I could picture Yvonne's face quite clearly in my mind: her rigidly blow-dried bob, which I supposed was the grown-up version of my own choppy, angular 'do; her smooth, plumped-out skin; the way her lips pressed together into a tight line when she looked at me.

So vivid was the mental image that it took me a few seconds to realise that, standing there on the pavement outside our block of flats, was Yvonne herself. Thank God we'd made up that story about the lock jamming and needing to be changed, otherwise she'd have let herself in. Again.

I stopped in my tracks, a few feet away from her, and tried to smile. 'Yvonne! This is a surprise.'

'Good evening, Natalie. I just dropped by thinking you might be in.' She held out a glossy white carrier bag. 'I brought you some reading material.'

Reading material? The bag looked really heavy, like she had the entire back catalogue of the *British Journal of Physiotherapy* in there.

'Come on in,' I said reluctantly, leaning in to kiss her cheek, feeling a faint dusting of her translucent face powder on my lips. 'It's freezing out here.'

'If you're sure it's no trouble?'

'Of course not.'

I unlocked the front door and heard the click of her heels as she followed me across the tiled lobby and through to our own door. Shit, I thought, what kind of state was the flat in? Had I left washing draped over the radiators? Were Archie's boxer shorts still on the floor by the sofa where he'd dropped them after our cosy cuddle in front of the telly the night before had heated up? Were the boxes of leftover pizza still curling and congealing on the kitchen counter?

But I needn't have worried. Clearly Archie had taken it on himself to blitz the place before leaving to open the shop that morning, and everything was immaculate. There was even a faint smell of bleach hanging in the air.

'Would you like a cup of coffee? Something stronger?' It was almost six thirty, that awkward in-between time that felt too late for a hot drink but maybe a bit too early for the gin and tonic I was longing for.

But Yvonne shook her head. 'I can't stop long. Keith will be expecting his dinner on the table in an hour, and although I put the beef in the slow cooker this morning, there's still the potatoes to mash. I do believe a woman's first duty is to keep her husband happy.'

Oh God. I felt totally seen. If Archie was expecting his dinner on the table when he got in from work, he was going to be sorely disappointed. The best he could hope for was scrambled egg on toast or whatever was on special offer through Uber Eats.

'Do sit down anyway.' I relieved Yvonne of the heavy carrier bag and gestured towards the sofa, sitting down myself with the bag on my lap. 'I'm sure Archie won't be long.'

'Actually.' Yvonne took a seat and carefully crossed one denim-clad calf over the other. 'It was you I came to see.'

I tensed, and the movement of my thighs caused the carrier bag to tilt on my lap, sending its contents slithering to the floor. It had been full of glossy wedding magazines, like the ones Tilly had given me in the salon, but loads more, and loads posher. Alongside *Inspired Bride*, there was *Perfect Day*, *Nuptials*, *Radiance*, *I Do!* and dozens of others.

'Blimey.' I bent over to gather them up. 'Uh, thank you. That's very generous of you.'

'The thing that I wanted to discuss with you is this, Natalie.' Yvonne leaned forward, fixing me with her wide hazel eyes. I could see the shiny copper-coloured eyeshadow she had applied to her upper lids. 'You know Keith and I had our children late in life.'

I nodded awkwardly. If this was going to lead to a lengthy discussion of my future in-laws' sex life, I was totally not here for it.

'Keith was working all hours establishing the business, and then expanding it. And I was working too, for a local estate agent. We thought we'd wait until the right time came, and then, when it did come, it felt as if it might be too late. When Poppy came along, it was like a miracle. I was already thirty-seven.'

Which was no age at all now. But maybe thirty years ago people had felt differently.

'Of course, all three of our children were so very much wanted. And now we have Linus to enjoy too,' she went on.

I couldn't help thinking she made him sound more like a large slab of carrot cake than a much-loved first grandchild. 'Of course,' I agreed.

'But Archie is our only son. And his wedding day will be a very special one for Keith and me.'

And for me, and for Mum, and I kind of hope for Archie too, I thought. But I just said, 'Of course,' again.

'I want you to know,' Yvonne said, reaching out and giving the pile of magazines on my lap a little pat, as if they were a pet she was entrusting me with before going on holiday, 'that Keith and I would be honoured to meet the cost of this wedding. We want it to be a day to remember. And we know that your family is not really in a position to…'

'I've told Mum I'm not going to ask her for a penny,' I said firmly. 'She's given me so much over the years, she needs to spend her money on herself now.'

'That's your prerogative, and hers. But please understand: we want the best for Archie. Only the best.'

As in, not me. I felt my stomach sink inside me. Was there anything I could do that would make this woman think I was good enough?

'I'm ever so grateful for your help,' I said. 'Really, I am. But I'm not sure Archie and I want to have a fancy wedding.'

Yvonne stood up, a bright smile on her face. 'You don't know what you want yet, and that's why I brought you those! Just a bit of inspiration – or hashtag Inspo, as Daisy would say! You and Archie have a little look through them, and we'll talk again. I bet you'll find ideas you love in there! I've got a few magazines of my own at home, and Daisy's got a Pinterest board. Between us three girls, we'll come up with something really special that you'll just love.'

'But I was—' I began. But before I could finish – before I could try and explain that having a small, quiet wedding and a party afterwards at the pub wasn't just cutting my coat to suit my cloth but what I genuinely wanted – Yvonne was in full flow again.

'Oh, and I brought something else for you, Natalie.'

She rummaged in her Louis Vuitton bag and pulled out a shiny white cardboard box, tied with an oyster-coloured silk bow, and placed it almost tenderly on my lap.

'What's this?' I asked. Yvonne's generosity couldn't be faulted, but her taste in gifts could. If this was another of her carefully chosen tokens of her lack of esteem for me, I was going to have to fix a polite smile on my face before I opened it.

'Just a little something I thought you might like,' she said. 'Although it's not for you really. Go on, open it.'

A present for Archie, maybe? But then why was I being asked to perform the unboxing? I untied the ribbon and slowly lifted off the lid. Inside, nestled in tissue paper, was a carefully rolled-up bundle of the same oyster satin, which I guessed from its visible collar was a dressing gown or kimono. Next to it was a card holding three white, oyster and gold hair ties; a gold-rimmed champagne flute; a strongly violet-scented bath bomb; and a sachet of creamy-pink dried rose petals.

So not a present for Archie, then. Flummoxed, I retrieved the lid of the box from the floor and examined it. Printed on the inside in twirly gold script were the words *I can't say 'I Do' without you.*

'Bridesmaid proposals!' Yvonne exclaimed. 'They're the latest thing, according to *Inspired Bride.* You can get them personalised for each of the girls, with their names embroidered on the robe and printed on the glass. Aren't they adorable? I can just picture Daisy's face when she opens hers.'

'But I've already asked her to be my bridesmaid,' I said stupidly. 'And Lara and Precious, too. Surely I don't need to, like, propose?'

'Oh, Natalie.' Yvonne shook her head, as if dealing with someone particularly hard of thinking. 'One thing you don't seem to realise is that there's doing things, and there's doing them properly. Now why don't you just pop me over Lara and Precious's – such an unusual name; is she foreign? – addresses in an email and I'll get these ordered and sent out.'

'But I…' I began, and then gave up. 'Thank you, Yvonne, that's a lovely idea. I'm sure they'll all be thrilled.'

'Don't mention it! Is that the time? I really must shoot off now, Natalie. Lovely to see you. Mwah, mwah.'

And she hurried out. I listened to the clack of her heels receding into silence, and then I put the stack of magazines away on the top shelf of my wardrobe, behind the beach towels and bikinis I wouldn't be touching until summer.

Chapter Five

When it comes to wedding plans, are you and your betrothed on the same page?

A. Totally. We've got this shared vision of our dream day and we can't wait to make it happen.

B. Not really! We've got a bunch of ideas, and some of them are contradictory, but I'm sure we'll figure it all out as we go along.

C. Er… No! But my day, my way, right? He'll come round to my way of thinking eventually.

D. I haven't got a clue! When it comes to the detail of planning the wedding, he's just not interested in discussing anything.

'The thing is,' I said, pushing a wooden spoon around the pan of bolognese sauce with more force than was strictly needed, 'I'm just a bit worried that if your mum and dad are paying for the wedding, and Daisy's helping to organise it, it's all going to snowball and end up being nothing like what we thought.'

'But why did you ask Daisy to be a bridesmaid if you didn't want her to help?'

'I just… I felt so bad for her. She was crying.'

Archie leaned a hip against the kitchen counter and took a sip of red wine. 'Honestly, Nat, I think you're being unreasonable. I mean, it's our wedding. They know it's our wedding. And anyway, six months is ages. By the time it happens, Daisy will have lost interest in it and moved on to the next thing.'

'What if she doesn't, though? Could you grate some parmesan? It's just… you know how hard I find it to say no to your family.'

I turned to get the spaghetti jar out of the cupboard. Its door was bright red and gave me a headache every time I looked at it. On a Pinterest board I hadn't added to for over a year, there were still pictures of other kitchen cabinets: sleek, handleless white ones; glossy charcoal grey ones; even navy blue ones with copper knobs.

But at the end of the day, the choice had been taken out of my hands. Archie's parents had put down the deposit on the flat for us, and Archie's dad had told us not to worry that it needed work; he'd 'send some of the boys round' to plaster and paint, and Archie's uncle Ray would sort out the plumbing for us.

And it had all gone on from there.

'You'll be wanting a new kitchen, won't you?' Keith had asked, sucking a pencil. 'Best way to add value, by far.'

I hadn't asked what point there was in adding monetary value to a place Archie and I would be living in for at least ten years, because there was no way we'd be able to afford to take the next step up on the property ladder on our own, and no way I would be able to live with myself if I accepted any more financial help from his family.

But Keith had ploughed inexorably on. 'I'll talk to my mate Brandon. He'll be able to sort you out with something from his showroom. Don't you worry, Natalie, he owes me a favour so it won't cost me a penny. I know you have your pride.'

And Yvonne had given him a look that was like, *Don't be ridiculous – she's got nothing of the kind*, and said they were getting rid of an almost new cream three-piece leather suite and we might as well have that too.

And there I'd been, thinking that my deep discomfort at accepting all their help had been so well hidden. So when the kitchen arrived and was totally and utterly not to my taste, and the sofas were too big for the room and anyway I hated leather furniture, all I'd been able to do was smile and thank them graciously and profusely, and suppress the knowledge that for the next however long, every time I made a cup of tea, I'd be doing so in a room whose shiny scarlet cabinets made it look like it was permanently sunset, or something out of the red light district. And then I'd felt guilty because not liking what he'd given us seemed like a rejection of Keith's generosity and made me feel like an ungrateful brat. And every time I got up off the sofa, my legs would stick to the leather and the brief smart of pain would remind me of the searing way Yvonne looked at me.

At the time, I'd promised myself that this was the absolute last time I'd accept any major financial help from Archie's parents. And yet, it seemed, here we were again.

I opened the pack of spaghetti and slid half of it into the pan of boiling water. Archie carried plates and cutlery over to the kitchen table – a cheap, basic one from Ikea that couldn't have been more ordinary but of which I was inordinately fond because I'd chosen it and paid for it myself – and splashed some red wine into a glass for me.

'Hey, Nat,' he said. 'You really don't need to stress about this, okay? Happiest time of our lives, it's meant to be, right?'

He came up behind me and put his arms round my waist, and I could feel his chin digging into the top of my head and the warmth of him against my back. I stirred the pasta, and for a second I thought tears would start trickling down my face into the boiling, salty water.

'I am happy,' I said. 'Honestly, I am. I'm so bloody lucky to have this place, and you, and your family being so kind. It's just…'

'You know what your problem is?' Archie said. I could feel his mouth moving against my hair. 'You're a pessimist.'

'I'm not! I'm a realist.'

'Pffft. You always expect stuff to go wrong, and it never does.'

Not so much, I thought, remembering the blithe confidence with which Archie had embarked on the launch of Craft Fever, and how we'd literally had to live on my wages and beans on toast for four months before the doors of the shop finally opened and it went from making no money whatsoever to making a tiny amount of money.

Since then, to be fair, it had developed into quite the success story, and Archie had even been interviewed by our local paper and shortlisted for a young entrepreneur award. So maybe he was right? Maybe all my misgivings had been baseless then, and maybe they were baseless now?

Still, I couldn't make myself share his unfounded, yet unshake-able belief that everything would turn out for the best. Archie, who

never carried an umbrella even when it was blatantly about to piss
it down, who only allowed fifteen minutes for journeys he knew
perfectly well always took half an hour, who thought we didn't need
to close the curtains before we had sex because no one would see.

'I'm not saying it'll go wrong,' I said. 'I'm just saying, I don't
know whether I'll like whatever ideas Daisy has in mind. I mean,
remember what you were saying about the palomino horses and
the meringue dress and everything? What if she thinks that's what
I should have?'

Archie laughed. 'That was years ago! Daisy will have got other
ideas now. Besides, I can put my foot down if she comes up with
anything too bonkers. I was thinking, palomino horses are a bit old
anyway. I fancy a coach drawn by six black stallions.'

'What? It's a wedding, not a funeral.'

'Come on, think big! We could go for a whole kind of *Bride
of Dracula* theme. You could wear a black lace frock with a traily
thing on the ground and black roses and I could have a cape with
a stand-up collar. And we could find a really spooky castle to have
the reception in. You know I was a goth when I was a kid, don't
you? It would be my dream come true.'

The spaghetti water bubbled furiously over onto the hob, and
I seized the pan a second too late, pouring it into the colander to
drain. Archie grabbed a cloth and started to wipe up the mess.

'I never knew you were a goth. Wasn't it kind of challenging,
with your hair being ginger and everything?'

'We all have our cross to bear. I bore mine round my neck – it
was this huge elaborate silver thing. I might see if I can dig it out
to wear under my cape.'

A few seconds before, I'd been worried, but now I figured he was joking.

'Actually,' I said, 'doesn't it kind of depend what time of year we have the wedding? I mean, if it was in winter your whole Dracula idea might just work. But if it was summer and still light at ten in the evening, we'd have a bit of an issue.'

'True. Also, aren't vampires' victims meant to be virgins?'

'Are they? Guess that's a bit of a non-starter, then.'

'Just as well too.' He came up behind me again and I felt his warm breath where my hair met my skin. Then he leaned into my neck and nibbled gently.

'Oi! Stop with the vampire action and get dinner on the table.'

He grinned. 'Shame, I thought you were enjoying it.'

'I was. But I'll enjoy a bowl of pasta more.'

Archie carried the dishes, salad and cheese, and I took the garlic bread out of the oven, releasing a blast of buttery-smelling heat.

'And this garlic would be a no-no obviously,' I said. 'But I was thinking, we could go for more of a *Snow-White*-type vibe. Your best man – is that going to be Dominic or Mo?'

'One of the two. Although my old mate Billy – you've never met him, but we were at school together – got in touch the other day and asked me to be best man at his wedding the year after next, so I might have to return the favour. But anyway…'

'Yeah, so anyway, you'd need to recruit four extra ones, and they could all grow beards and carry spades. And I could have birds flapping round my head and twittering.'

'Hi ho, hi ho, it's up the aisle we go,' Archie sang, out of tune.

'Exactly! And you could hack your way through an enchanted forest to kiss me.'

'Wrong fairy tale, babe. Anyway, wouldn't Mum have to poison you with an apple first?'

She might just want to try, I thought, taking a massive forkful of pasta, laden with the rich tomatoey sauce, and a gulp of wine.

'It would be really original and cool and different. Express a bit of our personalities.'

'Or how about a James Bond theme?' Archie said, spooning salad onto his plate. 'I could wear a dinner jacket and carry a pistol, and we could serve all the guests dry martinis.'

'And the vicar could have a white cat that he held right through the ceremony.'

'And instead of you walking up the aisle like normal, boring brides do, you could come out of the sea in a bikini.'

'We'd have to have the wedding on a beach then, though. Could be tricky to manage, with the tides and everything.'

'True. A pond, maybe? Or someone could just chuck a bucket of water over your head.'

'Yeah, that would work just as well.'

We both cracked up. Archie asked if it was okay if he polished off the cheese and I said that was fine as long as I could have first dibs on the remaining garlic bread, and we finished our dinner chatting about things unrelated to our wedding.

But once we'd cleared up and were slumped on the sofa watching *Line of Duty*, I felt the cloud of apprehension begin to hover over me again.

'Archie?'

'Mmhmm?' He glanced up from his phone.

'We're not going to have a crazy, over-the-top wedding, are we?'

'You mean, apart from the vampire teeth and bucket of water?'

'Those are just the basics. Your everyday run-of-the-mill marriage starts with a bat release and tame birds.'

Archie grinned. 'Seriously, Nat. We can have whatever kind of wedding we want. It's not my mum's decision or my sister's, no matter who's paying for it. It's our day.'

'So, if we were to, like, thank your parents for their kind offer and say that, actually, we'd rather have forty people for pints and a barbecue at the Ginger Cat, you reckon they'd be okay with that?'

'Course they would. Why wouldn't they? Save them a few quid, we get to do things our own way – everyone's a winner, right?'

'Right,' I said.

Archie put down his phone and reached for my hand, and I felt the reassuring warmth of him next to me as we sat in silence until the programme finished.

'I'm going to head to bed,' he said. 'Coming?'

'Sure.' I levered myself off the sofa and followed him through to the bedroom, pulling my jumper off as I went. But as I was brushing my teeth a few minutes later, I couldn't help remembering the stack of magazines Yvonne had delivered, still unread and hidden away in the wardrobe. If she'd bought those for me, I wondered, what if there was a similar stack in her own home, which she and Daisy were poring over? I thought of the magazine page with the quiz printed on it, folded in my handbag – what if Yvonne, too, was tearing pages out of magazines to remind herself of ideas she liked for our wedding?

And an hour later, with Archie sleeping next to me, I still lay awake staring at the ceiling, even though it was too dark for me to see it.

'So we haven't really planned anything yet,' I told Mum the next day, wriggling my bum more comfortably into the depths of her sofa and taking a gulp of my gin and tonic. 'And if I'm honest with you, I'd like to keep it that way for a bit. I mean, if we're going to have the wedding next spring because of Grandpa, and if we don't book anything until fairly late in the day, then there'll be nothing left except the Ginger Cat, and the problem will just kind of go away.'

'That doesn't sound like you,' Mum said. 'My little control-freak daughter.'

'I know, I know. But it's like the only way I can be in control of this is by not being. Don't think I haven't thought this through.'

Mum poured white sauce over a dish of cauliflower and sprinkled cheese over it all. The sauce had gone lumpy, I could see, but she didn't know I'd noticed and thought the cheese would hide the lumps. Which it would, a bit.

I could only see the back of her head, her highlighted blonde hair scraped back into a ponytail secured with a tie-dye print scarf. But there was something about the set of her shoulders that told me she was deep in thought.

'Don't go leaving it too late,' she said at last, sliding the glass dish into the oven.

'What? Why not? Is Grandpa okay?'

'Like you health professionals say, he's as well as can be expected. But he's not getting any younger, you know. He gets confused sometimes.'

'It's not unusual, in someone his age. Could be a bladder infection, could be the beginnings of dementia, could be nothing much at all. Has he seen his GP?'

Mum nodded. 'He was in the other day for a prostate check. Ugh, old age is no fun.'

I thought of my grandfather: his little two-storey house where he and Granny had lived for forty years, where Mum had been brought up, a precious only child born after they had given up hope of being able to have a baby at all. I could picture the place in my mind as clearly as if I was there: the brown velvet sofas, the net curtains on the window that Granny used to put through a boil wash every month, 'Whether they need it or not,' as she said, and which Grandpa now faithfully did as well. I could smell the carefully tended rosebushes in the back garden, and see beyond them to the rows of carrot tops and tomato plants, the sun glinting off the glass of the greenhouse, a cat basking on the warm paving slabs of the path.

What I couldn't picture was Grandpa anywhere else, certainly not stuck in a hospital bed or in a care home, waiting for the next meal to be served, or for it to be time to go to bed, or just because waiting was what he was there to do.

'I'm not even fifty.' My thoughts returned to Mum, who was still on a gloomy train of thought. 'And I feel ancient sometimes. It's like you get given an invisibility cloak as soon as there's a four in front of your age. Just like that. And no one tells you it's going to happen.'

'But you still look amazing!'

'That's very sweet of you. But it's not the point. Even if I was Cindy Crawford I'd still be forty-nine and over the hill as far as men are concerned. Especially men my age, who all seem to think they're somehow entitled to date women in their twenties.'

'Ewww!' I grimaced and forked up some of my dinner, blowing cautiously on it first because I knew Mum's habit of serving molten lava. Then something occurred to me. 'How do you know, anyway?'

'Just do.' She pulled the scarf out of her hair and leaned forward so the curtain of it hid her face.

'Mum! Seriously. How. Do. You. Know? You haven't dated anyone for at least ten years and even that was—'

'Short-lived.' She sighed. 'Oh dear, Dylan wasn't my finest hour. He seemed like such a good idea when I had my beer goggles on in the pub after work, but he turned out to be the world's biggest loser. Thank God I realised it after just a couple of months, before it was too late.'

'Before I'd even met him.'

'And quite right too. Everyone knows you've got to take these things slowly, and you were in your A-level year so the last thing you needed was massive emotional upheaval. You wouldn't have liked him anyway.'

'Why not?'

'Oh, he was just useless. Attractive and funny, but useless. God knows how he even managed to hold down a job when he had at least two spliffs with his morning coffee. And his clothes never fitted him properly. Once I'd seen his bum crack over the top of his jeans for the hundredth time, he didn't feel so attractive any more.'

I realised she'd distracted me from my original question. 'But anyway. How come you know all about what men your age are looking for in a woman? Your age now, as opposed to ten years ago?'

Mum forked up some cauliflower, a bit with loads of crisp cheesy coating, and ate it. 'Ow, that burned my mouth!'

'Emma! Answer the question!'

When I was little, I used to call Mum by her first name. I think it made her feel younger or something – not that she needed to feel any younger, given she was only twenty-two when she had me. Anyway, as soon as I started primary school I realised that calling my mother 'Emma' as opposed to 'Mummy' marked me out as weird right from the get-go, and I pretty soon switched.

It was the first of many such tiny rebellions against Mum's ideas of free-thinking, liberal parenting and a bohemian lifestyle. Most girls rebel by discovering counterculture, having unsuitable boyfriends and dropping out of university; my version was liking Atomic Kitten, losing my virginity at the ripe old age of twenty and getting a degree that would land me a safe, responsible, dependable job.

'Oh, all right then. I had a look at online dating, after what I said about being single for your wedding. I thought, *Hold on, I don't actually have to be.* I could find someone in time. So I set up a profile on OkCupid.'

'Amazing! I bet you got loads of likes.'

'Yes, loads. Four men in their seventies, two in their twenties looking for a cougar for some hot loving, one Royal Marine currently stranded in Turkmenistan and looking for a loan of five thousand pounds to help him get home, and one guy my age who I thought had potential until I saw he was looking for an additional partner for his polyamorous relationship.'

'Oh blimey. But I'm sure if you persisted, someone decent would come along.'

She shook her head. 'I'm not going to persist. I gave it a try and decided it isn't for me. I spend way too much time on social media anyway.'

'But, Mum! What about finding your plus-one for my wedding?'

'Ugh, it's not that big a deal. I'll come on my own and style it out. That would be a better look than turning up with my partner John and his other partner Jenny, right?'

'That would certainly give Archie's parents' friends something to talk about over their salmon mousse.'

Like they wouldn't have enough to talk about when it came to Mum anyway, I thought nervously. I tried to imagine her fitting in at the McCoys' tennis afternoons or one of their cocktail parties, but my brain just couldn't do it.

'Exactly. So John and Jenny didn't make the cut.'

'But someone else might. Come on, Mum. I can totally see why you think online dating isn't for you – it's a bear pit, my mate Lara says, and Zoe, who works at the Ginger Cat, did it for a bit and hated it. But there are other ways to meet men.'

'Such as what? I could sign up to a Russian brides agency, only I'm not Russian.'

'Like… Oh, I don't know. Loads of things.'

'Name three.'

'Okay. Parkrun. Wine-tasting clubs. Ballroom dancing classes. There you go.'

'But I can't run with my dodgy knees. And I've never drunk any wine that's cost more than about a fiver a bottle in my entire life so I'd look a right plonker – gettit? – at a wine-tasting club. And I certainly can't do ballroom dancing or any other kind of dancing – I've got two left feet.'

'But you used to dance loads, didn't you, when you used to go clubbing, before I was born?'

'That was different. That was to dance music at raves and I was… a lot younger.'

A lot younger and off your face on ecstasy, I thought. Mum's stories of her clubbing days had been carefully edited, but over the years I'd been able to fill in some of the blanks. I mean, if she'd been piling into a car with five friends and hitting the motorway on a Saturday night with no idea where they were going until a notification came through on Ceefax – whatever that used to be – and then partying until Sunday evening, there was no way she'd done it on the sheer joy of being young and free.

Often, I'd wondered what it had been like for her, all that being taken away by an unplanned pregnancy. But she'd never given any hint at all that she regretted having me – quite the reverse.

'Okay, maybe not those. But there are other things. Surely there must be stuff you've always wanted to try and never got around to?'

'Maybe.' Mum pushed her plate away and slid the cooling glass dish over so I could help myself to more, but I shook my head. 'I've always wanted to learn to cook properly. I could try a Thai cooking course or something.'

'Perfect! Or how about yoga? You've done a few classes and enjoyed that.'

'Yessss.' Mum sipped her tea.

'So why not give it a go? Try some new things, meet some new people? Even if none of them ends up being a date for my wedding – whenever it eventually happens – you'd have fun.'

'Ah, fun.' Mum smiled. 'I remember fun.'

'So go on, do it! What do you have to lose?'

'About ten pounds,' she said. 'I can't fit into any of my decent clothes any more.'

'So buy new clothes.'

'That's easier said than done. You know how tight money is.'

'Mum! You were saying just the other day you've almost paid off the mortgage on this place. You've done without nice stuff for so long, you deserve to treat yourself.'

'Perhaps you're right,' she said. 'It feels like a pivotal moment somehow, you getting married. Maybe now is the time to reinvent myself. After all, I might be a grandmother soon. I can't carry on wearing Zara skinny jeans forever.'

'You might be a what?'

'Oh, Nattie. Forget I said that. There's no pressure from me – if you want to have babies soon or not for ages or not ever. Or one baby or two or lots or none. But now, with you and Archie getting married – you know, it did cross my mind that that might be on the agenda.'

I stared at her for a few seconds, literally feeling my jaw drop.

'Never mind.' Mum stood up, piling our plates on top of each other. 'I can see you don't want to talk about it.'

I found my voice at last. 'It's not that. It's that Archie and I haven't ever talked about it. I mean – I don't want to have kids now. I'm pretty sure about that. I've always assumed I'll change my mind at some point, though, and suddenly start feeling broody. Isn't that how it works?'

Mum laughed. 'You're asking the wrong person, sweetie. As soon as I knew I was having you, I loved you and wanted you, you know that. It never crossed my mind to – you know, not have you. But before that, having a baby was the last thing on my mind.'

'But Archie…'

'Would have a say in the matter, obviously. Although ultimately of course it's your choice. But it's something you two should probably discuss, don't you think?'

'We probably should.' My voice sounded serious – not surprisingly, because it was a pretty heavy subject. But mentioning it had reminded me about something just as serious.

Even though Archie and I had lived together – shared every aspect of our day-to-day lives with each other – for almost a year, it still wasn't a long time. Twelve months was barely anything, now I thought about it. It wasn't long enough for me to have found out this fundamental thing about him and his plans and dreams for his life. It wasn't long enough for us to know what plans and dreams we shared either.

I thought of the crumpled magazine page in my handbag, and the twenty-three quiz questions that were supposed to tell me whether I was ready to commit to Archie forever. One of them had mentioned children, I remembered. I'd felt a little jolt of shock when I saw it and skipped quickly on to the next one. If I didn't know the answer to that, what else didn't I know about the man I'd promised to marry?

Chapter Six

Spending the rest of your life with one person is a big commitment. Let's say it like it is: you're promising never to have sex with anyone else, ever. How does that make you feel?

A. Over the moon. Why would I ever want to be with anyone else? He's perfect and we are head over heels in love.

B. A bit daunted. Still, I got my single adventures out of my system and I'm ready to settle down.

C. Scared. We love each other and we have amazing sex, but forever is a long time. Still, we can only do our best.

D. Never mind the rest of my life, I've got a wedding to plan!

For as long as I could remember, Granny and Grandpa's house had had the same smells. After Granny died, some of the ones that were typical of her – the Je Reviens perfume she wore; the redbush tea she liked to drink; the warm, floury scent of scones if she'd been baking – gradually faded, and I realised that what remained were the smells of the house itself, and of Grandpa.

There was the bowl of potpourri that had stood on the hall table since I was a little girl, faded and dusty now but still releasing a hint of orange peel and rose petals when you walked past it. There was the smell of the soap flakes Grandpa's wool jumpers were washed in, the Pears soap he used in the shower and the polish he used to shine his shoes. Even in the evening, there was the smell of toast lingering from breakfast.

But today, when Archie and I arrived for Sunday lunch, the house smelled different. The air was tainted with something acrid that caught in my throat as soon as we walked through the door, and it was freezing cold. But Grandpa greeted us as cheerfully as he always did, shaking Archie's hand and kissing my cheek, and he looked just the same in his worn corduroy trousers and a jumper with suede patches on the elbows where the fabric had worn through.

Was he slightly more stooped than usual, slightly shrunken? It was hard to tell; the days when he had seemed like the tallest man in the world were long gone.

'Come in, come in,' he said. 'It's nippy, isn't it? I burned my breakfast and I've been trying to get the place aired, but it's not going well so far.'

'Is your smoke alarm working?' I asked. 'It smells like you lit a barbecue in here. You could have burned the place down.'

'Did it go off?' Grandpa asked. 'You know, I can't recall. I was too busy flapping a tea towel out of the back door to try and clear the smoke. It was quite dramatic, I can tell you. The front room's a bit warmer – I've got the gas fire on.'

We followed him into the familiar beige and brown cocoon, where we were met by the scent of lavender furniture polish. Teresa, Grandpa's tabby cat, regarded me with deep suspicion, even though she'd known me all her life, and stalked slowly out of the room, her long stripy tail waving like the banner of a retreating army.

'I brought a couple of things from the shop I think you'll enjoy, Robin,' Archie said, kneeling down in front of the coffee table and taking cans out of a paper bag. Slightly stiffly, Grandpa joined him. *He should be doing some calf and hamstring exercises if his knees are hurting*, I thought, but I didn't say anything; I'd been told off before by Grandpa for fussing over him like a mother hen, and it had made me realise that, in his mind, I was still his precious grandchild who needed protecting, not a grown woman who increasingly wanted to protect him.

'This is a session IPA,' Archie was saying. 'It's got seriously punchy pineapple and citrus notes. It'd be great with a curry.'

Grandpa held the can at arm's length, squinting at the abstract orange and lime-green label.

'"Dance with the Devil",' he read. 'Strange names they give beers nowadays. Back in my time it was all "Barmaid's Bosom" and the like.'

'It's to attract the female customer,' Archie said. 'Craft beer isn't as popular with women as it is with blokes, but the balance is shifting all the time. And girls don't want to drink things called "Skinny Minnie" or "Topless Blonde" any more, do they, Nat?'

'No, they don't, and quite right too,' I said. 'Since we're living in these enlightened times, why don't I go and set the table?'

I left them going through the contents of the bag Archie had brought. Grandpa had never been much of a beer drinker, but the first time I'd introduced Archie to him, my new boyfriend had packed a bag full of beers to take as a gift. Grandpa had pretended to be fascinated and the tradition had continued from there. I didn't know whether Grandpa ever drank anything Archie brought, but I loved listening to their male-bonding chatter while I got on with making lunch.

'There's a fish pie in the oven, Nattie,' Grandpa called. 'It's from that new shop on the high street that does posh frozen ready meals. Some of them are really awfully good, but I haven't tried this one yet. It's got prawns and scallops in, so it ought to be all right.'

I opened the door of the old-fashioned gas oven. The odour of burned toast still lingered in the air, but it was joined by a waft of buttery mashed potato smell that made my mouth water. On the hob, a pan of carrots and peas was waiting to be boiled.

Teresa the cat strolled into the room, meowed and wound her slinky body round my legs.

'Cupboard love, little girl,' I reproved, bending down to stroke her, which she just about tolerated. 'You wouldn't give me the time of day if you hadn't heard there were prawns on offer.'

I arranged plates and cutlery on the polished wooden table, opened the bottle of white burgundy I'd brought and put the box of chocolate eclairs in the fridge for later. As soon as the table was set, Teresa jumped up and sat on the chair at the end that used to be Granny's place.

'You've spoiled that cat rotten, Grandpa,' I said. 'Look at her, being the lady of the house.'

'And so she is.' Grandpa stood slowly up and came over to fuss the cat. 'And a hard worker too. She brought in two mice yesterday. One of them was even dead.'

'And the other?'

He shook his head. 'Gone to ground. She'll wake me up in the middle of the night chasing it around the bedroom, I expect.'

I sliced some butter over the steaming vegetables and carried the dish to the table, and Archie followed with the fish pie.

'This looks delicious, Robin,' he said. 'Thanks for having us.'

'You're always welcome.' Grandpa spooned fish pie onto our plates. 'And now you must tell me what you've been up to.'

Archie and I looked at each other across the table and smiled. Grandpa was the last person we needed to share our news with properly, face to face, before we could update our social-media profiles to say we were engaged and let the rest of the world find out that way. I noticed Grandpa's gaze settle on my left hand, and then return upwards to meet my eyes, a slow smile spreading across his face.

'You never!' he said.

'We are,' I confirmed. 'Just a couple of weeks ago, Archie asked me to marry him. We wanted to wait until we saw you to tell you, so we could celebrate properly.'

'Well.' Grandpa poured wine carefully into the three cut-crystal glasses and raised his to us. 'Congratulations. These were a wedding gift to your grandmother and me, you know. From her parents. There were eight originally, but the others all got broken. Still, it's not bad going to survive over fifty years, is it?'

I felt a pang of sadness, thinking how no one could have expected that the glasses would see their golden wedding anniversary, but Granny wouldn't. Would Archie and I still be together in almost half a century's time? It was impossible to imagine – but then, so was being without him.

'I hope you'll be as happy as Elizabeth and I were,' Grandpa went on. 'When's the big day?'

'Quite soon, we hope,' Archie said. 'Early next year. Before Easter, anyway.'

'And we hoped you'd do a reading at the ceremony,' I added.

'I'd be honoured,' Grandpa said. 'The Song of Solomon? "The flowers appear on the earth; the time of the singing of birds is come, and the voice of the turtle is heard in our land."'

'Voice of the turtle?' I laughed. 'What's that mean? Do turtles even have voices?'

'It means a turtle dove, you little heathen,' Grandpa teased back.

'That makes a bit more sense.'

'We won't be allowed a Bible reading, will we?' Archie said. 'We're planning to have a civil ceremony, Robin. Something quite small, just close friends and family.'

'Shakespeare then,' suggested Grandpa. '"Let me not to the marriage of true minds admit impediment"? Anyway, you just let me know what you want and I'll be sure to learn it off by heart, so I don't make a fool of myself on the day.'

'You could never make a fool of yourself,' I said. Archie's feet found mine under the table, and he gave my ankle a firm squeeze that was like a little foot hug. I looked at him and at Grandpa, and I felt a huge, happy smile stretching over my face.

'You're my two favourite men in the world, you know,' I said.

Archie grinned. 'I should hope so.'

'I'll drink to that,' replied Grandpa. 'Although you'd better look after her, you know, young man. Or I shall have to send the boys round.'

Archie knew perfectly well that Grandpa had no more connections in the gangland underworld than Teresa the cat, but all the same he looked alarmed.

'I'll do my best,' he muttered.

'And your family?' Grandpa asked. 'What do they make of Nat? Not losing a son but gaining a daughter?'

'They're made up,' Archie said, with more confidence than I felt. 'They think Nat's great.'

'They're helping to organise the wedding,' I said. 'And Archie's mum and dad have offered to pay for it all, which is really kind.'

I noticed Grandpa looking thoughtfully across the table at me and wondered if he'd heard the doubt in my voice.

'Very generous,' Grandpa said. 'Bit of a blessing you don't want anything extravagant though, Nattie, because I know you wouldn't want to start married life feeling beholden to anyone.'

It was almost dark when Archie and I walked home through the park under a lowering grey sky, our gloved hands intertwined. Soon the high street would be alive with glittering Christmas lights, carols playing in all the shops, the giant tree illuminated and decorated outside the station. But for now, it was a bleak November afternoon, and Christmas felt far away. Not that I cared – inside I was as glowing with happiness as if I'd just troughed half a dozen mince pies and a vat of mulled wine.

'Thanks for being so lovely to Grandpa,' I said.

'Why wouldn't I be?' Archie asked. 'He's your family, after all. And a decent bloke. A diamond geezer, my uncle Ray would say.'

'Still though. It's nice of you, and I want you to know I appreciate it.'

'Takeaway pizza tonight?' Archie suggested, quickening his stride as we reached the gate to the street.

'I don't know, I'm still stuffed from lunch. There's some soup in the fridge; I might just... Hold on, that's my phone. It's your mother.'

I passed my buzzing phone to Archie and he looked at it in confusion.

'What do you want me to do?'

'Answer it, obviously.'

'But she's calling you.'

'But she's...' The high-pitched ringing continued and, almost against my will, I put the device to my ear and said, 'Hello, Yvonne.'

The conversation lasted all the way back to the flat. Well, I say conversation, but it was mostly Yvonne talking and me listening, trying occasionally and unsuccessfully to get a word in.

I guess all Archie heard was me saying, 'Yes, Yvonne,' 'No, Yvonne,' 'I hadn't really thought of that, Yvonne,' and 'I'll have to discuss it with Archie, Yvonne.'

Lucky for him, he missed his mother telling me that if I wanted a bespoke tiara or made-to-measure shoes, the time to order them was now, in case I wasn't aware. He didn't hear her asking whether we'd thought about a rehearsal dinner, and how many guests we'd like to have attend it. He didn't get to find out about the lady in Canterbury who tailor-made morning suits for babies, which would just be too adorable on Linus, didn't I think.

'What did she want?' Archie asked at last, unlocking the front door.

We both hurried into the blissful warmth of the flat, shrugging out of our coats and kicking off our shoes. I sat down on the sofa, my phone still in my hand, feeling like it might explode at any moment, or possibly erupt into a bespoke glitter-filled balloon bouquet.

'She was calling about the wedding.'

'What about it?'

'Everything about it. All the things. Well, actually, I guess just some of the things, because I bet there'll be loads more.'

'Give me the executive summary then.'

'There's this place she wants us to go and see. A potential venue, in Kent somewhere.'

'You sound like that's a problem.'

'It's not, obviously. Only, Archie…'

'What?' He flicked on the kettle and pressed the button on the television remote, flipping through the channels at lightning speed.

'It sounds seriously swanky. Like, a proper stately home. With a chapel and everything.'

'What's wrong with that?'

'It's just… not really what we had in mind, is it?'

Archie poured boiling water into two mugs and handed one to me.

'No harm in having a look, is there? If we don't like it, we tell her it's no good. And if we do, then we book it and your gramps can do his Bible reading about the turtles, and everyone's a winner.'

'I suppose,' I agreed reluctantly. But, sipping my hot tea in the warm room, Archie's firm, familiar thigh next to mine on the sofa, for some reason a coldness washed over me. I couldn't help feeling anxious, as if I were swimming in the sea and a huge wave was approaching. I thought I'd be able to let it wash me safely back to the beach – but I couldn't quite be sure.

Chapter Seven

His family are…

A. Great! I feel like I'm part of it already and I can't wait to make it official.

B. Okay. I mean, we get on and everything, but we have our differences.

C. A bit of a nightmare if I'm honest. But I'll make an effort and I'm sure we'll all rub along okay.

D. No idea – I've asked him when I'll get to meet them but he's being really evasive about it.

The staff break room at Queen Charlotte's was nothing to write home about, if I'm being honest. Over the years, there'd been talk of upgrading the facilities to include unimaginable luxuries like sleep pods and even a proper espresso machine, but they'd never materialised and we hadn't really expected them to. This was the

NHS, after all – a health service that might be the envy of the world but one that certainly didn't have spare cash for fripperies to make its staff's lives more luxurious.

Still, it was Wednesday and so the small room, with its row of basic kitchen units down one side and islands of Formica-topped tables and plastic chairs, was crowded and humming with anticipation.

It was Cake Wednesday. And not just any Cake Wednesday – Bake Off Wednesday. Over the past few weeks, the cakes had been not only appreciated and inhaled as usual – they'd been judged. A secret ballot had been organised and marks awarded for appearance, taste and originality. And, physiotherapists being the kind of people they are, my colleagues had taken it seriously. Lara had made a batch of cupcakes with various parts of human anatomy – the scapula, the pelvis, the patella – carefully piped on them in buttercream, and won herself a place in the final. Joining her was Matt, our junior, who had surprised us all by turning up a couple of weeks previously with a perfect tarte au citron.

My effort – a gin and tonic cake, naturally – hadn't made the grade (possibly because I'd been too heavy-handed with the gin, and the cake had gone a bit soggy), and to be quite honest I was relieved, because the final was here and the pressure was truly on the four remaining contestants. And besides, I'd been able to give my remaining cake to Grandpa, who very sensibly agreed with me that there was no such thing as too much gin.

'What did you make?' I asked, craning over Lara's shoulder as she carefully placed a lidded plastic box on the table.

'No peeking! You can see it when the others unveil theirs.'

She looked sideways at Nisha, who was hovering protectively over her cake tin.

'Who's the other finalist?' I asked. 'I missed a week early on, when Archie and I were in Crete.'

'Me.' Precious hurried up to the table, a large plastic box cradled tenderly in her arms. She leaned in towards us and whispered, 'Or rather, my mum. I know that's cheating but she's visiting from Lagos and she's staying with us before she goes off to inflict herself on my brother in Belfast. I did help her make it, though.'

'Let's see.' Lara and I watched as Precious carefully lifted the lid. Inside was the most enormous, most over-the-top cream cake I'd ever seen, piped with massive swirls of snow-white frosting and topped with drizzles of chocolate, glacé cherries and candied pineapple, all sprinkled with flakes of coconut.

'Oh my God, that's insane,' I breathed.

'I know, right? She's been cooking non-stop since she's been over. She's basically practising all the wedding food on us, so she's up to speed on it all when we go over for the wedding. Our flat looks like a restaurant kitchen when we get in in the evenings. The other day she left a massive tray of jollof rice in the bath because she'd run out of worktop. She said she'd fill our freezer before she goes back home and I was, like, "Mummy, we've got a box of fish fingers, a bag of oven chips and two tubs of Ben and Jerry's in there and it's already full." But she won't listen.'

'I wish my mum could cook like that,' I said.

'I wish I could cook like that,' said Lara. 'I bake, and that's it.'

'Ah, bless her.' Precious rolled her eyes, but her smile was loving. 'We had to have Cyprian's parents round for dinner, of course, because they've never met before, and Mum went even crazier. She was really nervous to meet them – she's worried they won't approve of us getting married, because they're Catholic and I'm not. But I think it's going to be all right. They're even okay with having the wedding in Lagos.'

'It's next May, right?' I said. 'I can't believe you've been engaged for so long and Archie literally just asked me, and it looks like I'll get married first.'

'I don't know how you're going to manage it,' Precious said. 'Before she came out here, Mum was emailing me, like, every day with these massive lists of everything that needs to be done and all the people that have to be invited and stuff. It's going to be a massive three-day party and I reckon there'll be about three hundred people there. The invited ones, that is; loads of randoms will turn up – they always do at Nigerian weddings.'

'What does Cyprian reckon to it all?' Lara asked.

Precious laughed. 'Oh, he knows to keep out of it. He's working such crazy hours anyway. Newly qualified solicitors work almost as hard as junior doctors. Mum and I chat away about the wedding and he just smiles and nods.'

'It must be really stressful, organising a wedding overseas,' I said. 'I mean, I've got to go and look at a potential venue in Kent with my mother-in-law and that's bad enough.'

'Actually, I'm getting off lightly. Because the wedding's not happening here, Cyprian's mum can't really get involved at all. I mean, they've lovely people and everything, but it's never going to be like the relationship you have with your own mum, is it?'

'God,' Lara interjected. 'Listening to the two of you, I'm so glad I'm single. This wedding lark sounds like way more trouble than it's worth.'

Precious and I met each other's eyes. I knew she was thinking the same as I was: we were going to have to dial down the wedding talk, because it wasn't fair on Lara to either bore her with it or keep reminding her of her single status.

But that afternoon, when I was grabbing a quick cup of tea before returning to the ward, Precious came and sat next to me, taking a grateful gulp from a can of Coke.

'Can I ask you something, Nat?'

'Course you can. So long as it's not how to bake the perfect Victoria sponge, because as you know I haven't got a clue.'

'Do Archie's parents like you?'

The expression on my face must have given my answer away.

'Because Cyprian's mum… I don't know. I sometimes think they don't approve of me, because I'm not a Catholic like they are.'

'But Cyprian's not religious, is he?'

'Not so's you'd notice. But he turns up at church when it's his niece's first holy communion or whatever, and he knows the Latin words to the prayers… And, besides, he's her son so he can do no wrong, can he?'

'But they must know that you're…?'

'Living in sin? No way. I've still got my room in my flatshare, even though I'm almost never there, and when his mum comes round, Cyprian and I do a proper blitz of the place and hide my nighties and my toothbrush and… you know. Everything.'

I sighed. 'I know Archie's mum feels I'm a disappointment. It's so bloody hard, isn't it? Like, do you try and be the perfect daughter-in-law or do you just crack on and let them take you or leave you?'

'Sometimes she looks at me and I swear she's trying not to roll her eyes.'

'Yvonne does roll her eyes. Sometimes so much I worry they'll get stuck in the back of her head and never roll back again.'

Precious giggled. 'Ridiculous, isn't it? Here we are, these grown-up professional women, and we're getting our knickers in a twist about what people think of us.'

'Maybe that's what getting married does. Maybe it, like, destroys your brain. To prepare you for the horror of childbirth or something.'

'Oh my God, don't! When I worked on the maternity ward, I'd go home one day thinking that having a baby would be the best thing ever and the next swearing I was going to keep my legs crossed for the rest of my life rather than go through that.'

'I guess that's why they're so protective of their sons. We'll probably be mothers-in-law from hell one day, you wait.'

'Well, we'll have had the opportunity to learn from the experts.' Precious drained her Coke and stood up. 'I'd better get back.'

We exchanged a fist bump and she hurried back to the ward. It was some comfort, I supposed, to know I wasn't the only one having doubts about how warmly my fiancé's family were going to welcome me. I hadn't marked an answer to the quiz question about Archie's family yet – I didn't know what I would put. Even though of course I'd never be as close to her as to my own mum, there was surely plenty of time to build a good relationship with them, to find some way to get along with Yvonne that would be cordial and friendly.

'Look!' With a flourish, Mum produced a small object from the bookshelf. 'I made this!'

Reverently, she passed it to me and I took it carefully, turning it over in my hands and trying to work out what it was. A model sailing boat? A jug? A bowl? A bowl, I decided. Just a slightly wonky one.

'It's lovely,' I said. 'I love the colour, how it's got bits of red and bits of kind of silver. What are you going to use it for?'

'It wasn't meant to look quite like that,' Mum admitted. 'Something went wrong with my glaze in the kiln, Mara, the course leader, said. But I'm proud of it anyway. I can't decide whether having my morning porridge in it would be wrong.'

'Why would it be wrong?'

'Mostly because there's a hole in the bottom. But I think if I put it on a plate and eat really quickly I might just get away with it.'

'We could put our onion bhajis in it now,' I said, producing them from the bag I'd brought from the Indian takeaway, together with bottles of lager from Archie's shop. 'The hole won't matter then. I got us samosas, aloo chat, chicken dhansak and chana dal. And some salad – they always put it in; I don't know why. It's not like anyone ever eats it.'

'I keep thinking I ought to start a wormery, and make compost and grow tomatoes on the balcony,' Mum said. 'They're supposed to be dead easy, but I worry the whole flat would smell of rotting food and what if I killed the poor worms? Never mind the poor tomatoes; I'd kill those for sure. Thank you for bringing dinner, sweetie – it all looks delicious.'

'Let's get this lot on the table and then you can tell me all about your ceramics thing,' I said.

A few minutes later, we were sitting in our usual places on the sofa, beers in our hands, the flat filling with the spicy smell of curry.

'So good,' Mum said around a bite of samosa. 'So I went along – it was last Thursday. I thought it would be a great way to meet new people. And it was – everyone was so friendly and nice. And even though I'm totally cack-handed, Mara says I'll get the hang of the basics really quickly.'

'It looks like you have already,' I said, gesturing to the wonky bowl. 'But tell about the other people. Were there handsome men there?'

'Well,' Mum spooned rice and chickpeas onto her plate, 'there were seven of us altogether. Me, Mara, two women who I think were a couple, another single woman my age, a young girl who was seriously good – I have no idea what she was doing there, since the rest of us were total beginners – and one man.'

'One man out of seven,' I said. 'Sounds like about the ratio you'd expect from a ceramics workshop.'

'I suppose so. That sort of thing doesn't exactly attract the macho type, does it? But it's a skill I've always wanted to learn, and I'm glad I did it.'

'But tell me about the one man who was there?'

'His name was Lucien,' Mum said. 'And he was lovely. A couple of years older than me, I'd guess, but really attractive and so friendly.'

Yasss, I thought. Mum's first foray into getting out there and meeting new people, and she'd only gone and met a nice man! Smugly I helped myself to chicken and said, 'Go on.'

'We had a lovely chat,' she said, 'and afterwards when we all went to the pub together – except Mara; I think she knew we'd all want to talk about what we thought of the course, and she didn't want to cramp our style – he and I shared a bottle of rather nice sancerre.'

This was sounding more and more promising. 'Excellent taste. So tell me more about Lucien. Are you going to see him again?'

'The course is six sessions,' Mum said. 'So I expect I will. Unless he decides to drop out, of course. And I doubt he will; his bowl was much better than mine.'

'You see!' I crowed. 'Just one ceramics class and you've already met a man! That's a step in the right direction, isn't it?'

Mum laughed. 'Oh, sweetie, you're so funny. Lucien's gay. Of course he is. A perfectly lovely man but definitely batting for the other side. We'll have a laugh together on the course and maybe when it's finished we'll meet up and go to the ballet or something – or out for tea and cake; he says he loves cake. But as a romantic partner he's a total non-starter.'

'Right,' I said, deflated. 'But honestly, Mum, what did you expect? I mean, a ceramics workshop? Like, of all the things to pick. How many straight single guys are likely to be keen on learning how to make bowls? Even lovely ones like yours.'

'The ones with an iota of common sense,' said Mum.

'How do you mean?'

'It's about playing a numbers game, isn't it?'

'What numbers game?'

'Just think about it for a second. You want to meet people of the opposite sex, you look for them where the opposite sex go. No man with two brain cells to rub together would try and meet women at – I don't know, five-a-side football or whatever.'

'I play five-a-side football.'

'Yes, you do, but you're the exception that proves the rule. My friend Rosa met her other half at an immersive theatre thing. The other people there were ninety per cent women and gay guys, but he had it sussed: he reckoned he'd have the luxury of choice, and he did, and he chose Rosa. Everyone was wearing masks, and she said she'd been chatting to him for half an hour before he took the mask off and she saw his massive handlebar moustache, but it was too late and she'd already fallen for him.'

'Okay,' I said, 'I can kind of see the logic. But you'd have to go to a hell of a lot of ceramics workshops to find the one guy who's worked out that the way to meet women is to hang out where women hang out.'

'That's okay. I like ceramics, I've decided. And besides, I'm playing the long game. Your wedding isn't for another few months. I could make you a dinner service for your trousseau. I've got all the time in the world.'

What Yvonne would make of a collection of plates as wonky and full of holes as Mum's most recent attempt, I dreaded to think.

Not for the first time, I felt torn between my natural inclination to not rush into getting married at all and the pressure that had been put on me by Grandpa's age and declining health. Now, it felt like there was an additional deadline to be met: finding a man for Mum so she wouldn't have to be a single mother of the bride. And that reminded me of the other thought that had been niggling around the edges of my mind for the past couple of weeks, jerking me awake just as I was falling asleep, distracting me when I was trying to watch TV or read a book, almost making me miss the bus stop on my way to work.

'Mum,' I said, 'there's something else I've been wondering about. Do you think I should tell my father I'm getting married? I mean, I wouldn't want him to be at the wedding or anything. But I wondered if he should know. If he'd even care. If you even know how to get in touch with him.'

Mum put her plate back on the coffee table and scooted along the sofa to curl her arm around me. I tilted my head against her shoulder, feeling the familiar tickle of her hair on my cheek and smelling the familiar scent of her honeysuckle soap.

'Sweetie. I can't be the one to make that decision, not really. If you want, I can try and call him – we haven't spoken for years, as you know. But his mobile number might still be the same, or the email address I've got for him. Although it's a Hotmail one and no one uses those any more, do they, unless they want spam about erectile dysfunction and Nigerian princes asking for their bank details. But I can try. Or I could pass the details on for you to try, if you'd rather speak to him yourself.'

I took a deep breath, trying to push down the lump that had formed in my throat. I'd never had a father, not in any meaningful sense of the word anyway. There had been a point, right after I was born, when he and Mum had lived together. And a time after that, once they'd realised their relationship wasn't going to work, when he'd come round to spend Christmas with us. And there was one weekend I remembered him taking me to McDonald's for a milkshake.

But those occasions were too long ago for me to have a proper memory of them. I had only a couple of photos of him and me together, which Mum had carefully kept in a biscuit tin along with the bracelet that had been round my wrist in the hospital where I was born, a single squashed pink rose from the bouquet her mother had given her to mark my birth, a pair of crocheted booties that had once been white, and the first of my baby teeth to fall out.

She'd tried to keep the stump of my umbilical cord too, she'd told me once, but it had got too gross and she'd thrown it out.

One of the pictures showed me and my father together in a park. I must have been about three: a dark-haired, serious-faced, chubby child in blue leggings and a rainbow-striped top. I was sitting on the top of a slide and my dad was holding me, getting ready to release me and let me whiz down to the bottom on my own.

In my memory, the slide had been impossibly high, the descent to earth thrilling and seemingly endless. But in the photograph, it was only at about my father's chest height. He was a small man, shorter than average, and so thin his wide grin seemed to take up most of his face. His head was shaven and he had a goatee beard, and he was wearing a T-shirt with a bright yellow smiley face on it.

Sometimes it was hard to tell whether I had any memory of the day itself, of my father or the slide, or whether I'd constructed it all in my mind, based on the image on that faded, curling print, which had become blurred over the years by my sticky fingerprints on its glossy surface.

'I don't know,' I said now. 'I mean, would he even be interested? He wasn't interested in me when I was little – why would he be now?'

Mum squeezed me closer. 'I've said this to you often, sweetie, and I'm saying it again. Your dad loved you. He adored you. When you were a tiny baby, he used to hold you for hours and hours while you slept. You used to have to be held, otherwise you'd scream the place down. And he'd sit there for ages, not moving a muscle even if his foot had gone to sleep and he was bursting for a wee, so as not to disturb you.'

'But then he lost interest.'

'He didn't lose interest in you,' Mum said. There was a tone to her voice I'd heard countless times before: it was as if it hurt her to get the words out, to try and say what was true but also what would hurt me the least. 'It was me he'd had enough of.'

Hearing the remembered pain in her voice made my heart twist with sadness too, thinking of Mum, younger than I was now, left all alone with a baby. She'd coped – somehow – but would I, in her position?

I couldn't help making the contrast with Archie's father: the provider, the head of the family, devoted to his wife and children. I might feel uncomfortable about our wedding being bankrolled by Yvonne and Keith; I might suspect – okay, know – that, for reasons of her own, Archie's mother didn't think I was the kind of catch she'd have wanted for her son; my mind might boggle at Daisy's diva ways. But there was no denying that theirs was a happy, stable family, whereas mine was just me, Mum and Grandpa.

And another thought jumped into my mind: without the example of a father of my own, how would I know if Archie was a good husband or if we were even doing the whole marriage thing right?

What did right look like, anyway? Was it the McCoys with their immaculate house and their three children who'd never wanted for anything? Or was it the tiny flat I'd grown up in, with Mum and I living on beans on toast at the end of the month – and, one time, her selling the stereo on eBay to pay the gas bill – but in which I'd always felt surrounded by love?

Or was it something else, something Archie and I would have to make up as we went along?

'I don't think I'll tell him,' I said. 'I don't think he'd be that interested. I've got you and Grandpa – I don't need him.'

Chapter Eight

Individually, as well as in your relationship, you'll face challenges. Do you have each other's back?

A. He's my rock. Any time I need support, I know he'll be there for me.

B. I'm pretty independent and I can mostly get by without him. It's good to know he's around when I need support though.

C. We let each other down occasionally, like everyone does. But he's a great sounding board.

D. I fight my own battles. His too, quite often.

'Oh my God,' Archie said, scrambling out of bed and yanking the duvet off my sleeping form. 'I need to get my skates on or I'll be late.'

I jerked up, bemused. 'You won't be late. We're not meeting your mother until eleven.'

'What? Meeting Mum for what?' Archie looked wide-eyed and surprised – maybe a bit *too* wide-eyed and surprised.

I rubbed sleep out of my eyes. 'To go and look at the Finchcocks place, remember? It's in the calendar. I've booked a day off work.'

'It's not in mine – look.'

He passed me his phone. Sure enough, there was no *Yvonne – Finchcocks Manor* at eleven o'clock – but there was another entry. *Machel – gin* at nine.

'Hold on, you can't come and look at a potential wedding venue because you're meeting some bloke for a gin?'

'Not for gin. About gin. This guy's a local artisan producer and he's just released a batch of gin, and I want to get some for the shop. If I don't buy it he'll sell out. The stuff's won loads of awards.'

'So buy it then. Why do you have to meet the guy?'

'You don't understand.' He looked at me pityingly. 'It's all about forging relationships with suppliers. Next time, I want to be top of his list instead of right near the bottom.'

'And besides, you want to taste it.'

Archie tried not to look shame-faced, and failed. 'Well, yeah.'

'But, Archie – come on. Just last night, when we were having dinner, I said we had this thing on today. You knew about it.'

'Nat, I'm really sorry. I must not have been listening properly. I've got so much on at the moment.'

I bit back a furious retort. 'Should we ring your mum and say we can't make it? Rearrange for another day?'

The prospect of visiting a venue that described itself as 'luxurious', 'exclusive' and 'unique' with Archie by my side had been intimidating enough; going alone made me feel downright terrified. What if

I fell asleep on the train and missed the stop? What if they served us tea and I forgot to put the milk in first? What if Yvonne looked at me in that way she had that made me feel about two inches tall?

Actually, that last one I didn't really need to worry about. Yvonne would do that anyway. Having no clue what you were supposed to wear to go and look at a posh country house to hold your wedding in, I'd decided I was going to wear jeans. I could already imagine the way she would look me up and down as if everyone knew that the appropriate attire was a twinset and pearls, or a full-length mink coat or a massive hat like women wore to Royal Ascot, except me.

'Don't do that,' Archie said. 'You go with her. It'll be fun. And if you like it, I can go another time and see it.'

'But what if they want us to book it, like, today?'

'Tell them we can't.' Archie's voice was muffled by the jumper he was tugging over his head. 'Or go ahead and do it. I trust your judgement, Nat.'

I was glad someone did. 'Are you sure you don't want to tell her we can't make it?'

'Seriously, I have to run. If you want to ring Mum and cancel that's fine.'

He stepped into his jeans, putting both feet into one leg at first and hopping around a bit before he got himself sorted out. His hair was still all sticking up from sleep, and I could see lines of worry on his forehead alongside the creases left by the pillow. I felt a rush of affection for him that tempered my annoyance.

'Okay,' I agreed. 'I'll go. Good luck with the gin guy.'

'Good luck with the wedding place.' Archie bent over to kiss me, while simultaneously trying to force his left foot into his right trainer. 'I'll text Mum – she'll pick you up at the station, I'm sure. Love you.'

'Love you too,' I told his departing back.

Reluctantly, I got out of bed and headed for the bathroom. As I brushed my teeth, I imagined girls in cashmere jumpers and designer jeans wafting expensive perfume as they commented on the provenance of the art on the walls and the antique furniture. I didn't own a cashmere jumper and I wouldn't know the difference between a Chippendale chair and something from Argos.

Don't be ridiculous, Nat, I told myself. *You do you. Who cares what they think of you?*

Still, despite my inner cheerleader trying her best, I wished I'd given myself more time to sort out my hair, which was kinking outwards annoyingly at the ends, and put on more than a dash of make-up. At least my yellow coat was equal to the occasion. And at that point, I was going to choose coffee over make-up for sure.

It was half past ten when I arrived at Ellingfield station, which was not much more than a platform surrounded by rolling green hills through which the little two-coach train had been pottering along for the past hour, stopping at other, equally tiny stations every so often. I stepped off, turning my coat collar up against the icy air, and looked around.

There was only one car in the car park: Yvonne's gunmetal-grey Range Rover. She wound down the window and waved a scarlet-manicured hand at me, and I felt a jolt of annoyance when I saw that she wasn't alone. From the passenger seat, Daisy waved too, and I heard her carol, 'Here we are, Nat!'

Great. I was going to visit a potential wedding venue without my fiancé, but with my future mother- and sister-in-law. Diva central.

'Morning.' I opened the door and swung into the back seat, keeping what I hoped was a cheerful smile on my face. 'Thanks ever so much for picking me up – I really appreciate it.'

'No other option out here, is there?' Yvonne said. 'There isn't exactly a taxi rank. Why you and Archie don't get a car I don't know.'

Because we can't afford to buy one. Because we'd only use it three times a year. Because Archie's got the van he uses for work. Because it would cost a fortune to park and insure. But I said none of those things.

'Us Londoners,' I said lightly, 'always assume there'll be Ubers, even in the countryside.'

Yvonne opened her mouth as if about to say something, then snapped it shut again and rolled her eyes.

'I'm off work.' Daisy twisted around in her seat and smiled conspiratorially. 'I've had an awful cold, you see. But then this morning I felt much better and I thought I'd come along and help.'

She didn't sound like she had a cold at all.

'Thanks for joining us,' I muttered.

'Now.' Yvonne tapped the satnav. 'Finchcocks Manor. It should take us about twenty-five minutes. It really is proper countryside. But there's a village a couple of miles away where there are a few B&Bs for guests. And of course there are rooms in the manor itself – enough to accommodate about thirty, so that would take care of the bridal party and anyone else who wanted to stay over.'

And could afford four hundred quid per person for a room – sorry, a suite. I'd been on the website and checked, almost writing off the place there and then.

'I saw Finchcocks in *Brides* magazine, back when Donovan and I were planning our wedding,' Daisy said wistfully. 'But it was booked solid, and anyway when we saw Gosfield Hall we just fell completely in love. With it, I mean. We were in love with each other already. Or so I thought.'

Yvonne sighed. 'That lovely wedding. All planned down to the last monogrammed serviette and he had to go and ruin it.'

'Bastard,' hissed Daisy.

I hunted desperately for something to say – did I commiserate over Donovan's undeniable bastardness? Join her in mourning the loss of her wedding almost two years ago? Say I was sorry even though it was nothing to do with me?

'I hope it's not bringing back too many horrible memories,' I said. 'Helping to plan Archie's and my wedding. Because although I really, really appreciate everything you're doing, if it's too painful…'

Daisy sniffed, but I still wasn't buying the cold story. 'It's whatchamacallit. A catalyst?'

'Catharsis,' her mother said. 'Like in Greek tragedies. Keith and I went to see one when we were in Athens and couldn't make head or tail of it. The actors might as well have been talking Greek for all the sense it made to us.'

I wasn't sure that I wanted my wedding to bear too much resemblance to a Greek tragedy, comprehensible or not. But before I could say anything else, the satnav cut in with a series of complicated directions, and soon Yvonne was swinging the car through a pair of high wrought-iron gates set in a red-brick wall that seemed to go on forever.

We drove slowly along a narrow drive lined with tall trees, which meandered through a series of graceful bends, gaps in the trees offering glimpses of green fields, a glimmering lake, and what looked like a golf course. At last the trees parted and the manor came into view.

If I'd thought Keith and Yvonne's house was the ultimate in grandeur, I changed my mind right then. This place was humongous. It had towers on either end and a broad terrace stretching between them, a double staircase leading up to it. Its three storeys were studded with windows that regarded us like the watchful eyes of a crowd of strangers. In front of the central door was a huge stone fountain, water splashing down the lichened flanks of four leaping dolphins.

'Imagine,' Daisy said. 'You could arrive in a vintage Roller and step out in your wedding gown. You'd feel just like a princess.'

I'd feel like a total fraud, I thought.

'Crikey, it's enormous,' I said. 'And very beautiful.'

'Designed by Robert Corrington, I read,' Yvonne said. 'But the house dates back to the Norman Conquest. Now where on earth do you suppose I'm meant to park?'

But before I could offer a suggestion, a man in a buff-coloured tailcoat stepped out from the front door and came over to us at a pace that looked leisurely but was actually speedy as anything. He walked round to Yvonne's side of the car and opened the door. Yvonne looked startled for a second, as if worried she'd become a victim of the world's poshest carjacking, then she half-swung her legs out of the door.

'Madam,' the man said, 'allow me to park your vehicle in one of our secure bays in the former stable block.'

'Certainly,' Yvonne said graciously, standing up and cracking her head on the door frame, which rather killed the graciousness.

I opened my door and joined her, but Daisy waited for the bloke – footman, valet, chauffeur, whatever he was – to come round and let her out. Then he took Yvonne's place behind the wheel and swung the car away round to the back of the house.

'I hope he doesn't scratch the bloody thing,' she said. 'Keith'd have my guts for garters.'

Together, we approached the entrance to the house, where another liveried man was waiting.

'Good morning, Madam. How may I assist you today?'

I wasn't sure whether Yvonne was still dazed from the bash she'd given her skull, but she seemed to have been robbed of the power of speech, so I stepped in.

'We're here to have a look around, potentially for a wedding.'

'Ah, you'll be seeing Valentin.' The guy was suddenly wreathed in smiles. 'Follow me.'

I thought how funny it was that someone in charge of arranging swanky weddings should be called Valentin, but as soon as I saw him I stopped thinking about anything much.

He had to be the most drop-dead gorgeous man I'd ever seen in my life. He wasn't especially tall, and he wasn't dressed in the sort of sharp suit I'd have expected (had I not been too overawed to expect anything much). But he was just classically model-handsome: his black hair curving perfectly over the olive skin of his forehead, his eyes a sparkling, clear brown under the arches of his brows, his open-necked blue shirt showing just the right amount of toned, tanned neck. And when he smiled, all I could think was, *Oh my God, if it wasn't for loving Archie, I so, so would.*

'Ladies.' He gave a little half-bow. 'Enchanted to meet you all. I am Valentin Dubois, the events planner here at Finchcocks.'

His accent was subtle but noticeably French, and the hand he extended for us to shake was perfectly manicured and left the faintest sheen of hand cream on my palm. Daisy and Yvonne were looking at him as if he was the Promised Land or something, evidently too bowled over by his gorgeousness to speak.

'I'm Nat,' I said. 'It's me that's getting married. And this is my fiancé's sister, Daisy, and mother, Yvonne.'

He shook their hands too, and I saw Daisy glance at hers as if resolving never to wash it ever again.

'Would you care to follow me,' he suggested, 'and I will give you the grand tour.'

'That would be great, thank you,' I said, and Daisy and Yvonne nodded mutely. I saw Yvonne give her daughter a little dig in the ribs and Daisy wink back at her, and the two of them pushed ahead of me to climb the stairs behind Valentin, rivalling each other for the best view of his chino-clad bottom.

It was like being in one of those Diet Coke ads. The ones that were broadcast before #MeToo came along and we all realised it wasn't okay to objectify anyone, male or female. Clearly my future mother- and sister-in-law hadn't got that memo – but then, if I hadn't been engaged to Archie, I'd probably have objectified Valentin myself like a good 'un.

But he wasn't the only thing to admire on our so-called grand tour. There was the eighteenth-century chapel, clad in red-, gold- and bronze-leaved ivy, where the ceremony could take place, with a twenty-person choir available to provide musical interludes. There was the stone-flagged banqueting hall where champagne and canapés could be served, the intimate dining room where a hundred and fifty guests could be accommodated for a sit-down meal, and the ballroom, where three enormous crystal chandeliers would illuminate guests as they danced the night away on a black-and-white chequered marble floor. There was the taxidermy room, packed with stuffed dead animals, including a zebra and a lion, on which, Valentin told us, many couples chose to perch for photographs.

And what was the most memorable moment of your wedding day, Nat? I imagined some future friend asking me.

That would have been when the dead zebra collapsed under my husband's weight in a cloud of sawdust, I could reply.

There was the flock of white peacocks that roamed the grounds, occasionally emitting discordant shrieks. There was the wine cellar, with its wonky cobbled floor and ranks and ranks of bottles lining the walls, some of which Valentin said were worth hundreds of thousands of pounds.

The honeymoon suite, Valentin told us, was occupied at present – he gave Daisy a knowing little smile as he said this, and she practically simpered back at him – but we could view a video of it on their website if we wished.

A video of the couple's wedding night, Paris Hilton-style? Surely that wasn't what he meant.

The tour ended in Valentin's office, which had mullioned windows and a Persian carpet on the floor and looked far too luxurious to be a place of work, where a woman in a black dress and white apron brought us coffee.

'*Alors*,' Valentin said, 'I think you have seen everything. Do you have any questions for me?'

How much would all of this cost? my mind screamed, but I was too shy to ask the question, and not sure that it was my place to, anyway.

'I suppose you must be booked up months and months in advance,' Daisy said, almost longingly.

'Indeed. Years in fact – we already have one confirmed booking for… let me see… twenty-nine months in the future. The summer is most popular, of course. If you were to consider a January wedding we might be able to offer something a little earlier.'

January? That was just weeks away. Even given the sense of urgency Mum had imparted to me, that felt terrifyingly soon. I thought of the quiz – *Are you truly ready to say I do?* I believed I was – I knew I was certain Archie was the man for me. But at the same time, and in total contradiction to that, I was even surer I wouldn't be ready for a wedding by January – certainly not one as posh and luxurious and pricey as this place demanded.

'January next year?' Yvonne asked faintly. 'Like, right after Christmas?'

'Ah – *non*,' Valentin said, tapping his iPad. 'That would be the following January, thirteen months from now.'

That still felt awfully soon – but, at the same time, really too late.

'We'd hoped for the first half of next year, really,' I said. 'You see, my grandpa's getting on, and my mother and I want – we want him to be able to enjoy the day.'

'Of course.' Valentin treated me to a devastating smile. 'A wedding should be an occasion for all the family to celebrate, young and not so young.'

The smile stayed in place, but I got the sense Valentin's attention was straying. Sure enough, he asked us to excuse him for a second (except, enchantingly, he said, '*Excusez-moi*') and took his mobile phone out of his pocket.

'Madame Whittard! How are you? And how are Georgia and Simon?'

There was a longish pause. I could just about hear a woman's voice talking agitatedly, but I couldn't make out any of the words.

'This is such a pity,' Valentin went on. 'Really, I am so sorry to hear. But it is only a postponement, yes? Once your son is back from China, the wedding will be rescheduled and go ahead better than ever! We keep all the plans on ice, yes? And you, Madame, please pass on my best wishes to the happy couple.'

He put down the phone. I could see expectation lighting up Yvonne and Daisy's faces.

'Well,' Valentin said, 'this is – what do you call it? – serendipitous. Our client who had the venue booked for the first Saturday in April has been posted abroad for six months, and therefore…'

'You've got a free date!' Yvonne breathed. 'At the perfect time for us!'

'*Oui, Madame.*'

'Then we should book it straight away. Shouldn't we?'

'God, yes!' Daisy said. 'There's masses of time, and there's all the research we did for my wedding, and Valentin will help us organise it all.'

'If Natalie agrees, of course.' Valentin turned his gaze to me, the corners of his eyes crinkling in a conspiratorial smile.

I felt like his eyes were a pair of headlights and I was a rabbit. Part of me was giddy with excitement at the idea of getting married in this gorgeous place – at the prospect of the rose garden in bloom, the photographs on the terrace, the champagne reception in the great hall. And all in plenty of time, so Grandpa would be there and be well. But another part was impossibly daunted. What about the quiet registry office ceremony Archie and I'd wanted? What about the chilled drinks party afterwards in the Ginger Cat, with a buffet cooked by Zoe?

What about how much all of this was going to cost?

'What about Archie?' I said. 'He hasn't even seen the place. Can we really make a decision without him?'

'Archie,' Yvonne said, in a tone that brooked no argument, 'will want to do whatever makes his future wife happy.'

Chapter Nine

Think about those moments that make you go weak at the knees. How do you keep the spark alive in your relationship?

A. Light candles and play soft music. He provides the red roses, and sometimes we slow-dance round our living room.

B. Go for a nice meal together, country walk – whatever, we're pretty close all the time and we don't need to manufacture romance in our relationship.

C. I've never thought about it – the spark's there every time he looks at me, no firelighters required.

D. Sparks fly twenty-four/seven over here – it's just a question of when they burst into flames!

'You need a drink?' Mum said. 'I need a drink!'

'I also need a drink,' echoed Lara.

'Honestly, the two of you are a right pair of drama llamas,' I said. 'I'm the one who's going to be trying on wedding dresses. You're just here for moral support.'

'But I'm going to be seeing my baby girl in what might be her bridal gown,' Mum said. 'I might cry.'

'And I'm the maid of honour,' Lara said. 'Whatever you choose will determine what I have to wear on the day. What if it ends up being tangerine-coloured or something?'

'It won't be tangerine! Honestly, what do you take me for? Anyway, that looks like a decent wine bar over there, and the shop's just down the road, so let's get absolutely bladdered first, if it'll make you feel better.'

I was putting a brave face on it, but the truth was I needed a drink as much as anyone else. The conversation Archie and I'd had the previous night had left me rattled. It hadn't been a row, but it had seemed as if the potential for it to become one had been hovering over us like a cloud obscuring the sun.

When I got home, Archie had greeted me with a gin and tonic made with his new supplier's fancy gin – clearly a peace offering to make up for leaving me to go to Finchcocks Manor on my own. He'd cooked a delicious chicken risotto and when we sat down to eat, he asked me how the day had gone.

'It's like I thought,' I said. 'Your mum went ahead and booked the place, and there was nothing I could do about it.'

'Why would you want to do anything about it? Don't you like it?'

'It's not that. I mean, it's perfectly lovely and everything, if you're into that sort of thing.'

'Into that... What are you talking about? Is it a sex dungeon or something?'

'Of course it's not a sex dungeon. Come on. Can you imagine your mother? "Yes, and we'll have the canapés just here, with a view of the gimp cage."'

'The bride will be in a latex catsuit, with a couture whip in lieu of a bouquet.'

'As the happy couple tie the knot – literally...' But I realised I was letting Archie's goofy sense of humour distract me from the conversation we needed to have. 'Seriously though. I really don't think it's right for us.'

'Okay. What's wrong with it?'

I thought of the sweeping lawns, the yew hedge maze, the peacocks and all the rest of it. How could I explain to Archie what it was about the place – or not even the venue itself, the whole set-up – that made me feel out of my depth and uncomfortable?

'Nothing. Nothing specific. It's lovely. It's really posh.'

'So? We get to have our wedding somewhere dead posh. Get in.'

'But we talked about keeping it small and low-key. We talked about having a small reception at the Ginger Cat.'

'That was before Mum and Dad offered to foot the bill. If we can have it somewhere awesome, why don't we?'

'But I wanted the Ginger Cat.' I sounded like a stubborn, sulky child, I knew. What had begun as just an idea, a way of doing things quickly and inexpensively, had become entrenched in my mind somehow.

'Why though? If you can explain it rationally to me, I might understand. Look, this just seems like fate. They've had a cancellation on a date within the timeframe you wanted for Robin to be there. Mum's happy, I'm happy. What's not to like?'

I felt tears stinging my eyes. Maybe I was being silly. Maybe I was having what other girls would see as a dream wedding venue handed to me on a plate, and I was being bratty and ungrateful. Maybe, once we started planning things properly, I'd fall in love with Finchcocks Manor almost as fast and hard as I had with Archie, and everything would be all right?

Either way, I was sure I wasn't ready to pick a fight with Archie over it.

'The manacles looked like they weren't that secure on the dungeon wall,' I said, forcing a smile. 'We might have to get them to put some brackets in or something.'

And Archie had laughed and given me that look he had, and said something about maybe starting off gently, with silk scarves or something, just to get some practice in. And later on we'd done just that, and weak at the knees didn't even cover how I'd felt.

But I definitely wasn't going to share that with my mum.

So I told her and Lara that we'd found a venue and it was amazing, and I was dead excited and, half an hour later, fortified by a bottle of chardonnay, we approached Lavinia's, a low-key boutique on a quiet cobbled street in north London.

I'd never been in the shop before; I'd never imagined I'd have an occasion special enough to wear one of their dresses for. They weren't even wedding dresses, really, but that season's collection was based around silvery grey and pale neutrals. I'd noticed this while staring wistfully at their Instagram feed, as I often did, wishing I led the sort of life that involved having immaculately cut, rather severe frocks with clean lines, as opposed to spending my days in blue polyester that could withstand a boil wash.

'Just look at that,' I said, pausing transfixed in front of the plate glass window. 'I mean, it's only a trouser suit but it's just so chic.'

'It's a bit Hillary Clinton,' Mum said, 'but you can see how perfect the cut is. That would flatter absolutely anyone.'

'It would be so stunning on you, Nat,' said Lara. 'That kind of look is really you. A pair of killer heels and you'd be good to go.'

'Shall we go in?' Tentatively, I pushed the wrought-iron handle and the door swung smoothly inwards.

The shop was small, and it smelled of fresh flowers and expensive fabric. There were clothes rails on either side, hung with just a few garments, and a polished wood armoire in the centre, its drawers ajar with artfully arranged folds of cashmere spilling out of them.

Lara approached one of the rails and reached out a finger, brushing the collar of an ecru jacket as cautiously as if it might bite her.

When a voice said, 'May I help you, ladies?' she snatched back her hand as if it just had.

Mum said, 'My daughter's getting married, and we thought we might be able to try a few pieces.'

'For the mother of the bride?' The woman was as elegant as the clothes. Although she was dressed casually in jeans and a silk top, her fair hair was gathered up in a smooth chignon and there was a string of what I was sure were real pearls around her neck. A discreet brass pin under her left collarbone had the name 'Dawn' on it.

'No, for me,' I managed to say. 'I love your clothes and I thought maybe, if you've something that's kind of bridal, it might work.'

Dawn looked at me appraisingly. 'I wouldn't describe our designs as bridal exactly, but if you were in the market for something a bit different…'

'I've not really started looking yet. This is the first place we've tried. So I'm just kind of testing the water. I'm not a dress person if I'm honest.'

'Not a dress person' was understating the case to the max. Basically, my wardrobe contained one dress: a straight-up-and-down black number I'd bought to wear to an awards thing I went to with work a few years back, when I'd still been quite new at the hospital. I'd been so intimidated at the prospect of my first outing with my new colleagues that I'd played it massively safe. The dress was long and plain and high-necked, and when I'd shown Mum a photo of it she'd raised her eyebrows and said it was surely a bit early in my life for me to go around looking like the sixty-year-old widow of a Mafia don.

So, after its sole outing, the dress had hung in my wardrobe, reproachful and unworn. All my other clothes were trousers, jeans, shorts, leggings and a few miniskirts, which I liked because they showed off my legs – my best feature, at least when they weren't covered in huge purple bruises from playing football. The thing was, I just didn't have a feminine figure. 'Athletic' would be putting it kindly – sure, I had long legs and they were a decent shape, but I wasn't exactly blessed in the boob department either, and when waists were being dished out I'd clearly been at the back of the queue, while being in the swimming team throughout high school had given me a pair of shoulders a quarterback would have been proud of.

I watched Dawn looking me up and down, assessing the situation and no doubt realising that what she was dealing with here was basically someone who the faintest hit of floral or lace or frills would transform into a man in drag.

'You can't get married in trousers, can you?' I asked hopefully.

'You can get married in whatever you bloody well please,' Lara said.

'But maybe not at Finchcocks Manor,' Mum murmured. 'And almost certainly not to Yvonne McCoy's only son.'

'If you're willing to break the mould a little,' said Dawn, 'I'm sure we have lots of pieces that would be suitable. This, for instance.'

She lifted a chunky wooden hanger from the rail behind her. Suspended from it was a jumpsuit made from heavy fabric which gleamed and flowed like water in the process of turning into ice, or possibly jelly. It was the deepest possible shade of cream, almost buttermilk in colour. It had a halterneck and no embellishment on it at all.

I reached out and touched it and the fabric was cool under my finger, so rich and smooth the slightest hint of a ragged cuticle would have snagged it.

'Oh my God,' said Lara.

'That is one hell of a garment,' Mum said.

'Can I try it on?' I croaked.

A few minutes later, I was standing in my bra and pants in a palatial fitting room, surrounded by mink-coloured velvet curtains so long they pooled on the parquet floor. I looked at myself in the mirror and saw the usual me: make-up free, my hair in its choppy bob with the heavy fringe falling just above my eyebrows, the tan marks on my arms where the sleeves of my T-shirts ended, still left over from summer.

If I was going to wear this, I'd need a spray tan for sure. But it felt like a price worth paying.

I took the jumpsuit off its hanger, feeling the weight of it draping over my arm. There were two poppers at the back of the strap that fitted round the neck, and a zip down the back – although not a long one, because it was so low-cut. I undid them both, placed a foot carefully into each leg, then pulled up the zip and pressed the poppers home.

When I turned to look at myself in the mirror, I realised I'd been holding my breath, because I let it out in a gasp.

Ordinary, scruffy Nat was gone. In her place was a woman who looked lean, elegant, even imposing. The neckline made my shoulders appear statuesque instead of just chunky. The way the seams flowed down my body gave me the waist I naturally lacked. My legs seemed longer than ever. When I turned around, I could see the strong curve of my back, graceful instead of just muscular, and for once I actually looked like I had a bottom to be proud of. My shabby black bra would have to go but that didn't matter – for once, being flat-chested was actually a blessing.

The price tag, a large rectangle of heavy cardboard embossed in gold with the designer's name, was hanging by my right elbow. I picked it up and craned my neck to see it.

It was more than I'd ever spent on a piece of clothing before – more even than my beloved yellow winter coat or the boots I'd bought the previous winter, justifying their cost to myself because they were the holy trinity of warm, waterproof and comfortable.

For something I'd only wear once, it was extortionate.

But I found I didn't care: I was smitten. I wanted that jumpsuit so much it physically hurt, a ball of longing I could feel in my chest.

But then I imagined it in the context of Finchcocks Manor. I pictured myself walking down the aisle between the rows of little golden-legged chairs, with Yvonne's friends judging me from underneath the feathered brims of their hats. I imagined Archie in his tailcoat and top hat with a rosebud in his buttonhole. I thought of the sweeping lawn that curved down to the lake with the swans on it, and the peacocks on the terrace.

At that fairy-tale wedding, I'd look like the wicked stepmother.

It was right for me, but all wrong for the wedding.

I let the price tag fall, feeling its sharp corner tap my ribs. I tugged down the zip and released the poppers, stepped carefully out and reassembled everything on the hanger. And when I turned back to my reflection, I was just me again; the spell was broken.

I put my jeans back on, laced up my trainers and pulled my jumper back over my head, combing my fingers through my hair to smooth it. I picked up my bag and shrugged on my yellow coat, which now felt like an ordinary garment, just another part of me, rather than the wonderful and exciting purchase it had seemed only a few weeks before.

And then, giving the jumpsuit a final, wistful caress, I parted the curtains and emerged into the shop.

'Well?' asked Mum.

'Why didn't you leave it on?' Lara demanded. 'I bet you looked knockout stunning in it. Go and put it on again so we can see!'

'Do you perhaps need a size down?' suggested Dawn.

'I don't think it's going to work,' I said. 'It's just not weddingy enough. I'm going to have to keep searching, I think.'

I passed the hanger back to her, hardly able to look at the garment on it, and watched as she carried it back to its place on the rail.

'There was a wedding-dress shop we passed a couple of door down,' Lara said. 'We could try there? I mean, their stuff will be weddingy.'

'What with it being a wedding-dress shop, and everything,' Mum said, and the two of them laughed.

'How weddingy are we aiming for, on a scale of minimalist to meringue?' Lara asked.

'Maybe somewhere around macaron?' Mum said.

I laughed, shaking off the gloom that had threatened to engulf me. We thanked Dawn and left the shop, and I didn't allow myself one last, loving look at the rail where the jumpsuit I'd never buy remained on its hanger.

'Hmmm, we're definitely veering towards meringue territory here,' I said, as we peered through the windows of Bridal Paradise a few seconds later.

'Look at that lace number.' Lara pointed. 'That's the full Kate Middleton, right there.'

'And that fishtail frock with the sequins,' Mum said. 'Don't get me wrong, Nattie, you'll look lovely whatever you wear. But I do feel it's a bit excessive to spend thousands on something that's only going to be worn for a couple of hours.'

'I could say the same about that hat you talked about buying,' I retorted. 'You won't exactly wear it every time you pop to Sainsbury's, will you?'

'And the bridesmaids' dresses as well,' Lara said. 'I mean, I definitely wouldn't want you to spend loads on something I'll never wear again. Like that, for instance. I bet that costs a bomb.'

She pointed to the interior of the shop, where I could see a girl posing in front of a mirror in a bright citrine-coloured dress. It was cut so low at the back you could practically see her bum crack, but she could get away with it because she was so toned and curvy. The bias-cut satin skimmed her hips and fell like liquid to the floor, where it puddled in a little train. Clashing hot-pink and silver beading embellished the back of the dress.

As I watched, the girl scooped up her poker-straight platinum-blonde hair on top of her head and held it there while she did a little twirl, craning over her shoulder to see her back view in the mirror.

'Let's get out of here!' I hissed, dragging Mum and Lara away from the window.

'What? Why?' Lara protested. 'Weren't we going to—'

'That was Daisy,' I said. 'Archie's sister. Trying on bridesmaid dresses. For my wedding. Without me.'

'How do you know it's for your wedding?' Mum asked.

'She's not being a bridesmaid for anyone else. She said so. And it's not like she's even my chief bridesmaid – Lara is.'

'I don't mind,' Lara said. 'But I would kind of like to actually try on what I'm going to wear before someone else chooses it.'

'With Daisy around, you'll be lucky,' I replied darkly.

I didn't want to look at any more potential wedding outfits after that – my heart wasn't in it. Instead, we went and had hot chocolate and enormous slabs of cake that was allegedly made with spinach, but, apart from the fact it was green, you'd never have known. And

Lara chose a pair of shoes and Mum bought a lipstick in a shade that didn't suit her but which came with a free gift; she could never resist one of those.

Then Lara headed off to meet a Tinder date and Mum and I got the train home.

We were mostly silent, until Mum said, 'You do know, sweetie, it's just one day?'

'I know.'

'And you do know it's only a dress?'

'I know.'

'I mean, I can't speak from experience, never having been married myself, but when you were little all my friends got engaged, one after another, and there was a period when I was going to what felt like dozens of weddings, every summer. You were a flower girl at a few of them – I'm not sure if you remember?'

I nodded. I did have a vague recollection of scratchy lace in my armpits, fancy socks that kept falling down, photos of me scowling under a circlet of flowers, and being sick after eating too much fruit cake.

'And all of them, without exception, were lovely. No matter what happened. Okay, maybe not the one where the best man got drunk and revealed in his speech that the groom liked being weed on during sex. But apart from that.'

'I know,' I acknowledged, feeling too glum even to ask Mum more about the intriguing-sounding wee story.

'And afterwards – not immediately afterwards, because there was always a sort of hangover period when you'd go round to someone's house and they'd insist you watch their wedding video even though you'd seen it about five times before – all my mates said they couldn't believe how silly they were to have worried about everything so much when, in the grand scheme of things, none of it was really that important.'

'I know.'

'Apart from them being with the person they loved. Or loved for the moment, because if memory serves me right at least half of them are divorced now.'

'Mum. I *know*.'

And I knew I sounded like a sulky teenager, but I didn't care. Mum didn't say anything more, but when she got off at her stop she gave me an extra-big hug before saying she'd see me during the week, and I wasn't to worry because everything would be all right.

And I disembarked at the next stop and walked slowly home through the dark evening, past the glowing interior of the Ginger Cat and the brightly lit front of Archie's shop, where Freddie, his assistant, was serving behind the counter. It was cold and raining and even the sight of the first Christmas lights strung up along the high street couldn't lift my mood. I felt like I'd lost something important, as if I'd taken my engagement ring off to wash my hands in the loo in a pub and forgotten to put it back on, and when I'd returned to look for it, it was gone.

Still sunk in gloom, I slotted my key into the lock and pushed open our front door. I was greeted by the smell of roasting chicken and the *Hamilton* soundtrack playing on the stereo. Archie was slumped on the sofa, his feet up on the coffee table and a beer in his hand. He was surrounded by copies of *Caffeine*, *Brew* and *Barista* magazines.

'Hey,' he said. 'How was it?'

'Okay.'

'Did you find a dress?'

'Nope. But, Archie, there's something I need to talk to you about.'

'Sure, I'll just get the potatoes in the oven. Glass of wine?'

'Yes please.'

He levered himself off the sofa and I got an extra-strong blast of roast-chicken smell as he opened the oven. I picked up one of Archie's magazines and turned the pages, but none of it meant anything to me so I went to join him as he carefully arranged the potatoes around the golden chicken.

'This can come out and rest in a second,' he said, 'then the spuds will need half an hour. Will you do that amazing thing with the spinach?'

'It's not that amazing,' I said. 'It's just enough butter to clog your arteries after one bite. It's the only thing I can actually cook.'

'Well, it's off the scale, anyway.'

I took a knife out of the drawer and started hacking at the bunch of spinach, while Archie eased the cork out of a bottle of white rioja, sniffed it, and poured a glass for me.

'Archie?'

'That's me.'

'I want to ask you something. Will you talk to Daisy and your mum about the wedding?'

'What about it?' He leaned against the closed oven door and took a swallow of beer. 'This is a new range I'm going to stock. Coffee stout. They do a chocolate version too, and a smoked one, and one with the flavour profile of milkshake. Taste?'

He passed me the bottle and I took a sip. Amazingly, it tasted of both beer and coffee.

'Nice. But seriously. I'm worried they're going to take over the whole thing. I mean, we've already got to have it at Finchcocks Manor, but there'll be loads of other things as well. I saw Daisy trying on a bridesmaid's dress today.'

'So? This is Daisy we're talking about. Shopping's basically what she does. It's her core skill.'

'I know, but it should be me making decisions about what my bridesmaids are going to wear. Or Lara. Not Daisy.'

'If she's daft enough to buy a bridesmaid's dress you don't like, tell her she's got to take it back and change it.'

I chucked the spinach into a pan of water with more force than was really necessary, waited a few seconds for it to come back to the boil, then poured it into a colander.

'It's not just that. Your mum's chosen our wedding venue. Daisy's choosing her dress. I just feel like it's going to escalate and there won't be anything left that's just ours.'

'How do you mean? What else is there to choose?'

'Everything! I don't know. Flowers, food, invitations – all that stuff.'

'Do you care what flowers we have? Because, quite honestly, I don't.'

'Well – not really,' I admitted. 'I don't know much about flowers.'

'So what's the problem with letting them do the legwork? You're busy, I'm busy. Let them get on with it. Or, if it's such a massive issue, you talk to them.'

I squeezed water out of the spinach, which was too hot still and scalded my hands.

'Ouch! I can't talk to them. Your mother doesn't like me. If she thinks I think she's interfering, it'll only make things worse.'

'Of course she likes you. Who wouldn't like you? You're amazing.'

'Thanks. But when she gave me a copy of *The Fast 800* diet book for my birthday, was that just me being paranoid? Nothing to do with her implying I'm a fat heifer?'

'Maybe she thought you'd like it. She and Daisy both think it's great. And you know you're not fat.'

'Well I certainly felt fat when she dropped round that load of her old clothes for me. Skinny jeans I couldn't get past my knees and pointy shoes and that awful mock-croc blazer thing.'

'I think that was real crocodile skin actually.'

'That makes it worse! And when she came round that time a couple of months back and cleaned the whole flat from top to bottom while we were at work, she wasn't trying to imply that I'm some kind of slattern?'

'She was just being helpful. You know how much we hate cleaning.'

'Everyone hates cleaning. That doesn't mean they want someone else to descend on their home when they're out and go through their stuff.'

Archie raised an eyebrow. 'Okay, now you are being a bit—'

'I'm not being paranoid! Archie, please? Won't you just mention to Yvonne that they can't make all the decisions?'

He looked at me, his face stubbornly set. 'Babe, just chill out. If they try and make us do stuff we don't want to do, we'll deal with it. No point making a drama out of nothing.'

'I'm not making a drama out of—' I stopped.

I could hear my voice raised in anger and I thought, *Great. So guess this is our first row about the wedding.* Sparks were flying – but the wrong kind of sparks, and not in a good way.

Chapter Ten

Do you and your man have hobbies and interests in common?

A. For sure! We love doing all the same things. We're basically joined at the hip.

B. Uh… I guess so. He's interested in me and I'm interested in him. Why would we want to do anything that doesn't involve the other?

C. Yes and no. Sometimes we do stuff together; sometimes we go off and do our own thing.

D. God, no! His hobbies bore me to tears and quite honestly it's great to have the place to myself while he's off with his mates.

The cold air seared my lungs and ears, and the tip of my nose felt numb from the rushing wind but, under my waterproof jacket, I could feel sweat trickling down into the small of my back. My thighs were burning too, pumping out the very last of the energy left in them. Behind me, I could hear Archie's breath coming in ragged gasps, but I could see nothing except the stony track in between my bike's handlebars and its front tyre turning more and more slowly.

At last, just as I was about to give up and walk, the track levelled off, and suddenly the world was spread out around and below me. Fields of trellised hops, their bare branches shining copper in the bright winter sun, were interspersed with acid-green grass, the darker green of woodland, and the coffee-brown of ploughed earth. Above it all, the sky arched in a blue dome so bright it hurt my eyes.

'Fuck me, I thought that hill was never going to end,' Archie panted, hopping off his bike and standing next to me. 'My legs feel like jelly. I'm going to have to get fit next year.'

'Worth it, though, for the view,' I said softly, my words vanishing into the brisk wind.

'It'll be worth it for the pub lunch,' Archie countered. 'Where is this place, anyway?'

'Down there.' I pointed. 'I think it's in that village where you can see the church steeple. It's only about five kilometres away.'

'Only! Lovely, relaxing, romantic day out, you said. It'll be fun, you said. Quality time, you said.'

I laughed. 'Come off it, you big moaner. Anyway, we had quality time earlier, right?'

Our eyes met and I felt a glow of pleasure, remembering how we'd worked up a sweat in a different way earlier that morning. Afterwards, we'd lain together in bed, the duvet crumpled up by our feet, our naked bodies fitting close as jigsaw pieces.

'I suppose we did,' he admitted. 'Just as well we got that in earlier, though, because my arse is going to be too sore to do anything other than lie on the sofa in front of the telly when we get home.'

'Best we get moving then,' I said. 'Come on – I'll race you to the bottom.'

Because I hadn't dismounted my bicycle, I had a head start. Archie's protestations that I was the world's most massive cheat ringing in my ears, I pushed off and pedalled furiously for a few seconds before gravity took over, and I was flying down the hill, the wind feeling even colder now, but the exhilaration of speed and beauty keeping me warm from the inside.

The trees lining the track sped past me in a blur; the last gold and russet leaves muffled the sound of our wheels on the stony ground. I glanced up briefly and saw a bird of prey – a buzzard, maybe? – hanging motionless in the cold sky.

In that moment, I felt the purest happiness. It was Saturday, I was with the man I loved, I was strong and healthy, the sun was shining and soon I'd be stuffing myself with an enormous lunch. In that moment, it was as if Yvonne, Daisy, Finchcocks Manor and my growing sense of anxiety about our wedding didn't exist – or, better still, wasn't important. This must be how Archie felt all the time, as if all was right with the world and everything would turn out for the best, no matter what.

At times like this, I could see his point.

A few minutes later, we were locking our bikes into the rack outside the Four Horseshoes. I pulled off my cycling helmet, feeling the cold breeze on my damp hair and trying to smooth down the strands with my hands.

'I must look a right sight.'

Archie pulled me close and kissed the tip of my nose. 'You look gorgeous. Your cheeks are all pink and you've got a leaf in your hair. Hold on.'

He removed it and held it out to show me.

'Thanks. Can't have them chucking us out because we look like we've been sleeping rough in a field.'

'Not until we've had our lunch, anyway. Come on, Victoria Pendleton.'

'Oi! I wasn't going that fast. You basically caught up with me coming past the church.'

'Only because you slowed down to look in the window of that cake shop. And I was only trying to catch you up so I could check out your bum in those Lycra shorts.'

'That's not my bum, that's padding.'

'What? I'm going to report you to Trading Standards for misleading advertising.'

Arm in arm, laughing, we walked into the pub and were immediately hit by a blast of heat from the open fire and the smell of fresh beer and roasting meat. We found our way to a table in the corner and sat down, peeling off our layers as fast as we could.

'Pint of lager?' Archie asked.

'Yeah, choose something for me. You're the expert.'

While I waited for him to come back from the bar, I scanned the single sheet of paper with the menu on it. There wasn't much, but it all sounded delicious and I wanted to eat it all. My mouth watered as I thought of the crunchy triple-cooked chips, burger dripping with melty cheese and golden onions, and deep-fried mac and cheese bites that were in my future.

'There's a specials board,' Archie reported, carefully putting two brimming glasses on the table. 'Whitebait, steak and ale pie, and bangers and mash.'

'Oh no! Now I've got total choice paralysis. I was sold on the burger but, then again, when is anything with pastry a bad idea?'

'If you have the burger, I'll have the pie and we can share.'

'And if you order the chocolate and cherry cheesecake, I'll give you some of my apple crumble and custard.'

'Deal.' He leaned across the table and we sealed it with a kiss.

'So, I was thinking,' Archie said an hour later as we sat back, replete from the warmth of the fire, the huge portions of food – clearly made by a chef who wasn't afraid of butter or cream or carbs – and our third pint, 'about coffee.'

'What, now? That's not a terrible idea actually, otherwise I might fall asleep on the train and we'll miss our stop.'

'Yeah, sure, I'll have a cappuccino if you're ordering. But more generally. Well, specifically, really. About the shop.'

'You want to sell coffee at Craft Fever?'

'Not just sell it.' He propped his elbows on the table and rested his chin on his hands. His eyes were sparkling with the same intensity they always had when he'd come up with a big idea... 'Roast it.'

'Roast your own coffee beans? Isn't that massively complicated?'

'Won't know until I try, will I? But there's a massive market for ethically sourced coffee from small producers. I've been looking into getting a roaster. It could live in a shed behind the shop.'

'But…' I tailed off. Part of me wanted to say that surely now – with the wedding planning about to start taking over our lives – was hardly the time to embark on another hare-brained scheme, and that the idea of needing yet more financial support from Archie's parents, however willing they were to give it, left me cold.

Then I looked across the table again at Archie's face, all lit up with excitement and enthusiasm, and I remembered how he'd toiled up the long hill behind me on his bicycle, not complaining – well, not complaining much – and how he'd immediately offered to share his food with me, how he'd told me I looked beautiful even though I was all sweaty and had a bad case of helmet hair.

I reminded myself that those things – his spontaneity, his generosity, his kindness – were the reasons why I loved him and was confident that I'd carry on loving him for the rest of my life. If he was some steady guy who worked for a bank or whatever and thought he was living on the edge if he wore his socks with 'Wednesday' printed on them when it was Tuesday, he wouldn't be Archie.

And if I was the sort of woman who wanted to share my future with such a man – well, I wouldn't be me.

'Tell me more,' I said, smiling this time. 'Where would you get the coffee beans?'

'I'm not sure yet. But there are a few small, independent roasteries around the place. It's like craft beer shops were a while ago – they're springing up everywhere. But I don't think the market's peaked yet; if I get the branding right and market it properly, it could really take off. I've already chatted to Alice at the Ginger Cat and she's up for switching from the mass-produced stuff they use now.'

'I think it sounds like a great idea,' I said. 'Like you say, it's really zeitgeisty. It'll be a wonderful addition to Craft Fever, alongside the beer and Poppy's honey.'

'And maybe next year, we can go on holiday and check out some of the plantations where they grow the stuff,' Archie went on. 'They're in amazing places – Peru, Rwanda, Costa Rica. Fancy going to Costa Rica on honeymoon?'

God. All the talk of planning our wedding and the idea of a honeymoon hadn't even crossed my mind. I'd assumed we'd wait a few months – we were too skint to go anywhere nice, and it wouldn't have occurred to me to ask Keith and Yvonne to extend their generosity beyond the wedding to what was, after all, just a glorified holiday.

'Maybe we could,' I said. 'Maybe later on next year, when we've saved up a bit.'

'It would be a legit business expense too,' Archie said. 'Tax deductible and everything. We could—'

'Hold on, I think that's my phone.'

I reached into my bag, praying it wouldn't be Yvonne or Daisy calling to talk through some new and crazy idea they'd had about the wedding. But it was an unfamiliar number on my screen.

'Hello, Nat speaking.'

'Hello!' a woman's voice carolled. 'I'm so glad I caught you. My name's Fenella White, features editor on *Inspired Bride* magazine. Terribly sorry to bother you on a weekend, but I thought I'd give your number a try, just on the off-chance no one else had got to you first. Is this a good time for a chat?'

'I… Okay. Yes, I guess so.'

Across the table, Archie raised an eyebrow curiously. I made a *no fucking idea* gesture with my hands.

'I got your number from Yvonne McCoy, and I got her number from Valentin at Finchcocks Manor – isn't he the biggest hunk? They both mentioned that your wedding was going to be something a bit special. As you know, if you're an *IB* reader – and of course you are! – we feature real weddings in the mag, ones that are a bit aspirational, a bit different, but nonetheless authentic. When Val told me about yours – the peacocks, the floral archway – I felt this had the *IB* magic written all over it. Would you…'

I held the phone away from my ear, looking at it in horror. My wedding, in a magazine? Photos of me and Archie, printed thousands of times? People flipping through the pages on the train and seeing me?

'I'm awfully sorry,' I said. 'This is such a terrible line, I can only catch about one word in three.'

'As I was saying, we were hoping to feature your wedding—'

'I'm afraid I can't hear… you're breaking up.' I terminated the call and put my phone away, my hands trembling.

'What was that about?'

'Just one of those ambulance-chaser calls about me having been in a car accident that wasn't my fault. You know.'

Archie rolled his eyes in sympathy. If Fenella Whatshername called again, I'd think of a way to say no to her. For now, cowardly as it was, I'd do my best to forget all about her.

Chapter Eleven

When you imagine walking down the aisle in your wedding dress, you feel…

A. Elated. I've dreamed of that moment for the longest time and I know I'll find The Dress just like I've found The One.

B. Excited – but it's more about the rest of our lives than about that moment, and a dress is just a dress at the end of the day.

C. Mega stressed. How am I ever going to find something that makes me look as perfect as I want to be on the day?

D. Super confident. I'm going to throw everything I've got at looking my best on the day and I know I'll nail it.

'Oh my God,' I moaned. 'My head. I'm broken. I feel sick.'

'Want me to bring a bucket?' Archie asked. I heard the rustle of the duvet as he sat up next to me.

'Yes. Actually, no. A couple of paracetamol and a cup of tea, and then I might be able to get back to sleep. I might even feel okay in a couple of years.'

'On it.' He swung out of bed and I heard his footsteps hurrying towards the kitchen and the flick of the kettle's switch, which went through my pounding head like a hammer blow.

I pulled the pillow over my eyes and willed myself to go back to sleep – cold tea would be a price worth paying for an escape from this misery. But now that I was awake, my body seemed determined to stay that way.

I sat up. The curtains were closed but I could see a line of blue sky between them, which hit my eyes like a laser. It was a beautiful day. Perhaps Archie and I could go for a walk and get some breakfast, once I was reasonably confident that I wasn't going to spew – or die.

By some miracle of self-preservation – the same magic that had got me home in one piece and reminded me to take off my make-up before getting into bed – I had remembered to put my phone on to charge. Strong work by Drunk Nat – if only she'd been thinking ahead to the same extent when she'd ordered that last round of tequila shots. I picked it up and flicked through to my text messages.

Oh my God, I'm dying, Lara had posted a few minutes before. *In fact I think I am already dead.*

I've puked twice already this morning, Precious had replied. *Cyprian is laughing at me and I might have to call off our engagement because I think I hate him.*

Me too, I replied. *Sending this from beyond the grave.*

Thank God we're not working.

Definitely not leaving this bed for a long time.

If ever.

Slightly cheered by knowing that my mates were feeling every bit as rough as I was, I tapped through to my other messages, vaguely recalling that there was a WhatsApp from Daisy I needed to answer.

But – oh shit – I already had. At about ten the previous night, which would have been after Mr Saw had dished out the Secret Santa gifts and Precious and I had collapsed most of a bottle of Baileys, but before the dancing-round-our-handbags stage, I'd sent her a message saying I was at my Christmas party, but we'd chat in the morning.

Coolio, she'd replied. *Only Mum and I were wondering if you'd be up for wedding-dress shopping tomorrow? There's this amazing new boutique that's opened near us, and they're doing free champagne and canapés tomorrow.*

Sounds great! Drunk Nat had texted back. *What time shall I meet you and where?*

Eleven o'clock at Melinda's? We can have breakfast and head off for dress shopping afterwards.

Amazing! I'll see you there.

Not cool, Drunk Nat, I thought. *I won't be letting you loose with my phone again in a hurry, if this is the kind of stunt you're going to pull on Hungover Nat.*

'Tea with two sugars,' Archie said. 'And two paracetamol. Glad you're still alive.'

'I am now, but I won't be for long. I only agreed to go wedding-dress shopping with your mum and sister. Last night, when I was pissed.'

Callously, Archie laughed. 'Drunk texting, rookie error. Why not tell her you made a mistake, you feel like death and you'll have to rearrange for another time when you're not looking like a corpse and stinking of stale prosecco?'

I gulped down the pills with a mouthful of tea. 'Can't. She'll be offended and your mum will hate me. Even more than she already does.'

'Nat, for the one billionth time, she doesn't hate you.'

'Still, I said I'd go, and I'm going to have to.'

'Would toast help? With peanut butter?'

'Thanks, Archie.' I finished my tea and handed him the empty mug. 'You are a good, kind man and I love you very much. But right now, even peanut butter won't fix me. The only thing that would help me is staying in bed all day, and that's not an option.'

'I'll get out of your way then.'

I heaved myself out of bed, waited for the room to stop spinning, and dragged myself through to the bathroom, cursing my own stupid drunk texting, my inability to stop after four glasses of prosecco, and absolutely everything to do with weddings, but specifically wedding dresses. Oh, and the stupid novelty reindeer antler headband I must have somehow acquired during the night, which I tripped over in the doorway.

At least, I thought, remembering last night's chat with Precious, I wasn't alone.

'Oh my God, it is so stressful,' she'd said, as we perched knee to knee on two hard chairs in the Ginger Cat, our bottle of Irish cream liqueur and a plate of pigs in blankets between us. 'It's not just me, is it?'

I shook my head. 'It is so stressful. I knew it would escalate, and it has. Yvonne's already talking about booking a string quartet for the reception and a soloist to sing "O Perfect Love" while we sign the register. And it's not like I can tell her to just crack on and do it – I have to listen to tapes of them all and discuss which one's best, and make a decision with her. And I'm tone-deaf – they could all be playing out of tune and singing flat for all I know.'

'Mum keeps sending me recipes,' Precious said. 'I mean, I'm a shit cook and she's ace and I know whatever she makes for the wedding will be delicious, but that's not good enough. It's like, "Do we have this recipe for ofada stew or that one? I can't decide so you need to cook them both and tell me what you think."'

'We had to go for a meeting with a cake lady last Saturday,' I said. 'Or rather, I had to go, because Archie was working. And I mean – it was cake, right? What's not to like? But then I had to taste about seven different flavours of sponge, because apparently no one has fruit cake any more, and I had to make a decision there and then, except I didn't like the chocolate orange and Yvonne did, so now we're having a layer of that and a layer of lemon and lavender and a layer of Madagascan vanilla. And the decoration is going to look stunning. But then she told Yvonne the price and I legit almost fainted.'

'Don't get me started on that. Mum's feeding half of Lagos, and buying all the drink too, and it's going to cost a fortune. Thanks God Cyprian's parents are contributing or she'd have had to sell her car or something.'

'And the worst thing is, you're grateful. I mean, you actually are.'

'Of course I am. Everyone's going to all this trouble and expense for me and Cyprian and I'm like, I really love you all so much but you don't have to do this.'

I nodded so hard my head almost fell off. 'I'm hoping that doing all this wedding planning with Yvonne will bring us closer. She's always been a bit kind of frosty with me. But it means I can't ever say, "Look, don't you think this is all too much?" I don't need two photographers and a videographer and a bloody wedding website designed for me. I just don't. And yeah, the cost.'

'And the guilt.'

And we'd looked around, almost furtively, as if Yvonne and Precious's mum might have been standing there listening in on our conversation, although of course they weren't. But the Baileys and the pigs in blankets were finished, so we got up and returned to the party.

And now, paying the price for my overindulgence, I was going to be trying on dresses feeling as rough as a badger's arse. An hour later, showered, make-up applied and hair washed, I turned left out of the train station as Daisy had directed, walked a few yards down the high street and stepped into the seventh circle of hell.

That was how it felt, anyway.

Everything – but everything – in Melinda's coffee shop was pink. The floor was pale pink porcelain tiles that felt slippery under my feet. The walls were covered in bright pink flock wallpaper and hung with prints of overblown roses and peonies. The chairs were upholstered in rose-coloured velvet. The waitresses wore cerise aprons. In a glass cabinet, I could see arrays of cupcakes piped with huge swirls of strawberry-coloured buttercream.

At first, my eyes were too assaulted by the ambush of pink to spot Archie's mother and sister, but then I heard Yvonne call out my name and saw her waving from a table in the far corner of the room. Her nails, I noticed as she lifted her glass of rosé champagne, were painted pink.

'Morning, morning,' they chorused.

I leaned over the table and exchanged air-kisses with them both, hoping my shower gel and toothpaste had got rid of the last lingering smell of booze from the night before.

'Don't you just love this place?' Daisy said. 'It's new; it opened a couple of weeks before the wedding-dress shop. Our high street is really coming up in the world.'

'It's really… feminine,' I agreed, sitting down and helping myself to water from a coral-coloured glass jug, praying it wouldn't be laced with some mysterious essence of pinkness.

'Just wait until you see the dress shop,' Yvonne gushed. 'It's absolutely adorable, like something out of a fairy tale. But we thought we should have a bite to eat first.'

'Don't the cupcakes look incredible?' asked Daisy. 'They do waffles, too, with four different flavours of syrup and loads of cream.'

'And macarons and red velvet cake and tiramisu,' said Yvonne.

'It's almost enough to make us break our pre-wedding diets,' Daisy sighed.

'But not quite,' Yvonne said. 'So we've ordered strawberries with fat-free yoghurt – we all deserve a treat, don't we?'

I certainly didn't feel like I deserved anything at that moment, apart from maybe a lie-down in a darkened room. But I picked up the menu – which was neon-pink with gold lettering on it and made my eyes feel as if they'd been plunged into a bath of acid – and scanned it.

Where was the sausage sandwich? Where was the egg and cheese toastie? Where was the cold pizza every cell in my body was calling out for? Not here, that was for sure. I considered the sugary, creamy offerings – which normally, let me be completely honest, I'd have been right behind – and there was just no way. The very idea of putting any of that stuff in my body was a one-way trip to Vomitville, population: me.

The alternative – toughing it out and possibly falling into a hypoglycaemic coma or killing someone in a fit of hungover hanger – wasn't pretty, but it was all I had.

'Actually,' I said, 'I was also hoping to lose a few pounds before the wedding. I'll stick with a peppermint tea.'

So it was fortified with just a bit of fragrant hot water (that and a sense that if I closed my eyes, all I would be able to see would be pink, as if my brain was literally melting like fairground candyfloss on a hot day) that I tottered after Daisy and Yvonne into Mariée, the new bridal boutique a few doors along.

If the café had assailed my senses with all things pink and sugary, the wedding shop had its own lethal arsenal as a follow-up. Here, everything was white, cream and sparkly. It was roasting hot – and I say that as a seasoned veteran of hospital wards. The scent of floral room fragrance was so strong it made me want to sneeze.

But Daisy, pausing on the threshold, breathed it all in with something like reverence.

'Oh my God,' she gasped. 'Imagine if this place had been here when I was planning my wedding, Mum. I'd basically have moved in and lived here.'

'Isn't it delightful?' Yvonne clasped her hands in front of her as if she was having a religious experience. 'So tasteful and upmarket. Just think, this was a fabric shop before. Rolls and rolls of polyester everywhere, in such garish colours, and I'm quite sure they had a clothes moth infestation.'

Pity the moth that tried eating this lot. It would choke to death on a sequin before it properly got started.

But before I could express an opinion of my own, a woman came whisking over to us. She was wearing a little waisted powder-blue suit, and her hair was pale coppery blonde, sprayed into a rigid helmet around her equally immobile, Botoxed-to-the-max face.

'Ladies!' she trilled. 'Welcome to Mariée! I'm Davina, and I'm so excited to be part of your bridal journey! This must be the lucky girl! With your colouring and your figure, you were just born to be a bride!'

'That's my daughter, Daisy,' Yvonne said proudly. 'The bride-to-be is Natalie here, who's engaged to my son Archie.'

'Ah.' To be fair, Davina did seem a bit embarrassed. But she styled it out. 'Well, you have a different look, but no matter. Why don't I help you ladies to a glass of champers and you can have a little browse around, get a sense of some of the styles and designers we represent.'

No! Not more bloody alcohol! my body screamed, but it was too late – a glass full of cold bubbles was pressed into my hand. My stomach was churning, my head felt like a jackhammer was going off inside it and I could feel sweat breaking out all over my body.

Just get through it, Nat, I told myself. *Try on a few frocks and then you can go home to bed.*

Cautiously, as if the ranks of dresses might take it upon themselves to leap off and attack me, I approached one of the rails, Daisy and Yvonne at my side. There was no doubt that these were beautiful designs: ice-white satin, champagne-coloured lace, cream silk, all embellished with beads and brocade and diamanté. I reached out a hand to touch one of them but, before I could, Davina leaped forward and pressed a pair of white cotton gloves into my hand.

'If you don't mind,' she said. 'We try to keep our pieces in pristine condition.'

Feeling like a naughty child with chocolate smeared all over my face, I pulled on the gloves. They made my perspiring hands even hotter.

'Look at this.' Yvonne lifted a hanger off the rail. 'Backless lace! I could just see you in this, Natalie. So feminine – so different from your usual style.'

As if my usual style was a suit and tie, or a blacksmith's apron, or dungarees and a lumberjack shirt.

'Detailing on the back of a frock is such a wonderful touch,' said Davina. 'When you're saying your vows, the assembled congregation can only see your back, of course, and it makes for such a lovely effect in the photographs.'

'We've booked Stephan Austell to take the photographs on the day,' Yvonne said. 'Don't you just love his style? Reportage, but with a real couture touch.'

Stephan Austell? He must have been one of the photographers whose portfolios Yvonne had sent me to look at. At the time, still reeling at the idea that we would need not one but two photographers on the day, I'd flicked through to the price section on their websites and tried to find the ones that looked cheapest. But Stephan had stood out for me because his 'full bridal package' included an 'intimate boudoir album' for the bride to present to her groom as a gift the night before.

And quite honestly, the idea of Yvonne and Keith not only paying for pictures of me in my bra and pants, sucking an ice lolly in a sultry fashion, but of them proudly presenting it to Archie for him to knock one out over on his last night as a single man made me cringe so hard I practically split in half.

'Mum!' Daisy almost squeaked from across the room. 'Come and look at this!'

Together, Yvonne, Davina and I turned and hurried over. Daisy had taken a frock off the rail and was holding it against her body, her face alight with emotion.

'It's basically *my* dress! My dream dress that we bought for my wedding!'

In spite of myself, I felt a wave of sadness for Daisy. The dress was so perfectly her. It had a tiny, strapless bodice, encrusted with a billion sparkles. The skirt was an enormous cloud of tulle, sparkling too, caught up at intervals at the hemline with satin bows. It was over the top, it was absurd, and Daisy would have looked like a princess in it.

'You'll try it on, won't you, Nat?' she asked. 'Just for me? Go on.'

'Of course I will.' As much as the dress was pure Daisy, it was pure not me, but in my fragile state it seemed easier to comply.

'Just step this way,' commanded Davina, ushering me into an enormous fitting room equipped with a dainty chaise longue and a cluster of little tables holding accessories: a pair of white velvet shoes, a tiara, a pearl necklace. There was no mirror.

But I had no time to properly take any of it in, because Davina had pulled my coat off my shoulders and was standing by waiting for me to strip. Clearly, she had no intention of leaving me to get into the dress on my own, which was just as well, really, because I'd have put a foot through it for sure. Reluctantly, I took off my trainers and socks, then stepped out of my jeans and tugged my jumper over my head.

Standing there in my shabby bra and cotton knickers with Snoopy printed on them, smelling my deodorant, and probably last night's prosecco, I could have died of embarrassment.

Just try on the dress, I ordered myself. *Just get this over with.*

'Now, if you just pop one foot in,' Davina said in a tone reminiscent of me explaining to a particularly wobbly patient how to use the stairs, 'there we go. And the other one. We'll just get rid of this, shall we?'

And she unhooked my bra. I held it up for a second, mortified, but there was nothing I could do. I had to let the straps slip off my shoulders and, seconds later, my top half was encased in rigid, boned, beaded satin.

'You'll need someone to help you get dressed on the day,' Davina prattled on. 'These wee hooks down the back are fiddly. Six, seven, eight – there we go. Now if you'll just slip your feet into these – a bit on the small side for you, but we need the extra height to see how the dress falls – that's lovely.'

Just let me not sweat in it, I prayed. *If I do, she might make me buy it.*

I could feel the beads and crystals around the top of the dress digging into the skin on my arms. The shoes pinched my toes. My head was fuzzy with hangover and heat and I wondered if I might be about to faint.

'Let's step outside and have a little look, shall we?'

Davina pulled the curtain aside and led me out into the shop, towards a wooden plinth in front of a mirror. Gritting my teeth, I stepped onto it and looked up.

In front of me was a bride. A woman in a fairy-tale dress, magical and sparkling. Only something was wrong. It was like I'd found myself in some random reality TV show where someone who had never met me had picked my name out of a hat and chosen a wedding dress for me. The tiny bodice made my shoulders appear bony and brawny, both at once. The nipped-in waist emphasised the fact that my waist did not, in fact, nip in. My bare arms, toned from my physical job, looked bulky and masculine alongside the delicate embroidered fabric. And my legs, my best feature, were completely hidden by layers and layers of poufy tulle.

All at once, the heat and the hangover and the sense of helplessness overwhelmed me, and I started to cry.

'Oh bless you!' Yvonne hurried over with a tissue. 'You poor love! It's an emotional moment seeing yourself looking so very different.'

'But don't you see?' Daisy breathed. 'Nat can wear my dress! My actual dress! It's identical to this one and it's been in the loft in acid-free tissue paper all this time! It will be perfect!'

Oh, no, screamed my mind, just as Yvonne cooed, 'Oh yes!'

There was no way out of this, I realised. None whatsoever. My legs seemed to lose the power to support me and I collapsed onto the dais in slow motion, surrounded by clouds of tulle, sobbing my head off.

Chapter Twelve

So your wedding plans are beginning to take shape. Who's making the decisions?

A. We're choosing absolutely everything together, the same as we do in all parts of our life.

B. I'm deciding most things, but not everything. I'm not fussed about what socks he wears, for instance.

C. I'm listening to everyone's opinions and to be honest it sometimes feels like we can't ever decide on anything!

D. I am, of course. I mean, it's both of our day but I'm the bride, right?

'What do you reckon, Nat? This one or this one?'

I looked at the two Christmas trees. One was slightly taller than the other, one slightly bushier. I could smell their piney fragrance in the cold air of the pub car park. I thought of the box of decorations packed away in our airing cupboard: the cheap glittery baubles I bought when we had our first Christmas together; the posh etched-glass ones from Selfridges that Yvonne gave us when they decided to replace all their decorations with a new purple and gold colour scheme; the battered red cardboard heart I made in primary school, which I'd persuaded Mum to part with.

Normally, I'd have been giddy with excitement at the prospect of getting the tree home, decorating it, switching on its lights and celebrating with a glass of sherry and a mince pie, knowing it was almost Christmas.

But somehow I couldn't summon up any excitement this year. Everything I normally looked forward to so much – the tree, the present-wrapping, the cake-icing and mince-pie-baking – just felt like another stressful chore to get through.

It didn't help that Archie, who last year had engaged with all the frantic pre-Christmas activity, or at least indulged me in it, hadn't shown much of an interest this year. I'd had to practically drag him out to choose our tree, way later than I would have normally put it up, because he'd claimed to be too busy. And I suppose he was: when he wasn't working in the shop, he was in the newly installed shed in its backyard, playing with his stupid bloody coffee roaster.

Okay, that was unfair, and I knew it. The coffee was going to be a part of his business, a diversification, an additional income stream. It wasn't Archie's fault that I was feeling anxious and overwhelmed. Although actually, maybe it was, a bit.

'Nat? Are you going to pick one?'

'Oh… the one on the left.'

'Right then.'

Archie handed over some cash to the Christmas tree guy – a surly, unshaven bloke who looked as if this was just a side hustle and his day job was actually dealing heroin or people-trafficking or something – hoisted the net-wrapped tree onto his shoulder, and we walked home together through the blustery, drizzly streets.

'Aren't you going to stay and help me decorate it?' I asked as Archie, having unceremoniously dumped the tree on the living-room floor, put his keys back in his pocket and turned to leave.

'Can't, Nat. I've got that batch of Nicaraguan beans in the roaster. I overdid the last lot so I want to keep an eye on these ones. We can do it tonight.'

'But tonight we're meant to be going through the guest list for the wedding. Your mum sent me that long email full of stuff we need to do, remember? And we said we'd get that ticked off tonight.'

'We can do them both. Or you can do the tree and we can take a look at the wedding stuff tonight. Okay? I have to run. Love you.'

He leaned over and kissed me, his cheek still cold from the winter day and smelling piney from the Christmas tree, and then he turned and left, the door slamming hard behind him.

Wearily, I stripped the mesh wrapping off the tree and stood it upright. With Archie there to help, one of us could have held the trunk while the other tightened the supports on the Christmas tree stand – another donation from Yvonne. But this time there was only me to do it, and two hands were at least one too few.

After a half-hour struggle, during which I was poked in the eye with spiky branches, got sticky black pine sap all over my hands, shed needles all over the carpet and told the damn tree, the bloody stand and the stupid bastarding institution of Christmas exactly what I thought of them all, I gave up, deciding that if the tree was slightly askew, it was going to have to stay that way.

I got out the box of decorations and unwrapped them, one by one, arranging them on the branches with the smallest at the top and the largest at the bottom, the way Mum had always done it. Before, it had felt like a treasure hunt, each star or angel or bauble emerging from its wrapping as if I was seeing it for the first time. But today there was none of that pleasure – it was just a job to be done.

And when it was finished, I hadn't the heart to have our special festive snack alone. I made a cup of coffee, sat down on the sofa with my laptop and opened the email I'd received from Yvonne the previous day. Although it was clearly meant for me and Archie, she hadn't copied him in on it.

Hello you two!

Only just over a hundred days to go! It seems like a long time, I know, but we have a lot of ground to cover before then and so many exciting choices to make! I think I mentioned that Daisy has set up a thing called Pinterest – I'd never heard of it, but she says you will know what it is and how it works. There are lots of different 'mood boards' on there that you can add pictures to of things that you like. I know I don't need to say this to you but please let's bear in mind that we want this occasion to be tasteful and classy.

Also, we need to make decisions on the guest list, the flowers, the wedding transport, the guest accommodation, the bridesmaids' and ushers' (and of course our wee pageboy Linus's!) outfits, the readings for the ceremony, your accessories, Archie's outfit, the menu, the hen and stag parties.

Keith has put together a spreadsheet to help us all keep track of costs, and I have attached it here. I've also attached an initial guest list of our family and friends who we really hope can attend – there are just seventy-five of them so far and the venue can accommodate a hundred and forty, so there will be plenty of room for some of your friends and Emma's side of the family.

Please remember that we are here to help guide your decision-making so if you're unsure about anything, please do ask me or Daisy.

Love from Mum/Yvonne

PS – Has Fenella White been in touch at all?

I read the email again and then clicked on the two attachments and the link to Daisy's Pinterest page. The guest list was just a long row of names of people, of whom I knew about five. Once we'd invited Mum, Grandpa, a couple of my colleagues and a few of Archie's friends, there'd barely be room for anyone else.

I thought of my friend Suzie, whose wedding I'd been bridesmaid at a couple of years previously, and my other mates from football. And what about the people we played Dungeons and Dragons with at the Ginger Cat, the nurses from work – all the others I cared about. I wondered how on earth we could leave them out. What was even the etiquette? Did you send out some kind of 'Sorry, there's no room for you' email? Or did you just not invite them and say nothing?

All so that Craig Barlow and his wife Suzanne, old business contacts of Keith's who I'd never met and would never meet again, could be there?

But here was the thing: because Keith and Yvonne were picking up the bill, Keith and Yvonne got to invite who they wanted. I felt a familiar twist of guilt. Was I being bratty and ungrateful? Should I assert myself and say I wanted my friends at my wedding, not their friends, because it wasn't their wedding?

But then I thought about how helpful Yvonne was being, how generous she and Keith were in paying for everything, knowing Mum wasn't in a position to contribute. They were Archie's family; they'd be my family soon. This was a relationship that would last for the rest of my life – what was the point in souring it for the sake of one day?

I tapped over to Keith's spreadsheet and felt even sicker. The cost for the venue was there, an astronomical sum that didn't even include food and drink yet. There were provisional figures for other things, all of which seemed dizzyingly high to me.

I glanced up from the screen and saw the lights of the Christmas tree blinking cheerfully, casting their golden glow around our cosy flat. I noticed the photo Suzie had taken the first time Archie came to watch me play footie: I'd scored a goal, and he'd run onto the pitch, scooped me up in his arms and twirled me around, as overcome with excitement as if I'd hit the back of the net in a World Cup final. Suzie had captured the moment: Archie's pride and exultation; my face torn between embarrassment and pride.

I looked at the small porcelain figure of a cat Archie had picked up in a charity shop because it reminded him of Grandpa's cat,

Teresa. On the sofa was the woven cushion we'd chosen on our holiday together in Crete, bearing an indentation where Archie's head rested on it. Jostling for position on a shelf were several bottles of gin, because every time he spotted a new variety, Archie would buy it for me, even though we already had far more than I could drink.

They were all the tiny building blocks that already, in just months together, were forming the foundation of a life. Each thing represented a moment of love, and over time there would be more and more of those moments, too many to count or even remember.

The wedding shouldn't matter; it was just one day. Maybe I could make like Elsa from *Frozen* and let it go? Maybe I should embrace it and choose a cake costing hundreds of pounds and flowers costing thousands and designer dresses for my bridesmaids? That was what Yvonne expected; she wouldn't bat an eyelid. She'd plan everything enthusiastically with me and take pleasure in paying for it all.

I put the laptop aside and trudged gloomily through to the kitchen, where I opened the fridge and stared vacantly into it. It was my turn to make dinner but we had almost nothing in: a jar of pasta sauce I knew from experience needed serious zhuzhing up if it were to taste of anything, but nothing to zhuzh it with; a pack of sausages but no potatoes; some salad leaves it was too cold to summon up any enthusiasm for.

I slammed the fridge closed and put on my coat, decision made. I was going to go and find Archie and talk to him, properly, like an adult. I almost ran down the stairs and burst out into the cold street, hurrying towards Craft Fever. It was half past seven; almost time for Archie to close up the shop. We could go to the Ginger

Cat and have something to eat there, share a bottle of wine and discuss it all.

As I expected, he was inside, the lights above the counter making the racks of bottles sparkle and burnishing his hair like copper. I flung open the door and he smiled in greeting.

'How may I help you, Madam?'

'I'm after something a bit fiancé-ey to enjoy over dinner this evening.'

'I'm afraid we only have one fiancé in stock right now.'

'Is it any good?'

'It's aged and bitter with notes of coffee.'

I laughed. 'I'll take that one then. Are you free to pop to the Ginger Cat?'

He hesitated. 'I was thinking I might try a slightly darker roast on those coffee beans. The batch I did earlier was good but not perfect.'

'Please? It's just, there's that email from your mum and so much stuff we really need to talk about.'

'Okay. Why don't you head next door and I'll lock up and see you there in a few minutes.'

But half an hour later, I was still sitting alone at a table for two, one glass of merlot down and a second on the way, and there was no sign of Archie. I tried ringing him but his phone went to voicemail. I stuck my head out of the door to see Craft Fever was in darkness, the shutters pulled down over the plate-glass windows.

It was another half an hour before he arrived, the unmistakeable smell of coffee clinging to his hair and clothes.

'God, I'm so sorry, Nat. I just got caught up in things – you know how it is.'

'That's okay,' I said, gritting my teeth. 'You're here now.'

'And thirsty, and starving,' Archie said. 'Let's check out the specials board.'

'Turkey and all the trimmings, glazed ham, chestnut Wellington,' I read. 'Zoe's gone full festive in there.'

'Quite right too. Let's order.'

It would have to be a severe case of narkiness, I thought, once I'd got halfway through my chestnut wellington, which was fragrant with sage, wrapped in the flakiest pastry and doused in gravy that had apparently been made with white port, that the Ginger Cat's food couldn't cure – or at least allay a bit. It was just as well we'd both been too hungry to talk much before our food arrived, because judging by the way Archie was hoovering up his ham and roast potatoes, he'd been on the ragged edge with hunger as well.

But we needed to have a conversation, and I was determined to go ahead with it.

'So we're spending Christmas Day at your parents' place this year, right?'

'Well, we couldn't go last year because they were on a cruise, so we went to your mum's. So it's their turn.'

Did that mean we were going to have to spend every other Christmas with Archie's parents, assuming they weren't soaking up the Caribbean sun on board the *Antiguan Princess*? But I was going to pick my battles – that was an argument for another day, or better still another year.

'Of course. I'm looking forward to it. But you'll remember to buy their presents this year, won't you? Because last time you forgot and I was fighting my way down Oxford Street on Christmas Eve trying to find cashmere wristwarmers for Daisy.'

Shit. So much for not dying on the Christmas hill.

'Look, it's not my fault it was too busy for me to leave the shop. Come on, Nat, it was twelve months ago and you're still going on about it.'

'I'm not going on about it! I mentioned it, like, twice.'

'More like six times.'

'Bollocks was it six… Look, Archie, I really don't want to have an argument about presents. If I did, I'd be mentioning the limited-edition papaya enzyme cleansing balm your sister's asked for, which I can confirm from hours of research is out of stock literally everywhere. But I won't, because we need to talk about plans for the wedding.'

'And have an argument about that instead?'

I counted to ten, carefully putting my knife and fork together and taking another gulp of wine.

Then I said, 'Definitely not an argument. We're on the same side here, aren't we? We're getting married, aren't we?'

'For our sins.'

'Jeez, what's that supposed to mean?'

'Just what I said. I can tell you're stressing massively about this. Just don't, okay? It's all going to be fine. We're going to have an amazing day with our families and our best mates there. Why not just enjoy it, instead of moaning about flowers?'

'I'm not moaning about flowers! I don't want any fucking flowers! I wanted a tiny wedding and a few drinks here, job done. It's your mother who—'

'So argue with her about it, not with me.'

'But she. Is. Your. Mother. And Daisy's your sister.'

'What's Daisy got to do with it?'

She's only manoeuvred me into wearing her bloody wedding dress, I thought. But I couldn't say that. I didn't know whether Archie had had sight of the never-used fairy meringue that was now going to be mine, unless I could come up with some genius way to get out of it. But a stupid, deeply superstitious part of me wouldn't allow me to tell him that. Whatever I wore on our wedding day must surely be a surprise for him, even if it made him think he was entering into an incestuous union with his own sister, and so that was one conflict I couldn't involve him in.

'It's just that she and your mother are micromanaging everything, and it's all going to be the way they want it,' I said lamely.

'So tell them what you want, and have that.'

'But what about what you want?'

'Blimey, Nat. You know I couldn't care less. As far as I'm concerned, we're going to spend the rest of our lives together – and no doubt I'll be listening to you bang on about those bloody cashmere wristwarmers every Christmas until I'm ninety and too deaf to hear – but the wedding is one day. One day. Have what Mum wants, have what Daisy wants, have what you want. If you're all happy, I'm happy.'

You're always happy, I thought. It was one of the things I loved about Archie – his cheerfulness and easy-going nature. But right now, it was so exasperating I felt like I could scream.

'Archie, please. I just wish you'd have a chat to your mum and tell her we don't want a huge fancy wedding with seventy-five of your parents' friends there. We don't want Finchcocks Manor and Daisy's… all that stuff.'

'It's a bit late for that now, isn't it? Haven't they paid the deposit?'

And there it was again. The huge, insuperable barrier of money and the weight of obligation Archie's parents' generosity had placed on us.

'Couldn't they cancel?'

'Search me. Talk to Mum, if you want. Look, let's drop it. Shall we get the bill?'

Furious, I went up to the bar and paid for our meal. It was clear that Archie was going to be no help whatsoever. I thought of the quiz question about decision-making, and how clearly the answer you were supposed to give was that this was a collaborative process with both of you doing your share. Right now, it felt like anything but that, and I desperately needed that to change.

But I had absolutely no idea how to begin, or even whether I had the courage to try.

Chapter Thirteen

You're having a tough time and you need a shoulder to cry on. Who do you turn to?

A. My other half of course. I share everything with him.

B. I'm blessed to have loads of people I can rely on in a crisis – friends, family, my fiancé. So I try to spread the love a bit.

C. My mum – she's my rock and I can tell her anything.

D. I'm not much of a cryer and I tend to deal with negative feelings on my own.

'I'm not sure what was worst,' Mum said, 'four days of vegan food and no sugar, salt, wheat or alcohol, or all those bloody downward dogs. Honestly, I felt like my hamstrings were going to snap. Oh, and did I mention the silence? No talking at mealtimes, to encourage mindfulness of our bodies' natural processes, apparently.

We were sat there round this scrubbed pine table in a room with a stone floor and no curtains, and every time someone's tummy rumbled it was like a bomb going off. And don't get me started on the chewing sounds.'

I laughed. 'Sounds like I picked the right takeaway to bring tonight, then. There's this new American diner opened opposite the station, and I thought I'd give it a try. Look: one cheese, bacon and jalapeño burger, one blue cheese and chilli jam burger, two portions of fries, one portion of onion rings, two brownies and a few beers. Although those are from Archie's shop, not the diner.'

'You're a lifesaver, Nattie. My God, look at those chips! And smell the onions! There's definitely no butter in those.'

'None whatsoever. Calorie-free. And no sugar in the brownies. And I didn't bring extra sachets of salt and ketchup. And all that means I'm definitely not breaking the pre-wedding diet I'm meant to be on, according to Yvonne.'

I heard Mum give a sharp intake of breath, as if about to launch into one of her lectures about the evils of the diet industry. But that would have meant criticising my future mother-in-law, so she just said, 'Funny, isn't it, how when you have a trashy takeaway, your own normal salt and tomato sauce don't taste as good as the stuff you get from the takeaway. How does that actually work?'

'I'm not sure. Same way a milkshake tastes better through a straw, maybe?'

I unwrapped the burgers, put them on plates and cut each one in half.

'You cut, I choose,' Mum said, carefully eyeballing the burgers and picking a piece of each one before liberally salting her chips.

We sat down on the sofa and Mum flicked on the telly with the sound down.

'Sounds like you're glad to be home,' I said. 'I'm sorry you didn't enjoy the yoga retreat.'

'What do you mean, didn't enjoy it? It was brilliant. I loved it. I'm going to do another in a few months' time. I tell you what, this trying-to-find-a-man thing is definitely broadening my horizons. I'm going to a life-drawing class next week and a container gardening workshop the week after. And I'm thinking of enrolling in a British Sign Language course after that. I'll need all the junk food going to make up for that level of self-improvement.'

She took a massive bite of her burger and wiped sauce off her chin.

'But what about meeting men?' I asked. 'I mean, self-improvement is all very well, but are there actually any single blokes at these things?'

'Well, on the yoga retreat there were twelve of us. Eight were women – I'd say the youngest was in her early twenties and oldest must have been eighty, although you wouldn't believe how fit she was. She could do headstands and everything. She put me to shame.'

'And the other four?'

She sighed. 'The other four were men, obviously. There was Rico, who's a fitness instructor and absolutely gorgeous. He's twenty-three.'

'Which is a bit young, unless you were up for some hardcore cradle-snatching.'

'There's being open to dating men in other age brackets, and then there's flinging myself at a wee thing young enough to be my son. So no.'

'Hard pass on Rico? He'd be too young for me too, to be fair.'

'Exactly. And then there were Mitch and Stavros, and they were a couple so off limits.'

'Okay. That leaves one.'

Mum sighed. 'Niten, the course leader. Honestly, what a man. The kind of body you get from years of clean living and hours of yoga every day. You could've grated cheese on his abs, only they didn't allow dairy there either. And he was ever so intelligent, too, and the right sort of age, I think, although he looked younger from all the Buddha bowls and downward dogs.'

'Hmmm.' I watched Mum sprinkle salt on an onion ring then open another beer, and took a bite of my burger, thinking I'd rather have salt, fat and carbs than clean living any day. 'Sounds like you might be really compatible in some ways.'

'I gave birth to you, young lady! Don't you go judging my life choices.'

'Sorry.'

'So you should be. Anyway, it did cross my mind that a lifetime of getting up at four thirty in the morning and eating grated carrot with sprouted seeds for lunch and never drinking anything stronger than echinacea tea could be a price worth paying. And of course the silence at meals could end up being a total blessing in disguise. Think of the arguments you'd end up not having.'

I thought of the argument Archie and I had had over dinner, just a few days before. We weren't not speaking – neither of us had ever been sulkers – but since then there had been something between us, a distance, a coldness, which didn't seem to be shifting.

'Yeah, I get that,' I said. 'So he sounds like quite the catch.'

'Apart from one thing.' Mum wiped her oily fingers on a paper napkin. 'Shall we have our brownies now? So I was talking to Niten about all the places in the world he'd travelled to – practically everywhere; Nepal and Uruguay and Greenland – and I was wondering what it would be like to have a partner who was so serene and spiritual – not to mention bendy – when he told me he'd elected to live a life free of excess material wealth.'

'What, like a vow of poverty?' I asked, trying to drag my mind away from images of what Mum might have hoped to get up to with Niten's bendy body.

'Not poverty exactly – that's not a thing in Buddhism. In fact, some adherents believe the accumulation of wealth can come to pass as a result of good deeds done in a previous life.'

I imagined Mum staring up at Niten while he told her all this, drinking in his words, her eyes wide and fascinated, ready to quote them back like this was stuff she'd always known and cared about.

'I mean, come on,' she went on. 'I've lived on the sniff of an oily rag for most of my adult life. It's only the past few years that I've been anything close to financially stable. So what's living a life free of excess wealth to me? It's not like I haven't practised.'

'So you could get past that, and the carrots, and the early starts,' I said. 'He sounds perfect.'

'That's what I was thinking,' Mum said. 'I was just starting to wonder how I'd go about asking him out – maybe suggest we go for a stroll round the organic vegetable gardens together at sunset or something like that – when he said that it wasn't just wealth he'd opted to renounce to further the path of his spirituality.'

'Oh no.'

'Oh yes. He's been celibate for eight years, he says. He says freeing himself from the fetters of carnal desire has greatly enhanced his meditative powers.'

'How nice for him.'

'Yes, and how not-nice for me. But anyway, I had a lovely time at the retreat, and now it's time to try the next thing.'

'What's that going to be? After the life drawing and sign language and whatever the other one was, I mean?'

'Haven't decided yet. Maybe flower arranging? But talking of flowers, sweetie! I've been banging on about myself for ages and not even asked how the wedding preparations are going. Is everything okay?'

'Kind of,' I muttered.

'Have you and Archie had a row?'

I nodded miserably. Mum crossed her legs on the sofa, turning to face me as she so often did, so she could properly look at me and listen to me.

'Do you want to talk about it?' she asked.

'It's just so stupid. Yvonne and Daisy want to organise this massive, expensive wedding and I don't know how to stop them, and Archie says we should just go along with it. It's like he doesn't even care what I want.'

'What about what he wants?'

'He doesn't really say. I think he wants to just let everyone else get on with it, and whatever we – or rather they – decide is cool with him. He thinks it'll all turn out fine in the end.'

'Archie is a lovely man, but he's an incurable optimist. Although really, on this one, he might have a point, you know.'

'I know. I mean, part of me is like, "What's the worst that can happen?" I wear a dress that doesn't suit me for a day, and Keith and Yvonne spend a fortune on flowers and shit I don't want. It's not like they'd donate the money to charity otherwise, is it? It would just sit in their investment fund or whatever and I suppose eventually Archie would inherit some of it.'

'But then, it is your wedding day.'

'It's supposed to be. Right now it feels like it's Daisy's wedding day.'

'Now, sweetie. You know I don't often play the mum card, but I'm going to right now. Will you listen to me?'

I nodded.

'If there's one thing I've tried to teach you, it's to stand up for what you believe in. If you feel strongly about this, you need to talk to them. And you can't expect Archie to fight your battles for you, because it doesn't sound like he's going to. Explain to Yvonne how you feel. It's not an unreasonable position you're taking.'

'I know it's not.'

'So there you go. Next time you see her – face to face; a text message is no good – talk to her properly about it. She's going to be your mother-in-law for a long time and you need to get the relationship off on the right footing, otherwise it's only going to get worse.'

'And Archie…'

'Big life events are stressful, you know. They put a strain on the strongest relationships. And yours and Archie's – well, I'm not saying it's not strong; it is, but it's young, isn't it? You haven't had a lot of practice in dealing with difficult things together. You need to keep communicating, keep that bond between you. You know what I mean.'

I did know what she meant. But that bond – that attraction and chemistry that had pulled us together in the first place, so strongly I'd felt as if I'd never want to be with anyone else ever again – was being stretched to what felt like breaking point.

And in that moment, I made a decision. I was going to go along with what Yvonne wanted for our wedding. I loved Archie; I wanted his family to love me. And if that meant a dress that didn't suit me and a few peacocks, I'd just have to suck it up.

I still wasn't going to return Fenella White's call though.

Chapter Fourteen

Are we hearing the patter of little feet? Your attitudes to parenting (or remaining child-free) are an important point to cover before marriage. Are you there yet?

A. Totally! We can't wait to have a family, the more the merrier.

B. That ship has sailed! We're a modern couple and we've already had babies. But who knows – there could be more on the cards!

C. We've talked about it. We know for sure we're not ready yet, so we'll be revisiting that one in the future.

D. I know what I want, and he knows he's providing the equipment. Sorted.

'So we've got the knee replacement lady – Mrs Gomez – needing to go home today,' Nisha said. 'I know she's not that steady on her feet, but Mr Saw insists we need the bed. Nat, are you able to spend some time with her?'

I almost jumped at the mention of my name, although it was perfectly normal to be assigned tasks in the morning meeting. My mind had been miles away, though – thinking about Archie. Over the past week, we'd had no more rows, at least. I'd told him about my decision to embrace his mother's ideas for our wedding, and he'd seemed relieved – yet, also, not really engaged.

When I asked what he thought of Daisy's idea of having bubbles instead of confetti, he'd said it was up to me, really. When I asked if he'd made an appointment with his father's tailor to be measured for a suit, he said he hadn't got around to it yet because things were so hectic at the shop. When Yvonne sent through links to four different videographers' websites, he said he was far too busy to look at them.

So I ended up leaving decisions unmade, because the alternative was making them alone or having another row with Archie, and neither option appealed in the slightest.

'Nat? Mrs Gomez?' Nisha repeated.

'Sure, in theory, but doesn't she live in a third-floor flat with no lift? I mean, I can do a stairs assessment and probably get her up and down one flight safely but that won't really help her once she's back home and needs to go out for shopping and stuff.'

'Have social care been in touch with her family?'

'There's no family. Well, a daughter up in Aberdeen and a son in Winnipeg. Her husband passed away a couple of years back.'

'Really, she should be discharged into a care home environment.'

'But there are no spaces.'

We looked at each other in mutual frustration. Everyone else in the room was half-listening; it was a conversation they heard over and over, every day.

'I'll talk to Mr Saw,' I said. 'See if we can keep her in for another day or two until there's somewhere safe for her to go. She might not pass the stairs assessment, anyway, and there's no way he'll discharge her if she doesn't. You know how fussy he is about that.'

'And then we've the new gentleman. He had a fall at home. His neighbour popped in to check on him and found him yesterday, and he was brought straight in. Nasty hip fracture. He'll be going in for surgery this afternoon and you'll want one of your team to see him straight after.'

'Right, Lara or I will do that. What's his name?'

'Same as yours, funnily enough. A Mr Blake.'

I felt as if all the blood had rushed out of my face, then whooshed straight back again. Surely it couldn't be Grandpa? Surely he couldn't have been lying alone in his flat for hours, with no one to help him? And surely now he couldn't be here, in a bed just a few metres away, waiting for major surgery?

'It's not Robin Blake, is it?' I asked, my mouth so dry I could hardly get the words out.

'Robin Blake, yes. Do you know him?'

'He's my grandfather.'

Nisha shook her head sympathetically. 'Such a worry. You'll want to pop in and see him as soon as we've finished here, then. He's quite comfortable, he's had his breakfast and wash and his pain is being managed quite well.'

I'd never been so grateful for the habit I'd learned early on of noting down every single detail of the morning briefings, because if I hadn't, there was no way I'd have remembered anything that was said for the next twenty minutes. All I wanted was to get out of that room, go and see Grandpa, speak to Mum and find out if she knew what had happened.

I thought of all the platitudes we trotted out to the families of our patients. *He's in the right place. The outcome of this surgery is overwhelmingly successful. He'll be back on his feet in no time.* The words were true, I knew – but now, for the first time, I also knew what little comfort they offered when it was a person you loved in pain. How, no matter how much faith you had in the ability of the surgical team, the fear of something going wrong was still so real, so strong.

As soon as the meeting broke up, I hurried on to the ward and raced towards the curtained cubicle where Grandpa was. The ward looked the way it did on any typical morning: one of the registrars doing his rounds, a couple of students tagging along behind him; the nurses rushing from bed to bed making sure the patients were ready to be seen; the patients trying to get their attention; the smell of toast and tea lingering from breakfast.

Normally, I barely noticed any of that. It was just my place of work and, like anyone else, I was always too busy for reflection. But now it was as if I was seeing it for the first time, through the eyes of someone who'd never been here before – Grandpa's eyes. And I knew that what was familiar to me would be terrifying to him. The nurses' efficiency might seem like indifference; the students' diligence like ghoulish curiosity; the other patients' demands like despair.

I froze outside Grandpa's cubicle, suddenly frightened of what would be behind the curtains. And then they parted and one of the new young nurses emerged.

'Mr Blake isn't in surgery until the afternoon,' she said. 'So you won't need to see him just yet. He's a trooper though, strong as a horse.'

Beyond her, I could see Grandpa propped up against the pillows. He didn't look like a trooper to me. His face was as pale as candlewax and tufts of hair were sticking out above his ears. The hospital gown hung crooked over his bony shoulders.

But when he saw me, his face broke into a smile.

'Natalie,' he said. 'Fancy seeing you here.'

For a second, I thought, *He's so confused he's forgotten I work here.*

And then I noticed the crinkles at the corners of his eyes and realised this was his attempt at humour. I laughed, even while thinking how crazy it was that it should have to be him, in pain in this strange environment, who put me at ease.

'Never mind that,' I said. 'What are you doing, lounging around in a bed a sick person needs?'

'Where else am I going to get a bionic hip put in? The old one's no good, they say, proper smashed up. Not that it was anything to write home about before. Been giving me gyp for months and then, when I was getting my whisky and soda before dinner, I dropped an ice cube on the floor and stepped on it, and it sent me flying.'

'Oh, Grandpa.' I slipped through the curtains and perched on the bed, reaching for his hand. I could only spare five minutes, but I couldn't bear to leave him alone just yet.

'I tried banging on the wall but no one heard me, and I tried to crawl to the phone but I couldn't manage it. Teresa was meowing for her dinner and there was nothing I could do about it. And you know what the worst thing was?'

I shook my head. The pain? The fear? Being cold and alone for hours?

'That glass of Glenlivet was right there on the counter, and I couldn't get to it, could I?'

I laughed, more with relief than at his lame joke. 'You've got a Saw fracture, you know. Named after my consultant. It's quite rare, and he's developed a special technique for fixing it. You should be proud.'

'Is that the Asian gentleman? He came in to see me earlier. We had a good chat about Uttar Pradesh, where his family are from. You know I spent some time working there back in the 1950s. Your grandmother couldn't stand the mosquitoes.'

'Well you'll be able to compare notes with him again over the next few days, I expect.'

'And Lucia, who brought my breakfast, told me her mother lives three streets down from where I was born. Imagine that? Small world.'

'Basically, you've been here a few hours and you've got more mates in this hospital than I have. Strong work, Grandpa.'

Imagining him chatting away to everyone who parted the curtains, I wondered how lonely Grandpa had been and for how long. He'd always seemed quite content, and insisted he was managing quite well, cleaving to his routine. It started with the *Today* programme on the radio in the morning while Teresa ate her breakfast (and he shaved with the lethal cut-throat razor Mum always fretted would slip, leaving him dead in a pool of blood like something out of an Agatha Christie novel), followed by a brisk walk regardless of the weather, then a boiled egg and soldiers, a potter in the garden, a bowl of soup, a crossword in the newspaper, a trip to the local shops (no matter how often Mum offered to organise a supermarket delivery for him, he insisted it did him good to get out, and he liked choosing whatever posh ready meal he fancied for his dinner on the day), a shower, the news and finally bed with a book and the cat on his feet.

On Sundays he went to church and then had a gin and tonic in the pub, and after that Mum, or sometimes Mum and Archie and me, would go round for lunch. His world must have shrunk dramatically after Granny's death, I realised, when her book group friends suddenly stopped coming round every four weeks, her gossip from the library where she volunteered, her sewing machine humming as she made – quite frankly hideous – wrap skirts and blouses which Mum and I had to pretend to appreciate at Christmas.

'I'm quite looking forward to a few days in here,' Grandpa said, squeezing my hand with his. His skin felt cool and almost papery-dry but reassuringly strong. 'You get pudding with lunch, you know. And with supper. It's like staying at Buckingham Palace.'

'Watch what you say. If you give the nurses half a chance, they'll be squeezing out your toothpaste for you, just like Prince Charles.'

We laughed together, and I was relieved that was the sight that greeted Mum when she came bursting in through the curtains.

'Bloody hell, Dad,' she said, out of breath as if she'd sprinted up the stairs and across the ward. 'Thank God you're okay. My phone ran out of charge overnight so I missed the call from the hospital to say you were here. And then my alarm didn't go off so I was in a mad rush and I only got it plugged in once I was at work. And then there were a million messages from your neighbours and Nat and the people here. I came as quickly as I could.'

She leaned over to kiss him, and I saw the panic in her face ease when she realised he was comfortable, stable and, above all, alive.

'I'd better get on with my work,' I said. 'I'll leave Mum to hear all about your conquests of the nurses, and you can decide what tempts you from the lunch menu.'

'Speaking of lunch,' Mum said, 'shall we grab a sandwich on your break?'

'Sure. I won't vouch for the quality of it though.'

Mum turned back to Grandpa and I left the cubicle to get on with my working day. I knew she'd want to quiz me about Grandpa's prognosis – how dangerous the surgery was, how quickly he might get back on his feet, how much pain he would be in. They were all questions she could ask Mr Saw, and which he'd be in a better position to answer than me. But I knew, also, that her worry about Grandpa and fear of the worst things that might happen would cloud her ability to listen to him, and she'd find it easier to concentrate if I explained, as best I could, over coffee and a flabby sandwich.

But when I got to the café at twelve thirty, Mum wasn't alone. I could see that she'd been crying; the make-up she'd been wearing that morning was mostly gone, apart from a dark smudge of mascara under one eye. There was a half-finished cappuccino and a half-eaten panini on the table in front of her. I knew from experience that the former would be, somehow, both bitter and watery and the latter floppy and dry. As I watched she picked up the sandwich, took a bite, then grimaced and put it down again.

The man sitting opposite her smiled sympathetically, then stood up and went to the counter. In his absence, I hurried over to Mum with my own tray, which held a can of Diet Coke and an egg mayonnaise on wholemeal bread – the most palatable options my extensive research had found.

'Hey, Mum.'

Before I could ask who the strange man was she'd been sitting with, Mum answered the question. 'Hey, Nattie. It's the strangest thing. I just bumped into an old friend – Max. Well, actually, I was having a bit of a weep in the corridor, and he stopped to ask if I was okay and then we realised we knew each other. Max, this is my daughter, Natalie.'

Max had returned from the counter with a fresh tray, on which was a bottle of sparkling water and two chocolate brownies. Clearly the man had taste – the brownies were positively edible, good even, and I'd been planning to invest in one myself if I had time after my sandwich. And not only did he have taste, he was pretty tasty too, in a silver-fox sort of way. He looked about Mum's age, and he was wearing jeans and an olive-coloured woollen jumper. A battered brown leather jacket was slung over the back of the chair where he'd been sitting, and his eyes were brown too – amber like one of the craft beers in Archie's shop – and framed by laughter lines. He was tall, with the slight stoop to his shoulders that tall people often have.

'Am I interrupting?' he asked. 'I thought Emma could do with a bit of a sugar hit.'

I glanced at Mum. If she was happy for Max to join us and be party to our conversation about Grandpa, that was okay with me; if she wanted him to get lost, she'd have to be the one to tell him so.

But she said, 'Sugar is exactly what I need, thank you. Grab a seat.'

'Hospital's not exactly fun at the best of times.' Max secured a chair from a neighbouring table and pulled it over for me, then held out his hand for me to shake. 'I'm here dropping off a gift for a colleague who's just had a baby, so it's a happy occasion for me. But you must be worried about your grandfather.'

'I am, of course. But he's in the right place, and in the best possible hands.'

I launched into a brief explanation of what Grandpa's care would involve, and Mum and Max both listened intently. But I could see Mum's gaze drifting from me to him, as if she was getting equal reassurance from us both.

'So, really, after the surgery, he should be up and about within a couple of days,' I concluded. 'If everything goes well obviously, and there's no reason at all why it shouldn't.'

Again, there was that look passing between Mum and Max. It was just a glance, but if it'd had words, they'd have been something like, *Are you okay?* from him, then *Yes – but also not*, from her, and then, *I'm here*, from him.

'So how do you two know each other?' I blurted out.

'Back in the mists of time,' Max said, 'your mother and I were at secondary school together.'

'Chisleden Comprehensive,' Mum said. 'What a hole it was! It's an academy now and quite highly regarded.'

'Awful,' Max agreed. 'Emma and I were thought of as quite the swots, because we didn't spend every break time smoking behind the bike sheds.'

'We only smoked in the street, while we were walking home,' Mum said. 'After I'd turned up the waistband of my skirt a few times and tied my tie round my wrist.'

'I made your mother a compilation tape.' Max grinned, and I could see where those lines around his eyes had come from.

'I listened to it on my Sony Walkman – endlessly.'

'We went to the GCSE prom together, only they weren't called proms then.'

'It was a ball. I mean, it was called a ball. Not we had a ball.'

'Although we did. Remember dancing to "Tainted Love"?'

'In my emerald-green ruched satin dress that made me look like something out of *Dynasty*.'

'And I was in a tuxedo from Marks and Spencer's, only I got my mother to alter it so the trousers were proper drainpipes.'

'You could barely walk in them, never mind dance.'

They both laughed, and I found myself laughing too. I glugged the last of my Diet Coke from the can and finished the final bite of my sandwich, hoping that maybe they'd carry on and give me more of a glimpse into a part of Mum's past I knew very little about.

But Mum said, 'Christ, look at the time! I said I'd be back at work by half one and it's twenty to already. Nattie, is there any chance you could look in at Grandpa's and feed the cat? He's worried about her.'

'Of course,' I said, although I was pretty sure that self-possessed Teresa would already have either stocked up enough dead mice to last her until Grandpa's return or moved herself in with a neighbour. 'I'll go on my way home from work.'

I jumped up, returned our trays to the rack by the counter, hugged Mum and hurried away. But I couldn't resist stealing a glance back over my shoulder, and I saw her and Max standing together by the empty table, each with their phones in their hands.

Slipping the key into the lock of Grandpa's front door felt strange – almost furtive, like I had no business being there on my own, no right to let myself in. The curtains in the houses on either side were drawn against the icy December night, but I could see Christmas lights twinkling behind them and I imagined that any moment a door might fly open and an irate householder emerge demanding to know what the hell I thought I was doing.

But my presence here was clearly necessary. Even through the closed door, I could hear frantic mewing. Poor Teresa had missed her breakfast that morning and it was probably long past her dinnertime too – never mind the snacks Grandpa would no doubt have slipped her way during the day. Clearly there'd been a bit of a mouse shortage too; the poor thing must be starving.

'I'm coming, little girl,' I said, pushing open the door slowly so as not to send her flying. 'Bear with me just a second. Room service is on its way.'

Dumping my bag and coat on the hallway floor, I squatted down to fuss the cat. Hunger made her friendlier than usual – she twined round my ankles, purring thunderously in between urgent squeaks. Her fur was silky soft, I noticed, and the stripes in her coat were the same colours as a fresh espresso where the pale crema breaks apart to reveal the deep brown coffee beneath.

'Where does Grandpa keep your food then?' I asked her, getting to my feet. Teresa trotted purposefully ahead of me to the kitchen, making a beeline for the cupboard under the sink and scratching at it with a paw.

'In there, is it? Let's have a look.'

I pulled out a box of cat food pouches – expensive-looking ones that claimed to be made with ninety per cent organic chicken; clearly only the best would do for Grandpa's furry princess – and tipped one into the ceramic bowl with a picture of a fish on it, which had been resting on the draining board. Teresa's eager cries increased in volume when she smelled the food, and her claws scrabbled at the leg of my jeans.

I set the bowl down on the floor and silence descended as she buried her face in the food. Sitting at the kitchen table, I watched her eat, feeling the same kind of satisfaction I knew from when a patient managed the walk to the bathroom unassisted for the first time, or told me a movement that had been painful before was easy now.

Teresa would need breakfast in the morning, I realised, and dinner tomorrow. And then the same again for the next seven days, or however long Grandpa remained in hospital, and the journey from our flat to Grandpa's house took half an hour on the bus or an hour by foot. Mum would help, of course, but she was allergic to cats; when she visited Grandpa, Teresa had learned to tactfully take herself out into the garden, but even so Mum often left with her eyes and nose streaming. One time a few years back, when Grandpa had had a bad case of the flu, she'd stayed over and woken up to find the cat asleep on her pillow and practically had to be hospitalised herself. I could ask a neighbour to drop in, but I'd worry they might forget, and I knew Grandpa would ask me whether his cat was okay whenever I dropped by his bed at work.

'Fancy a homestay, Teresa?' I asked. 'I can't promise mice, but our flat's nice and warm, and you'll get regular meals. What do you reckon?'

The cat didn't respond; she was laser-focused on her food.

I tapped out a quick text to Archie, then went to investigate the house. In the spare bedroom upstairs, I found Teresa's litter tray, which I emptied and cleaned. In the cupboard under the stairs were a bag of cat litter, more boxes of food and her carrier. Her water bowl was in front of the fireplace in Grandpa's bedroom.

I lingered there for a second, looking at the neatly made bed and the imprint of Teresa's body on the duvet. It would be some time before Grandpa would be able to climb those stairs again, before he could settle down here for the night, his cat purring at his feet, and take up one of the thrillers from the pile on the bedside table to read a few chapters before he fell asleep.

Next to the pile of books, I noticed a few faded photographs in mismatched frames. There were Granny and Grandpa on their wedding day. There was Granny in high-waisted, flared jeans, holding the baby who would grow up to be my mum on her hip. And·there I was, aged about eight, grinning and clutching a football, my socks and knees encrusted in mud.

I sat down on the bed and took the frame in my hands, my throat suddenly closing and tears stinging my eyes.

A memory I didn't know I had came rushing back, as clear as a video clip. A summer Sunday, after Granny had cooked lunch for us. She and Mum had settled down to drink tea and have a catch-up, while Grandpa and I had gone for a walk. I don't know what it was that had made me confide in him – probably the fact that he was the only constant male presence in my life and best placed to advise me on the dilemma that had been troubling me throughout the school term.

'Grandpa,' I said, slipping my hand into his large, warm one, 'girls can't be footballers, can they?'

'Who says that, Nattie?'

'The boys at school. Edward and Jamie and Steve. They don't want me to play with them at break any more, even though I score the most goals.'

I looked up at him and saw him smile. 'I think you'll probably find it's because you score the most goals.'

'Really? Not because I'm a girl?'

'Well, both. If you were a boy and a better player than them, they wouldn't mind nearly so much. But as a girl, you're more of a threat. Their egos can't take it.'

'But all the famous footballers are men,' I argued. 'Ladies have to play… I don't know. Tennis.'

Grandpa sighed. 'You know, less than a hundred years ago, ladies' football was hugely popular. Women's teams drew massive crowds and raised thousands of pounds for charity. And then the Football Association banned it.'

'Banned it? But why?'

'For the same reason Edward and the rest of them don't want you playing with them.'

I thought about this for a second, smarting at the injustice of it.

'It changed then, and it can change back again,' Grandpa went on. 'You keep playing, Nattie. We'll get your teacher to have a word with those boys. Don't let them stop you doing things you love, things you're good at.'

And that Christmas, I remembered, I'd received a pair of shiny new football boots and a Queens Park Rangers shirt from Granny and Grandpa. I wasn't sure what Grandpa had said to Mum, or what Mum had said to my head of year, or what Mr Grainger had said to the boys, but a couple of days later they casually asked me to join them on the pitch as if nothing had happened. I kept playing, and I kept scoring goals, and even after I realised I'd never be good enough to play even semi-professionally, I never lost my love for the game.

Lewis, my boyfriend at university, had said that the moment he first fell in love with me was when I explained the offside rule to him. The relationship had fizzled out, of course, and now I had Archie, who barely knew one end of a football from the other.

I brushed away my tears, smiling now, and put the photograph back on Grandpa's bedside table.

'Come on, Teresa,' I called to the cat. 'We're getting an Uber home.'

Over the next few days, Grandpa's cat established her position in our flat. After disappearing under the sofa and staying there for eight hours, driving me to distraction with worry that I'd made the wrong decision, she emerged and woke us up demanding her breakfast. Archie, who normally needed a forklift truck to get him out of bed in the mornings, sprang up as soon as he heard her meow.

'She's come out!' he said. 'She must be settling in!'

I lay back on the pillows, listening as he chatted away to Teresa, explaining that the humans were going to have to go to work and leave her in charge but that we would be back in time for her tea, and that there would be a delivery arriving that day from Amazon which might interest her.

'You'll have to wait for us to open the package,' he said. 'Because you don't have opposable thumbs, you see.'

When I got home from football practice that evening, I found Archie surrounded by boxes. One of them had held an enormous cat tree that reached almost to the ceiling of the flat, which he was painstakingly assembling with his cordless screwdriver. Another contained an assortment of feathery, rattly, catnip-scented toys. Another was full of locally produced, organic cat food.

Teresa was watching him from the back of the sofa, an expression on her face that clearly meant, *Well, I've got this human where I want him.*

Who would have thought it? I mused. *Practical Archie, going doolally over a cat.*

'You know she's only here for a couple of weeks?' I said.

'Yes, but we want her to enjoy it, right? We want this to be like a stay at The Ritz, not a holiday at Butlin's. I came back and checked on her at lunchtime, and I cooked some chicken for her tea.'

'I'll be able to tell Grandpa she's making herself at home. He'll be pleased.'

And I was pleased too. This was a side of Archie I'd never seen before – a soft, nurturing side. Watching him sit immobile on the sofa because the cat had deigned to settle down on his lap, hearing him singing to her, noticing the fastidiousness with which he washed her food bowl and cleaned out her litter tray, made me feel something I'd never felt before.

It wasn't quite broodiness. It wasn't the primal urge I'd heard other women describe. It was more a realisation that, when the time came, if we decided it was something we both wanted, Archie would be a loving, involved, hands-on father.

It didn't help me answer the question in the quiz, but it reassured me all the same.

Chapter Fifteen

Division of domestic duties can become a bone of contention in a marriage. How have you addressed it?

A. Call me a '50s housewife but I love doing housework! He doesn't have to lift a finger.

B. Bone of contention is right! Fortunately we've both got low standards so we make it work okay.

C. Strict division of labour here – if he doesn't do his share, it doesn't get done.

D. I got him properly housetrained from the get-go and now I get to be a lady of leisure.

The first time Archie cooked a meal for me, I couldn't believe my luck. We'd only been going out for a couple of weeks, and he'd invited me round to the flat he shared with Mo, who was away with work. Sensing that this was a bit of an occasion, I'd worn a skirt and high heels and bought a bottle of Argentinian malbec the man in the wine shop assured me was superb quality for the price and would go brilliantly with any food.

We didn't drink it that night though, because Archie had carefully selected wine to go with every course, and gave me a gin and tonic with rose petals in it when I arrived. He'd made his own pasta, served with an intense seafood sauce he said had involved roasting the shells of prawns. There were fillet steaks with proper bearnaise sauce and dauphinoise potatoes. There was a passion-fruit mousse, which I was too full to eat more than a spoonful of.

At last, I'd pushed back my chair, thanked him for about the millionth time, and said, 'Let me give you a hand clearing this lot away.'

'No!' Archie jumped to his feet. 'I'll do it. You stay here.'

I sat back down, but as soon as he opened the kitchen door, I piled up some plates and followed him. It was nice he was being gallant, but I couldn't just sit there while he did all the work.

But the minute I stepped into the kitchen, I understood why he'd refused. The place looked like an explosion on the set of *MasterChef*. Every surface was crowded with dirty pans, plates and bowls. The sink was choked with potato peelings and eggshells. Unstoppered bottles and jars threatened to topple onto the floor. Cookbooks were propped open against the wall, their pages splattered with grease and red wine.

'Blimey.' I surveyed the carnage and started to laugh.

Archie looked mortified for a second, then joined in. 'Sorry. I'm not the most organised cook.'

It might have been the understatement of the decade. Since then, I'd learned there was a price to pay for Archie's gourmet cuisine:

at least a day of total chaos, which someone would have to clear up. And that someone obviously couldn't be the head chef, who'd done all the thinking and recipe researching and tracking down of obscure ingredients in specialist shops.

When I told Lara about it, she snorted with derision and said, 'Ha! Male performance cooking! My dad does this and it drives Mum crazy. Pulls out all the stops and gets all the glory on special occasions, so long as someone else cleans up after him. But does he do the daily slog of shopping and cooking? Does he fuck.'

And so, delicious as his more ambitious meals were, I tried to restrict Archie to simple cooking most of the time or foisted my own even humbler efforts onto him.

But Grandpa, Mum and Max coming over to ours for dinner was clearly a special occasion, and one that warranted Archie going all out and producing one of his feasts, particularly because it was, as he pointed out, just three days before Christmas.

It was three days since Grandpa had been discharged from hospital, almost two weeks since his surgery, and he was doing, as I would have said if he was one of my patients, better than expected. He'd been working like a trooper on his exercises and could make it up and down the stairs at home with the help of a stick. The pain medication he was on was keeping him comfortable.

And now he was sitting in an armchair in our living room, Teresa on his lap and a whisky and soda by his side, the Christmas tree lights turning his white hair alternately silver and gold.

Across from him, Mum and Max were on the sofa. Mum was wearing a little black dress I'd never seen before, and red lipstick. The lipstick was extra noticeable because she kept smiling – a smile that lit up her whole face as brightly as the Christmas tree lights illuminated the room. She had her hand on Max's knee, and every time she said something, even if it was just a banal comment about how cold it had been the past few days, Max looked at her with a kind of adoring reverence, as if a goddess had spoken.

'So what's young Archie got up his sleeve for our dinner then, Nattie?' Grandpa asked. 'The hospital food was pretty good, it really was, but it'll be even better to have some proper home cooking.'

'You know what Archie's like. I wouldn't call this home cooking – more like Michelin-star dining. I've hardly been allowed into the kitchen all day but I believe there's some sort of terrine to start, and venison wellington, and something for pudding that involved about six bars of dark chocolate, judging by the wrapping that was in the recycling.'

'That sounds delicious,' Max said. 'It'll certainly be an improvement on what my sister comes up with on Christmas Day. I love her dearly but she is very much of the "buy something from Iceland and stick it in the microwave" culinary school.'

I wondered whether he had yet experienced Mum's cooking and decided he was so smitten with her, he wouldn't care what she put on his plate, even if it was her special lentil stew.

'We'll be at Archie's parents' place. Apparently they really push the boat out. I guess it runs in the family,' I said as a crash came from the kitchen, followed by a muffled curse from Archie.

'Is he okay in there?' Max asked. 'Should we go and see if he needs a hand?'

'No point,' I said. 'Trust me, I know from experience. You've just got to let him get on with it and deal with the carnage afterwards.'

'That's the advantage of having a new bionic hip,' Grandpa joked. 'No one expects you to do any work. The lady from the community nursing team comes once a day and checks up on me, and offers to make me a cup of tea and a sandwich. I ought to have had this done years ago – I'm living a life of leisure.'

'But you're keeping up with your exercises, aren't you?' Mum asked anxiously.

'I get no choice in the matter. The young woman – the community physiotherapist – comes every few days too, and what a slave-driver she is. "Are you keeping up with your ankle pumps and your buttock contractions, Robin?" And she fixes me with a gimlet eye. I never thought I'd be discussing my buttocks with a twenty-something girl, but that's old age for you.'

'She's right though, Grandpa. That's the only way you'll get better. It might feel uncomfortable at first, but—'

'And you're just as bad, Natalie,' Grandpa scolded. 'Never a moment's peace.'

'The sooner you're properly mobile again, the sooner you can have Teresa home again,' I said. 'Archie and I have loved having her, but once you're able to bend down to give her her food and clean out her litter tray, you'll want her back, won't you?'

Grandpa rested his hand on the cat's head, and she blinked slowly and started to purr.

'I'll need to get better at looking after myself before I can look after you again, my girl,' he said. 'You stay here with Nattie and Archie for the time being, all right?'

Archie emerged from the kitchen, accompanied by a waft of delicious smells.

'Food will be ready in a couple of minutes,' he said. 'Shall we open another bottle of fizz or move on to wine?'

'How about both?' Max stood up and followed Archie back into the kitchen, reappearing a moment later laden with bottles. 'It's quite the production line in there. I've never seen so much food.'

'I hope everyone's hungry. Archie always over-caters and it's always amazing.' I lifted Teresa off Grandpa's lap and helped him to his feet. With his stick, he was able to move quite comfortably over to the table, and he lowered himself easily into his chair.

Archie lovingly arranged plates of terrine, decorated with frilly lettuce and dotted with some sort of shiny sauce, at each place. In the centre of the table was a basket of bread he'd made himself and a dish of butter that had been whipped into peaks and flavoured with – if I remembered correctly – anchovy and capers.

I imagined the scene of devastation behind the kitchen door and the hours it would take to restore order after everyone had left, but it was worth it to see the pride on his face at hosting my family.

Max filled everyone's glasses but, just as Mum was toasting a thank-you to the chef and everyone was preparing to dive into the food, my phone rang.

'It's Archie's mum,' I said. 'She'll be calling about something to do with the wedding, I expect. I'll ring her back.'

'Answer it,' Mum said. 'It's all right – we don't mind waiting a minute.'

I'd be lucky if it was a minute, I thought, knowing how Yvonne's calls to chat about flowers or cake or whether I'd considered a balloon arch at the entrance to the chapel could go on for ages.

But this wasn't about the wedding, and I was back at my place within a couple of minutes.

'She wanted to know if you'd like to spend Christmas Day with them,' I said. 'With us, I mean, since Archie and I will be there. I said I'd ask and let her know, but you can't, really, can you?'

'Why ever not?' Grandpa asked. 'I'll be perfectly all right. The Dawsons next door have already invited me over for lunch. It's only right you should meet Archie's family.'

Mum looked from Grandpa to me. I could see the indecision in her face, and I knew she was torn between her duty to Grandpa and her duty to me. What she would really have wanted – for Max to abandon his plans with his sister and the two of them to spend the day together – clearly wasn't an option.

'I suppose you're right, Dad,' she said. 'I mean, if you're sure? You'll ring me if you need anything?'

'It's only a couple of hours' drive,' Archie said. 'We'll go in the van, and I won't drink so we can get back if we need to.'

'You won't need to,' Grandpa said. 'Don't you worry about me. I'll be perfectly all right.'

I remembered his words afterwards and wished with all my heart that they'd been true.

Chapter Sixteen

Your wedding isn't the only big day you'll celebrate together. How do you mark other special occasions?

A. Christmas, birthdays, anniversaries – they're all a big deal for us. I still get flowers once a month on the date we met.

B. So long as we're surrounded by close family, we're happy.

C. We love a party! Massive group of friends, plenty of food and drink – just like our wedding's going to be, really.

D. It's all a lot of commercialised nonsense, isn't it?

'Blimey,' Mum said, as Archie swung the van round the corner into the road where his parents lived. 'I bet you can see that lot from space.'

Even though Archie had warned me that Christmas in his family was a big deal, I was taken aback by the extravagance of the display that filled their front garden. There was a vast outdoor Christmas tree festooned with rainbow lights. There was an illuminated sleigh drawn by eight neon reindeer. There was a life-size Father Christmas disappearing head-first down the chimney. There were stars and holly wreaths and angels and even – for some reason I couldn't begin to comprehend – a wicker goat, its head lowered as if it was cropping the lawn.

'It must be really impressive at night,' I said.

Archie nodded. 'Mum and Dad, bringing light pollution to suburban Kent since the year 2010.'

'Are you sure I look all right?' Mum fretted. 'I'm sure your mother will be much smarter than me, Archie.'

'You look lovely,' I reassured her. Her caramel-coloured leather skirt (though knowing Mum and her budget, it was more likely plastic from Primark, but it looked great all the same) and scarlet mohair jumper were festive and just the right amount of glam. She'd taken some persuading to accept Yvonne's invitation, and now I could tell she was just as nervous about this meeting with Archie's family as I was.

But Yvonne, surprisingly, was all smiles when she flung open the front door as the van's wheels crunched over the gravel. She picked her way over to us in her four-inch heels, wrapping her hands around the arms of her bottle-green velvet dress against the cold – but she seemed to be warmed from within by the Christmas spirit. Either that or she'd been at the sherry already.

'Come in, come in. You must be Emma. Merry Christmas! How lovely to meet you,' she gushed, enveloping Mum in a hug. 'Keith's just getting the cork out of a bottle of Krug, and the canapés will be ready in five minutes.'

'Do let me know what I can do to help,' Mum said, her eyes widening as she took in the eleven-foot Christmas tree that dominated the hallway, its branches draped with white, blue and violet lights.

Archie followed, laden with two Sainsbury's Bags for Life stuffed full of presents. In her eagerness to please, Mum had splashed out at the local Christmas craft market on screen-printed tea towels for Yvonne, a nubbly knitted scarf for Keith, handmade soap for Daisy, hemp hand cream for Poppy, chocolate truffles for Freya and a teddy bear made from recycled jumpers for Linus.

'Oh, there's no need for you to lift a finger,' Yvonne said. 'We got caterers in this year. Ever so lazy, I know, but who wants to spend Christmas Day up to their elbows in sprout peelings? Come and join us in the lounge.'

We all trooped through to the white and gold sitting room, where a fire was roaring and yet another Christmas tree twinkling. I saw Mum's cheeks flushing in the heat and noticed her tugging at her jumper as it started to itch. But she smiled bravely, accepted a glass of champagne from Keith, and sat down on one of the vast, squashy sofas with Poppy and Freya to admire Linus and ask how he was enjoying his first Christmas.

Over the next couple of hours, I felt like someone in one of those competitive eating competitions you read about sometimes – only it wasn't soggy hot dogs I was stuffing myself with, it was blinis with caviar, prosciutto and chestnut bonbons, and pumpkin and goat's cheese tartlets. And that was before the main event, which featured a three-bird roast, two kinds of potatoes, three different stuffings, a ham and a vast beef roast, just in case anyone didn't fancy pork or poultry.

Clearly, Yvonne's normal penis portions policy got put on hold just once a year.

I saw Mum's eyes widen as the leftovers were ferried back to the kitchen by the caterers, and a huge, flaming Christmas pudding brought in, alongside a trifle and a Yule log, and I knew she was thinking longingly how welcome all that would be at the local soup kitchen where she volunteered twice a month.

At last, feeling as stuffed as pythons, we all staggered back to the sofas, where a platter of mince pies and a bottle of pudding wine were waiting. Mum sat down and glanced at her phone with a secret smile that must mean Max had texted her. Poppy and Freya settled on the carpet with Linus, who was more interested in playing with discarded wrapping paper than with any of his presents. Keith flicked on the TV ready for the Queen's Christmas address, and I thought longingly of a nap.

But Daisy had other ideas. As soon as the sovereign's familiar face appeared on the screen, she said, 'Her Majesty will have one fewer audience member this year – I'm going out for a cigarette. Coming, Nat?'

Taken by surprise, I was on my feet almost before I could think about it.

'Sure,' I said, and followed her out through the warm, silent kitchen, the lights dimmed over the island and the smell of gravy still hanging in the warm air.

Daisy threw open the door to the garden and we walked outside, pulling on our coats. It was dark already, a persistent drizzle was falling and the grass was wet under our feet. Daisy lost her balance in her sparkly red court shoes and almost stacked it before righting herself and leaning against one of the stone planters. She took a packet of cigarettes out of her pocket and lit one, then offered it to me.

'I'm good, thanks.'

'You don't smoke. Of course you don't.'

I wasn't sure what that was supposed to mean, so I said nothing.

'I told Mum I wanted Guerlain L'Interdit perfume,' Daisy went on. 'I told her, like, over and over and over again. What did she do? Get me Coco bloody Mademoiselle, same as every year.'

'Maybe she forgot.'

'Maybe she just thinks she knows best, about bloody everything. You know, a couple of months back, I said I wanted to redecorate my bedroom. I wanted navy blue paint and a coral and forest-green feature wall, and what did I get? Magnolia.'

'Couldn't you have painted it yourself?'

'Me?' She gave a laugh that was totally without humour. 'Course not. Never mind that Dad's been in the construction trade all his life, I've never been able to so much as pick up a bloody paintbrush.'

'You could learn. It's not that hard.'

'It's only a place to sleep. I don't really care. God, you're lucky though. To be getting married.'

'It's pretty stressful, if I'm honest. Just wait until you try it.'

As soon as the words were out, I regretted them, remembering that Daisy had in fact tried it, several times, before Donovan's infidelity had put paid to her third engagement and, it seemed, her dreams of having any kind of independent life of her own.

But she ignored my blunder. 'I'm so wretchedly sick of my life, Nat. Living here, working in that boutique in town for Mum's friend Carole, seeing the same fucking people every fucking day.'

'But you don't have to, surely? You could change stuff. Get a different job.'

'Yeah, right. With my ambition and experience, I'm like crack to employers.'

'You could move out? I'm sure your mum and dad would help you with a deposit on a flat, like they did for Archie.'

'Sure they would. But what then? I'd still have to pay the mortgage and I've got no cash. At least as long as I'm here I live for free, and Dad lets me buy stuff on his credit card.'

A billion thoughts jostled in my brain. Daisy's situation might have been mostly of her own making, but I sensed she didn't feel she had the power to change it. And I suspected any helpful suggestions I might make would fall on stony ground.

So I just listened while she stubbed out her cigarette on the grass, lit another and carried on.

'It's all right for you. You've got a man. And Poppy's got a baby. I've got no one. No one cares about me.'

'You know that's not true.'

But she wasn't listening. 'I tried modelling, you know. I got on the books with an agency and everything. And then the first job they sent me on, I overslept and I was late. It wasn't my fault – my phone was dead and my alarm didn't go off. But they wouldn't offer me anything more after that. I mean, how unfair? It was only an advert for deodorant, for God's sake. Not exactly London Fashion Week.'

'That must have been disappointing,' I said, thinking but not saying that whoever had booked the studio, the photographer, art director, client, agency and anyone else involved in the shoot must have been significantly more disappointed than Daisy herself. 'You could try again with a different agency, if that's what you really want to do?'

'I'm too old now. I'm twenty-four. Twenty-five in April. My whole life is basically over.'

I managed not to laugh. I could remember saying pretty much the same thing to Mum when my first boyfriend dumped me, closely followed by, 'I didn't ask to be born.' But then again, I'd been fourteen at the time.

'I get that Donovan broke your heart,' I said. 'I'm sorry about that. But there are decent guys out there – really there are. You just have to get out and find someone. If that's what you want to do.'

'Christ, I don't know what I want to do. It's like, I'm so sick of everything. I get up every morning and work out with my personal trainer before work and go shopping and go to Dubai for the weekend with my friends and post on my Instagram like I've got this fabulous life. But it's not, really, is it?'

You go to Dubai for the weekend? Just like that? My mind boggled. I thought of what Mum's life had been like when she was Daisy's age, trying to juggle a full-time job and toddler me on barely any money while living in a one-bedroom flat on a dodgy estate, never being able to go out with her friends because she couldn't afford to pay a babysitter, and I thought Daisy had it pretty easy by comparison. I debated saying this to her, then I remembered my fourteen-year-old self and that feeling of the whole world being against me, and thought better of it – Archie's sister wanted someone to listen while she vented, not to be given helpful advice.

'God, it's freezing out here. Let's go in,' she said, as if standing out in the cold had been my idea, not hers. Then she added, 'You can try on my dress.'

'What, you mean now?'

'Sure. No time like the present, right? We'll get Dad to get it down from the loft.'

I wondered whether Keith, digesting his Christmas lunch in front of the TV with a whisky, would tell his younger daughter she had another think coming, but I should have known he wouldn't. No one ever said no to Daisy. Both her parents leaped into action. Archie was ordered to go and fetch a ladder from the garage and Yvonne led the way upstairs, leaving Mum, Freya and Poppy drinking sherry and debating whether to have another chocolate truffle or a slice of Yule log.

'Remember, Daisy, how excited we all were?' she asked. 'I'll never forget that day, when we had only a month to go, when your father went and picked up the dress and you tried it on. Poppy helped you into it and you walked down the stairs into the living room, and you looked just like a princess.'

'Dad cried, didn't he, Mum?' Daisy said.

'He did. First and only time in forty years of marriage I've known that man to shed a tear. But he's an old softie at heart, your father.'

'Ah, bless him. Remember how he drove all the way to Ipswich because that was the only place he could find a pink Rolls-Royce for our bridesmaids to be taken to the church in?'

'That car! It sat in the garage for four days, and I've never been so terrified in all my life. I couldn't put my own car in there because I was too worried I'd scratch it.'

'And those horses.' Daisy sat down on her parents' bed. The duvet cover was a glossy expanse of oyster-coloured satin, a battalion of assorted silk, satin, pleated and lace-trimmed cushions piled up against the pillows, a white fur throw carefully arranged over its foot. I wondered how long it took Keith and Yvonne to get that lot sorted before they got into bed, and whether they were ever in a hurry to do so – but then, thankfully, my mind veered away from that thought.

'Ah, those horses were just glorious,' Yvonne said. 'The pièce de résistance, that's what the journalist from *Brides* magazine said about them. She said it was set to be one of the most spectacular weddings she'd ever have the pleasure of covering.'

'And then it never happened.' Daisy sniffed, picking at the satin bedcover with her blade-shaped nails.

'All that planning for nothing,' agreed her mother. 'I never thought there'd be another wedding in the family so soon. It's just such a pity—'

She broke off, and I wondered what had been going through her mind. Such a pity about the bride?

'Are you sure you won't have horses, Nat?' said Daisy. 'I've still got the number of the lady we were going to hire them and the carriage from.'

'Honestly, I'd love to,' I said. 'I think it's such a great idea. But unfortunately I'm allergic to horses, like I told Yvonne. I'd start sneezing if I got within a few yards of them and not be able to stop.'

'Couldn't the bridesmaids have the horses and carriage?' Daisy suggested. 'And Nat have the pink Rolls-Royce?'

'Your father already contacted the Rolls-Royce man,' Yvonne said. 'And he's painted it mint-green now. So unless we were to change the whole colour scheme…'

'And Nat totally wants coral and gold, don't you?' said Daisy.

I couldn't remember expressing an opinion, except maybe to say I'd prefer it to the sage-grey that had been Daisy's other suggestion. But if it meant I didn't have to have a custom-painted Rolls Royce, I was all for it.

'Coral and gold will be really gorgeous,' I agreed.

'And I keep meaning to ask whether Fenella from *Inspired Bride* has been in touch? She was ever so keen to feature you.'

I was tempted to say that my allergy to wedding magazine journalists was even stronger than my allergy to horses, and that having one there would bring me out in unsightly hives.

But I said, 'It's such a lovely thought, Yvonne. But I just know I'll be so overwhelmed with everything on the day, it would be too stressful and I'd be really shy about all the photos.'

'Well, if you're set against the idea,' Yvonne said. 'Such a pity, it would have been great publicity for Archie's shop. Oh well.'

'Where is Dad, anyway?' Daisy demanded. 'He hasn't got lost up there in the loft, has he?'

'He'll have found those boxes of old Marvel comics he keeps up there,' said Yvonne. 'He spends whole Sunday afternoons browsing through them, like a little boy. Keith!'

Her call brought an answering, indistinguishable shout from above our heads.

'Do hurry up with those boxes, Dad,' Daisy called. 'Nat wants to try on the dress.'

I heard another shout and then a series of thumps.

'Don't drop them!' Daisy shouted.

'They're just dresses.' Keith's voice was clearer now. 'Unless you've got a pair of glass slippers in here somewhere, like Cinde-bloody-rella. Someone come and give me a hand.'

'Hold on,' I said. 'I'm on my way.'

I left the room and made my way down the passage to the loft hatch, where I could see Keith's face peering over like Father Christmas having second thoughts about making it down the chimney.

'If you can pass them down through the hatch, I think I can just about reach,' I said.

I stretched up my arms and felt the weight of a cardboard crate in my hands.

'Got it?'

'Got it.' I lowered the box carefully onto the floor. It was carefully sealed up with brown tape and smelled of cedar. On it there was a large sticky label in Yvonne's handwriting, saying 'Frocks'.

'Hold on,' Keith said. 'There's more.'

The box was followed by three more, and then by Keith himself. 'The wife won't ever throw anything away,' he told me, glancing nervously towards the bedroom door and lowering his voice a bit. 'Want a hand with these?'

'Yes please.'

Together, we carried the boxes back to where his wife and daughter were waiting.

'Oh my God, you've brought all of them down,' Yvonne said. 'We only needed the one! This one!'

She pointed to the smallest of the boxes, and I saw its label read 'Daisy wedding dress'.

'Well I wasn't to know, was I? You said to get the dress box from the loft, so I got—'

'Honestly! Men!'

'What's in the others then?' Daisy asked.

'Oh, all sorts of old things,' said Yvonne. 'Nothing you'd want to see.'

'But I do want to see. Go on, can't we open them?'

'Oh, all right. Keith, fetch the Stanley knife.'

Keith hovered, clearly not wanting to miss out on the excitement. Impatiently, Daisy grabbed a nail file from her mother's dressing table and attacked the tape on one of the boxes. She parted the cardboard flaps and pulled out a wad of yellowing tissue paper, followed by what looked like a pair of nude tights with gold sequins stitched to them.

'Oh my God, Mum. What the hell is this?'

'It's the jumpsuit I wore to my friend Karen's twenty-first birthday. That was the night I met your father.'

'Jumpsuit?' Daisy rearranged the garment and held it up in front of her. 'Jesus. There's hardly anything there. Were you Cher?'

'I had a lovely figure in those days,' Yvonne said defensively. 'I could get away with that sort of thing. And it certainly turned Keith's head, didn't it, darling?'

'I'll say.' He reached over and patted her bottom fondly.

'Can I try it on?' Daisy asked.

'I'll leave you ladies to it.' Keith backed hastily out of the room and closed the door after himself.

'Come on, Nat,' Daisy said. 'There's loads of stuff here.'

She wriggled out of her tight velvet trousers, tugged her jumper over her head and stood there in her bra and tiny lace thong, and seconds later Yvonne did the same and stripped down to her rather more substantial bra and Spanx.

Shit. Were they really expecting me to get my kit off and play dress-up? It looked like they were. Desperately conscious that my bra had a hole in the back where I'd put my thumbnail through it and my knickers didn't match it, I undressed, grabbed the nearest garment and pulled it on. It was a ruched dress in violet satin with a massive frill on one shoulder.

'Ah, I wore that to your auntie Elaine's fortieth,' Yvonne said. 'It was just a couple of months after Archie was born. I had to do the cabbage soup diet for two weeks to get into it, but it was worth it.'

I caught a glimpse of myself in the full-length cheval mirror. Apart from my rather startled face peering out, surrounded by stiff, shiny purple fabric, I was the very spit of the hazelnut and caramel chocolate from a box of Quality Street.

'It's dated, of course,' Yvonne said. 'But the colour suits you. If you were to make an effort a little more often, you could be quite—'

Again, she stopped herself, leaving me wondering what barbed comment she'd bitten back.

'Holy shit, Mum, this is a bit racy.' Daisy had managed to get into the gold sequinned jumpsuit. It was so sheer I could see the dolphin tattoo on her left bum cheek.

'I was quite the party girl back then,' Yvonne said smugly. 'Ah, look! Here's my wedding dress!'

'Oooh!' Daisy and I leaned over as Yvonne slit open the tape on another box. Out came a cloud of tissue paper and then a cloud of silk.

'Oh, Mother! It's Princess Di-tastic! Look at those sleeves!'

Look at those creases, I thought, as Yvonne shook out the voluminous skirt.

'It could do with a press,' Yvonne admitted, 'but the workmanship on it – all those beads! I wonder if I can still get into it.'

'I bet you can,' Daisy said.

'We'll do up the back,' I encouraged.

Together, we helped Yvonne into the dress. Whether it was down to her hold-it-all-in knickers or sheer willpower over the years, the dress did still just about do up at the back. And, creases or no creases, it was gorgeous – pure old-fashioned extravagance.

'I had a tiara too,' Yvonne said. 'I expect that's in another box, still up there in the loft. But look.'

She did a twirl in front of the mirror. At once, I could see the bride she'd been – the young woman, alight with excitement, embarking on her new life with the man she loved. I wondered whether there would ever be a time when she looked at me with that happy smile on her face.

'Knock-knock,' came Keith's voice from outside the door. 'Your Stanley knife, ladies.'

'Oooh, I'd better get this off,' said Yvonne.

'Don't!' urged Daisy. 'Go on, Mum, let him see.'

Yvonne looked doubtful for a moment, but then she turned to her reflection and smiled.

'Come in!'

Keith pushed open the door – and froze.

'Oh. Oh, look at you.'

Yvonne tilted up her chin and glided across the carpet to him as if they were about to dance. He held her at arm's length and gazed down into her face, and I could tell that, as far as he was concerned, she was still the twenty-something woman he'd fallen in love with. I caught Daisy's eye and we both smiled.

'Right,' Yvonne said. 'Enough of this nonsense. Let me get out of this thing and pack it away.'

'Wait,' Daisy said. 'Let me get a pic of you first, for my Insta.'

'Don't be ridiculous,' Yvonne said, but I could tell she was delighted.

'Just the one, and then Nat can try on my dress.'

'Oh, all right. If you insist. Mind you put a filter on it though.'

A few minutes later, they were both back in their normal clothes and I was posing by the mirror in what would have been Daisy's wedding dress. Like the one I'd tried on in the shop, it was strapless, its heavily beaded bodice cut in a sweetheart neckline, its skirt a huge confection of tulle and lace and sparkles. Like the one in the shop, it was over the top and didn't suit me, and I felt more like a contestant on *RuPaul's Drag Race* than a bride.

'You look so amazing.' Daisy dabbed at her eye with a tissue. 'If only I'd got to wear it.'

'Let me just have a look at the fit here.' Yvonne leaned in, so close I could smell her hairspray, and tugged at the seam over my bust. 'Of course, you're quite a bit smaller than Daisy, so it doesn't quite…'

She wasn't wrong. The fabric jutted out over my chest, where Daisy's impressive assets would have filled it and my not-so-impressive ones did not.

'We'll have to get it taken in,' Daisy said.

'Yes, that's an option,' agreed Yvonne. 'Although there is still time, if Nat wanted… No, that might be a bit drastic.'

Did I hear that right? Did Archie's mum just suggest I get a boob job before my wedding?

'We'll get it taken in,' I said firmly.

'Yes, that's probably best,' Yvonne conceded. 'It's a beautiful dress. Natalie, you look quite radiant.'

And that was it – there was no getting out of it. For the first time I'd had a glimpse of what it would be like to be truly part of Archie's family. I wanted to please them, and it seemed like a relatively small sacrifice to make.

And, besides, I knew that whatever I wore, when he saw me walk down the aisle, Archie would look at me the way I'd seen Keith look at Yvonne. Because that was the whole point really: we were in love.

I stood in front of the mirror for a second, staring at my reflection. The dress was hopelessly absurd, but my face at least was alight with happiness. Then I was jerked out of my reverie by a hammering on the door and Archie's voice calling out, 'Nat? Are you in there?'

'You can't come in!' Yvonne snapped. 'You're not allowed to see Nat in her dress until the big day!'

'It's not that.' Archie's voice was muffled, but I could hear the urgency in it. 'We have to go back to London. Your granddad's had a stroke.'

Chapter Seventeen

In sickness and in health – whether it's a bad cold, a hangover or something more serious, what happens when one of you is ill?

A. I go the full Florence Nightingale! Cook him soup, mop his brow – you get the picture.

B. I'm the one who gets man flu in our house! Thankfully he's very good about looking after me.

C. We're both grown-ups – we take responsibility for our own heath.

D. Oh my God, the hypochondria! A touch of hay fever and you'd think he was dying. I've learned to ignore it now.

Mum opened the door with a finger to her lips. I nodded and followed her into the house – not into the living room as usual but into the kitchen. It smelled, as always, of toast, but there was another smell too, one so familiar I barely registered it at first. Then

I realised: it might have been familiar, but it didn't belong here, not in Granny and Grandpa's house.

It was the smell of work. The smell of hospitals.

'He's sleeping,' Mum said, softly closing the kitchen door behind us and flicking on the kettle. 'He sleeps a lot. Well, during the day he does. He wakes often during the night and needs me. The social care people have been great – they've set up a bed for him in the living room. It's all kinds of weird, being back in my old bedroom upstairs. Like being fifteen again. I wake up in the morning and expect to see U2 posters on the wall.'

She poured boiling water into two mugs. It wasn't her usual fruit tea but the regular builders' tea Grandpa drank. I guessed she hadn't had a chance to get sorted with supplies of the stuff she needed. Her hands were shaking, I noticed, and there were dark circles under her eyes. Grey roots were showing on her parting and around her temples, and her skin looked dry and dull.

'So Grandpa's being looked after,' I said. 'And Teresa can stay with us as long as she needs to. How about you?'

Mum sat down abruptly on one of the wooden chairs, like a puppet with the strings cut, as if her legs suddenly couldn't hold her weight any more.

'I'm all right,' she said.

'Really?' I probed. 'Because it's hard, caring for someone. Along with everything else you're doing. You must be shattered.'

'Okay, I am shattered,' she admitted. 'I've not been up so often during the night since you were tiny, and I was almost thirty years younger then with all the energy in the world. But – you know – needs must.'

'How about work? Are they being decent about letting you take time off?'

'They're being amazing. I've gone down to three days a week, compressed hours, but that means I don't get to take a lunch break, and I have to dash back here in the evenings to relieve the carers. But I'll manage.'

She poured milk into our tea, but it curdled and separated.

'Bollocks,' she said. 'This is off. I'm so sorry, Nattie, I meant to get to the shops, but…'

'You haven't had time,' I said. 'Of course you haven't. Why don't we get a supermarket order delivered? I'll do it now – just tell me what you need.'

I took out my phone and tapped through to the Tesco app, adding Grandpa's address for the first time.

'Of course. Online shopping. God, I've been doing my own for years, I don't know why I didn't think to get a delivery sorted for here.'

You didn't think because you're run ragged, I thought.

'So,' I said. 'Milk. I'll pop down the road to the corner shop and get some in a second to see you through in the meantime, or I can stay here with Grandpa while you go, if you'd like a bit of fresh air.'

'Milk,' Mum repeated. 'The carers seem to drink gallons of tea, not that I blame them. But it just makes it harder to keep track of everything. Bread, I suppose. The loaf I used for Dad's breakfast this morning was on its last legs. Butter. Biscuits – the carers again. They seem to like chocolate digestives but they haven't touched the Hobnobs.'

'How about some pots of soup? Ready meals? And things you need – shampoo and shower gel and stuff like that?'

'And a box dye for my bloody hair.'

'Why not go to the hairdresser? Seriously. You need to look after yourself. I can easily stay with Grandpa while you do that.'

'I know. I know. That's what everyone's been saying. Max rang earlier and offered to help, but it just seems like it's so complicated keeping track of everything I need to do, never mind trying to delegate to other people.'

'How is Max, anyway?'

Just the mention of his name seemed to give Mum a bit of a boost; for the first time since I'd arrived at the house, she actually smiled.

'He's amazing. But we haven't seen each other since Christmas Eve, when we went for that walk and pub lunch. He rings every day but there's just no time.'

'Mum! Listen to me. We're in for the long haul here with Grandpa. You know what the neurologist said. He might well get better, but it's a slow process. It could take weeks before he's back on his feet and independent again.'

If he ever is. Unspoken, the thought hovered between us.

But I carried on. 'So you need to prioritise yourself. Not letting work get on top of you, getting a decent amount of rest. Seeing Max. Having your hair done. All that stuff.'

'Well I can't see Max before I've had my hair done, that's for sure.' Mum managed a shaky giggle.

'Don't be daft! I bet he wouldn't even care.'

'But I'd care.' She ran her fingers through her hair, and a ragged nail caught in it, snapping off a strand. 'I know you're right. I know it's ridiculous. But I just feel like if I was out with Max, or at the salon or out for a walk or whatever, and something happened to Dad, it would be my fault.'

'Of course you think that.' I heard my professional voice – my work voice – taking over. 'It's totally normal to feel that way. But you're no use to Grandpa if you're exhausted, are you? Or to work. You have to give yourself some TLC. It might seem like a waste of time, but it really isn't.'

'It's funny how things change, isn't it?' Mum said. 'Just a couple of months ago, I thought I'd be single forever. All those things I did – the yoga and the ceramics and everything – you were right. I was never going to meet a man doing that stuff. It was all about me, really. And then Max came along out of the blue, and he makes me feel like I'm sixteen again.'

'Like it was fate or something. Like the universe was telling you to bloody well be happy.'

Mum laughed again. 'The universe talks a lot like a certain daughter of mine. But being with him just made me realise how much I'd been missing out on. And I thought, with Dad back from hospital and on the mend, we'd be able to take our time, get to know each other, see how things went. And then that damn stroke changed everything.'

Again, I heard Work Nat talking. 'Of course it's a massive change. And it's a massive burden for you to take on. But there's loads of support out there, and you need to use it. And ask me for help too.'

'I know you want to help, sweetie. But you've got enough on your plate. You've got your own work, and Archie, and a wedding to plan. And I haven't even asked you how that's going.'

'Ugh, Mum. I know it's meant to be the most exciting time of my life and all that stuff. But it just feels like there's so much to do. I know I can't complain really, not with Grandpa ill and everything, but—'

'Just because Grandpa's ill doesn't mean the rest of the world's problems have vanished.'

'I know. And I also know how lucky I am to have them paying for everything and wanting to be so involved, and I know I sound like a diva, but it's like Yvonne and Daisy are planning their dream wedding, not mine. Yvonne keeps asking me about things we need to decide and Archie's just not interested. He says he's happy for me and Yvonne and Daisy to do everything, but then when we do make decisions about things, he says he isn't happy. Like, we had a meeting last week with the florist, and we decided to have these roses that are right for the colour scheme Daisy picked, and when I told Archie he was like, "Roses? But aren't those a bit weddingy?"'

'A bit weddingy?' Mum laughed again, sounding more like herself, and I wondered if, perhaps, talking to her about my wedding-planning woes wasn't as selfish as I'd thought at first. 'What does he think you're organising here, a bloody funeral?'

Our eyes met and the smiles faded from our faces. But I pretended I hadn't noticed.

'And then Yvonne's been putting together the guest list, and there are all these people on it I've never met and there's not really enough space for all of Archie's and my friends. But when I suggested that maybe he didn't invite this Billy bloke, who he was at school with but basically hasn't seen for ten years, he said not only has Billy got to be there, but he's got to be an usher, because Billy asked Archie to be best man at his wedding. And I just feel like I'm being pulled in two directions at once all the time.'

'I know the feeling,' Mum said.

'And this weekend we've got to go to the venue for a menu tasting. I mean, I never even knew that was a thing. I was happy to just get them to email me a list of options and we'd pick whatever sounded nicest. But Archie said we've got to try the food and choose wines that match, like he's suddenly gone full control freak about it.'

'It sounds like a fun day out at least,' Mum said, a bit wistfully, and again I felt terrible for moaning about my first-world problems.

'Well it'll be more fun than the afternoon we spent looking at stationery,' I said, trying again to lighten her mood. 'I had to take the afternoon off work and Nisha looked like a bulldog chewing a wasp, but it wasn't like I had a choice. Honestly, it was mental. Archie refused point blank to come – he said he had to roast some coffee, which is his go-to excuse whenever he doesn't want to do anything these days. So Yvonne and Daisy and I went to this swanky shop in Chelsea, and they spent ages trying to decide whether they should have the word "Invitation" blind embossed or foiled or engraved, or embossed and foiled, and whether the foil should be gold or silver, and matte or shiny, and whether the edge of the cards should be scalloped or plain, and I was standing there going, "God, can't we just send them emails?"'

'Oh sweetie.' Mum was laughing properly again. 'You're such a tonic. And you're right, I'm going to head out and pop to Sainsbury's and I'll stick my head round the door of Hair by Leo and see if they can squeeze me in. If you're okay to wait here in case Grandpa wakes up?'

'Of course I am. I'll go and sit with him and finish off the Tesco order while I'm here. And ring Max while you're out, okay?'

'Okay. Promise.'

Mum kissed the top of my head, the way she'd always done since I was a little girl, and hurried out, shoving her arms into her coat sleeves as she pulled the front door closed.

I took a deep breath, and then I opened the door of the living room as quietly as I could.

The hospital smell was stronger in here. The sofa had been pushed back into a corner to make way for the big bed by the window. The antique leather-topped side table was covered with a paper towel, and there were boxes of surgical gloves, a roll of cotton wool and various bottles of pills on it. On the coffee table were about five elaborate flower arrangements, which was comforting – at least lots of people were thinking about Grandpa. I put the card I'd brought next to them, opening it so he would see the little trail of Teresa's paw prints we'd managed to get her to make across the card by putting a sprinkling of my face powder on one side of it and a bowl of cat food on the other.

And he was, as Mum had said, asleep. His face on the pillow appeared peaceful, but even in repose I could see the uneven droop of his eye and mouth. His hands on top of the covers looked gnarled and old.

I remembered how cheerful he'd been the last time I saw him, tucking into the dinner Archie had cooked. I remembered his promise that he would be at my wedding and would start practising the reading from the Song of Solomon straight away so he was word-perfect.

I hoped with all my heart he would be able to keep that promise.

*

'So how's all the planning going?' Tilly asked a few days later, brushing colour onto the roots of my hair.

I hesitated, wondering which version of events to give her. I could remember the last time I'd visited the salon, when I'd torn out the quiz page from the magazine, eager to have it confirm that I was primed and ready for my happy ever after. Now, whenever I thought about the crumpled page at the bottom of my handbag, I was assailed by fresh doubts. But should I share them with Tilly? I could say what she was expecting to hear: that I was the luckiest girl in the world, having my dream wedding bankrolled by my in-laws, with a venue to die for and a dress that had cost thousands of pounds, even if it hadn't been meant for me originally and either it or I would need some serious surgery for it to fit. I could say the kind of things I read in the wedding magazines that Yvonne had subscribed me to, which made me feel slightly queasy when I heard the telltale weighty thunk as they came through our letterbox.

In the bridal suite at Grade I-listed Finchcocks Manor, Natalie and her bridesmaids will be coiffed and made up to look their dazzling best by celebrity hair and make-up artist Sonia Peters, whose radiant bridal look makes her the choice of royalty and A-listers. In her fairy-tale gown, Natalie will make her way to the chapel, passing beneath a bower of coral-pink roses, their leaves gilded to match the colour scheme.

At the altar, her groom will await, his bespoke suit tailored by Rodney Rodgerson of Savile Row. A fleet of vintage motors, likewise liveried in the bridal colours, will have transported guests from their nearby accommodation. The mother of the groom sports a lilac and cream disc fascinator embellished with silk roses and marabou feathers, by the Duchess of Cambridge's milliner du choix, *Philip Treacy. The couple will be serenaded by a twenty-strong choir, accompanied by soloists and the organist from King's College.*

The ceremony over, guests will stroll through the rose garden towards the terrace, setting of the couple's pre-wedding photo shoot the previous day, where a string quartet plays and champagne flows. Solar-powered light balls decorate the estate's famous maze, and a dove release greets the couple as they join their guests for the pre-reception…

And so on and on, through the wedding breakfast to the balloon drop; the change into a different frock for the evening reception; the cutting of the cake; the first dance. (*As Archie sweeps his bride into his arms, the strains of Ed Sheeran's 'Perfect' will bring tears to the eyes of many in the two-hundred-strong assembly.*)

Or I could tell Tilly the truth. Hairdressers were like priests taking confession, weren't they? What was said within the salon was sacred; I'd be heard and forgiven. And besides, she might not really be listening.

I could say the things here that I'd only really hinted at to Mum and to Precious, because I could barely admit them to myself. I could tell her about the spreadsheet Keith had shared with me, the numbers on it rising higher and higher until, I realised, the wedding was going to cost almost as much as my annual salary.

I could tell her that whenever I suggested to Yvonne and Daisy that maybe we didn't actually need a cake made of cheese as well as the actual cake; that bringing in a flock of pink flamingoes to complement the white peacocks that lived in the grounds of Finchcocks Manor was not only unnecessary but unethical; that the idea of a floating selfie booth on the lake was impractical bordering on dangerous, they looked at me with such disappointment on their faces, and Daisy said, 'But Valentin says…' and I found myself shutting up, smiling and nodding.

I could tell her I'd barely made it to a football match in weeks, because every Saturday afternoon seemed to be taken up with wedding planning stuff.

I could tell her that, just the previous night, I'd been in tears, begging Archie to ask his mother to please, please just tone it all down a tiny bit, and he'd hugged me and told me not to get upset about it, because they were just trying to make our day as special as they could, and we ought to be feeling grateful and excited.

I could tell her that the haste with which all this was being arranged in order to accommodate Grandpa might all count for nothing, because he might not be well enough to be there at all.

I could, at last, admit that I was having doubts not only about the fourth of April – now just weeks away – but about my whole future with Archie.

It was that last thought – so huge and terrifying – that decided it for me.

'Oh my God, Tilly,' I said, sipping the coffee she'd brought me, which was almost cold now. 'You know what wedding planning is like! So stressful.'

'So stressful!' she echoed, wrapping clingfilm around my head. 'I'll never forget my mum's neighbour's daughter Louise. She came in here a month before her wedding for balayage, and she was in such a state about it all that her hair was literally falling out in handfuls. I had to fit a full head of micro ring extensions. It took six hours. But it was all okay on the day. Your wedding will be too – you watch.'

Chapter Eighteen

Exciting as it is, getting married can be a stressful time, too. As a couple, how are you dealing with that?

A. Stress? What stress? We've never been happier.

B. It's a bit intense at times, but we share the organisation and outsource what we can.

C. When the going gets tough, the tough go shopping! We're spending a fortune on random stuff.

D. I have an epic meltdown and leave him to sort out whatever it is.

'Oh my God, I am so excited about this,' Daisy said, swinging her car onto the gravel drive of Finchcocks Manor. 'I haven't eaten all day. I'm going to totally stuff myself with whatever they give us to try.'

She seemed to have entirely forgotten her gloom on Christmas Day. She was dressed for the occasion (I supposed, if there was a dress code for going to a menu tasting for your brother's wedding) in coated skinny jeans and a cashmere hoodie, and her blonde hair had been straightened into a gleaming curtain that draped over the headrest of her sporty little red Mazda.

She'd been chatting away non-stop since picking Archie and me up from the station, about how excited she was to see the 'floral designs' and the layout of the room where the reception was going to be held; about whether we'd considered having crab terrine rather than smoked salmon mousse; about what cheeses would be served after the cake; and mostly about what Valentin thought about it all, which he appeared to have confided in a series of private WhatsApps.

'Of course, Val says everyone's doing doughnut cakes this year; fruit is so over. And really too heavy for most people. All that marzipan, ugh. Val says no one in France ever has fruit cake at weddings – they've literally never heard of it there. He suggested we could maybe look at having a croquembouche instead. Although that's something for us to discuss with the cake designer. Val reckons the new colour scheme will work so well. Coral and gold – it's traditional but fresh enough to look really contemporary.'

I couldn't help noticing that she'd pretty much stopped talking about what Archie and I were going to choose. Which didn't seem to bother Archie at all, so I tried my best not to let it bother me either.

'*Bonjour, bonjour.*' Valentin appeared at the entrance, his dark suit immaculate, his black hair as glossy as his black shoes.

Daisy hopped out of the car and hurried over to him, accepting kisses on both cheeks and then a third for good measure.

'This is how they do it in Belgium, where my father is from,' he said. 'So I indulge myself sometimes with an extra kiss, especially for a pretty lady.'

I only warranted two kisses, I noticed, and Archie, looking faintly appalled, extended his hand to be shaken.

'It's gorgeous, isn't it?' I asked him. 'I keep forgetting you haven't seen it before.'

'It's smashing.' Archie stood in the doorway for a moment, taking in the huge hallway with its sweeping double staircase, the huge bowl of roses on the table, the towering Christmas tree arrayed with silver lights. 'Off the scale.'

I took his hand and he squeezed it. I wondered if he was feeling as daunted as I did when I first saw the manor, trying to picture us, ordinary Nat who worked in a hospital and ordinary Archie who ran a shop, being lord and lady of this place for a day.

But maybe he was able to take it in his stride in a way I wasn't.

'Can we show my brother the chapel first, Val?' Daisy asked. 'It's so romantic, even now, in winter – and in April when the daffodils are out, it'll be just stunning.'

'Of course. It's this way, round the side of the main house. Follow me please.'

There must have been a wedding the previous day, because the little chapel was still filled with flowers. Bouquets of red and white, interspersed with holly and pine cones, lined the aisle, and there was a huge arrangement by the altar. The winter sunlight streamed in through the stained-glass windows, spilling like ink over the wooden pews and the stone floors.

I've never been a spiritual person, and Mum never made me go to Sunday school when I was growing up or anything like that. But, standing in the quiet of that building, I felt a new sense of the importance – the significance – of what Archie and I were going to do.

I thought of all the people who'd waited where we were now, over the years and centuries, poised to walk up that aisle and undergo a mysterious process that would make them husband and wife. I wondered how many had been brimming with excitement, love and happiness, and how many had felt fear or even just a cold sense of duty.

And I thought, *None of the other stuff matters. Not really. It's about the commitment we're going to make to each other up there underneath that gilded wooden cross.*

Archie squeezed my hand tighter, and this time I knew that he was thinking the same as me.

'With my body, I thee worship,' Valentin said. 'My favourite part of the marriage ceremony.'

Archie gave an awkward laugh and let go of my hand.

'Isn't it weird,' Daisy said, 'saying something so sexy in a church, with the vicar right there?'

I laughed. 'I'll let you know once I've said it.'

'Never mind all that,' Archie said. 'I thought we were here to talk about food, not bedroom shenanigans.'

'Ah, but the bridal suite!' said Valentin. 'This I must show you, and then we'll proceed to the dining room where chef is ready for us.'

We followed him back into the main house, and he led us up a flight of stairs, along a corridor and then up more stairs, narrow and winding this time. *We'd better not get too pissed at the reception*, I thought, *or we'll never find our way up here and end up getting lost forever and haunting the place.*

'*Voilà!*' Valentin flung open a door and stood back to allow us into the room. It was large, but still seemed to be filled almost entirely by an enormous four-poster bed, surrounded by red velvet curtains and covered by a gold brocade spread.

'This room was designed by the first owner of the house, in the 1800s,' Valentin said. 'He had the room created for his first wife, and it is thought likely their marriage was consummated in this very bed.'

'That's so romantic!' Daisy said.

Archie caught my eye and mimicked sticking his finger down his throat to be sick.

'Of course, she was his first wife but not his only woman,' said Valentin. 'If these walls could talk they would have stories to tell that would most certainly be – ah – racy.'

'You'll have to invent some for us,' said Daisy, flicking her hair over her shoulder and smiling at Valentin from under her eyelashes. 'I do love a racy story.'

Great. Now I was going to spend my wedding night thinking not only about some poor Victorian woman being deflowered in this bed, but also about the events planner talking dirty to my sister-in-law. Archie, next to me, looked outraged.

'It's certainly a gorgeous room,' I said.

'Indeed. And now we have some gorgeous food.'

Valentin locked the door behind us, and we retraced our steps back to the main hall and into the dining room. Most of the tables were occupied by groups and couples, all different ages but all apparently graduates of the Duke and Duchess of Cambridge school of personal styling.

'This is the main dining hall, where your reception will take place,' he went on, 'but for today, we have the intimacy of a private room.'

'Oooh, intimacy, how fab,' said Daisy.

I glanced at Archie, who rolled his eyes. Fair enough, Daisy was being annoying, but then annoying was pretty much her default setting. This might not be what either of us would have chosen for our wedding but, now that we were here, couldn't he at least try and enjoy the experience? Or just pretend to enjoy it?

Instead of gazing around in wonder at the flagstone floor, mullioned windows and velvet soft furnishings, Archie was staring down at his phone. I hung back, squeezed his elbow and gave him what I hoped was a look somewhere between imploring and furious.

'I'm missing football for this. You could at least try and enjoy it,' I whispered, and Archie guiltily put his phone away in his pocket.

'And here we are. Our stylist has dressed the table as it will be on the day, although of course we welcome your feedback.'

The table was set with gleaming cutlery, a tall silver candelabra and gold plates. Swags of orangey-pink roses were draped across the front of it. Each crisply starched napkin was rolled up and tied with rustic twine holding another rosebud.

'Stunning!' Daisy said. 'I knew you'd be a good lay. A good layer, I mean.'

'We do what we can to please,' said Valentin. 'Now, I will just tell Chef you're ready, and the sommelier will be with you shortly to discuss the wine menu.'

'Would you mind showing me where the bathroom is?' asked Daisy, and Valentin led her away, a solicitous hand under her elbow.

'Is that sleaze hitting on my sister?' Archie demanded as soon as they were out of earshot.

'What? I think you've got it the wrong way round.'

'Daisy's just being friendly.'

'Okay, right. If you insist. But if they are flirting a bit – so what?'

'He's a professional. He's meant to be doing his job.'

'And his job surely is: if a client flirts with him, flirt back.'

'Well if he so much as—'

'Jeez, Archie! Have you suddenly turned into the Pope or something, expecting girls to be virgins until they—'

'Sir, Madam.' Shit. I had no idea how long the wine guy had been standing in the doorway, listening to a conversation that was somewhere between a lively discussion and the beginning of a row but possibly coming down on the row side of things. 'Would you care to discuss the *carte des vins*?'

'Yes please. Of course.'

We sat down, and the wine guy, who had an impressive waxed moustache, leaned over us, pointing out various bottles of red wine, white wine and champagne, all of which seemed dizzyingly expensive. I was getting light-headed just looking at the prices; God only knew what would happen if I actually drank any of the stuff.

Fortunately, the prospect of showing off his knowledge of wine – which although not as extensive as his knowledge of beer was a whole lot more extensive than mine – made Archie stop acting like a spoiled six-year-old for a bit. He leaned in and pored over the list with the sommelier, and they had it narrowed down to a selection of two of each for us to try before Daisy returned from the loo looking smug and smelling of freesia hand cream and perfume, her lipstick freshly applied.

Small tastes were poured into our glasses, the wine guy expounding about tannins and terroirs and other things I hadn't a clue about, and then Valentin reappeared with a basket of bread and a little wooden thing like a ping-pong bat with various different-coloured pats of butter arranged on it.

'Here at Finchcocks Manor, we bake all our own bread from sourdough starters made with our own wild yeast,' he said. 'Today's selection includes malted fennel and caraway seed, slow-roast tomato and mixed olive, and the butters are anchovy, chicken skin and dill. Enjoy.'

'Personally,' Daisy said, 'when it comes to bread, I like a nice, soft floury bap. How do you feel about baps, Val?'

Surely, I thought, that wasn't an accident. But also, surely Valentin, being French, wouldn't get an innuendo based on a slang term for breasts?

But I'd underestimated him.

He cupped his hands in front of his chest as if cradling two warm, soft… well, bread rolls, and said, 'If Madam likes warm baps, this of course can be arranged.'

Archie looked like he might be about to explode. But his sister either didn't notice or didn't care. As the menu tasting progressed, she kept up a steady stream of borderline smut. She said how much she liked fresh oysters – they reminded her of something; she couldn't think what. She licked melted butter off an asparagus spear in a way that bordered on pornographic. She pointed out how delightful it was when a nice firm sausage exploded in your mouth. She even asked Valentin if his meat was well hung, because she did insist on well-hung meat.

And at last, after Archie and I had cringed our way through two hours of this and made our menu selections based entirely on whether the food in question had no sexual connotation whatsoever, Daisy led us back out to her red sports car looking like a cat that had not only got the cream but made a display of suggestively licking it.

'You know,' she said, swinging her tiny, pert bum into the driver's seat, 'I think he might fancy me.'

Chapter Nineteen

When it comes to his friends, you…

A. Treat them as my own – which they are, of course.

B. Do absolutely everything I can to make them like me.

C. Get on great with some of them – others not so much. It's cool, we're different people after all.

D. Ugh! I try to avoid them.

'Is this a thing then?' I asked Archie. 'Like, a combined stag and hen do before the actual stag and hen dos? What's it called? A sten? A hag?'

'A staggen?' Archie suggested. 'Shift up a bit, would you? You're hogging the whole mirror.'

We were in the bathroom of our flat and I was leaning over the basin, painstakingly applying mascara to my newly lifted eyelashes. It was practically mandatory now, Lara had said, and I might as well get it done, because it lasted months and would save me getting lash extensions for the wedding. But I was still getting used to the new angle I had to use for the mascara wand, and Archie digging me in the rib with his elbows so he could see to trim his beard wasn't helping.

'Ouch! You nearly made me poke my eye out.'

'Sorry. You look great, though. I love that top.'

'You think?' I finished my make-up and did a little twirl in front of the mirror. The bright red polo-neck bodysuit was new, and I was wearing it with wide-legged black velvet trousers and matching bright red lipstick.

'Foxy,' Archie said. 'Love the boots too.'

'Poppy passed them on to me. She says she never wears heels any more and never will again, so I might as well have them. They make a nice change from work shoes and football boots, but I'll probably break an ankle and end up having to oversee my own rehabilitation.' And if I had to wear hand-me-downs from Archie's family, at least there was one member who had similar taste to me.

Archie laughed, put down his beard trimmer and headed for the bedroom, emerging a few minutes later buttoning up a black and grey shirt.

'Too much?' he asked.

'No, I like it. It's not like we go to fancy places very often, so we may as well get dressed up for a night down the Ginger Cat.'

'I hope Billy finds the place okay. He hardly ever comes to London any more, he says.'

'I expect he'll work it out. He's got Google Maps like everyone else.'

'Yeah, but…' Archie tailed off. 'Right. I guess we'd better get going; it's almost seven.'

I glanced at him, but his face was unreadable. He'd been acting a bit strangely, I thought, ever since he'd suggested this night out with our respective hens and stags as a way for them all to get to know one another. And I sensed that at least part of it was about this Billy, his childhood friend who'd recently resurfaced in his life. When I'd asked what Billy had been like at school, Archie had said only, 'You know. Pretty cool.'

I couldn't help thinking that Billy's opinion mattered a lot more than Archie was willing to let on, but I wasn't going to make a big issue out of it. When I'd answered the question in the quiz about Archie's friends, I'd happily ticked option A – Dom and Mo did feel like my mates, even though I hadn't known them that long. And I was really praying Billy wouldn't make me want to revise my answer.

'I hope he doesn't mind crashing on the sofa,' he said. 'I said he could stay over but he might think I meant we had a spare room.'

'Why would he mind? Is he the Princess and the Pea? Does he have a bad back?'

'Dunno,' Archie said, pocketing his phone and keys and opening the front door. 'He just might. No, Teresa, you've had your dinner. You park yourself on the sofa and guard the place while we're gone. Ready, Nat?'

Rain lashed my umbrella and the wind threatened to blow it inside out – or possibly carry me off over the rooftops like Mary Poppins – as we walked arm in arm to the Ginger Cat. It felt good to be having a night out with friends again . Almost every weekend so far this year seemed to have been taken up with something to do with the wedding or helping out with Grandpa so that Mum could have some much-needed time off to spend alone or with Max.

Even though this, strictly speaking, was wedding business too, it was still just a normal night down the pub. Although, I reminded myself, I had an appointment at Davina's studio tomorrow to see how the alterations of Daisy's former wedding dress were coming along. If I wanted to avoid a repeat of last time, I'd have to be fairly restrained; I still felt faintly queasy remembering standing on that dais in the enormous dress, successfully battling down nausea and unsuccessfully fighting back tears.

'Archie! My man! Still a ginger minger, I see? And this must be the lucky lady. Nice rack.'

And this random stranger, accosting us in the street outside the pub, must be Billy, I realised. He was tall and powerfully built. His head was completely bald, or shaven, and went straight down into his neck so that he looked like a thumb – or the head of a penis. He was wearing a full-length leather trench coat. He had a row of gold earrings in his left ear and a diamond ring on the little finger of his right hand.

'Billy? I'm Nat.'

'*Enchantée*, as they say. Not your usual type, is she, Arch? Nice pins though.'

He leaned over under my umbrella and smacked a kiss on my lips before I had a chance to turn my head. Out of the corner of my eye, I saw Archie wince and force his face into a grin.

While I was still recovering from the shock, Billy went on, 'Well, no point standing about here coffee-housing! There's a bottle of Chivas with our name on in there, mate.'

Archie pushed open the door of the pub and we trooped inside. I liked Archie's friends – shy Mo, who was going to be his best man and who Archie had said was already having sleepless nights over the prospect of making a speech; friendly Dom, who used to work with Archie when he was selling advertising space; Freddie who helped in the shop sometimes.

But I had an instant conviction that I wasn't going to like Billy.

Before I could analyse why, we were shown to our table, where Lara was already waiting with a gin and tonic. Archie went to the bar and came back with two pints for Billy and himself and a glass of merlot for me.

'What's this about then?' Billy demanded. 'You're not expecting to party on lager, are you? Come on, mate, let's get that bottle of Scotch in. Got to drink these girls pretty.'

And – I'm fairly sure for the first time in the Ginger Cat's entire history – an entire bottle of Chivas Regal was purchased for our table.

Who the fuck does he think he is? I wondered. *Lil Pump?*

Billy splashed whisky into his glass and Archie's, but didn't offer Lara or me any. Lara gave me a sideways glance that told me exactly what she thought of that.

'Eighty quid this cost,' Billy said. 'Bloody London. I don't know why you bother, mate. You could have a four-bedroom house with a massive garden up in the north-east for the money you paid for that flat of yours. And it's not like this pub's all that either. We should go on somewhere later. Stringfellows maybe? Or are we saving that for the stag night, haha?'

Over my dead body. But before I could say anything, Daisy, Poppy and Freya arrived with Linus, and even Billy had to stop showing off for a few minutes to coo over the baby. And soon after, Dom and Mo turned up and Billy embarked on a male-bonding session by talking earnestly about football.

'Of course, now we've got Maguire we're a shoo-in for the Premiership,' said Billy. 'Eighty-seven mill doesn't buy you rubbish; it buys you trophies.'

'Actually, I think he's overrated,' I said. 'I mean, I know Manchester United have form for spending silly money on players, but that's just beyond.'

Billy gave a patronising laugh. 'Got her well trained, have you, Arch? Nice to have a bird who can pretend she knows about footie.'

Archie opened his mouth to say something – I hoped in my defence – but I didn't give him a chance.

'He was great when he was at Leicester. But although he knows how to read the game, his slow pace is always going to be a problem. He's got a great head on his shoulders, but his legs let him down.'

'And besides, the bloke looks like a fridge,' Lara added.

'He totally does,' said Freya.

'He can't help that, to be fair,' Mo said. 'I mean, come on. Be kind. Cut the man some slack. Plenty of my best friends have a touch of the domestic appliance about them.'

I tried to decide whether to point out that Billy, in his long, shiny black coat, looked like a high-end double oven, but I thought better of it. He was Archie's friend, after all. And, as Mo had said, be kind.

'Football's all so dull, anyway,' said Daisy, looking up from her phone. 'Aren't we going to order some food? You're always saying how great the chef here is, Archie.'

Relieved, I jumped up and got some menus, and for a few minutes we all perused them, Billy unable to resist saying he couldn't believe they had the brass neck to charge fifteen quid for a burger and Poppy pointing out that it was certified organic grass-fed beef, after all, and she for one was happy to pay a bit extra to ensure high animal-welfare standards.

'All that bollocks will be history after Brexit, you watch,' Billy said. 'We won't be governed by diktats from Brussels any more. We'll be able to make our own way in the world, finally.'

'Actually, those are British standards,' Poppy said. 'I only hope we'll be able to uphold them, regardless of politics.'

As another almost-row hovered in the air, Alice turned up to take our orders. Her presence seemed to remind Billy that he was hungry, and he happily ordered the fifteen-pound burger, plus an extra patty, fries extra crispy if Alice didn't mind. And he'd like a bottle of whatever their best champagne was, if there was one. Alice smiled sweetly as she took the order, but I could see by the set of her shoulders that she was deeply pissed off – her reaction to anyone casting aspersions on her pub was akin to someone telling a mother her first-born baby wasn't much to look at.

The arrival of the food and more booze – plus the fact that the original bottle of Scotch had been more than half-finished, mostly by Billy – calmed things down a bit. Lara asked to hold Linus and he fell asleep in her arms. Freya enquired after Dad. Poppy chatted to Mo about the beehives she kept on the roof of her apartment building.

Billy made a valiant attempt to flirt with Daisy – at least, I assumed that making a comment about how hair extensions made girls look like My Little Pony and asking if she could actually see through those eyelashes of hers was flirting in neg-hit form – but Daisy gave him a look that would have reduced most men to tears, and he shut up.

It's all going to be okay, I promised myself. He's a bit rough round the edges, that's all. He's with Archie, who he hasn't seen in ages, and a bunch of other people he's never met before – he's just showing off.

But before the end of the night, my breezy optimism was shattered.

It wasn't my pounding head that woke me, or the vile taste in my mouth, or even the fact that my eyelashes were stuck together from my un-removed mascara. (Actually, I'd have considered it a bit of a blessing in disguise if my eyes could have stayed glued closed forever.)

It was a deep, lingering, sick-making sense of something being wrong. Something to do with Archie. Something I'd done. In my dreams, we'd been having a horrible row – not the regular snapping-at-each-other-and-then-feeling-annoyed-for-a-few-days kind of rows we had in real life, but a massive, terminal-feeling row. I'd reached my arms out for him, trying to pull him close and begging him to make everything all right again, but he'd moved away from me, cold and implacable.

And then I'd woken up.

I rubbed black gunk out of my eyes and opened them, feeling the morning light stab my brain like a laser. Low winter sun streamed through the gap between the curtains, falling in a wide, cold stripe across Archie's empty pillow. So I must really have reached out for him in my sleep, and he hadn't been there. He wasn't there now.

What have I done? My poor battered brain scrambled to piece together the events of the previous night. Archie and I hadn't had a row. We'd come home together – with Billy, that was right – and everything had been fine. But then something had happened.

With a lurch of nausea, I remembered. Billy. Billy had tried to kiss me. Right there, next door, in our living room.

We'd all been quite drunk by the time we got back to the flat. Lara, Poppy, Freya and Daisy had called it a night relatively early and gone home; Dom and Mo had left shortly after. I'd been pretty keen to head off, too, but there was no stopping Billy from ordering round after round of drinks – flaming Sambuca had been involved at one point, I remembered queasily – although when it had come to settling up, he hadn't been anything like so enthusiastic. But the result was that Archie had staggered to bed as soon as we got in and fallen asleep, leaving me to sort out a makeshift bed for Billy on the sofa.

I'd tried to keep up a flow of casual conversation as I shoved pillows into pillowcases and wrestled our spare duvet into its cover, but it was hard to be breezy and pleasant with Billy slumped on the sofa, watching my every move but making no offer to help and slurping away at the can of pale ale I'd given him because he insisted the party wasn't over, and it was the only booze we had in the house.

'Right then,' I'd said eventually. 'Can I get you anything else? Cup of tea?'

Then he'd stood up and, before I could move away or react at all, he'd pulled me into his arms and kissed me. A full-on kiss, his mouth on mine tasting like an unwashed ashtray, his stubble grating against my cheeks, his arms so tight and strong around me I'd had to wrestle free, and even considered whether it would be necessary to knee him in the crotch.

And then he'd laughed. 'I was wondering what Archie saw in you, and now I know. Feisty lady.'

I hadn't known what to say, so I turned and went into our bedroom without a word.

I sat up, now, feeling like I might spew. When I was reasonably confident I wasn't going to – not just yet, anyway – I allowed myself to return to what had happened. I hadn't been afraid or anything. I hadn't worried that he was going to hurt me. I'd been safe in my own home, Archie in bed next door.

But what Billy had done was so way over the mark. So horribly inappropriate and gross. I was his friend's fiancée. He was going to be at Archie's stag do. And never mind that, he was going to be an usher at our wedding, showing our guests to their places in the chapel and handing out order of service cards with a Special Memories rosebud in his buttonhole, when just a few weeks before he'd made a drunken pass at the bride.

What the hell had he been thinking?

And what the hell was I going to say to Archie?

If I told him what had happened, he'd surely want to sack Billy as a groomsman. It was the only possible thing to do in the circumstances. Perhaps he'd even want to end their friendship. I would, if it was a mate of mine who'd made a massive play for Archie. And it wasn't even like Billy was a particularly close friend, or even a particularly nice person. He was what my grandpa would call an oaf.

But still, he was Archie's oldest friend, and I wasn't sure I wanted to carry the responsibility for creating a rift between them. And there was another lingering thought trying to edge its way into my brain: what if it was somehow my fault? What if I'd led him on in some way – let him think I'd be totally up for a sneaky shag on the sofa while my husband-to-be slept on the other side of the wall?

But that was crazy thinking. Never mind that I'd been a bit pissed too; never mind that I'd offered to chuck a couple of pillows and a duvet on the sofa for him; never mind that I'd offered him a cup of tea, because he was a guest in our home and I thought it was the polite thing to do. There was no way anyone who wasn't a total creep would take that as a sign of anything other than hospitality.

This lengthy internal analysis certainly wasn't making me feel any better, that was for sure. I leaned my pounding head back against the pillow, wishing I had a glass of water. Maybe Archie would bring me one. And then my thoughts snapped back to Archie. Where was he? Was Billy still here in the flat?

The thought made me feel suddenly exposed and vulnerable, and that in turn made me realise I desperately needed a wee. But I wasn't sure I was ready to venture to the bathroom until I knew the coast was clear.

The bedroom door was firmly closed, but I shut my eyes and listened, waiting to identify the familiar sounds of the flat – the flush of the toilet, the whoosh of the boiler, the ping of the microwave, Archie's feet on the wooden floors – and any unfamiliar ones that might give me a clue whether Billy was still there.

But I could hear nothing. Only the honk of a few geese making their way to the pond in the park; the tick of the radiator; the swish of car tyres along the street outside, which told me it had been raining; a mother calling her child to get back on the pavement.

The flat, as far as I could tell, was empty apart from me and Teresa.

I pushed the duvet aside, pulled on my dressing gown and went to the living room. The sofa was unoccupied, the spare bedclothes I'd given Billy piled tidily over one arm, the cat curled up on top of them. In the kitchen, I saw the empty can of beer he'd drunk standing on the draining board, and two used mugs in the sink. Archie's keys were missing from their hook on the rack by the front door. Billy's black leather trench coat was nowhere to be seen.

So they'd gone out. And with a bit of luck, I wouldn't have to see Billy again today. Maybe I wouldn't have to see him again, ever.

I went to the bathroom and cleaned my teeth, had a shower, blow-dried my hair and put on some make-up. I was going to take myself to the café on the high street, self-medicate my hangover away with a good old fry-up and decide what to say to Archie before heading to Davina's for my dress fitting.

I'd pulled on my coat and was just tucking my keys into my bag when I heard footsteps outside. My stomach gave an unwelcome jolt and I felt my heart pounding.

The door swung open and Archie stepped in, bringing a blast of cold morning air with him. Behind him stood Billy, a huge bunch of pink roses in his hands.

'Just a little something for the lady of the house,' he said, passing them over to me. Their heady scent filled my nostrils and a fresh wave of sickness washed over me.

'Thanks,' I heard my voice say, coming out in little more than a squeak.

'To thank you,' Billy went on, 'for letting me stay over. And – you know – all the rest of it.'

Archie had already gone into the flat, so there was no way he saw Billy wink at me and lick his lips. By the time I'd taken them inside and found a vase, I was running late, and inevitably I found all the trains into town had been cancelled owing to a points failure. I hadn't thought to check the app on my phone first, so I joined the throng of angry, damp people standing on the platform looking at the unhelpful digital departures board, which showed no departures whatsoever, then turning and traipsing out onto the street again, muttering darkly about how it was all going to hell in a handcart and there were probably the wrong kind of leaves on the track.

But once I'd resigned myself to being late and having to skip the fry-up, I found I was quite looking forward to a forty-five-minute bus journey. I'd be in the warm, I had my phone for company, and if I was really lucky there'd be interesting conversations to eavesdrop on, like the one memorable time I heard a girl telling her friend at length about how she was going to dump her sugar daddy because he'd bought his wife a bigger diamond bracelet for Valentine's Day than he'd bought her.

The bus arrived at last, and I climbed the stairs to the top deck, pleased to see a vacant seat right at the front. I settled into it and waited to begin the leisurely crawl towards my destination.

And a crawl it was. The streets were congested with traffic and after ten minutes we still hadn't even reached the next stop. The day was miserable, a slate-grey sky making midday look like evening, and all the people I could see hurrying along the rain-slicked streets were huddled under umbrellas, their coat collars and scarves pulled high around their necks.

The brightly lit buildings, though, all looked warm and inviting. From my vantage point, I could see into the first-floor flats we passed: in one of them, a man was playing a board game with his two small children; in another, a woman was taking a tray of what looked like scones out of the oven; in a third, a shirtless young man was ironing, steam fogging the window so I couldn't give his bare chest the appreciation it deserved.

At street level, too, there was a sense of inviting warmth. In the window of a pizza restaurant, a group of friends were drinking red wine. Inside the Ginger Cat, I could see what looked like a kids' birthday party under way, candles sparkling on a white-frosted cake. And in the chichi new café, the one that sold cupcakes with actual miniature doughnuts on top, a man and a woman were leaning across a table, their hands clasped and their heads almost touching.

Neither of them were young, but there was something about the way they were leaning towards each other that suggested the passion and intensity of a new relationship. They didn't look like a long-married couple having a chat about the mortgage or the children's university tuition fees; they looked like two people newly in love.

The bus had stopped at a traffic light, so I was able to get a good long stare at them: his head pewter-grey; hers dark blonde; his shoulders in a dark blue jumper; hers in bright red. I could even see the silver earrings that hung almost to her shoulders, but I was too high up to make out their faces.

Then, as I watched, they released each other's hands. The man stood up and turned away, passing out of my view for a second before emerging from the café into the street. Now that his face was visible, I instantly recognised him. Max.

That meant that the woman was Mum. Of course – I thought there'd been something familiar about the earrings. As the bus pulled away, I turned to get a last look at her, some instinct telling me I needed to see. Her head was resting on the table now, cradled by her arms.

She was crying.

Oh no. What was I going to do? I was already going to be at least quarter of an hour late for my dress fitting. But what if something was badly wrong? Clearly, the intense conversation I'd witnessed just a few seconds of hadn't been a happy one, like I'd initially thought. What if they'd had a huge row, or he'd told her he was still married or something? What if something had happened to Grandpa?

I hesitated for just a few seconds before taking out my phone and texting Yvonne to say I was really sorry, but I wasn't going to make the dress fitting. (I wasn't sorry, not really – I was too worried about Mum. But equally, there was no point pissing Yvonne off more than I had to.) There'd been a crisis, I said, not specifying any details because I didn't know them. Could Daisy try the dress on instead of me, I asked, since we were both almost the same size? *If she can't squeeze her pneumatic boobs into it, they've probably pretty much nailed the alteration*, I thought, but I didn't put that in my text.

And then I abandoned my seat on the warm bus and went downstairs, waiting by the door as it inched its way with excruciating slowness towards the next stop. After what felt like an eternity crawling through the choking traffic, the doors opened and I ran back the way the bus had come, considerably faster on my two feet than it had moved on four wheels.

Mum was still at the table. Her head was lifted now, and she was dabbing at her eyes with a tissue. Max was nowhere to be seen.

I pushed open the door and went over to the table, taking the seat he'd left.

'Hey, Mum. I was on the bus, and I saw you. Are you okay?'

She looked up at me. Her mascara was streaked down her cheeks, and I took the tissue from her and gently wiped it away. She opened her mouth to speak, but no sound came out.

'Mum?' I asked again. 'What's happened?'

'Oh, sweetie,' she said, her voice hoarse with pain. 'I just broke up with Max, and I feel like my heart is breaking too.'

'Oh, Mum! Oh no! Wait, let me get us something to drink and you can tell me all about it. Chamomile tea?'

'You know what I want? I want a glass of prosecco. If I was at home, I'd open a bottle, but I'm not and this is an emergency after all.'

'Right. I'm on it. Have you eaten?'

She nodded. I went up to the counter and ordered two glasses of prosecco – my hangover was just going to have to deal with it – and a bacon and avocado panini for myself, because there was toughing it out and then there was pure self-sabotage.

And then I returned to our table, sat down and waited for Mum to explain.

'You're like a guardian angel, you know, sweetie,' she said. 'If angels arrived on buses, which I suppose is about as likely as them arriving any other way.'

'The angels must be in charge of the Overground's points system,' I said, 'otherwise I'd have got to my dress fitting ages ago on the train. But Max. What happened? It was all going so well.'

She lifted the tissue to her face and wiped her eyes again. I saw the wet black imprint of her lashes on its white surface, but she didn't seem to have any more tears to shed.

'It was,' she agreed. 'He's a good man. I didn't think I'd ever meet one, but I did, and I'll always be grateful for that.'

'But then why—'

'The last couple of weeks,' Mum said, 'have been… well, I've never known anything harder. I love Dad, I love him completely and unconditionally and I know caring for him when he's so frail isn't just a duty, it's a privilege.'

'I'd do the same for you, Mum,' I said. 'You know I would.'

Her eyes blazed with sudden fierceness. 'Promise me one thing, Nattie. Promise me you won't ever, ever do that. No matter what. Even if the alternative is sticking me in some hellhole of a nursing home where there's only one staff member for twenty patients and I get fed gruel and lie in my own shit all day, or me taking myself off to Dignitas, promise me you won't be my carer when I'm old.'

'Oh, Mum! It's not that bad. The nurses at work…'

'They've chosen to do it! It's a profession, a vocation, whatever. It takes a massively special person to sign up for that. And they're not doing it for people they love.'

She was right, of course. However much care and compassion my colleagues lavished on all our patients – and they did lavish it, skilfully and unstintingly, even weeping when a patient they'd grown close to passed away – they didn't have the same deep bond of love and duty tying them to the people they cared for. And, as she said, they'd chosen the role and found it endlessly fascinating and rewarding.

'You didn't sign up for it,' I said.

'No. But here we are. And I've got to do my best for Dad, however hard it is. And it's relentless. He wakes up at night, even though he's got pills to help him sleep. He wakes up all frightened and confused, and sometimes he falls out of bed. Often he can't get to the toilet. I never thought I'd have to help him in that way, but I do – because how can I not?'

'But the carers – could someone not come at night?'

'We're getting all the help there is,' she said. 'People come during the day while I'm at work, otherwise I'd have to give that up. And then what? Sell my place and move into Dad's house permanently, I suppose.'

I thought of Mum's beautiful flat, which she'd saved so hard to buy and made so perfect, shining clean and tranquil. And I imagined how it would feel to move back into her childhood home, like stepping back to a time when she wasn't independent, wasn't an adult.

'I could help more,' I offered desperately.

'Nattie,' Mum said flatly. 'You couldn't.'

'But I—'

'You've got enough on your plate. You've got an important job, doing vital work. You've got a wedding coming up. And you've got a life. You're twenty-seven and you need to bloody well live it.'

'Like you need to live yours.'

'Sure I do. But for now, I have to prioritise your grandpa. I'm spread pretty thin, but I'll manage. Only something had to give. And it couldn't be work.'

'So it was Max?'

The fierceness faded from Mum's face, and her eyes welled with tears again. 'Yes. It's not fair on him to see him for a coffee once a week when I can spare the time. I can't invite him round to the house, because that's not fair on Grandpa. And when I do get a few hours to myself, I need to spend them resting, or getting to a yoga class or something, because otherwise that's not fair on me. I'm in for the long haul here, Nat. Like you said, I've got to look after myself.'

'But Max makes you so happy – you said so! Isn't that looking after yourself?'

'Yes, perhaps. But it would also be stringing him along. Dad could live another ten years – and I really, really hope he does. I hope he makes a full recovery, and I can move back home and we can both pick up our lives like they were before. But I wouldn't lay money on that happening soon, if it does at all.'

'Wouldn't Max understand, though? That things have to be kind of on hold? Just for the minute, until you know how the prognosis is for Grandpa?'

'That's what he said. I said no. I said I wasn't going to keep him hanging on on the off-chance that things might change in the next few weeks, or even the next few months. I won't do that to him, and I can't give myself the extra burden of thinking that he's hoping my life will go back to how it was when I don't know when – or even whether – it will. So that's that.'

The waitress brought my food; I'd barely noticed our glasses of prosecco had arrived a few minutes before and we'd both taken just a couple of sips. I took another now – the wine was warmish and tasted a bit sour, and made my stomach churn a bit.

I thought of how Mum had looked when I first saw her and Max together at the hospital – the sudden, shining happiness in her face. I thought of her saying, wistfully, how she'd like it if she could bring someone to my wedding. I thought how she'd said Max made her feel sixteen again.

And I thought about reading her the riot act – calling her Emma, as I sometimes did, telling her she only had one life and she needed to live it, urging her to… do what?

The reality of her situation was as she'd laid it out. She had to prioritise Grandpa and his care. No matter what she'd said earlier, I knew I'd feel the same if it were her lying in that bed in the front room, confused and frail and needing help. I knew that if I tried to do more myself, I'd be putting my own job and my relationship with Archie and my mental health in jeopardy.

As if she'd read my mind, Mum said, 'Eat your breakfast, Natalie. You need to keep your strength up.'

And, obediently, I did what my mother asked.

Chapter Twenty

Under the duvet with the lights out, or swinging from the chandeliers – how compatible are you in the intimacy department?

A. We're super-compatible in bed just as we are in every other area of our relationship. Lucky me, huh?

B. We don't always get turned on by the same things, but we're willing to experiment and have fun together.

C. Sometimes it's great, sometimes it's not so great. Sometimes I want it more and sometimes he does. We have our ups and downs, same as any couple.

D. It's one of the things we argue about the most. But it'll get better once we're married, right?

'Are you okay, Nat?' Archie asked.

'Fine.' I tried to keep the irritation out of my voice and probably failed. 'Why do you ask?'

'It's just… you don't look comfortable. Would you like to move to another table?'

'Here's great. I'm okay.'

And it was true – there was nothing wrong with the table. It was our usual spot at the Ginger Cat, in the corner, where Archie's uncle Ray and his friends played their dominoes game every morning. The chairs in the pub were all mismatched, but the straight-backed wooden one I was sitting on, which looked like it might have started life in a classroom, back in the days before anyone had heard of ergonomics, was no harder or more rickety than its fellows.

Archie was right, though. I was uncomfortable. Underneath my green jumper and denim skirt, my skin felt like it was being pricked by a thousand tiny razor blades. Instead of the usual smoothness of woolly tights beneath my thighs, I could feel ridges digging into my flesh. Something sharp spiked me in the armpit every time I lifted a forkful of lobster mac and cheese from my plate to my mouth.

Not for the first time, I cursed Precious for persuading me and Lara to go along with her to the home lingerie party her sister had hosted the previous week, and cursed myself for thinking that this boned black lace basque with built-in suspenders was anything other than a terrible idea.

But – as I'd reasoned to myself at the time – something had to be done. Archie and I had never had anything to worry about when it came to our sex life: we'd fancied each other from the moment we first met, and that attraction had translated into sex that, right from the get-go, had been pleasurable at worst and mind-blowing at best.

Now, though, not so much. It seemed like every time I reached for Archie's body in bed, or he slipped his arms around me when

I emerged from the shower, tugging at my towel to send it slithering damply to the floor, something got in the way. And not just something – the niggling list of wedding worries that sprang into my head like buzzing mosquitoes the second I closed my eyes.

A WhatsApp from Daisy: *Nat, Valentin sent me a link to a company that does rose petal cannons. Don't you think that would be so awesome for your first dance?*

A voicemail from Yvonne: 'Natalie, I was flicking through *Inspired Bride* the other day and I saw a pic of an open-topped marquee in the grounds of a venue. It looked perfect for getting a bit of fresh air if the evening is warm, or for those who still – you know – smoke. I thought we should get some quotes, so you should really start ringing round.'

An email from Valentin: *Chef has located a supplier of English Wagyu beef and suggests it as a canapé with Guinness sourdough croutes and balsamic pearls. This will add another 25p to the cost per head – please let me know if you'd like to go ahead.*

And with those worries would come a swarm of other feelings – resentment of Archie for not putting his foot down and instead allowing his mother and sister to get caught up in this ever-escalating spiral of excess. Worry about whether it would all come together and be okay or whether something might go wrong and spoil it, so all the hassle and expense would be for nothing. Concern about Grandpa and whether, after rushing to hold the wedding quickly, he would be well enough to attend at all. Waiting for the right moment (which never seemed to come) to tell Archie what had happened with Billy. And, most overwhelming of all, the fear I was rushing into a commitment I wasn't ready to make.

Passion-killer much?

So, whenever things between Archie and me looked like getting even a bit steamy, I found myself making some kind of excuse. I was knackered after work. My period was due. I hadn't shaved my legs. Every time, I'd see a shadow of hurt and bewilderment cross his face. And when my guilt at making him feel unwanted led me to make overtures towards him, he'd often turn away, giving me an affectionate peck on the lips, and say, 'It's okay, Nat, I know you're not feeling it right now.'

It was no good at all and it had to change, I'd realised. When I'd seen Precious, her sister and their mates giggling over the lacy lingerie, sex toys and ridiculous French maids' outfits at the party (there was even a sexy nurse's uniform, so different from our own practical polyester it had brought us to tears of laughter), I'd told myself that now was the time to rekindle the spark, and splashed out fifty quid on the alluring underwear that was currently torturing me.

'So I had an order for coffee from the café over the road,' Archie was saying. 'I gave them a few packs for free and they reckon the customers love it. It's better than the mass-produced stuff they were buying before and lower in cost, and the reusable packaging was a big hit too. And the artisan gin's been flying off the shelves. Poppy brought in another load of honey last week and it's almost all sold. I kept a jar back for your grandpa though – I know he loves having it on toast for breakfast.'

'Thanks.' I shifted on my chair, wishing I could prise the underwire of my basque out from my armpit, where it appeared to be trying to drill through my skin. 'I'll drop it off when I visit him tomorrow. Sounds like you're heading for world domination.'

'Well, maybe not quite.' Archie ate the last of his chips and the final bite of his burger. 'But there's a unit for rent over in Bermondsey that I thought I might have a look at. It's more expensive than here, obviously, but it's a much swankier area and the footfall's higher. Craft Fever two point zero – what do you reckon?'

'Maybe after the wedding?' I suggested. 'When we've both got a bit less on our plates?'

'Place won't stick around that long. The estate agent says they've had loads of interest in it already.'

'But…' I began, and then stopped. The angry words that threatened to flood out of my mouth were the same ones that jostled through my head every time Yvonne rang and said she'd tried to reach Archie first but he hadn't answered his phone; every time I looked at the pile of florists' brochures on the kitchen table, which he'd promised over and over to look through and hadn't; every time I had to give up another Saturday morning for yet another dress fitting, Davina's tutting reminding me that my waist was too big, my shoulders too broad, my cleavage too non-existent.

I hadn't said those words, because I was worried that once I began, I wouldn't be able to stop. And I didn't want to ruin this attempt at a much-needed romantic evening.

'How about another drink?' I suggested. 'One of those gin cocktails you like?'

Archie shook his head. 'Early start in the morning. I've got a seven o'clock delivery and I need to get a load of beans in the roaster before then. Shall we call it a night?'

I tried to conceal my relief. The sooner we got home and I got the seduction I was determined to go through with over and done with, the sooner I could get out of my tortuously uncomfortable underwear. Did other women wear this stuff and feel sexy and empowered or was it all a horrible conspiracy? Were there women like me, all over the world, feeling itchy and annoyed and not one bit sexy, wondering if there was something wrong with them?

Archie paid the bill and I stood up, tugging my skirt down over my stocking tops and putting on my coat. We walked out into the night together and I reached for his hand.

'Look at that moon.' I pointed up at the slender crescent floating in the cold, clear sky, surrounded by a thin haze of cloud. 'We should make a wish.'

Archie pulled me close and the strong length of his body next to mine brought a surge of the old, familiar love and desire for him, and an accompanying rush of relief. Once this was all behind us, we could get back to just being us again.

'What'll it be?' he asked.

Anxiety rushed back into my mind. What should I wish for? That everything with the wedding would go smoothly and my worries prove unfounded? That Grandpa would make a full recovery and live a healthy, independent life again? That Mum and Max would live happily ever after? That Archie's precious Craft Fever would grow and flourish into a little empire spanning south London?

Before I could stop them, the words flashed through my mind: *I wish I could get out of this ridiculous fucking basque.*

That was it – it was done and too late to be changed.

At home, I waited until Archie had cleaned his teeth and got into bed before taking off my make-up and brushing my own teeth. I pulled off my skirt and jumper, before peering into the bathroom mirror. The lace of the basque was slightly baggy over my left breast, the boning had buckled down one side and my stockings were sagging between the clips of the suspenders.

If I was a femme fatale, I was a pretty low-rent one. For a second, I considered ripping the whole lot off, dropping it at the clothes recycling bank in the morning and putting this absurd idea behind me once and for all. But then I would have spent the night in acute discomfort for nothing.

The flat was cold, and I pulled on my towelling dressing gown and pushed my feet into my sheepskin slippers, then flicked off the bathroom light and padded through to the bedroom. Archie looked up from his phone and smiled at me, pulling the duvet aside for me to get in bed next to him.

I took a deep breath and eased the dressing gown down off my shoulders, letting it fall to the floor.

Archie's eyes widened. In a good way. 'Oh my God, Nat. Look at you. Come here.'

I took the single step towards the bed and lay down, fitting myself into the curve of his arm. He pushed himself up on his elbow and looked down at me, running his finger along the shoulder strap of the basque to where the lace met my skin, which I could feel come alive at his touch.

'You like it?' I asked.

'Sure,' he said. 'You look amazing. Hot. It's really… different.'

His lips met mine and parted, and I felt his beard brushing my skin as his tongue caressed my lower lip. His hand found my breast and cupped it, tenderly and lovingly, unlike the pinching wire below it.

All of a sudden, inexplicably, I felt tears squeezing out of my eyes.

'Nat! Hey, what the matter?' His hands moved to my shoulders, holding me so he could see my face.

'I thought this would be all sexy,' I muttered. 'But it's not. I've felt bloody miserable all evening. It's itchy and horrid and awful and I've just wanted to rip the stupid thing off, and possibly my own skin with it.'

'You've been wearing that all night? Christ, you poor thing. I thought you were meant to put this clobber on before you came to bed and take it off right after... you know.'

'I thought it would get me in the mood.' I buried my face in his shoulder. 'But it hasn't. Actually, the total opposite.'

'Hey, Nat. Don't cry. Come on, let's set the girls free.'

He pulled me upright and carefully undid all the hooks down the back of the basque, craning over my shoulder so he could see what he was doing. When the last one came loose, he eased the garment away from my body. I could see the imprint of the lace on my breasts and a red, angry indentation on my sternum where the wires had pressed.

'How do these little bastards work?' He lowered his head to my thighs, fumbling with the fiddly catches on the suspenders.

'God only knows. It took me about half an hour to get the stupid things done up.' In spite of myself, I started to laugh.

'I'm not surprised. You need a degree in engineering to... there we go. Only five more.'

His fingers worked rapidly, and soon he'd peeled the stockings off my legs. His fingernail snagged in one of them and I saw it ladder.

'Bollocks! Sorry about that.'

'Don't worry. Trust me, I wasn't planning to wear them again.'

He pulled me close and suddenly we were both giggling, our mouths pressed together in a mutual smile. All at once, the desire I thought had deserted me came rushing back, and I felt myself dissolve inside in anticipation of his body close to me, over me, inside me.

'You don't need kit like that to be the sexiest woman in the world, you know.'

'And nor do you,' I said. 'Which is just as well, because quite frankly…'

'I dunno,' he said. 'Don't knock it till I've tried it.'

Half an hour later, tangled in each other's arms, Teresa watching us suspiciously from the foot of the bed, we were still laughing.

Chapter Twenty-One

Do you still enjoy wild nights out without your man, or have you got your single adventures out of your system?

A. What single adventures? Marriage is the only adventure I've ever wanted.

B. I still have nights out with friends, but they're a lot more sedate now we're all coupled up.

C. Of course! My friends are just as important as my other half, only in a different way.

D. Hell to the no. I intend to carry on having all the fun and he wouldn't dream of stopping me.

'Now, listen up.' Lara looked around at the assembled faces, which were wearing varying expressions of apprehension, eagerness and – in Daisy's case – something that reminded me a bit of a small child on her first day of school, who'd been persuaded to put on her uniform and pick up her sandwiches only after a major meltdown. 'There are a few rules for this hen do.'

'Everyone get shitfaced?' Suzie piped up.

'You seriously need me to tell you that?' said Lara. 'Now, first off, we need to keep together. I don't want anyone going astray on the mean streets of London. If you do decide to bow out early, that's cool, but just let me or Nat know. Second, we've all got some accessories to wear.'

There was a chorus of groans and laughter, and Lara handed out neon-pink T-shirts with 'Nat's Hens' written on them in glitter. She also passed me a gold sash that said 'Bride to be'. Then there were – of course – cock deely-boppers for everyone, and a naff plastic tiara for me.

'I don't want to wear this,' Daisy grumbled, almost but not quite under her breath. 'That is seriously tacky. I mean, come on.'

'It's a hen party, for God's sake,' I just made out Poppy saying. 'And it's not about you. Stop being a diva and wear it.'

'Second thing,' Lara said, 'I've sent you all an email with all the addresses for where we need to be and at what time, so if you do get separated from the group, you'll know where to catch us up. Not you, Nat, it's all a surprise for you, and the rest of us will just have to make sure you don't get lost.'

'I'll chain Nat to me with these,' said Precious, brandishing a pair of pink furry handcuffs.

I laughed. 'Don't even think about it.'

'I'm not reading that,' Daisy muttered. 'Seriously, does she think we're six?'

The way you're behaving, she'd be quite justified, I thought.

'Third – and I guess this only really applies to me, Nat and Precious, but especially to Nat – I know work has been kind of crazy lately. But this is your day, babe. You need to relax and enjoy it, okay?'

'Don't you worry about that,' I said. Funnily enough, I'd had exactly the same conversation with Mum the previous day, and with Archie before I left the flat that morning. *There'll be plenty of time for you to get back to worrying about work and your grandpa and the wedding on Monday morning*, they said. *Today is your day and it's all about having a good time*, they said.

I'll put a puke bucket by your side of the bed, Archie said.

And, funnily enough, now I was here, in the central London coffee shop where Lara had arranged for us all to meet, I found I could quite easily put the worries that had been mounting up over the past few weeks if not behind me, at least to one side. It was just one day, after all. The world wasn't going to end because I went out and had fun for one day.

I just wished Daisy had got the memo.

'And finally, let's all have a great time!' Lara said.

There was a little chorus of whoops and squeals around the table, which even Daisy joined in with, albeit half-heartedly. I wished I knew what was wrong – over the past few weeks, her irritatingly excited messages about wedding planning details had dried up. When we'd met up the previous weekend for my final dress fitting, instead of gushing about how stunning I looked in it, she'd sat in silence, staring at her phone.

It wasn't that I needed her approval, but if I'd done something to upset her, I just wished she'd tell me.

Glancing over, I could see Poppy leaning close over her sister, whispering intently in her ear, her face stern. Daisy stuck out her lower lip, looking like a child caught on the brink of some misdemeanour – *Wasn't gonna!* – but then, reluctantly, she nodded. Hopefully, whatever problem she had with me, or with being here today, she'd been told to bloody well forget about it for the time being.

I couldn't help wishing I could have been a fly on the wall of the WhatsApp group I'd set up to introduce my hens to one another, before leaving it so they could get on with their planning. I wondered how much of the organisation Daisy had actually engaged with, and how much had been left up to Lara and Precious.

'Right then!' Lara was saying. 'If we've all finished our coffees, let's get this show on the road!'

Her words, and her eager smile, reminded me of my earlier promise to stop worrying and have fun, and I resolved to do just that.

And an hour later, I was wholeheartedly keeping my promise to myself. We'd all been issued with knitted legwarmers in neon colours, and Abba was playing at full volume as we dashed around a dodgeball court lit with flashing disco lights. I was sweating and out of breath, I was sure my make-up had run, and I didn't care one bit. I was having the most fun I'd had in ages.

I grabbed one of the foam balls and threw it as hard as I could in Precious's direction, scoring a direct hit. She shrieked with laughter and pelted it back at me, but I ducked just in time and grabbed the missile, sending it flying across the court in the direction of the opposing team.

Ooops. A bullseye right in Daisy's face.

The balls were far too soft to cause any damage but, as I watched, she crumpled to the ground, burying her face in her hands like she'd been whacked with a brick.

'Woman down!' Suzie shouted.

We all paused, and I saw Precious go over to her and put a hand on her shoulder, suddenly not a twenty-eight-year-old woman having fun but a healthcare worker, concerned that someone might need help.

'I'm fine!' I heard Daisy snap. 'I just hate this stupid game. And I've only got two weeks left of my Invisalign braces – it had better not have knocked my teeth crooked again.'

'Is she always like this?' Suzie whispered to me.

'A bit. Not this bad though.'

'I mean, to be fair, it is a stupid game.'

'But it's supposed to be a stupid game.'

Daisy retreated to the side of the court and sat down. Precious and Lara briefly conferred, then Lara called out, 'Right, looks like the green team are a woman down. Sorry, guys! Advantage to the yellow team. Let's crack on.'

And we did, but a bit of the fun seemed to have gone out of the morning. Everyone threw the balls a bit more softly, and missed their targets a bit more often, and the remaining half of the game passed in an altogether tamer fashion than it had begun.

By the time our session was over, though, Daisy seemed to have recovered her equilibrium, and she came up to my side as we made our way to the next stop on our hens' odyssey.

'Do you know where we're off to?' I asked.

'Lunch, obviously,' Daisy said. 'But it's a surprise. And there's another surprise for you.'

'Awesome!' I said. 'I love surprises. You sure you're okay? That ball didn't do any damage?'

'Nah, not really. I'm just not a games kind of person.'

Which was fair enough, I supposed. And by the time we were all sitting in a red vinyl booth around a steel-topped table, studying menus packed with every kind of retro junk food known to man, she definitely seemed to have perked up a bit.

'Boozy milkshakes all round!' Lara said.

'Double-thick Oreo with sprinkles for me,' I said. 'And a shot of Baileys.'

'Bubblegum with a flake here please,' said Precious. 'And… Oh go on, make it a rum.'

'Strawberry and mango, vodka shot.'

'Mint Aero with extra chocolate buttons and crème de menthe.'

'Salted caramel peanut butter with bourbon.'

'Just a Diet Coke please.' This was from Daisy.

There was a second of silence during which I imagined everyone thinking, *Really? Does she have to?* And then segueing to, *Well, it's her body. No one's going to force her to drink milkshake if she doesn't want to. Be kind.*

And then the chatter resumed, our drinks arrived (not that you'd call the thing that landed in front of me a drink; it was so thick I could barely get my penis-shaped straw into it), and we all ordered burgers, hot dogs, mac and cheese bites, fries and onion rings. Even Daisy, although she said she wouldn't have any sides because she was sticking to her pre-wedding diet even if the bride wasn't, but she'd have some of her sister's. Like food eaten off someone else's plate somehow magically had the calories removed.

'Like hell you will,' Poppy said.

'Well, if you want to be so selfish…' Daisy began.

'The portions here are absolutely huge,' Precious said. 'I've ordered fries and onion rings, like a greedy bastard, so I'll have plenty to share.'

And so that crisis was averted.

After we'd all eaten (and Precious was right – there was more than enough to go around), Daisy said, 'Now, I've got a surprise.'

Lara looked alarmed. 'What's that? Because we've got our next activity booked in forty-five minutes.'

'It won't take long,' Daisy said. 'It's just a game for Nat.'

'You know me,' I said. 'Always up for a challenge. Hit me with it, Daisy.'

'Okay. So you know how you play Mr and Mrs?'

'Like, when you ask the man questions about his partner, and he answers them, and you see if his answers match hers?'

'Yeah, like that. Only Archie isn't here, obviously. But I am.'

'And you're his sister,' Suzie said.

'Exactly. So, in theory, I should know him better than anyone.'

'Except maybe me,' Poppy said. 'Given I've been his sister for four whole years longer than you have. But I'm afraid I'm going to have to love and leave you all, because Freya's got to work on an assignment and I promised I'd get home to look after Linus.'

'And maybe Nat,' said Lara, but I didn't think anyone heard her, because we were all kissing Poppy goodbye, and she was saying how gutted she was to be missing out on the rest of the day, and how, really, babies were more trouble than they were worth.

'Right, so,' Daisy said once we'd all settled down again, 'are you ready, Nat?'

'Ready as I'll ever be.'

'What was the name of Archie's first pet, and what was it?'

I racked my brains. 'Was it Willow, the Jack Russell terrier?'

'Wrong! Archie's first pet was an imaginary Dalmatian called Spotty.'

'I'm not sure that counts,' Suzie protested.

'It totally does. He was obsessed with this pretend dog, and imagined it following him around everywhere until he was, like, eight.'

'Okay.' I laughed. 'Fine. You've got me on Spotty. I'll have to ask Archie about him and see if he remembers.'

'About *her*,' Daisy said. 'Spotty was a girl imaginary dog.'

An imaginary bitch, I thought, but stopped myself right there.

'What was the name of Archie's first girlfriend?'

I thought back. He'd said something about a girl in high school – what was her name? 'Debbie?'

'Wrong. Archie's first girlfriend was Megan Brown, in primary school. They used to sit next to each other in class.'

'Isn't that cute?' I said. 'Imagine, little Archie and Megan. I'll definitely be taking the piss out of him for that.'

My friends around the table were all beginning to look puzzled and a bit embarrassed. What was the point of this? Why was Daisy coming up with these random questions, designed to prove she knew obscure facts about her brother's childhood that I didn't and, really, couldn't be expected to?

'What's Archie's favourite food?'

'That's easy. Sunday roast at the Ginger Cat.'

'Nope. It's pickled onion Monster Munch.'

In all the time I'd known Archie, he'd never so much as mentioned Monster Munch, pickled onion or any other flavour. But this was my hen night, and I wasn't going to get into a row with my future sister-in-law about my fiancé's taste in snacks.

Daisy looked at me across the table, her eyes narrowed, a little smile on her face. Lara signalled the waitress for our bill, handed over her credit card and started tapping at her phone, I guessed checking details of our next destination.

'What's Archie's guilty secret?' Daisy asked.

There was no denying it, this game had got very old very quickly. But I wasn't going to play into Daisy's hands by revealing that I was annoyed and – if I was honest with myself – a bit embarrassed by her behaviour.

'Evidently,' I said lightly, 'it's that he likes pickled onion Monster Munch. But I'm sure he has others.'

'Just the one,' Daisy said.

'Right. And that is…?'

'Well, I couldn't possibly tell you, could I?' Daisy said, with a smug little smile that made me wish I had another foam ball handy to pelt her with. 'Otherwise it wouldn't be a secret any more.'

'Okay,' Lara said, 'we really should be making a move. So if you're done with the questions…'

'There's one more. We've got time for one, haven't we?'

'Go on then,' I agreed reluctantly.

'What annoys Archie most about you?'

I heard myself give a forced little laugh. 'Where would you like me to start?'

Of course I knew there were lots of things I did that annoyed Archie. It would be weird if there weren't. There was the way I left the bathroom cupboard open after I'd finished getting ready in the mornings, every time, no matter how hard I tried to remember to close it. The way I put my work clothes in the washing machine every evening when I got home, without checking whether there was other stuff that needed doing to make up a full load. The way I sent him to the late-night chemist to buy wax strips for my bikini line when I'd forgotten I needed them.

And there was something else: something he'd never told me but had confided in his sister. And which she was about to reveal to my best mates.

'Come on,' Precious said. 'Enough of this. Lara's worried we're going to be late, and you're upsetting Nat.'

'I'm not upset,' I lied. 'But we need to make a move anyway.'

The feeling of stilted awkwardness persisted as we left the burger bar and headed out into the street. Daisy tagged along at the back of the group, looking at her phone. Precious and Suzie walked together, their heads close, talking softly. Lara fell into step next to me.

'Are you okay?' she whispered.

'Sure. I'll be fine.'

'Bit bloody off, trying to make you look stupid on your hen do.'

'Yeah, well,' I tried to sound casual, 'no one can make me look stupid unless I actually – you know – do look stupid. So I'll try my best to avoid that.'

Lara laughed. 'Or save it for later, at least. We've got a nice relaxing couple of hours now, before we head out for the evening. Don't let her stress you out.'

She squeezed me into a half-hug and I hugged her back, whispering, 'I won't.'

And she was right. Next stop was a spa, where we were all whisked off into separate cubicles for massages and pedicures. I let myself sink down into the bed, the therapist's hands easing knots of tension I hadn't even known were there – or maybe they'd been there so long I'd stopped noticing them any more – from my back and shoulders. I enjoyed the bubbles in the foot spa ticking my feet. I watched as my toenails were painted a perfect, glossy rose-pink.

I showered and put on a fluffy white robe and was reunited with my friends in the luxurious locker room, where we all put on our make-up and got dressed for the evening.

Daisy, I noticed, was doing her face extra carefully, smoothing on primer and then foundation and then concealer, then using three different contour and highlighters, and sticking on false eyelashes over her winged eyeliner.

But, as we all got ready to leave, she said, 'I'm really sorry, but I'm not going to be able to come on with you for the rest of the evening.'

'That's a shame,' Lara said. 'Why not? Are you okay?'

Daisy shook her head. 'I think I've got a migraine coming on. It must've been being hit on the head with that ball earlier on. My vision's all blurry and I've got a pain just here.'

She pressed a finger to her temple and looked forlorn.

'You wouldn't have got concussion from being hit with a piece of foam rubber,' Precious said. 'I did three years in Accident and Emergency and I've seen just about everything, but never that.'

'Still, if you're feeling poorly…' Suzie said, shooting a concerned took at me. I rolled my eyes and shrugged – Daisy was going to do Daisy, whether it upset me or not, so I wasn't going to let it.

'I really am,' Daisy insisted. 'I think I'll go home and lie down.'

'Will you be okay?' Lara asked. 'Do you want to get an Uber?'

Daisy shook her head. 'I'll get the train. Don't worry about me.'

We said goodbye and watched as she walked off towards the station, slowly at first, then quickening her steps as she turned a corner and disappeared.

'Who puts on false eyelashes to go home and lie down?' demanded Precious.

'I guess there's a first time for everything,' Suzie said.

'Wouldn't it be boring if we were all the same?' said Lara. 'Personally, I never start the ironing unless I've got my diamond earrings in.'

I laughed. 'I blow-dry my hair before I put my swimming cap on at the gym, just so it looks its best for all the people who won't see it.'

'Come on then,' Lara said. 'At least there are four of us still standing, and we've got cocktails, dinner and then a VIP table in a club. Everyone up for that?'

We managed a chorus of only slightly half-hearted cheers. I resolved to text Daisy the next day and check she was okay, and maybe text Poppy too and ask if I'd done anything to upset her sister. But, for now, I could enjoy the rest of the evening without giving her another thought.

Chapter Twenty-Two

He's heading off on his stag night/weekend/week. Set any boundaries around that?

A. Why would I need to? I know I can trust him not to behave in a way I wouldn't approve of.

B. Yeah, we've talked about it. I'm cool about most stuff, and I know he'll have a great time without overstepping the mark.

C. What happens in Vegas stays in Vegas! So long as I get him back in one piece, he's welcome to have a wild time.

D. Well I'm tracking his phone and I know all his passwords so if he gets up to no good, I'll find out about it – and I'll know what to do about it.

'So what happened after that?' Archie sat down on the bed where I was reclining, propped up by pillows, after carefully placing a laden tray on my knees. 'Here you go: can of full-fat Coke, bacon and egg muffin, packet of pickled onion Monster Munch. What's with those – some new hangover cure you read about in *Orthopaedics and Trauma*?'

'I'm not sure *O and T* covers hangovers,' I said. 'It damn well should, though. And actually, I've never really got why some of our patients say they look forward to a stay in hospital before, but I do now. I might be feeling like shit, but I'm living my best life, right here in bed with you nursing me.'

'So long as you return the favour next weekend.' Archie ripped open the crisps and ate one. 'God, these haven't got any better, have they? They minged last time I ate them – must be a good ten years ago, mind – and they ming now.'

'I thought they were your favourite food.'

'What? You know perfectly well it's that vegetable and chickpea soup you make when there are loads of bendy carrots and soggy spinach in the fridge and we're skint. Actually it's not – it's Sunday lunch at the Ginger Cat.'

'I knew it! So why was Daisy going on about pickled onion Monster Munch?'

'Search me. Must be confusing me with her secret other brother. But anyway – what happened next, after you left the spa place?'

I picked up my bacon and egg muffin and took a bite. Archie had cooked the egg perfectly, so just-set yolk and runny butter dripped down my chin. I mopped it up with a square of kitchen roll before any got on the duvet, trying to decide what to tell him, and in what order.

And a niggling part of me remembered what his youngest sister had said about Archie having a guilty secret, and what that might be. But I pushed the thought away. If the Monster Munch fiasco was anything to go by, it was probably just Daisy being Daisy – playing mind games and trying to make me feel uncomfortable.

'So then we went for cocktails,' I began. 'Lara found this amazing place that does, like, drinks served in massive shells with smoke coming out of them and negronis made with barrel-aged… But I can't talk about that now – I'm still feeling a bit fragile.'

'Save it for later. Especially the barrel-aged negroni whatnot – I might want to get some for the shop.'

'I think I've got pictures of it on Insta,' I said. 'Just can't look at them right now.'

'Take your time,' Archie said. 'No point rushing your recovery, as I bet you say to the geriatrics.'

'Don't call them that! They're not all old, anyway. There was a fourteen-year-old on the ward the other day. Wiped off his skateboard doing a three-sixty hardflip – whatever that is – and smashed up his elbow. Anyway, we went for dinner after that, only it wasn't really dinner, it was a restaurant that does a pudding tasting menu.'

'Oh man. Lara knows her market.'

'I know, right? It was awesome. We had lemon tart and chocolate fondant and cupcakes with cherry buttercream and these shortbread things, and—'

'Okay, stop that. You're torturing me. All we've got in the house is half a bag of Percy Pigs that have gone all hard. So what was the highlight of the evening?'

I finished my muffin and took a big gulp of Coke. 'Definitely, one hundred per cent, it was when we were leaving the club, right at the end of the night.'

'Really? What happened?'

'So we were all a bit pissed by then, but Lara had really been giving it some. And when we were leaving the club, she tripped up on her shoes – she was wearing these massive five-inch stilettos and she never wears heels normally, and she was totally shitfaced, so you can imagine. Anyway she did this total staggering thing across the pavement and she almost collided with a police officer who was going past on his beat.'

'Oh no!'

'Oh yes. But it gets worse. She looked up at him and she was like, "I never knew we ordered a strippergram! He's hot! Come on, get your kit off, you sexy beast." And we all had to restrain her and explain that he was a real policeman, not a male stripper dressed up as one, and hope he didn't decide to arrest us for being drunk and disorderly.'

Archie looked bemused.

'Maybe you had to be there. But then, there's another thing I need to tell you. Daisy bailed out early. She said she wasn't feeling well, but I thought it was a bit weird because she'd seemed fine the whole rest of the day, and she put her make-up on and stuff when we did, after we had our spa treatments. But when we were leaving the restaurant…'

I paused for breath, a big gulp of Coke and another bite of my muffin.

'When you were leaving the restaurant…?' Archie prompted.

'Yeah, so it's not like it's a massively posh place. But it's in Covent Garden, and you know there are loads of quite posh places round there.'

'Like that one I took you to for your birthday.'

'God, yes. Where the waiters were all about ninety and we thought we'd get chucked out for not knowing how to use a fish knife.'

'Yeah, that place. What was it called again?'

'Rules, I think. Appropriately enough, because we certainly broke them.'

'Yes, when we swapped over our main courses because you didn't like the grouse, I thought the waiter was going to have a heart attack.'

'Just as well I did a stint in cardiac rehab, back in the day. I could have saved his life.'

'He would still have wanted to chuck us out, though.'

'Probably. Anyway, we were waiting for our Uber to take us to the club, and we noticed there was this other restaurant across the road, even posher.'

'And you thought we could go there for your next birthday?'

I laughed. 'No thanks. But this place had these massive windows, so you could see right into the room. It's that whole industrial vibe, I think. Lots of bare walls and polished concrete.'

'Nat?'

'You called?'

'Are you going to go into an in-depth analysis of restaurant interior design trends or are you going to tell me what happened?'

'Sorry. So we were waiting for our Uber and kind of looking through the window, like you do. And we saw Daisy.'

'Daisy my sister?'

'No, Daisy Duke. Of course your sister.'

'But she'd gone home with a headache.'

'Except she hadn't. She was having dinner in a swanky restaurant with…' I took a deep breath. 'Valentin.'

'Valentin from Finchcocks?'

'No, Valentin…' But I couldn't think of another person with that name. 'Of course him. They were eating oysters, right by the window. I don't think they saw us.'

'Jesus. That dude. I knew he was hitting on her, and now look!'

'Archie, calm down. I know she's your sister, but she's an adult. If she wants to go on a date with an attractive man, that's okay, isn't it?'

'Even though she was meant to be on your hen do? Even though he was feeding her oysters like he's Casa-fucking-nova?'

'Well, that's not ideal, obviously. But it's not like forcing her to be there when she'd rather be somewhere else would have meant anyone else having a more fun night. And she can eat oysters if she wants to. I mean, I was a bit hurt, but Lara said I should just let it go. So that's what I'm going to do.'

'You're not going to sack her as your chief bridesmaid?'

'Would you sack Billy as one of your groomsmen if he did a shitty thing on your stag night?'

Archie looked down at his hands and, to my surprise, I saw a deep red blush creeping up his neck.

'Depends how shitty,' he muttered.

Suddenly, even though I was snuggled under the duvet and the bedroom was warm, I felt a chill spreading through my body.

'Archie,' I said, 'there aren't any plans for your stag do that you think you should tell me about, are there?'

'What? No, of course not.'

'Really? Because I remember when we saw Billy last, he happened to mention taking you to Stringfellows.'

'He did? He must have been kidding.'

'Okay, cool. But if – just perhaps – he wasn't, I think you probably ought to know my views on that.'

'God, Nat. Isn't it just a thing blokes do sometimes?'

'Some blokes, maybe. Not the kind of bloke I'd want to marry, though.'

'But it's just—'

'Just what? Just commodifying women? Just disrespecting the person you're about to marry with the idea that you're entitled to some kind of last hurrah looking at other girls naked because you'll be tied to your one boring wife for the foreseeable? Just colluding in the exploitation and—'

'Woah. Steady on. Since when have you felt so strongly about this?'

'Since forever. I guess I've just never really spoken to you about it because it never crossed my mind you were the sort of person I'd need to speak to about it.'

Archie looked down at his hands again and said nothing.

'And I bet Dom and Mo would feel the same as me.' I tried to imagine shy, gentle Mo with a stripper's boobs in his face, or nerdy Dom being herded behind a curtain for a private dance, and failed entirely. They'd drop dead with embarrassment, I reckoned.

'I don't know what they've planned,' Archie said. 'Seriously, Nat. It's all a surprise. If I'm honest I'd think something like going to a strip club would be cringe as fuck, never mind a massive rip-off. I'm not some wanker City boy. I don't have hundreds of pounds to spaff on shit champagne, even if that was my idea of a fun night out, which it isn't.'

'So if Billy were to tell you that was the plan, what would you do?'

'I'm sure Mo would tell him it's a terrible idea. And Dom would back Mo up.'

'And what about you?'

'Nat!' He sounded almost pleading. 'I don't know what you're getting so worked up about. It hasn't happened. I haven't been near a lap-dancing club ever in my life and you're acting like I'm some kind of cheating low-life.'

'I'm not acting like anything,' I said. 'I'm making clear what my boundaries are, in case there's any confusion. Just so you know. I trust you. I trust Mo and Dom. But I don't trust Billy, and I guess I'm worried that if he did suggest something like that you might go along with it because you're a nice person and you hate saying no to your friends.'

'How can you not trust Billy? He's my oldest mate, and anyway you're only met him the once.'

I took a deep breath. There was still about a quarter of my muffin left on my plate, and all the crisps in the packet apart from the one Archie had eaten. But the egg yolk was cold now, congealed and unappetising, and the harsh, vinegary smell of the Monster Munch was making me feel queasy again.

Too much time had passed for me to reveal to Archie the real reason I had for not trusting Billy. In my head, in the weeks since the night when he'd clumsily lunged at me in our living room, I'd successfully minimised the whole thing in my head. I'd told myself nothing had actually happened. Billy had clearly felt remorseful –

he'd bought me roses, after all – and if I were to tell Archie now, he'd worry I'd been hiding something more serious than what had actually taken place – or, worse, suspect me of making it up because I didn't like Billy and because of the argument we were right in the middle of having.

'I just don't,' I answered lamely. 'Look, Archie, you know how I feel about this now. I'm sure nothing will happen. I know you'd do the right thing. But it's a bit of a deal-breaker for me, and I wanted to make that clear.'

'No overstepping the boundaries?' he asked, his face serious.

'No overstepping the boundaries.'

'No lap-dancing club?'

'No lap-dancing club.'

'No strippers' tits in my face?'

'No strippers'—Ugh, Archie! No strippers' tits in your face.'

Archie stood up, grinning, and lifted the tray off my lap.

'Okay. I'd better head off now and open the shop. Hope you get some more rest.'

I shook my head. 'I'm getting up as soon as you're done in the bathroom. I'm going to spend the day with Grandpa to give Mum a break. He can almost write again, although it's harder than it used to be for him. That book of large-print crossword puzzles you bought is great.'

'Tell him I said hi,' Archie said. 'I'll look in after work, bring a takeaway for us, if you like.'

'Thanks. That would be great.'

I lay back against the pillows and closed my eyes, listening to the pattering of water on the tiles as Archie had his shower. Instead of enjoying the last few minutes luxuriating in bed, my mind was in overdrive. I trusted him – I was as sure as it was possible to be that I did. I knew that Archie, even though he could sometimes be inconsiderate and have his head in the clouds with whatever his latest grand plan was, was a kind and decent man, and he loved me. I trusted Mo and Dom. But Billy? Billy I didn't trust as far I could have kicked him, if I was having an off-day playing five-a-side footie.

And then I remembered what Daisy had said about Archie having a secret, a secret she knew and I didn't. Maybe she'd just been trying to make me feel awkward – and succeeding, if I was honest with myself – but maybe there was something important Archie had never told me. And if he could hide one thing from me, why not another?

If something happened on his stag night that he knew would be a deal-breaker for me, would I ever even find out about it?

Chapter Twenty-Three

How do you feel about secrets in your relationship?

A. Secrets? What secrets? We tell each other everything.

B. You mean like surprise birthday gifts and stuff? What's wrong with that?

C. I guess some things are best kept private. But when it's something important affecting our relationship, I'd tell him.

D. What I don't know won't hurt me. I don't care if he's got more skeletons in his closet than a Halloween party planner, so long as he keeps them there.

'Bye, Nat.' Archie leaned over and kissed me, but I could only mumble a response.

'Have fun,' I said, then buried my head in the pillow again and tipped back into a weird dream in which I was walking up the aisle to get married, only I was in my work uniform instead of my wedding dress, and it wasn't Mum next to me holding my arm but Mr Saw.

You didn't have to be Sigmund Freud to decode that one, I thought, when I eventually woke up. But some of the other dreams I'd been having recently had been downright bizarre.

In one, I was walking up the aisle with Mum, feeling radiant and happy in my sparkly dress, a circlet of flowers on my head and a huge bunch of them in my hands. But when I arrived at Archie's side, he and Mo turned to me and they both started to laugh and laugh, and I knew that it had all been a cruel, elaborate hoax and Archie had never wanted to marry me after all.

In another, I was alone in a taxi, trying desperately to find Finchcocks Manor, but I couldn't. Whichever country lane we turned down seemed to lead to Yvonne and Keith's house, and the circle of lawn round which their gravel drive swept had a funfair carousel set up on it, and all their friends were going round and round, perched on the brightly painted horses, laughing at me.

In another, I was getting dressed in the bridal suite and, instead of Daisy's former wedding dress, she came into the room carrying one of the pink flamingoes, insisting I was going to wear that with a peacock attached to my bottom by way of a train.

'It's totally normal,' Precious had assured me at work. 'Wedding stress dreams! Man, you won't believe the ones I've been having. Cyprian too – the other night he dreamed he was standing waiting for me at the altar wearing a clown's outfit. Awful. And the hours we're all working don't help. Make sure you get some rest this weekend.'

'Archie's off on his stag do,' I'd said. 'Basically I'm planning to not leave my bed from Friday night until Sunday morning and I can't wait.'

'Mind he behaves himself,' Lara had warned. 'Or rather, mind his stags behave themselves. My brother's best man had them all doing tequila shots at seven in the morning and when Duncan eventually got home the next day, he'd lost both his shoes, shaved off his eyebrows and got a tattoo of Venus Williams on his—'

Then we'd seen Mr Saw striding purposefully towards us and we'd all scattered off back to work.

At last, having slept until I could sleep no more, I rolled over onto my back and opened my eyes. My phone told me it was eleven thirty, which was pretty good going: a solid twelve hours of oblivion. On the pillow next to me, Teresa gave me a disapproving glance that told me exactly what she thought of humans who slept even more than their cats. I pushed myself up on the pillows and checked my Instagram. Archie had posted a pic of him and his four stags boarding the Tube, all grinning with excitement.

I had nothing to worry about, I assured myself. I could trust Archie. Then I noticed Billy, his fingers making bunny ears above Archie's head, a huge grin on his face, and some of my confidence drained away.

But I was being silly, I told myself. Yes, things between Archie and me had been strained recently. But that was just the stress of arranging a wedding. It was normal. The row we'd had earlier in the week was – well, it wasn't anything to worry about, was it? Not really? It wasn't something that would send him dashing off into the arms of a lap dancer (not that they were allowed to touch their clients, as far as I knew) just to spite me, was it? It wasn't... terminal?

And Billy... Billy could hardly force Archie and the others into a strip club if they didn't want to go, could he? Would he? But my own experience had shown me that Billy's respect for boundaries was not exactly robust.

As fully awake now as if I'd just stepped out of a cold shower, I got out of bed. My longed-for day at home alone suddenly didn't feel as welcome as I'd expected. The flat felt peaceful without Archie there, of course, but more than that... it felt empty. The hours I'd been looking forward to spending relaxing, getting in some self-care (okay, binge-watching *Glow* on Netflix, but that counted, didn't it?), felt wasteful and pointless instead of indulgent.

And in the back of my mind was the wedding to-do list, which never seemed to get any shorter, however many items I ticked off on it. There was the schedule for the day that Yvonne had asked for. There were thank-you notes to write for the presents that had already been received by friends of Archie's parents who lived abroad and couldn't attend. There was my own speech to write. There were gifts to buy for Yvonne, Keith, Mum, my bridesmaids and Archie's groomsmen.

When I'd shown Archie the list, he'd laughed.

'What is all that bollocks? We don't have to do this. A visitors' book? What the fuck for?'

'Apparently we're meant to have one.'

'Meant by who? It's our wedding, isn't it? We make the rules.'

'But your mum said—'

'If Mum wants it, let her buy it.'

'Yes, what about the hair and make-up trial? She can't do that for me, even if she wanted to.'

Archie had laughed. 'I bet Daisy would do it, if you gave her half a chance.'

'Archie, it's not funny. I feel like I'm drowning here. All this, and work, and I can't ask Mum to help because she's drowning too and I promised I'd help with Grandpa this weekend.'

'Nat, just say no. Just say we don't want a visitors' book and you don't need your hair and make-up practised and people can sit where they want. Look, I've got fifty orders of coffee to get packed and delivered. I've got no time to argue about trivial crap like that.'

And then – and I'm not proud of this – I totally lost my shit.

'Do you think I've got time to argue about it? Do you think I don't know how trivial it is? Do you think I care whether the menus are printed in Christmas Wish Calligraphy or French Script and whether they're in coral ink on a white card or gold ink on a coral card? Let me give you a clue, Archie. No, I do not fucking care. But someone has to make these decisions and, because you're refusing to engage, your mother and your sister are asking me to make them. No, I don't care. No, I don't have time for any of this. But I'm having to make time because you're refusing to. How do you think that makes me feel?'

'Jeez, calm down. Fine, we'll have the Christmas whatsit and the gold on coral.'

'No, we won't. Because I already told Yvonne we're having the French Script, coral on white. Because she said the printers needed an answer and you weren't reading my messages.'

'So the decision's made then. What's the problem?'

'The problem,' I said, through gritted teeth, 'is the other six million decisions that have to be made – and yes, they're all equally trivial. Do we want the guest book with the marbled cover or the plain one? Do we want floral arrangements on all the pews, or just one big one at the altar? Do you want to be wearing a coral or a gold cravat, bearing in mind that your groomsmen will have the other? Can we rubber-stamp the canapé selection and confirm whether we'd prefer organic smoked salmon with the blinis or locally sourced smoked trout?'

'Can't you just get Valentin to decide? Isn't that what we're paying him for? As opposed to, you know, hitting on my sister?'

'Archie, that's really not the point. If he decides, he'll want to discuss it over email. And someone has to answer his emails, because if you don't, he gets on the phone to you. Or rather, he gets on the phone to me. Do you know how many voice messages I had when I took my lunch break today? Twelve. Three from him, four from your mother, three from Daisy and two from the cake woman. And all of them said they'd tried getting hold of you.'

'I'd have answered, only I was busy,' Archie said defensively.

'And I wasn't?' I'd felt my heart literally pounding with anger, as if I'd run up a flight of stairs. The words were on the tip of my tongue: *As far as I'm concerned we'd be better off just cancelling this whole fucking wedding.* But I knew that once I said them, there'd be no unsaying them. The genie would be out of the bottle – the idea that I didn't want to go ahead with the wedding and therefore, by extension, I didn't want to be married to Archie.

I wasn't ready to allow that suggestion to be voiced, not even in my own head.

So I'd said I didn't want to discuss it any more, and I was off to bed. And I'd gone and lain there in the dark, seething, my eyes firmly closed but sleep eluding me, until long after Archie joined me, facing away and as far away from me as he could get.

And I'd thought, *How has it come to this? How come just a few months ago we were so in love we couldn't keep our hands off each other, and now we can barely have a conversation without getting into a row? How come my husband-to-be is off on his stag do and all I can think about is whether he'll be tempted to cheat because he's so angry with me?*

I was still sitting on the bed, sunk in gloom, too tired even to stand up. But I couldn't sit there forever. If I was going to salvage anything from this day – whether it involved wedding planning (please God, no) or not, I needed to move.

I stood up, my whole body aching like I'd done a boxercise class, then walked slowly through to the bathroom. I ran a boiling hot bath with the last of my geranium oil and lay in it until it was lukewarm, staring blankly at my phone.

Archie had posted another picture of himself and his stags, now splattered with red and yellow dye from their paintballing experience. On his face – along with smears of dye – was an expression of pure, uncomplicated happiness that twisted my heart. It was the way he'd looked when he got the keys for the shop; the way he looked after we had sex; the way I imagined him looking when he saw me in my wedding dress for the first time.

But it suddenly seemed like a long time since he'd smiled at me like that.

I thought of the three seasons of *Glow* waiting to be streamed on Netflix, of the new Lebanese place that had opened a couple of doors down from the Ginger Cat and did deliveries by bicycle, of making our bed up with clean sheets and getting back in and staying there – all the things I wanted to do with this day alone.

I thought of the long list of tasks I ought to be doing, too: the work admin I'd had to put off during the week because I'd been too busy, the endless wedding to-do list, the everyday chores around the flat I'd let slide and been too wary of yet another argument to remind Archie about.

But, I decided, all that would have to wait. Right now, I needed my mum.

And it turned out Mum needed me. When I texted, she told me she was back at her flat, not at Grandpa's house, so I got the bus there, swishing through the rainy streets, my phone determinedly tucked in my pocket rather than in my hand reminding me of all the essential things I ought to be doing and my mind whirling with worry.

I remembered how cheerful Grandpa had been the previous Saturday, eating nachos with Archie and me and knowing all the answers on *Who Wants to be a Millionaire?* I remembered how much steadier he'd been on his feet when I'd popped in to see him in between work and football practice on Thursday, how he'd climbed the stairs with just a light touch on the handrail. I'd said that Teresa would be able to return home soon (although I felt a pang of anticipatory loss at the thought of how much Archie and I would miss her). I'd joked that we could do with a new midfielder on our team, and he was just the man for the job.

Something must have happened. Something must have gone wrong.

Mum opened the door before I could ring the bell, as if she had been listening for the sound of my footsteps on the walkway outside. Her flat looked neglected, somehow – there was a vase of dead flowers on the kitchen table, a thin film of dust everywhere, and it was cold, as if she'd only recently turned the heating back on after being away for a long time. There was a sour smell of unemptied rubbish bins in the air, and she looked neglected too. Her baggy sweatshirt had a stain on the front, her lips were dry and cracked, and she smelled of antiseptic soap rather than her usual Estée Lauder Pleasures body lotion.

'There's no milk,' she said wearily, pulling me into a hug. 'Again. Will black coffee do? Or black tea?'

'Of course. Whatever you're having. Why aren't you at Grandpa's?'

'Come and sit down, sweetie.'

I flopped onto the sofa and she joined me a moment later, two mugs of instant coffee in her hands.

'Nat, I'm sorry to have to tell you this. He's back in hospital.'

'Oh no! Oh, Mum.' I steadied myself and tried to sound calmer than I felt. 'What happened?'

'He had a funny turn yesterday afternoon. They think another stroke. It was minor, not life-threatening at all – don't worry about that. I'd have told you straight away if it was. But it was worse than before. He can't talk properly.'

'But a speech and language therapist…' I began, and then I shut up. Grandpa wasn't in my care. Whoever was looking after him would be doing all the right things.

'Someone will be seeing him on Monday. They say the prognosis is good – we caught it early. I was at work but one of his carers called an ambulance and he was taken in straight away.'

'Why didn't you tell me?'

'Sweetie, I didn't want to worry you. And I wanted some time to think about things.'

'What things?'

Mum finished her coffee and stretched her arms above her head, then ran a hand over her face as if trying to smooth away the new lines of worry and weariness that had settled there.

'I don't think I can do it any more, Nattie. Living there, managing Grandpa's care. Especially not now. Before, I told myself I could just about cope. But now his needs are going to be more complex.'

'But people often recover well from strokes. He could be back on his feet in a few days.'

'He could – I pray he will. But he still needs so much help. His shopping doing, his meals cooking, the house cleaning. And the other stuff, too. Stuff I never thought I'd have to do for my own father. Getting dressed, getting to the toilet, in and out of the shower, washing even. And I think he's in pain quite a lot of the time, and I can't always understand what he's saying. There's only so much support available – you know that.'

'I do know.' I reached for her hand and squeezed it, feeling the roughness of her skin. I felt a deep weight of guilt settle on me. I'd tried to pretend that this was all temporary – that somehow, really soon, Grandpa would be living independently again, Mum could get back to her old life and everything would return to normal.

But I knew that couldn't possibly happen. What was wrong with Grandpa wasn't just a fall and a successful hip replacement operation. It wasn't just a minor stroke that he'd bounce back from with appropriate treatment. It was a steady and irreversible decline. It was age.

And I knew that Mum had been carrying the burden of my hopes, my denial that he wouldn't live forever, as well as her own sense of obligation and her love for him, which by definition was even more intense and complicated than my own.

'Nattie, when he leaves the hospital, I'm going to have to arrange for him to move into a care home. It's too much for me. I feel so selfish – I know if I was a good daughter I'd be sacrificing everything to look after him at home. But it's just too difficult. I can't.'

I thought of Max, who she'd already sacrificed. I remembered how she'd glowed with happiness when she talked about him; how different she'd looked from the weary, defeated woman sitting next to me now. How she'd given him up, even though it broke her heart.

'You're not selfish,' I said. 'You're the least selfish person in the whole world.'

'You'll have to keep the cat,' she said. 'Dad couldn't bear it if she went to a shelter.'

'We couldn't bear that either,' I said. 'Teresa can live with us as long as she wants.'

Mum pressed her hands to her face again, and this time I saw tears leaking out from between her fingers. I pulled her into my arms and held her tight, and we both cried until we didn't have any tears left.

Then I said, 'Why don't we give this place a bit of a clean?'

By the time we were done, it was evening. The flat was sparkling again, the fridge stocked after a trip to the supermarket. Fresh tulips stood in the vase on the table, although I knew Mum would have preferred the dead ones, because they'd been a gift from Max. I ran her a bath, sloshing some of her favourite freesia bath oil into it, and brought her a glass of wine.

'Do you want me to stay tonight?' I asked. 'Archie's on his stag do and won't be home until late. I can sleep on the sofa. I can make us some food. I left Teresa with a full bowl of cat biscuits and she's taken to helping herself to the neighbourhood mice already, so she'll be okay.'

'That's lovely of you, sweetie. But I'm not hungry, and I'm knackered. I'll ring the hospital and check that everything is okay, and then go to bed.'

After she'd finished her bath, made the call and reported that Grandpa was doing as well as could be expected and was fast asleep, I kissed her and left, feeling a huge weight of sadness. It was nothing, I knew, compared to how Mum must be feeling – I could only hope that, for her, the sadness was mixed with a sense of peace.

I decided to walk home even though it was late, dark and beginning to rain. I could have waited for a bus, or got an Uber, but I just wanted to be alone, the dark weight of the night sky as heavy as my heart and the drizzle mixing with my tears before they could properly fall.

The walk took almost an hour, and by the time I got home, it was raining in earnest. I'd gone out in such a rush I hadn't picked up an umbrella; the hood of my yellow coat was totally inadequate for the task of keeping me dry and my fringe was dripping water persistently down onto my nose. My trainers were squelching, my jeans sticking to my legs, my fingers wrinkled like I'd just got out of the bath, and it's fair to say I was as pissed off as I looked like I'd been pissed on.

But my plans to get in, get dry and go to bed were destined not to come to fruition.

When I approached the building, I saw a familiar little red car parked outside, at a random acute angle, as if it had squealed into the space at speed. As I watched, the driver stepped out, climbed the stairs and rang the bell, waited for a few impatient seconds and then rang it again.

'It's no good, Daisy,' I said. 'We're out.'

Then I felt guilty when she jumped about three feet in the air and let out a little squeal of fright.

'I thought you'd be home,' she said.

'I've been at my mum's place and Archie's on his stag night. Remember?'

Although there was no real reason why she should – the stag party was the only aspect of our wedding in which Daisy had shown no interest whatsoever. It wouldn't have surprised me if she'd insisted on going along, but maybe the mention of paintballing had put her off.

'It's okay,' she said. 'It's you I wanted to see. I tried calling but you weren't answering your phone and nor was Archie.'

So you just rocked up on the off-chance you were exactly the person we wanted to see on a Saturday night, I thought.

But I said, 'You'd better come in.'

She looked at me more closely. 'You're wet.'

'It's raining.'

She sniffed like that was somehow my fault, and followed me up the stairs.

'Have a seat,' I said. 'I'm just going to change.'

Maybe it was rude to leave her parked on the sofa on her own without even offering her a drink, but I was too wet to care. In the bedroom, I stripped off my soaking clothes and pulled on leggings and a sweatshirt. I scrubbed my hair dry with a towel as best I could, stuck my feet into my furry slippers and went back to join my future sister-in-law.

She wasn't in the living room where I'd left her, though; she was standing by the table in the kitchen, which was littered with the beginnings of the seating plan, samples of place cards and menus, rolls of different-coloured ribbon and wedding magazines. It had been like that for days now, and looking at it made me feel a bit sick with the enormity of how much was still left to do. Archie and I had been eating our dinner on the sofa in front of the telly, when we ate together at all.

'Would you like a cup of tea, Daisy?'

'I'd like a gin and tonic. Slimline, obviously, with a twist of grapefruit.'

'I can do regular tonic and lime. But aren't you…?'

'Driving?' She shrugged. 'I'll leave my car here and get a taxi to Poppy's place. After we're done here.'

Done with what? I wondered, but I wasn't going to ask – I knew for sure she would tell me when she was good and ready.

I poured two drinks, added ice and slices of lime, and handed one to her. Before I could lead the way out to the sitting room, she'd pulled out one of the kitchen chairs and plonked herself down on it.

'Cheers,' she said, taking a large gulp of her drink. 'I guess.'

'Cheers,' I said, taking a gulp too and feeling the fizz filling my mouth and a welcome hit of alcohol making its way to my bloodstream. I remembered reading somewhere, ages ago, that clinking glasses had developed from the days when people used to swap their drinks to make sure they weren't being poisoned by the other, and was a sign that a swap wasn't needed because you trusted your companion.

Daisy and I didn't clink glasses.

'You should go for the coral cards with the gold lettering,' she said, picking one up and holding it out at arm's length. 'And this font is much better than the other one. That's naff.'

'Okay,' I agreed calmly, locating the dreaded list in among the clutter on the table and making a note next to the entry about place cards. 'That settles that then.'

'And the canapés. Smoked salmon blinis, sundried tomato tartlets, fresh asparagus spears wrapped in prosciutto, quail's eggs and harissa lamb skewers.'

Another tick went on the list. 'Okay. Sounds good to me.'

'I've chosen the bridesmaids' dresses.' She took out her phone, flicked through the photos and passed it to me. 'The maid of honour can wear gold, and the others coral. They can choose their own styles, but they can't have the floor-length one with spaghetti straps because I'm wearing that.'

The most flattering option, naturally. And with her pale colour-ing, blonde hair and freckles, Lara would look like a ghost in the wheat-coloured satin. But, as my chief bridesmaid, she could overrule Daisy if she wanted to, I supposed, and wear coral too. If there was going to be a handbags (or rather, metallic snake-effect mini-totes) at dawn situation between my bridesmaids, I was going to steer well clear.

'I'll pass that on to them and let them decide,' I said.

Daisy finished her drink and held her glass out to me for a refill; I splashed more gin and tonic water into both our glasses and turned to the fridge to get fresh ice cubes.

'You know Valentin and I are going out?' she asked from behind me.

I dropped ice into our glasses and turned to face her, but she was looking down at the table, her fingers twiddling a card bearing samples of ribbons in almost-identical shades of coral pink.

'Yes,' I said. 'I saw you two together on the evening of my hen do. Remember, when you had to leave early because you had a migraine coming on.'

To my surprise, Daisy blushed. 'I didn't plan to meet up with him.'

'Of course you didn't.'

'Okay,' she snapped. 'I did. He hardly ever gets a Saturday night off, and the one time he did it was on your hen night. What was I meant to do?'

'Tell him you had a prior engagement?' I suggested. 'Look, it really doesn't matter. Poppy left early too. We had a great time anyway. I just wish you'd said that was why you didn't want to stay.'

'You know his parents have a chateau in France?' she said. 'He's only working at that place to gain experience in the hospitality industry. He's going to go home and run their place as a luxury hotel next year. He's going to inherit the whole thing when his father dies.'

So he's a sleaze, but it's okay because he's a rich, handsome sleaze.

'I'm pleased things are going well with you two,' I said.

'We've only been on, like, three dates,' Daisy went on. 'But we've already had the exclusivity talk. I'm going to go out there with him in summer and meet his family, after we've spent a few days in Paris. He's soooo romantic. He sent me seventy-five red roses at work on Tuesday, one for every day since we met, and a teddy bear almost as big as me.'

'That's nice,' I said, but she carried on like she hadn't heard me.

'I think it's serious with us, you know. I've been single for so long – longer than you've been with Archie. You don't know what it's like.'

'Actually, I do. I was single for ages before I met Archie.'

'That's not the point. You're not single now.'

Daisy was already more than halfway through her second drink. I didn't know what she was doing here; I wanted her to leave but I couldn't exactly kick her out. And I was hungry – there was totally a takeaway out there with my name on it, but I wasn't about to invite her to stay and share it and listen to the inevitable lecture about how many grams of carbs there were in a garlic naan bread.

Call me selfish – and I guess I was – but my relaxing evening alone had been hijacked, and I didn't like it.

'Daisy,' I said, 'I wish you'd tell me what the point is, then. I'm pleased you're happy with Valentin. I don't know him well – only professionally, really – but it sounds like you really get on, and I hope it works out well for you.'

'So do I.' Daisy looked at me, her eyes narrow slits of blue under her extravagant lashes. 'Only problem is, if it does go well and he asks me to marry him, I can't have my wedding.'

'You can't what?'

'I can't have my dream wedding,' she hissed, 'because you've stolen it.'

For a second, I was speechless. Then I heard myself gasp, 'I what?'

'You've stolen my wedding. Everything – the colours, the dress, the menu, the flowers. Everything. It was all what I wanted, for me, and now you're having it!'

She tipped the rest of her drink into her mouth, swallowed it, and then buried her face in her hands and started to cry.

Archie's sister wasn't my favourite person in the world, and she might have been spouting absolute nonsense, but there was no way I could just sit there when she was so distressed. Almost without thinking, I found myself on my feet, hurrying around the table and squatting down next to her, my arm around her heaving shoulders.

'Daisy. Come on.' I patted the shoulder of her velvet dress. 'I'm sorry you're upset. But you can't steal a wedding.'

'You can!' she wailed. 'You have! I chose everything, so that it would all be perfect, and now I can't have it because you are.'

'Look, you're being daft. There's no reason why you can't have all the same things when – if – you marry Valentin. And you wouldn't even do it at the same venue; you'd do it at his family chateau, right? It would be completely different.'

'You're wearing *my* dress!'

'I can find another dress. I don't care. I'll go to Monsoon and buy one. And even if I did wear yours, no one will remember.'

'They will! Everyone will know. All the same people would be there – Mum and Dad's friends – and they'd all think I copied you.'

'Come on, Daisy. Seriously. I know all these things were your ideas, but that's just because I didn't really care and you did. If there was time to change everything, I'd change everything. There probably still is time.'

'There isn't! It's taken months. It's all going to be perfect.'

I stood up again, passed her the roll of kitchen towel, and returned to my chair. My mind was whirring: could I really cancel everything? Give it all back to Daisy somehow? But that would be impossible, and absurd – even if I did think her bonkers behaviour deserved to be indulged, all the deposits had been paid, everything had already been booked. Only the final details remained to be chosen.

I finished my own drink and, after a second's hesitation, made us both a fresh one. She'd had way too much to drive anyway – one more wasn't going to make much difference.

Then my phone buzzed on the table. I glanced at it, resolved to ignore whatever – whoever – it was, then remembered. Archie. Archie was out on his stag night; it was after midnight and, last time I'd checked, he hadn't updated his Insta story for several hours. The feeling of sick dread – of something inevitable, unavoidable, being about to happen, which Daisy's histrionics had driven from my mind – returned in a rush.

The WhatsApp message wasn't from Archie, though. It was from Mo – sweet, trustworthy Mo, who was Archie's best friend but who I believed was as loyal to me as he was to my fiancé.

Hey Nat, he'd written. *Hope you're okay. Just checking in – has Archie come home? Only me and Dom lost track of him and Billy, and we're kinda concerned.*

Concerned. It was the mildest word he could have used in the circumstances, and it didn't come close to doing justice to the feeling of churning anxiety that had been making my stomach turn over and over all day, until I'd been distracted by Mum and then by Daisy.

I didn't feel it now though. I just felt resigned, almost numb. Archie knew how I felt about Billy's strip club suggestion – he knew, and if he chose to disregard my feelings, there was nothing I could do about it.

'What's happening?' Daisy demanded. 'You've gone all quiet.'

She was right; when I took a deep breath, it sounded loud in the silence. The patter of Teresa's paws on the floor as she approached the table and jumped up to begin her favourite game of hunt-the-coral-ribbon sounded loud too. Our accidental cat – I hadn't planned to bring her here and we hadn't known how long she would stay. And now it looked like at least one relationship in my life truly would be until death parted us.

I blinked away the tears threatening to fill my eyes, and suddenly it was as if I could see everything more clearly, not just the table in front of me and the cat's questing stripy paws. I felt like I'd been sleepwalking, allowing myself to be swept along by events and by other people, relinquishing control over my own life.

It was time to take charge again.

'Daisy,' I said, 'you need to stop worrying about my wedding. Don't you think you've given it more than enough head space? Because I do. Now shall I order you an Uber and you can go to Poppy and Freya's place?'

Maybe it was that she was pretty pissed, maybe it was the note of flat finality in my voice, but Daisy didn't object. She stood up, shrugged her arms into her little pink denim jacket and nodded mutely. We went outside together, and when the car arrived, I pulled her into a hug before opening the door for her and making sure the driver had the right address.

Then I went inside and lay down on Archie's and my bed, staring at the ceiling, tears trickling down into my ears.

But I couldn't cry for long: the restless anxiety I was feeling was too much. I thought I knew where Archie and Billy were, but I wasn't sure. I sat up, picked up my phone and started calling.

Chapter Twenty-Four

How do you deal with conflict in your relationship?

A. We're so lucky – we don't have to worry about that stuff! There's literally never a cross word between us.

B. If we have a disagreement, we discuss it calmly then kiss and make up.

C. We've been known to have some epic rows, but we're working on our communication and trying to lower the temperature when we argue.

D. I guess you could say we have a volatile relationship! But it's totally worth it for the mind-blowing make-up sex.

I called Mo first. He told me that they'd been to a craft beer tasting after the paintballing, and then on to have a curry before heading to a club. So far, so innocent. But then, he said, Billy had asked Archie to join him outside for a cigarette. When fifteen minutes or so had passed and they hadn't reappeared, Mo and Dom went to look for them.

'We walked to the Tube station and back, and round the block,' he said. 'But you know, Nat, it's Shoreditch on a Saturday night and it was well crowded and they could've been anywhere. So we went back to the club and we had another beer and hoped they'd turn up. But they didn't and neither of them were answering their phones. So that's when I texted you.'

He was back at Dom's place now, he said. It was after one in the morning and their hearts weren't really in it any longer, so they were going to call it a night.

'If he turns up here, I'll ring you straight away,' Mo promised, and I knew that he would.

Next, I tried ringing Archie myself, but, as Mo had said, his phone went straight through to voicemail. My stomach twisting with tension, I tried Billy's number, which Mo had given me, but he didn't answer either.

I called Poppy and apologised profusely for waking her, but she said she'd been up with Linus anyway.

'Daisy's here,' she said. 'And in a bit of a state. She says you and she had an argument, but she didn't say what about – she was a bit pissed and she's gone to bed. But we haven't heard from Archie.'

I got up, left the flat and hurried the few hundred yards to our local high street. The Ginger Cat was dark and shuttered, and so too was Craft Fever next door, so Archie hadn't somehow ended up back at the shop. Walking home, I felt myself veering between anger and concern. I could call the police, but what would I tell them? That my fiancé was on his stag night and hadn't returned home at three in the morning? They'd laugh at me. If I was a friend of mine, I'd laugh at me, too. Clearly, Archie and Billy were simply carrying on the party elsewhere. It was naïve to think anything else.

My stomach and my mind churned with gin, anxiety and helplessness. There was nothing I could do now. My only option was to go to bed, attempt sleep and try not to think of what I would say to Archie when he eventually returned. Although rationally I knew that he would, still I couldn't block the visions crowding my mind: of him having been mugged and beaten up, him having been run over by a bus, him having somehow fallen into the river and drowned.

He hadn't been run over by a bus, or any of the other things. Of course he hadn't. When I checked his Instagram before I went to sleep, for one final time, there was the picture I'd been dreading: Archie seated on a red velvet banquette, a look of glazed bemusement on his face, and a blonde woman, naked except for a tiny thong, writhing on his lap.

Her skin was tanned and shone under the spotlight above them. Her body was – well, it was the sort of body that, if you had it, you wouldn't doubt for a second that you could make money from it. There were tattoos, too indistinct in the photo to identify, on her back and thighs. Her heavily made-up face, glancing over her shoulder, bore an expression of deep weariness and boredom.

It was that, more than anything, that made me feel sick to my stomach. There was Archie, punch-drunk with booze and no doubt lust, gazing in amazement at her naked body. There was someone – Billy, I presumed – behind the camera, recording this moment, knowing it could bring our relationship, our wedding, our whole future, crashing down in smithereens.

And that woman didn't give a shit. Why would she, after all? To her, Archie was just another sleazy drunk guy on his stag night, whose exact level of sleaziness and drunkenness would determine whether she could feed her kids or pay her university tuition or send money home to her family in Lithuania, or whatever it was that was driving her to do a job that I felt cold and sad inside imagining.

None of this was her fault, that was for sure. And equally certain was the fact that if I looked at the picture for much longer, it would be indelibly printed on my mind forever.

I flicked my phone off. I didn't cry; I felt strangely empty, as if the part of me that had been anticipating this moment with leaden dread had now fallen away, because the worst had happened. From the end of the bed, Teresa regarded me solemnly, as if she knew the turmoil I was feeling.

Then I picked up my phone again. I didn't open Instagram; I felt like I never wanted to look at it again. But I tapped through to WhatsApp. There were no more messages from Dom or Mo – I hadn't expected there to be. And much as I longed for and feared a message from Archie, there was nothing.

I tapped on Daisy's name and, almost without thinking, I typed a message.

You know that secret you said Archie had? What was it?

She wouldn't read it until the morning, of course. It was gone three; she'd be out cold. But I was amazed to see two blue ticks appearing next to my text. Perhaps she'd got up to puke or drink water; perhaps Linus had been kicking off and woken the whole household.

But awake she was, and I could see she was typing.

The message popped into my feed after a couple of minutes. I supposed Daisy had needed a few goes to type it, and it was still riddled with mistakes. But I could make out the gist with no problem at all, even in between the random emojis she'd inserted.

Acrhei used tto die his hair brown [hairdresser emoji] wen he was at uni. And wax his chest [chestnut emoji], so noone would kno he was ginger [orange emoji]. Then he gotta girl fiend an he decided to dye his – ykno – pubes, before they'd did the deed [aubergine emoji]. Only he left the dye on too long and gve himself chemical burns [multiple flame emojis] Ahahaha.

Oh. I wondered what the person who'd compiled that silly quiz had had in mind when they came up with that question about secrets. I'd known, of course, that there were things about Archie's life and his past that I wasn't aware of – after all, how could you possibly reveal twenty-nine years of history in just over a year? I'd imagined aspects of him I hadn't seen gradually revealing themselves to me over time, the way the facets of my engagement ring caught the sunlight when I turned my hand.

What I hadn't expected was for something like this, silly and sad as it was, to be revealed to me when I knew there was another, far bigger thing Archie had set out to conceal from me.

But then, he hadn't really. That Instagram post was public – anyone could see it. And what that said about Archie, about the level of respect he had for me and my boundaries, I found my mind shying away from thinking about.

Wearily, I put my phone aside, turned out the light and lay down under the duvet. Soon, I felt Teresa's weight on my thighs, warm and familiar, as different as possible from the new, cold weight that had settled on my heart.

It felt like I'd only been asleep for about five minutes when I was woken by the scrape of a key in the front door, followed by the thud of the door hitting the hallway wall and the crash of it closing. Then I heard Archie's heavy footsteps on the floor and felt the mattress sag as he sat down on the bed.

He was home. He was here, at least, and safe. I kept my eyes squeezed shut for a few seconds, hoping he'd believe I was asleep and I could put off the moment when I would have to find out where he'd been.

But he said, 'Nat?' and reached over to touch my shoulder, and there was no way of pretending any more.

I sat up, my heart hammering in my chest. 'Where were you?'

'I was kidnapped.'

'You what? What the fuck?'

'Billy and I went out for a cigarette, and these two blokes in balaclavas walked past us. I thought it was kind of weird, but I was drunk and didn't really think anything of it. Then a couple of seconds later I felt them grab my arms from behind. They put a blindfold on me, held on with gaffer tape, and they tied my hands up too. Look.'

I leaned towards him, and in the half-light I could see livid red marks on his forehead and wrists. I could also smell stale booze on his breath and fag smoke on his hair and clothes.

Torn between anger and disbelief, I waited for him to carry on.

'They took my phone and my wallet out of my pocket, then they put me in a car and drove away.'

'Drove where?'

'I didn't know, because I was blindfolded. But it turned out to be Covent Garden.'

I pushed myself higher up on the pillows. 'Where, exactly, in Covent Garden?'

'Nat, I need you to know I didn't mean to do it. Seriously. I know how strongly you feel about the whole stripper thing and I genuinely wouldn't have… But when the blindfold came off, there was this girl, right in front of me. And I guess Billy must've taken photos on my phone. It was a prank, the whole kidnapping thing. I guess it's kind of funny when you think about it.'

'You think? I think it's the least fucking funny thing I've ever heard of in my life. Even if I believed it, which I don't.'

'Nat, it's true. I swear it is. Look at this.'

He tapped his phone a few times, then passed it to me. On the screen was an unfamiliar app – TikTok, which I knew Archie used to promote the shop, but which I'd never downloaded. He was viewing an account called BillysBantz, and as I watched a jerky video appeared on the screen.

I could see the back of Archie's head, his bright hair above the collar of his tweed coat unmistakeable even in the semi-darkness. And then, just as he'd described, two black-clad figures, their faces covered, rushed in from the side of the frame and grabbed him, bundling him into a waiting car.

Text flashed onto the screen: #stagpranksofficial.

'There's a company that does stuff like this.' Archie took the phone out of my hand. 'Fake arrests, fake kidnaps. Fake brides, even. It's a thing, Billy said, once we were out of there.'

'It's a stupid, juvenile, dangerous thing. And it's exactly what I would have expected from Billy.'

'Steady on, Nat. It was just a joke.'

'You mean you're going to let him get away with doing that to you? Do you know how worried Mo and Dom were? How worried I was?'

'I'm sorry. But I mean, nothing actually happened, did it?'

It was true. Nothing had actually happened. So he'd had a naked woman up in his face. It was something guys did every day. And did I believe the kidnap story? Now I'd seen the evidence, I couldn't not. All the same, I was furious.

'Billy,' I said, 'is a total shit. And I don't want to see him ever again.'

'Come on, Nat. You're overreacting. He's going to be an usher at our wedding, remember?'

'Archie! Jesus, how can you even consider… After what he did? You know that night when he stayed over here, he hit on me? He tried to kiss me.'

'Yeah, I know.' Archie looked down at his hands, his expression unreadable.

'What? How?'

'He said he couldn't remember much about what happened that night after we got back here, on account of being a bit tired and emotional.'

'Right. But…?'

'He said he might have been a bit over-friendly to you.'

'Over-friendly? Is that how he put it?'

'Yeah. He apologised to me. Said he didn't mean to tread on anyone's toes.'

'He apologised to you?'

'Uh… yeah. Shouldn't he have done?'

'He should have apologised to me! Not to you! I'm not your property. It's not like he smashed a glass or vomited on the floor or something. He groped me, Archie. He kissed me. It was gross, and if you hadn't been in the house, it would actually have been frightening.'

'I'm sorry, Nat. I'm really sorry that happened.'

'Sorry? So sorry you didn't even mention it to me?'

'I didn't know what to do. I felt really embarrassed for him. I'm sorry, Nat. It's not cool.'

'Not cool? No, it really is not.'

'But, like I said, Billy did apologise. He said he was really, really drunk and he could hardly remember what happened, but he thinks he might have overstepped the mark. He said it wouldn't happen again. And the prank last night… Well, that won't happen again either, on account of me only having one stag night. And the thing is, I owe him something.'

'Owe him what?' I could feel my anger building and building, so I could hardly get the words out.

'You know I told you how I met Billy?'

'You were at school together, weren't you?'

'Yeah. In Kent. It was back when Dad's business was still getting off the ground. We'd just moved to the area and I was the new boy, in year eight. I was thirteen.'

I nodded. Archie had told me before how Keith had built up the business from nothing, starting out as a jobbing builder on other people's projects, then gradually bidding for work on his own, developing a reputation for hard graft and fair prices, and over years and years achieving success and all the trappings that went with it. It was a classic rags-to-riches tale, and Archie's pride in what his parents had achieved shone out whenever he mentioned it.

I felt my anger abate a bit. 'Yeah, you've told me about that.'

'I don't know what you were like when you were twelve, Nat. Actually, I can imagine. You were popular, you were sporty, you studied hard, you had loads of friends. You were one of the cool girls.'

'No one thinks they're cool when they're thirteen,' I objected. But, to be honest, he had a point. In spite of all the normal teenage angst – never mind the handicap of a mother who was mortifyingly young and pretty – I'd had a fairly easy time of it, I had to admit.

'Maybe not,' Archie said. 'But I was seriously, properly not cool. I've got red hair. I mean, come on. And if that wasn't enough, I had really bad acne. And I was about three inches shorter than any of the boys in my class. I might as well have shown up at the school gate that first day with a sticker on my head saying "Bully me".'

'Oh, Archie. That's shit. Poor you.'

'Yeah. It was shit. I don't know what girls are like at that age but boys are pretty direct about it. They don't pull any punches –

literally. They started calling me copper crotch on the first day and escalated to beating me up twice in the first week.'

'My God. Surely the teachers put a stop to it?'

'I couldn't tell anyone. I felt too ashamed. When my new school bag got chucked in a pond, I told Mum I'd left it on the bus, and she docked my allowance to buy a new one. She always said she wanted us to know the value of money. Same thing happened with my cricket bat and even the bloody violin they bought me. Although I wasn't too gutted about that because, if the ginger hair and the pimples weren't enough to get me bullied, that violin would've sealed the deal.'

I reached over and took his hand, my heart breaking for the little boy my cool, easy-going, kind, funny fiancé had been sixteen years before. All the things I loved about Archie – his sensitivity, his quirkiness, his modesty – must have been meat and drink to those boys.

'And what happened then?'

'It went on for months. I just put up with it. I tried standing up for myself, but that wasn't any good. I tried making myself invisible, but that didn't work either. I started bunking off school and going and sitting in the park on my own, but then I got in trouble for that and was given detentions. And then Billy joined our year.'

'Right,' I said.

'No one would have messed with Billy. He grew up in a rough area, and he was tough. He knew what it was like to be an outsider, but he also knew how to handle himself. And he saw straight away what was going on.'

'And he stood up for you?'

Archie nodded. 'It didn't take much. You know they say you should stand up to bullies? When I tried, I got nowhere. But Billy was different. He smacked the worst of them around a bit, and it stopped. Just like that.'

'And you were mates, after that?'

'Of course. Really, really good mates, right up until he left after his GCSEs and I went to sixth-form college. And I was okay there, because I'd got taller and my skin was okay and I didn't care any more what shit anyone said about my hair and I'd got good at cross-country running.'

'And then after that you lost touch?'

'Yeah, pretty much. I mean, there was Facebook and stuff. We were never really not in touch, in the sense we could contact each other if we wanted to. But he moved up north and I went to uni then moved to London, and we just didn't have so much in common any more. And then he messaged me back in November and asked me to be his best man.'

'And that must have brought it all back.'

'It did. I was like, "That was all so long ago but he still feels that close to me, and wants to give me that honour." And I remembered what a massive debt I owed him. I'm not being melodramatic, Nat, but he was a massive part of my life.'

I thought about it for a second. It was really hard to reconcile the brash, arrogant Billy with a boy who'd defend an outsider against bullies, at huge potential cost to himself. But now, at least, I understood why Archie had been so willing to welcome this near-stranger back into our lives. And I understood, too, how Archie must have felt when he confided in his sister about dyeing his hair.

It wasn't just a ridiculous, vain experiment that had backfired. It was something deeper, a way of hiding pain and shame, and my heart broke for the boy he'd been.

I understood – but, deep down, it didn't really change how I felt. I thought of the past months – the snowballing of a massive wedding I hadn't wanted, Archie's distance and lack of support, my desperation to please his family at any cost – and I felt a fresh surge of the certainty and resolve that had strengthened me the previous night.

I reached out my hands to Archie and he took them, and we looked at each other. Teresa jumped onto the bed and greeted Archie with a butt of her head, and he bent down to kiss her, without letting go of my hands.

'Archie,' I said. 'We need to talk.'

'We are talking.'

In spite of myself, I almost laughed. 'Oh, for God's sake. Archie, please listen to me for just one second. There's no easy way to say this. I don't want to marry you. I've changed my mind. Or maybe I never knew my own mind in the first place. I'm sorry.'

'Are you serious?' Archie's eyes widened in shock and hurt, and I felt myself waver.

'Yes,' I managed to say. 'I really, really am. I can't go ahead with it. It doesn't mean the end for us, just the end for the wedding.'

He let go of my hands and stood up. There was a look on his face I'd never seen before – pain changing before my eyes into anger.

'You think? You think you can just cancel the whole wedding like that, after what I've just told you, and I won't feel like it's me you're cancelling?'

'It's not,' I pleaded. 'Seriously, Archie, of course it isn't.'

He shook his head. 'I guess you think I'm not good enough for you. Not good enough to marry you. Fine. I'll go.'

'What? Go where?'

'Mo's place, I guess. Give you some space.'

'I'll tell your mum and dad,' I said. My voice sounded flat and sad, and a bit hoarse, as if I'd been crying. 'It's only fair, since it's my decision.'

'Nat, you know I…'

'You what?'

'Never mind.'

He reached out his arms and I reached out mine, but somehow we couldn't connect in an embrace. We just paused there for a second, hugging the air that separated us, and then Archie turned and left.

Chapter Twenty-Five

I couldn't remember ever having sat down in Yvonne and Keith's kitchen before. There was a table and chairs in there, where I presumed they and Daisy ate their breakfast and maybe even dinner on nights when the formal dining room wasn't deemed necessary. But I'd only been in there before to ferry plates from the table, or to stick my head around the door while meals were being prepared and offer help, only to be shooed out by Yvonne in her Dolce & Gabbana apron.

But today I was seated on one of the plain wooden chairs, turned away from the table to face the window overlooking the garden. The trees weren't in leaf yet, but I could see a faint green haze on their branches that I knew would soon burst into spring foliage. A cold blue winter sky arched over everything and the sun, still low at three o'clock in the afternoon, illuminated sweeps of daffodils on the lawn, each one itself like a miniature sun.

'Of course the light is so much better in here,' Yvonne said, putting a tray of coffee and a home-made coffee and walnut cake on the table. I could just see it out of the corner of my eye, and the smell made my mouth water. But there would be none for me for a while – shoving cake and buttercream into my face wasn't an option while make-up was being trowelled onto it.

'I do think it's important to have a proper trial before the big day,' said Sonia, the hair and make-up artist Yvonne had recruited. 'I like my brides to be one hundred per cent happy with the look, and we have the opportunity to make any tweaks now, rather than amid the excitement of the wedding morning.'

I half-watched as Daisy cut herself a slab of cake and sat down at the head of the table, scraping up frosting with a fork while rummaging through Sonia's make-up kit with the other hand. I'd almost expected her to insist that she have her trial done before I had mine, but she seemed unusually subdued – and unusually keen to ram sugar and saturated fat down her neck.

When she met me at the front door, she'd seemed reluctant to meet my eyes at first, and then she'd looked at me, like it was a really difficult thing to do, and said, 'Listen, I'm sorry about the other night, right? I shouldn't have barged in like that and given you a hard time about the wedding.'

And I'd told her it really didn't matter, which was one hundred per cent true.

Sonia pulled over a chair and sat opposite me, leaning forward to scrutinise my face.

'Lovely strong bone structure, Natalie,' she said, as if this was something I'd achieved through hard work, rather than just the way nature had made me. 'The hair is a little harsh, but I'm sure we can create a more bridal look. I'll just pop the heated rollers in, and then we can get started on the maquillage.'

I nodded, wondering for the umpteenth time why on earth I'd agreed that this should go ahead. I should have called Yvonne and asked her to cancel it, but her text had arrived during a particularly brutal shift at work the previous day and I hadn't had time to reply. By the time I got home the previous night after spending a couple of hours sitting with Grandpa, well after nine, I'd lain down on the sofa to decompress for a bit and the next thing I knew I was waking up at seven in the morning, freezing cold with a crick in my neck and the echoes of a nightmare filling my brain, and it had been too late to change anything.

I stared out at the garden while Sonia wound my hair around a series of plastic cylinders. They were uncomfortably hot against my scalp, and the tightness of my hair pulled painfully, but I barely felt it. While she practised my bridal beauty look, in my head I was rehearsing the conversation I was going to have to have with Yvonne. There was a squirrel trying to break into the bird feeder, and a magpie moving across the grass in a series of jerky hops. In among the daffodils, I could see purple crocuses and the last of the winter's snowdrops, their white heads overblown and withering.

I'm so grateful for everything you and Keith have done, I said inside my head. *But I'm afraid I can't…* And that was as far as I could get.

I'm so grateful for everything… The words spun around again and again like a GIF that wouldn't stop playing, tangling in my mind with the guilt I was feeling, knowing I should have had this conversation days before.

'Now, foundation!' Sonia said. 'We'll moisturise thoroughly first – close your eyes for me for just a second, Natalie – and I'm going to use a slightly pink shade to warm you up. Your skin is a

little sallow, if you don't mind me saying so, and I like my brides
to really glow.'

*Nope, I don't mind being told I've got the wrong colour skin for a
bride. You crack right on,* I thought, as her fingers smoothed lotions
and potions into my skin. The foundation had a smell I remembered
from Granny's cheek the last time I kissed her; even in hospital,
she'd insisted on doing her face every day.

'And a touch of rouge – let's make you a blushing bride! I always
think the natural look is best for a wedding. You don't want to look
like you're off out clubbing, do you?'

Maybe, once this was all over, I could go clubbing. I'd wear
a miniskirt and trainers and dance around my handbag and get
shitfaced. Maybe I wouldn't even wait until this was all over – I'd
crack open a bottle of wine that very night and have a glass in the
bath, and it might make me feel better.

'I'm going to use a grey-blue eyeliner. I always feel black is too
harsh.'

'Not to mention a bit tarty,' said Yvonne.

'Don't be ridiculous, Mum,' Daisy interjected. 'I wear black
eyeliner every day of my life. If black suits Nat, she should have black.'

'I don't mind,' I said. 'Sonia's the expert.'

'Grey it is then,' Sonia said. 'Look up for me please, Natalie.
That's great.'

And she carried on doing things to my face, and I carried on
looking out at the garden, feeling the stickiness of my eyelashes
when I blinked, half-listening to Yvonne and Daisy chatting about
who was going to collect the orders of service from the printer, and
smelling the hairspray Sonia wafted over my head.

'And *voilà*!' she announced at last. 'We are all done! Take a look.'

She whisked the old-fashioned nylon cape thing off my shoulders and passed me a plastic hand mirror.

It was all I could do not to burst out laughing.

My face was coated in foundation so heavy my skin looked like pink wax. My lips were sticky and shiny and coral-coloured. My eyelashes looked like spiders' legs and there were wings of blue eyeshadow going up towards my eyebrows. My hair was set in bouffant curls like the Queen's.

'What do you think?' Sonia demanded. 'Quite an improvement, isn't it?'

'I… it's certainly different from what I was expecting,' I muttered.

'Isn't it a bit heavy?' asked Yvonne.

'She looks like she's off to do Drag Queen Story Time,' Daisy said.

'Wedding make-up isn't like normal make-up, young lady,' Sonia lectured. 'In order for it to look healthy and glowing in the photographs, especially if there's a flash, you need to have full coverage and plenty of emphasis on individual features.'

'Even if that means looking like a Kardashian?'

Sonia bridled. 'I've been styling brides for twenty years and I've never had a customer not satisfied. If you'd like a second trial, that can be arranged. And if you feel my work is not right for you, I shan't charge you for this session. Why don't you have a think and let me know?'

'I'm awfully sorry,' I said. 'I'm sure it's lovely really. It's just kind of a surprise, when I'm not used to looking like this. I hardly ever wear make-up normally – I work in a hospital and it's hot and…'

'The examples you showed us of your work were lovely,' Yvonne soothed. 'I just wonder if you're used to working with girls with Nat's colouring? I can see how on more of the English-rose type the colours would be really fresh and pretty, but…'

'They make Nat look like she's been embalmed,' said Daisy.

Sonia literally huffed, and finished packing away her gear. I thought of her little red Ford Fiesta parked outside and imagined her accelerating away down the driveway, feeling – what? Hurt? Offended? Furious we hadn't been taken in by her schtick?

'If you decide you require my services after all, Mrs McCoy, do give me a call. But be warned, I am extremely busy and I won't hesitate to take another booking if I don't hear from you within seven days.'

'I'll see you out,' Yvonne said, her back rigid as she escorted Sonia from the room.

'Thanks awfully for your time,' I said.

Both of them left, and Daisy and I stared at each other, wide-eyed, for a couple of seconds, and then, both at once, we started to laugh helplessly.

'Oh my God, you look fucking hideous.'

'I know! Imagine getting married looking like this?'

'When the vicar asked if there was any just impediment to you two getting hitched, someone would have said, "Yes! He can't marry a sex robot!"'

'I'm going to need a paint scraper to get this lot off. And my hair!'

'Don't brush it, whatever you do. It'll go like Worzel Gummidge.'

We doubled over and laughed until I thought I would throw up. I could feel the mascara dissolving and running down my face, and

I couldn't have cared less. It barely occurred to me that, for once, Daisy's taste and mine were entirely aligned.

Once I was able to speak again, I said, 'Thank God you were here. I'd never have been brave enough to say I hated it.'

'Seriously? You'd go to your own wedding looking like that so as not to offend some woman you'll never see again in your life?'

'Well…' I began.

'Good grief, woman. You need to grow a pair.'

Before I could respond, Yvonne came bustling back into the room.

'Well that was unfortunate,' she said. 'I'm ever so sorry, Nat. Sonia had such good reviews and I really thought it would work out, and of course lots and lots of people are already booked. I'll do my very best to find someone else. I thought, since her work appeared in *Tatler* and *Inspired Bride*, she'd know what she was doing, but clearly not.'

Daisy's words echoed in my mind. *You need to grow a pair.*

I took a deep breath. 'Yvonne, I'm so grateful for everything you and Keith have done to plan this wedding. I should have asked you to cancel Sonia and not wasted everyone's time. But I wanted to speak to you face to face because I'm afraid the wedding isn't going to go ahead.'

'Not going to… What do you mean?' Yvonne picked up a teacup, her trembling hands rattling it against the saucer.

'You haven't dumped Archie, have you?' demanded Daisy. 'Is it about what happened at his stag do? Because I thought—'

'It's not that. It's just… Planning the wedding has really made me think about a lot of stuff.' As had that silly magazine quiz, still crumpled at the bottom of my bag. Maybe it had been written by the work-experience girl, her mind on whether she was going to have a Pret chicken and avo sandwich or a Costa panini for her lunch. But even so, it had made me think. It had made me realise that going ahead with the wedding Daisy and Yvonne wanted for me would be a massive mistake. It had made me realise that I didn't know Archie well enough to commit to spending the rest of my life with him. It had made me realise that in my eagerness to please him and his family, I'd lost sight of who I was.

'Do you mean it isn't what you want?' Yvonne asked. 'We can change things, if it all seems like too much. We could have simple spring flowers and a buffet instead of a sit-down meal and a DJ instead of a string quartet. I can cancel Fenella White and the horses, even though it took me ever so long to—'

'Mother, listen to yourself! No wonder Nat didn't say what she wanted – we'd just have taken over and made her have what we wanted instead. She said no to the ponies. She said she didn't want a journalist there. And we cracked on and booked it all anyway. We've been the in-laws from hell, quite frankly, and I'm sorry.'

Daisy couldn't have surprised me more if she'd said she wanted to engage Sonia to do her make-up for her own wedding.

'Don't be sorry. It's not about the wedding. It's not about you or anything you've done. It's just that I'm not ready to get married. Archie and I haven't been together long enough. It all feels too rushed. There have been times in the past few months when I've felt like I hardly know him.'

Daisy's eyes widened and Yvonne's jaw dropped. 'Are you saying you've dumped Archie?'

'No. But we're not together right now. He's staying at his friend Mo's place. We both thought we needed some time to think about things. It hurt him, me calling it all off. That's why I wanted to talk to you myself… I feel responsible for it all, for letting it go so far. Even having this make-up trial – I should have let you know it needed to be cancelled.'

I felt a tear working its way down my face. I imagined it creating a furrow in the heavy make-up, like rain in a dry riverbed. And suddenly, all the tears I hadn't shed over the past months came gushing out of me.

I heard myself saying, wretchedly, over and over again, how sorry I was. For the hurt, the expense, the time and effort they'd spent on something I ought to have put a stop to long ago – maybe as long ago as the first time I'd glanced at that magazine in Tilly's salon.

And, to my amazement, Daisy and Yvonne gathered round me, their hands on my shoulders and my hair, patting and comforting me as if Yvonne was my own mother and Daisy the sister I'd never had.

'I blame myself.' Yvonne wiped away a tear. 'And now I've driven you and Archie apart.'

'You haven't—' I began, but she carried on talking as if I hadn't said a thing.

'You know, when Keith and I moved here from Eltham, I had no idea how difficult it would be. I thought we'd made it in the world. Keith had sold McCoy Construction and we were finally able to build our own dream home. It was like we'd arrived. We were comfortable for the first time, after scrimping and saving for all those years and every spare penny going into the business.'

'You wouldn't let me choose what colour scheme to have in my bedroom, even then,' Daisy said. 'Not that I'm bitter or anything.'

'And you were a little madam, even then.' Her mother's words were sharp, but the hand that smoothed Daisy's hair back from her forehead was tender. 'We didn't understand what was going on at first. Well, Keith did, but I think he tried to hide it from me, to protect me. He got blackballed when he tried to join the golf club – that was the first thing.'

'What? I never knew that!' Daisy burst out. 'The fuckers! How dare they be mean to Dad?'

'We had a party,' Yvonne said. 'It was summer, and we thought we'd invite some of the neighbours over for a barbecue, to start to get to make friends. We were expecting about fifty. I got a company in to do a hog roast, and there was going to be stuffing and apple sauce and a salad buffet. But no one came. Well, no one except the vicar and his wife.'

'Oh my God,' Daisy said. 'That's why we had to eat cold pork for, like, weeks. I can't stand the stuff now.'

'I learned my lesson after that,' Yvonne went on. 'I learned my place. It took a good few years before people started inviting us to things, before they let Keith in the golf club. I know we should have had our pride, we should have said no, but you've got to make a life for yourself, don't you?'

'That must be why they bullied Archie at school,' I said.

'What?' Daisy demanded. 'I never knew that either.'

'Because of his hair,' I explained. 'I mean, it wasn't that really, of course. If he'd had different hair, they'd have found something else.'

'And that's why he did the dye thing at uni.' Daisy hung her head, so her own hair fell over her face. 'Oh my God, I'm such a bitch.'

'We tried so hard never to put a foot wrong,' Yvonne said. 'All these years. And with Archie getting married, I was too focused on what people would think. On having a wedding for my son that would impress my friends. And when he found true love, I ruined it.'

'Mum,' Daisy said gently. 'It's not about you. Listen to Nat. She's just saying she isn't ready. And Archie – well, he's my brother and I love him, obviously, but he can be an annoying tit at times.'

The words sprang into my mind: *But he's my annoying tit!* But I couldn't say them, because I didn't know whether they were true any more.

'You could have the wedding, Daisy,' I said. 'All of it. The cake and the flowers and the flamingoes and the dress, obviously. It was yours first.'

'Pfft,' Daisy said. 'I'm not getting married any time soon.'

'Really? But you and Valentin…'

'Kicked him to the kerb.' Daisy flicked her hair over her shoulder. 'It's the weirdest thing. I was reading *Inspired Bride* – you know, Mum, one of those magazines you keep – you kept – buying for Nat? And there was this quiz in it, to test whether you're compatible with someone. I did it for me and Val, and it came out like, *No way, José.* And it got me thinking. I've been rushing into relationships and I don't really know who I am or what I want. So I'm taking some time to find out. I might go and volunteer at an orphanage in Tibet, or something.'

Yvonne looked from me to her daughter and back again. Then she said, 'What I think we ought to do is have a gin and tonic.'

'And another bit of that cake,' Daisy added.

And so, when Archie's father got back from the golf course two hours later, the three of us were half-pissed, laughing helplessly, and there were only a few crumbs left on the cake plate and nothing in the gin bottle.

Chapter Twenty-Six

I'd never dreaded going to work before. Sure, there had been times when I was hungover, or knew I was going to be working with a particularly difficult patient, or we were short-staffed and all run off our feet, stressed and bad-tempered. But those had always been minor things, easily overcome, and the satisfaction work gave me far outweighed them.

The past few days had been quite different. The changes had happened gradually – first, we'd been told non-emergency admissions were being reduced, and for a few days the ward was suddenly quiet. Then Lara had been moved to the critical care department. Then we'd been told we needed to ensure as many patients as possible were discharged.

Now, as I waited for my bus, I felt as if I had to physically steel myself for the day ahead. But I also felt as if I were running a marathon or something – perhaps that grim-sounding multiple-day race that people do across the Sahara Desert, where they have to carry all their own food and if they get even a tiny grain of sand inside their sock they end up with a weeping open wound and probably sepsis.

I felt like I was running that race and I'd been running it for over a week, and yet I had no idea how long the race was or when it would end.

My back and shoulders hurt. The backs of my ears hurt. My hands and feet hurt. I felt deeply weary, even though I'd fallen into bed at half past eight the previous night and slept for nine solid hours.

The bus pulled up and I got on as usual, seeing the same familiar people I saw every day. The group of teenagers on their way to school, bantering and flirting and sharing headphones to listen to music on each other's phones. The woman who worked in the hospital kitchen, who I'd never spoken to but exchanged smiles with every morning. The couple who got off at the station together after spending the ten-minute journey holding hands, except when they couldn't get seats next to each other.

It was all so familiar, part of the steady rhythm of my working days, and yet it all felt so different – as if things had changed, or were about to.

But when I alighted outside the hospital, my feet carried me on autopilot to the locker room and I changed into my uniform as usual, and as usual I made my way into the morning briefing. I half-listened as the priorities for the day were outlined. There were fewer patients than usual going in for surgery, but there was a new admission of a young woman who'd been diagnosed with an aggressive bone cancer, a handful of road traffic accidents and an elderly lady who'd had a fall while walking her dog and broken her wrist.

It felt just like a normal morning – and yet it didn't. Too many of the faces who should have been there weren't. There was an air of tension that differed from the usual bustle of the ward. The bed where Grandpa had been just a few weeks before was empty, reminding me that he would have woken up today in an unfamiliar bed in Cedar Views, and that he would never return to the home he and Granny and Mum had shared for so long.

Still, the business of the morning would proceed as usual.

'Mrs Bridges could use some help getting to the shower, Natalie,' Nisha was saying. 'You could give her a hand, maybe, and show her how to use her crutches at the same time.'

'Sure.' I scribbled a note on my pad.

'And the lady Mr Saw's operating on this afternoon – it's not an elective procedure; it's removal of cancerous bone in her tibia and insertion of a prosthesis – will need to be seen once she's out of theatre this afternoon.'

'No problem. I'll get on to Ms Melrose's stairs assessment first, shall I?'

Nisha nodded, and I waited for the meeting to end before hurrying off to find my patient.

Melissa Melrose worked in fashion, she'd told me, and her annual skiing trip was the highlight of her year.

'My husband got me into it,' she'd said the first time I met her, 'and he was none too pleased when I turned out to be better at it than him! I guess I got too cocky, going ahead of him down that black run, and here I am.'

Here she'd been, indeed, with a complex fracture of her tibia. She'd had it strapped up by medics in Italy and had soldiered on until the pain got so bad she realised something was seriously wrong. Her surgery had been performed a couple of days previously.

Like many people, once Melissa was back on her feet, she'd been apprehensive about getting around, moving cautiously on her crutches over the shiny floor of the ward as if it too was an icy slope down which she might tumble at any moment. But she'd gained confidence quickly and was carrying out the exercises I'd given her diligently and determinedly.

'Morning, Nat!' she called as I approached her bed. She was sitting up, dressed in her everyday clothes, a copy of *Vogue* magazine open on her knee.

'Hello. Good to see you up and about. Have you had breakfast?'

'I have not. There was only porridge left by the time they got round to me, and I can't stand the stuff. But I don't care because I'm out of here! I've been told I'm free to leave and Duncan's on his way to pick me up.'

'But…' I looked around. Mr Saw was walking down the ward towards us, deep in conversation with Nisha. 'Just one second.'

I hurried over to join my colleagues and said softly, 'Ms Melrose tells me she's been discharged.'

'That's correct.' Mr Saw looked up at me, his eyes bright under his bushy white eyebrows. 'Have you got a problem with that?'

'It's just – I was going to do her stairs assessment this morning, and—'

'Natalie,' he said, 'that lady is getting off the ward within the hour, stairs assessment or no stairs assessment.'

He hadn't given me a bollocking. He hadn't even raised his voice. But as I smiled, said, 'Yes, Mr Saw,' and turned back to Melissa, I felt like a bucket of icy water had been chucked over me.

Stairs assessments were sacred. No patient ever left the ward without one – until now. I'd been trained to deal with crisis situations, but I'd never found myself so deep in one until now. It would be another week – two at most, the newspapers were saying – until the whole country went into lockdown. No one knew what that would look like, what we'd be allowed to do and not allowed to do, and for how long.

But there were a few things I knew for sure. My work would change. I'd be helping people who needed not just to learn to walk again but to breathe again. I'd be under more pressure than I'd ever been before. I might be saving lives.

And I knew, also, that the wedding Archie and I had been going to have couldn't have gone ahead, even if I hadn't chosen to cancel it. But still, I knew that I'd done the right thing. I'd found the courage to stand up for myself, to say no.

But, deep in my heart, I knew that I was missing Archie.

I'd made the right decision – I knew that for sure. I'd chosen not to go ahead with a wedding that wasn't right for me, with a man I wasn't sure was right. But other people wouldn't have that choice. I thought of the other women buying *Inspired Bride*, poring over the ads and answering the quiz, same as I had. I imagined them trying on dresses that really did make them feel like princesses, planning every last detail of their special days from music to flower to cake, the samples of ribbon and acetate boxes of sugared almonds cluttering up their kitchens like they had mine.

I imagined the bitter disappointment they'd be dealing with – all those women I didn't know. And one who I did know.

As soon as my shift was over, I hurried to the staff locker room, knowing I'd find Precious there. As I'd anticipated she would be, she was crying.

'Hey.' I sat down next to her and slipped an arm around her heaving shoulders. 'It sucks, doesn't it?'

She nodded, sobbing even harder.

'It'll be okay. It doesn't seem that way now, but it will be. You've got this.'

'I just found out this morning,' she said, barely managing to get the words out.

'I know. We thought things would be okay. We thought they'd tell us to keep washing our hands and somehow we could carry on like normal. But we can't.'

'I can't get married. I can't go to Nigeria for my wedding.'

'I know. I'm so sorry. But it'll happen. Maybe not this year, but it will. Cyprian's not going to change his mind, right?'

She took her hands away from her face and looked at me, stricken. 'But his mum might.'

'His mum? What? Why?'

'Oh my God, Nat. Like I said, I just found out this morning for sure. I'm pregnant.'

'That's amazing! That's huge! I'm so happy for you both.'

'Nat, it's not that simple. Cyprian's parents – you know what strict Catholics they are. They'll freak out.'

'They'll understand, surely?'

She shook her head. I put my arm around her again, my mind racing. I couldn't imagine a family that wouldn't be delighted by the arrival of a grandchild – but then, I didn't know any families whose views were so strict.

I remembered Daisy saying, 'You've stolen my wedding.' It had been a ridiculous idea – she must have known it herself, even at the time.

But it had given me an idea: I could give Precious my wedding. Not the one at Finchcocks Manor, with all its crazy excess – the other one. The one I'd wanted in the beginning.

'You can do this,' I said. 'You and Cyprian. There's still time. You can get married at the registry office and have a little party afterwards at the pub. Keep it small, just close friends and family. There's still time to organise it if we hurry. Your mum can come out and be here with you. It'll be perfect.'

She looked at me, her eyes still liquid with tears.

'You really think so?'

'I know so. We'll need to get our skates on, but we've got this. We've got – what – ten days? Masses of time. Trust me. If there's one thing these last few months have taught me, it's how to plan a wedding.'

Chapter Twenty-Seven

It took me a week to teach Teresa to like going in her cat carrier, and about twenty quid's worth of chicken. That was okay though – I had nothing else to do after work, and no one else to share my dinner with. When I'd brought her from Grandpa's house for what I thought was a temporary stay, I'd unceremoniously bundled her into the cage before she could realise what was going on and suspect that perhaps she was going to the dreaded vet, but a more subtle approach was called for now. If the cat was going to be making social calls, she needed to be her most composed, charming self.

Like I say, it took a while, but we got there in the end. On a Sunday morning, I was able to open the door, make the clicking noise I'd trained her to respond to, and she happily strolled into the carrier and settled down, her paws tucked under her chest, her green eyes regarding me serenely as she waited for her chicken reward.

'Come on, sweetie,' I said. 'We're going on an adventure.'

While I waited for our taxi, I tapped through to my messages from Archie, but there was nothing new. He was okay. I was okay. Mo was okay. Teresa was... You get the picture. But nothing had changed because neither of us had been able to find the words to change it.

And, with every day that passed, every morning of waking up alone in our bed (and, I have to admit it, being the one to respond to Teresa's increasingly urgent demands for her breakfast), I missed him more and more. I missed the way he smiled almost all the time, even when he was sleeping, like he had happier dreams than most people. I missed the sound his boots made on the floor when he kicked them off as soon as he walked in the door. I missed his kisses and his arms around me and the way he could turn a hug into a seduction just by looking at me a certain way, moving his hand from my back to my waist. I even missed how he dripped toothpaste onto the bathroom floor, so that now I instinctively wiped it while I was cleaning my own teeth, only to find there was no need.

But I couldn't get away from the fact that I'd behaved badly. I'd let the juggernaut of our wedding plans rumble on even as my doubts about it all grew and grew. I'd projected my worries about our relationship – that this was all too fast, too much, too soon – onto the wedding itself – too big, too flash, too expensive – rather than talking honestly to Archie about what I was really feeling.

But even though Archie was never far from my thoughts, I had a different man on my mind now. The taxi glided to a stop and I got out, carefully lifting Teresa in her cat carrier out from the seat and putting her down while I popped yet another piece of chicken through the bars and pulled on my coat.

It was early March and the sun was shining, making the white gateposts almost too bright to look at. The lawn sloped away from me, sparkling with the rain that had fallen earlier and studded with sweeps of daffodils, the same stinging yellow as my coat, bordered by a smooth grey pathway. Although the day was cool, the air was still and just mild enough, so I knew exactly where to go.

Grandpa was in his favourite spot underneath a chestnut tree, his wheelchair positioned alongside a stone bench where visitors could sit or tea trays be placed. There was a newspaper on his lap and his head was lowered over it, whether in concentration or slumber I couldn't quite tell. A pencil rested loosely in his fingers, and I could see the crossword puzzle was half-completed. A tartan rug was tucked over his knees and he was wearing his favourite, shabby corduroy jacket, a scarf Granny had knitted years ago nestled into its collar.

He must have heard me approaching, because he looked up, his face lighting up with pleasure.

'Nattie! What have you got there?'

I leaned over and kissed him, smelling his familiar shaving cream and the toffees he liked to suck, much to his dentist's despair.

'I brought you a visitor. They said it wasn't really allowed, but I asked extra nicely and they said maybe, just this once. Thin end of the wedge, I reckon.'

I squatted down and opened the cat carrier. Along with her transport training, I'd also bribed Teresa to enjoy wearing a harness, a fancy black velvet affair that matched the darkest, plushest parts of her coat. I needn't have worried, though – she wasn't afraid and didn't want to run away or hide.

She emerged from the cage slowly and stood still for a second, her whiskers twitching as she took in the unfamiliar scents – and the familiar ones. With a little chirrup of greeting, she approached Grandpa's chair and hopped up onto his lap, butting her head into his hand before settling down on the newspaper.

'That's my girl!' Grandpa's smile was still slightly crooked, his voice not quite distinct, but love and pleasure shone from his eyes. 'Always wanting to help with the crossword. What's three across then? It's an anagram but I can't quite figure it out.'

His gnarled hands moved tenderly over Teresa's fur, and I heard the soft creaking sounds she always made when she was about to start purring in earnest.

'She's missed you,' I said. 'I told her she could visit, but she had to be on her best behaviour, and she listened.'

'She's a good girl,' Grandpa said. 'And so are you, Nattie. Coming twice a week, ringing most evenings – between you, your mother and your young man I've got quite the social life here.'

'My young man?'

'Archie. He dropped in last Sunday, and the Sunday before. Brought me some newfangled milkshake-flavoured stout and a pack of coffee. I shared that around – they love a coffee after dinner here. It's amazing anyone gets a wink of sleep.'

'Did he... did he say anything to you? About us?'

'Other than backing up what you and your mother said about the wedding being off? Not much. But I know a lad with a broken heart when I see one, Nattie.'

'I didn't mean to break his heart.' My voice sounded small in the sweeping space of the garden.

'I daresay you didn't. But you know what I think? I think you should have thought less about rushing into getting married and more about rushing out of it.'

'What do you mean?'

'Look, your mother explained how you didn't think the wedding was the right thing for you. And I can see why – personally I can't bear big weddings. Lot of show and a waste of money. And of course you couldn't have gone ahead with it now anyway – it would've had to be postponed.'

'Yes,' I said. 'Until the autumn, I suppose, or whenever things return to normal. But it was all just too much. It wasn't right for me.'

'So you drew the conclusion that Archie wasn't right either?'

'No. Yes. I guess maybe I just wasn't sure enough to go ahead with it all. I wasn't ready.'

'Better to realise that sooner rather than later, I suppose.' Grandpa paused, and then he laughed, so suddenly and loudly that Teresa started awake on his lap.

'What's so funny?'

'You know me and your grandmother were married almost fifty years?'

I nodded.

'But did you know we almost didn't make it to five months?'

'No way! Why not?' Horrible visions crowded into my mind – had Grandpa had an affair, or one of them come into the marriage with some terrible secret the other didn't know? I couldn't begin to imagine what that might have been.

He looked down at the cat and rubbed her under the chin, his lopsided face suddenly shy. 'She threw me out, you know.'

'No *way*! What happened?'

'Elizabeth was a modern woman, you see, Nattie. She'd been to university, and after we were married she kept her job, and she planned to return to work after we had children too, although that didn't happen as quickly as we imagined it would. But when she was a student she got involved with the women's liberation movement, as it was called in those days, and went to a lot of consciousness-raising meetings and that sort of thing.'

I remembered the photo of Granny in her flared jeans, holding Mum on her hip, and tried to imagine her as a young woman – younger than me – a fiery activist fighting for the rights her daughter and granddaughter would take for granted.

Grandpa went on, 'She asked me, of course, before we got engaged, what I thought of it all. Whether I believed in equality of the sexes, all that sort of thing. And I said, of course I did. I'd have said the sky was green back then, just to please her. But I didn't think I wasn't being straight with her.'

'Then what happened?'

'We didn't live together before we got married. My parents were old-fashioned and wouldn't have held with that. So when we got back from honeymoon and moved into our first flat together, neither of us really knew what to expect.'

I shifted on the stone bench, which was making my bum go numb, and carried on listening, fascinated.

'Well, I suppose what I expected was that things would be the same as they were in my mum and dad's home. Dinner on the table when I got home from work, my ironing done for me and all the cleaning. It didn't cross my mind that it wasn't a woman's job, even though she had another job to do as well.

'Elizabeth asked me to help at first. And I tried, but my heart wasn't really in it, and I made a hash of things so she'd end up having to do them anyway, and after a bit I stopped trying. And eventually she stopped asking, and I thought that was that.'

'And then what happened?'

'Elizabeth must have been along to one of her meetings. Because I got home one day and there was a bag packed waiting by the front door, and she said, "Robin, unless you can be an equal partner in this marriage, it's over." I'll never forget the look on her face – proper blazing mad.'

'Did you go?'

'I did. I went back home to Mum and Dad's with my tail between my legs, and Mum was horrified. She wanted to know what kind of woman wouldn't think it her duty to look after her husband and her home.'

'That's outrageous!'

'Well, I thought about it, and I realised I knew the answer. A strong woman. A woman who knew her own mind and her own value.'

'Good for you.'

'It was almost too little, too late. But after that, I promised Elizabeth I'd change. And change I did.'

I thought of Grandpa's house, always immaculately clean, his shirts always carefully ironed, the smell of furniture polish in the air, even after Granny had died. He'd kept his promise.

'I suppose what I'm saying, Nattie,' he said, easing Teresa off his lap, 'is don't throw the baby out with the bathwater. Now I'd better be going in for my lunch.'

Later, Teresa and I made our way home, where she strolled out of her carrier and settled down to wash her face, looking quite proud of her journey and happy to have reconnected with her favourite human. I found it harder to settle down. I half-heartedly pushed the Hoover around, put a load of washing on, ate a cheese and tomato sandwich and thought about watching the football, but my heart wasn't in it. The flat – Archie's flat, it would be, if we were to separate, in spite of it having been my home for over a year – felt empty without him, incomplete.

I wondered what would have happened if Grandpa hadn't returned to Granny, contrite and determined to step up and do his share. Mum would never have been born and nor would I. But, almost more importantly, the love they'd shared for all those years would have withered on the vine, their relationship over before it had properly begun.

I rummaged in my handbag and found the page I'd ripped out of the magazine all those months ago. I hadn't looked at it for ages. The paper was worn now, crumpled and dull. Ingrained creases where I'd folded and unfolded it over and over again had worn the print away so it was almost invisible in places.

I looked at the questions again, seeing my answers ringed in pencil and various shades of ballpoint ink. Had I been ready for marriage? According to the person who'd compiled the quiz – work-experience girl or intuitive genius, or possibly both – I hadn't been. Not for that marriage, that wedding, at any rate.

Was I ready to commit to Archie, to loving him with all my heart and making our relationship grow stronger and deeper, until the time came when we were able to promise to be together forever?

That was a harder question, but I was almost certain I knew the answer.

Chapter Twenty-Eight

The wedding Archie and I had dreamed of took place before lunch on a Wednesday, which was the only time that was available – the town hall official had said when I rang up to book that there'd been quite a rush of people wanting to tie the knot before everything shut down. They'd made me wait on hold for an agonising ten minutes before saying that, yes, they'd be able to fit us in so long as we didn't mind a mid-week morning and short notice, which we didn't.

I dressed quickly, thankful I wasn't wearing Daisy's enormous frock, because there was no one to help with the countless tiny buttons down its back and relieved that Tilly, too, had been able to find a slot in her massively overcrowded schedule so my hair looked its sleek, flippy best. I did my make-up the way I usually did, remembering with a rueful smile Sonia's heavy-handed bridal look, then slipped my feet into the shoes I'd bought for the occasion, flat but sparkly with delicate straps around the ankles and pointed toes.

I went to find Teresa, who'd settled down for her morning nap on the side of the bed that I still thought of as Archie's, scratched her behind the ears and told her I'd be back later on.

And then, just as I was tucking my keys into my bag, my phone rang.

'Nattie!' Mum's voice was almost squeaky with excitement. 'You won't believe what's happened.'

'What? Is everything okay?' I glanced at my watch. I didn't have much time, but I had enough, so I perched on the edge of the dining table to listen to her.

'I don't remember if I told you – I signed up for an interpretive dance workshop. It's meant to be a way of getting in touch with your natural rhythms, releasing pent-up emotions, and expressing your truth through lyrical movement of the body.'

'And meeting new people?' I suggested. 'I'm getting a sense of déjà vu here, you know.'

Mum giggled. 'Well, you know. It's something I've always thought was a bit hippie and bonkers, but I told myself, *Don't knock it till you've tried it, Emma*. And who knows when we'll be able to do this sort of thing again, given the state of everything. So I went along.'

'And? Don't tell me you met someone?'

'No. I didn't meet someone.'

I mean, come on, Mother. What were you thinking? How many eligible men in their forties and fifties would be seen dead at an interpretive flaming dance workshop? Take up golf, for goodness' sake.

But mixed with my amused impatience was a real sadness for her. Mum had found love in the most unlikely place in the world – I'd been in a fair few hospital cafeterias in my time and never felt the faintest flicker of passion, yet it had worked for her and Max – and given it up for another, deeper kind of love.

More than anything, I hoped for her happiness.

'Are you still there, Nattie?'

'Yes, I am. I can't talk for long, though, because I—'

'I didn't meet someone, because I'd already met him. Max was there.'

'What? Your Max? At some wafty modern dance thing?'

Mum burst into giggles. 'I know, right? You could have knocked me down with a feather. There were feathers actually, massive ostrich fans we had to – well, waft with. It was all Max and I could do to keep a straight face.'

'But what was he doing there? Was he unhinged by grief at losing you and the only way he could think of to express it was through the lyrical movement of his body?'

'Don't be ridiculous.' I could hear that she was smiling. 'He'd had a tip-off.'

'A tip-off? From who?' I asked, although I had a strong suspicion that I already knew the answer.

'Your grandfather. Imagine, taking to playing Cupid at his age! He tracked Max down, on LinkedIn of all places, and he invited him round to Cedar Views. Basically ordered him to come, Max said. So Max reported for duty with a bottle of Glenmorangie and they sat in the lounge and Dad gave him a good talking-to, he said.'

'But why? Max did nothing wrong. You broke up with him.'

'Yes, and I hadn't contacted him once I'd moved back home and everything was kind of getting back to normal because… well, it's not going to be normal for some time now, is it? We're going into lockdown and it'll be weeks – months even – before people can see each other like before. And I thought how selfish it would be to do that to Max again, after what happened when I was caring for Dad.'

'And he didn't try and contact you?'

'He did, at first. He left a few voicemails on my phone, but I didn't return his calls because what was the point? As far as I knew I could be in that situation indefinitely. And then Dad moved to Cedar Views and it all felt like it was too late, like I'd treated Max so shabbily he'd never want anything to do with me again.'

'But Grandpa didn't agree?'

'Apparently not. Or at any rate, Max said, it seemed like he wanted to sound him out, get a sense of how he was feeling. Because of course when Dad asked me about it, he could tell how sad I still was. It was after that that he started quizzing me about the dance thing. I thought it was because he could see I was going to cry, but actually he must've already been planning to pass all the details about what time it was and where – a dingy church hall in Catford, as a matter of fact – on to Max.'

'So Max turned up there and the two of you wafted together?'

'We did! We wafted like anything, and when the class was over, we wafted to the pub and then back to mine. And Max has just left.'

'Oh, Mum. That's incredible news. So is that it? You two are back together?'

'It looks like it. I mean, it's early days and I know you're not meant to rush these things, but at the same time…'

'You know when someone's right for you. You just do. Mum, I have to go or I'll be late.'

'Run along then, sweetie. Love you.'

'Love you too,' I said, realising as I switched my phone on to silent that if I didn't get my skates on, I was going to miss my dream wedding.

It wasn't my wedding, of course. Archie wasn't even there. It was Cyprian, tall and serious in his impeccably cut charcoal suit, a purple tulip in his buttonhole, waiting by the lectern at the front of the room for his bride.

I gave him a little wave and slipped into the last remaining seat, which Lara had been saving for me, hoping my face didn't give away that I'd already seen Precious. I was so late that she'd been getting out of the taxi with her mother as I arrived, joyful and flustered in her ice-white satin dress, her hair wound in a matching head tie. We'd only had time for a quick hug and for me to wish her luck.

In the couple of minutes I had to wait, I looked around the room. There in the front row must be Cyprian's parents, his mother serene and dignified in a lime-green coat and fascinator, his father tightly gripping her hand. I wondered if they knew the true reason this wedding was going ahead in such a hurry, and if they'd mind.

I suspected that, once their first grandchild arrived, any thoughts of exactly when he or she had been conceived would be instantly forgotten.

And soon my thoughts were forgotten, too, as Precious sailed into the room on her mother's arm, her smile so radiant it put the spring sunshine to shame. I heard Cyprian give a little gasp of admiration, and then his face also lit up in a grin of pure happiness.

I couldn't help imagining how Archie's face would have looked had it been me walking up the aisle on our wedding day, and my heart felt like it might split in two: a sad half and a happy half.

Then the registrar cleared her throat, the room fell silent, and I had no thoughts for anything other than the words my friend and her fiancé were exchanging, the promises of love and faithfulness and care and respect, which I knew they wanted more than anything in the world to honour for the rest of their lives.

It seemed to be over in seconds. They were married; the small crowd burst out of the town hall into the sunshine, laughing and chattering. Lara handed round little bags of rice and everyone chucked handfuls over Precious and Cyprian as they came down the stairs. Then everyone filed through to the garden for photographs.

There was no professional photographer that day, just Cyprian's uncle Benedict, who had a cool vintage Nikon and wasn't afraid to use it. We all posed and smiled, and hugged and chatted and posed and smiled some more. But I felt as if there was a force strong as a magnet pulling me away from that happy sunlit garden. Soon, I knew, everyone would be leaving for the Ginger Cat, where the feast Zoe had prepared would be ready on the dot of noon.

It wasn't hunger that made me want to leave, though – not even the promise of a posh gin and tonic with a sprig of rosemary in it. It was something else.

I sidled up to Lara.

'Do you think they're done with the photos?'

She glanced around. 'I reckon. Look, Precious's little nephew is having a total paddy. They'll be wanting to get a sausage roll inside that kid, stat.'

The bride was squatting down on the grass, her white dress spread around her as she tried to console the screaming toddler. Even though Uncle Benedict was still snapping determinedly away – the moment was total wedding album goals after all – I agreed with Lara.

'I'll catch you at the reception later, okay?'

She looked at me, her head on one side. 'Got something to do?'

'Yep.'

She pulled me into a hug. 'If anyone asks, I'll say you're on your way.'

I left the garden, noticing as I hurried back past the town hall steps that a small flock of hungry pigeons had descended and were hoovering up the grains of rice. I paused for a second and watched them: some nondescript grey, some grey and white, one speckled tawny brown, and one particularly handsome bird with a ruff of iridescent purply-green feathers round his neck.

'I'd rather have you lot than all the peacocks and flamingoes in the world,' I told them.

And then I turned onto the main road, where cars and lorries and buses roared along, filling the air with their fumes, and I walked as fast as I could. It took about fifteen minutes, so I was glad of my flat, comfy-ish shoes. I could have got there quicker in an Uber or a bus, but I wasn't going to give myself time to think.

Outside the Ginger Cat, I saw the chalkboard outside had been lovingly lettered with hearts and bells, and the words 'Closed for a private function'. I could see bunting and flowers filling the inside of the pub, and Alice, arranging champagne glasses on the bar, spotted me and waved.

But I didn't push open the door. I didn't even allow myself to hesitate. I carried right on down the pavement to the next-door shop. Craft Fever. Archie's shop.

He was there, of course, as he always was on a working day. His back was to me as he ran a duster over the display of artisan gins, bottles of beer and jars of honey arranged behind the counter. There was a new display in the shop, I noticed: a rack laden with bags of coffee, bearing a cool new logo I'd never seen before.

The bell pinged as I pushed open the door, and Archie turned to greet his customer. When he saw me, there was a flicker of the beaming smile I'd fallen for all those months ago, but then his face closed into wary neutrality.

'Hi, Nat.'

'Hi.' I felt as awkward as Archie looked, almost shy around him.

He put down the duster and walked around the counter towards me, his arms half-extended. I held out my hands too, but we didn't hug; we just clasped hands like two people about to dance.

'How've you been?' he asked.

'Okay. Busy. Sad. Missing you. Teresa is too.'

'I've been missing her.'

'But not me?'

His face opened into a faint shadow of his normal smile – not much, but something.

'Yeah, I've been missing you as well,' he said. 'Why aren't you next door at the wedding party?'

'Because I wanted to see you.'

'I'm glad you came.'

He released my hands and we moved together to the counter, leaning our elbows on its burnished copper top, looking at each other. Although we were two feet or so apart, I could feel that magnetic pull again, drawing me towards him. But I resisted; there were things that needed saying before I could throw myself into his arms as I so longed to do.

And I didn't know, of course, whether the embrace I craved would mark a new beginning, or the end of everything.

'I hoped you—' Archie began.

'I just wanted to—' I said at the same time.

'Carry on.'

'No, you go.'

'I hoped you'd come.' Archie's words came out in a rush, as if he'd practised saying them and wanted to get them out before he forgot the order they needed to be in. 'I wanted to apologise.'

I nodded. 'Me too.'

'I'm sorry I left you in the lurch to deal with the wedding and everything. I'm sorry I let Mum and Daisy railroad you into stuff you didn't want. I guess I thought it didn't matter; it was just one day and we might as well go along with whatever would make them happy. I guess I also thought all girls – all women – want a big fancy wedding really, and you were just being weird about it because of the money. I should have realised that wasn't like you.'

'I'm sorry I cancelled it all at the last minute. I shouldn't have let it get so far. I just wanted your mother to like me, and I thought if I stood up for myself, she never would.'

Archie looked down at the counter, his finger inscribing slow circles on the copper. I could see where its warmth left a faint trail of condensation on the metal, which evaporated almost straight away.

'She didn't at first. I mean, she liked you for you, if you know what I mean? But she worries because… you know. She doesn't want any of us to get hurt. And after Daisy had been so many times, and then we moved in together so quickly…'

'She thought I was just in it for an easy life?'

'I dunno. A bit of that, maybe. And just being overprotective and stuff.'

'And she was right. I did hurt you.'

He nodded. 'Yeah. But I hurt you too. I made you feel alone and unsupported, and I could kick myself for that. I thought if we could just get through the wedding, then they'd have to accept you. They'd realise I was serious about you – about us.'

'I was always serious about you,' I said. 'I guess all the wedding stuff just made me panic a bit and wonder if we were rushing things.'

'Maybe we were. I never expected it all to happen so quickly when I gave you that ring.' Archie's eyes dropped to my left hand, the third finger unadorned.

'I took it off. I thought, after I'd cancelled everything, and when you left, it wouldn't be right to wear it any more. I gave it to your dad, to keep in the safe with their passports and your mum's jewellery.'

'So that's it then.' He sighed, looking so desperately unhappy that I wondered if I'd ever see that smile again, feel the warmth it spread through me. Again, the weight of sadness and guilt over how much I'd hurt Archie, even though I'd never meant to, settled heavily on me.

'Do you want me to move out?' I asked in a small voice. 'What about Teresa?'

'She's your cat really,' he said.

'But she loves you the best.'

'No, she really, really loves you.'

'Only because of the chicken.'

'Nat, I… Lots of people love you, right? And I reckon in almost every case, chicken has nothing to do with it.'

'Do you mean you weren't first attracted to me because of my culinary genius?'

It wasn't quite the trademarked, unbeatable Archie smile – more a poor facsimile. But it was something.

'Nah. Amazing legs, check. Cleverness and kindness and ambition, check. Making me go "Phwoar" when you bend over to empty the washing machine, check. Skills with a chicken? Not so much.'

'Teresa thinks my grilled chicken tastes great. Clearly she has a more refined palate.'

Now Archie did smile properly. I tried to imagine a future in which that look, the total lighting up of his face, the crinkling of his eyes at the corners, the confidence and optimism that radiated from him, wouldn't give me all the feels in the world.

But I couldn't.

'Just because the wedding's cancelled, does it have to mean we are?' I asked. 'I mean, of course I'll move out if you want. But we could, like, go back to how it was before, maybe.'

'You can't ever go back to how things were before,' Archie said sombrely, his face serious again, his words twisting my heart.

'No. No, I suppose you can't.'

'But we could start again.'

'We could?'

'Sure. Like, I could bring you breakfast in bed tomorrow and not tip cornflakes all over you.'

'The next time I saw your mum I could not be covered in mud from playing footie.'

'The next time we planned our wedding we could not forget how to talk to each other like normal—'

'Steady on. Archie, I'm not ready for that.'

He smiled again, and this time there was something in his face that looked almost like relief.

Now, I stepped forward and so did he, and we opened our arms and pulled each other close. Our kiss might have been up there with the most awkward ones ever, but it filled me with so much happiness I thought I might burst.

'I'm meant to be at a wedding right now,' I said, once the kiss had settled into something more like normality.

'Then we should go,' Archie said.

'What about the shop?'

'Freddie's out the back, bagging coffee. He can mind things here while we go and celebrate.'

And so, ten minutes later, we made our entrance into the Ginger Cat, hand in hand, our faces making our feelings clear to everyone. Even though it wasn't our wedding, it felt as if we were embarking on our new life together, stronger and happier, surrounded by our friends, just like we'd planned way back in the beginning.

Chapter Twenty-Nine

Two months later

The zombies are coming! Run away very fast! But first, you grab your...

A. Fiancé, obviously. He's my world and I don't want him turned into an undead corporeal revenant, thanks all the same.

B. Um... I'd expect my other half to rescue me! But if he wasn't about I'd take care of vulnerable members of the household like elderly people, children and pets.

C. Phone. I'm not getting landed in a post-apocalyptic dystopia without Instagram, that's for sure.

D. Wedding dress. If I'm going to be shambling around with bits of me hanging off, at least I'll do it in a killer frock.

It was a significant celebration by anyone's standards, and it had been planned down to the last detail. Champagne had been delivered, the world's most sumptuous afternoon tea ordered, and decorations handmade and put up under cover of darkness so as not to spoil the surprise.

And it was worth all the stressy texts from Daisy. Worth being interrupted in the middle of a hectic shift at work by a call from Poppy saying that if someone didn't tell her sister to calm the hell down, she was literally going to murder her, first chance she got. Worth the logistical nightmare of getting me, Archie, Mum and Grandpa all together on schedule.

Keith and Yvonne were sitting next to each other on one of their marshmallow-soft cream sofas. Yvonne was wearing her wedding dress, which Daisy had sponged and ironed herself, noting that there was a bit at the back that a moth had got at, but it wouldn't matter because no one would see. Keith was in a morning suit, but the top hat his younger daughter had tried to make him wear was on the coffee table in front of them, next to the champagne bottle, glasses and vase of crimson roses.

On the wall behind them a host of scarlet balloons had been pinned, surrounding a banner that said 'Happy 40th wedding anniversary, Mum and Dad'. They were holding hands, looking slightly dazed by all the fuss being made of them. Yvonne had cried at first, but now she was wreathed in smiles.

Poppy and Freya, even more reluctant than usual to wear anything that wasn't loungewear, had compromised and were in ruby-red satin pyjamas, sprawled on the carpet with Linus, who'd recently learned to crawl, between them.

Max and Mum were on another sofa, also holding hands. Mum looked younger and more relaxed than she had for ages, although she was clearly overdue a trip to the hairdresser. She had her feet up on Max's lap and they both had glasses in their hands. In spite of me giving Mum a tongue-in-cheek lecture on the folly of rushing into things where relationships were concerned, Max had moved in with her a few weeks before. He'd told me her lentil stew was one of the best things he'd ever tasted, especially when eaten out of one of her handmade ceramic bowls, so clearly either things were going well or the man had taken leave of his senses.

Grandpa was still in his wheelchair, but the community physio whose care he was under had said that the weakness on his left side was improving, he was regaining some mobility and, all being well, would be back on his feet soon. He looked slightly bewildered to be part of this over-the-top gathering, never having met the McCoys before, but he was already more than halfway through a glass of champagne and had told me he couldn't wait for the scones with strawberry jam and clotted cream.

Archie had tried to argue that his red hair was surely enough to fit the dress code, but his sister was having none of it. To keep the peace, I'd ordered a red and black checked shirt for him and, although I had to admit that it clashed with his beard, he was still the most handsome man I'd ever seen. Reaching over to squeeze my leg before topping up my glass, he gave me one of those smiles I knew I'd never be able to resist.

'Where the hell's Daisy?' he asked. 'She organised this whole thing – she could at least show up.'

'I'm sure she won't be long,' I soothed. 'We said two o'clock and it's only a couple of minutes past.'

Right on cue, Daisy plonked herself down on the sofa next to her parents. She was wearing a scarlet silk dress – well, it was scarlet-ish. I couldn't see very clearly, but the colour looked a bit patchy in places, where the scarlet faded to a shade that was more like coral. And there was something familiar about the cut of it, the way the fabric draped from spaghetti straps that criss-crossed her slim shoulders.

'She's wearing her bridesmaid's dress!' I told Archie, whispering even though I was almost sure Daisy wouldn't be able to hear me. 'She must've dyed it in the washing machine. How cool is that?'

'So next time we decide to get married, we're going to have to have a red theme,' Archie said. 'Then she can wear it again.'

I elbowed him in the ribs. 'Don't even go there. If we ever do get married, it'll be—'

'Registry office ceremony, few drinks in the Ginger Cat, close friends and family only?'

'Correct. Although I haven't entirely ruled out eloping to Vegas.'

Archie grinned, his whole face lighting up. 'Seriously? So I might get to see Elvis after all?'

'We can go to Vegas and see Elvis any time we like, doofus. We don't have to get married.'

'I guess we can. At any rate, as soon as all this—'

Daisy tapped her glass with a pen, making a sharp pinging sound and sending it rocking on its coaster.

'Good afternoon, everyone,' she said. 'Sorry I was a bit late – I couldn't get my eyelashes to stick. Anyway, as you all know, we're here to celebrate Mum and Dad's ruby wedding anniversary. Mum tells me that when they met, she decided straight away she wanted to marry Dad because he had kind eyes. Dad tells me that when he met Mum, he decided straight away he wanted to marry her because she had amazing bo—'

'Daisy! There's no need to be vulgar!' her mother interrupted.

'What? Amazing book-keeping skills – what's vulgar about that?'

Laughter rippled over everyone's faces.

'So it's been forty years since they tied the knot. In that time, they built a business from nothing, built this gorgeous house – even if they're a bit too keen on magnolia paint – and raised three incredible children. Well, two above-average ones and an off-the-scale third attempt.'

More laughter. I wondered how long Daisy had spent preparing and practising this little speech, and felt a surge of fondness for her.

'And we're all here to celebrate that. So let's raise our glasses to Keith and Yvonne.'

Everyone clinked glasses and gulped champagne, and Daisy's clear voice began to sing 'For They Are Jolly Good Fellows'. Archie and I mouthed along with her.

Keith and Yvonne sat there next to her, staring straight ahead, rigid with self-consciousness but also looking like they might burst with pride and pleasure.

'Thank you for those kind words,' Keith said, once the last 'And so say all of us' had died away. 'As Daisy said, Yvonne and I have raised three wonderful children. But the family has grown beyond that, and we're overjoyed to have not only welcomed our first grandchild, but also to be able to count Freya and Natalie as part of the family.'

'And Emma and Robin, too,' Yvonne said. 'We're so glad you were able to be here, and you, Max. I think it's fair to say it has been an eventful year, but times like this serve as a reminder of the importance of family, and the power of love.'

'Hear, hear,' said Keith, and the two of them exchanged a look just like the one I'd seen pass between them on Christmas Day – a look that told me forty years had only deepened and strengthened their feelings for each other.

'So I guess that mostly concludes the formalities,' Daisy interjected. 'At three o'clock, we'll enjoy our afternoon tea together. But first, I've prepared a short quiz.'

'Oh God, not another fucking quiz,' Archie said.

'What? Archie, you're on mute.'

'Sorry.' Archie leaned forward, careful not to disturb Teresa, who was sleeping on his lap, and tapped the trackpad. 'I just said, aren't we all pretty much over quizzes already?'

'Don't be ridiculous,' his sister said. 'It's a family Zoom – there has to be a quiz. It's practically the law. Besides, I had to write one anyway.'

'Why's that then?' Freya asked, also unmuting herself.

'Didn't Poppy tell you? I couldn't go and work in an orphanage in Tibet, on account of there being a global pandemic and everything, so I got a job. Well, an internship.'

I felt something click into place in my mind and had to stop myself from laughing – or perhaps crying.

'It's with *Inspired Bride*,' Daisy went on. 'They were hugely impressed by all my contacts in the wedding industry, as well as my drive and enthusiasm. And the first thing they gave me to do was the monthly quiz. So if everyone's got a pen and paper handy, I'll share my screen and we'll get started.

'Ready? So, "Have You Found True Love?" Question one…'

A letter from Sophie

As I write this, we are taking our first tentative steps out of a long and arduous lockdown, preparing to resume normality: seeing friends and family, returning to work, going to the pub and the gym and the hairdresser.

Hold on – isn't that exactly what I said when I wrote my last author letter?

The past year has been relentlessly tough for pretty much everyone, life-changing for many of us and tragic for some. For me, the past four months have in many ways been the hardest: the long, dark evenings; the miserable weather relieved only by a couple of glorious snowy days; the never-ending sameness of it all.

That made it extra hard to recall those early months of 2020, when we were all so sure that this would be a mere blip, a temporary disruption of everyday life, after which normal service would resume. I remember having a sense then that the whole country – even large parts of the world – was sleepwalking into a crisis, desperate to pretend it wasn't serious, or even that it wasn't happening at all.

For many people, the most difficult thing has been enforced separation from our families: grandparents unhugged, weddings cancelled, trips abroad put off until some unspecified future date. *He's Cancelled* is fundamentally a book about family as much as it is a love story, and I hope that by the time this novel emerges into the world, those hugs and celebrations and reunions will be taking place once more.

If you enjoyed *He's Cancelled* and want to keep up to date with all my latest releases, just sign up at the following link. Your email address will never be shared and you can unsubscribe at any time.

www.bookouture.com/sophie-ranald

I hope that, wherever you are, you're at last enjoying a sense of renewed optimism: a feeling that, even if we'll never go back to how things were, we can create a better normal. I hope that, when we look back at this past year, what we remember most clearly will be the small acts of kindness, the courage of our frontline workers, the new closeness that has grown within communities.

One thing that has brought so much joy to me over this time has been the messages I've received from readers telling me that my books have had a small part to play in getting you through this. Thanks to every single one of you – and to those who haven't been in touch but who have joined me and my characters in the world contained in these pages for a few hours.

Please stay in touch, stay safe and stay smiling.

@SophieRanald

SophieRanald

@SophieRanald

Any horrific clangers are entirely down to me, and no reflection on their expertise.

At Bookouture, I am supported by an absolute dream team. My editor, Christina Demosthenous, has kept me going through the existential crises that threaten to overwhelm me during the writing process, making me hoot with laughter at her comments on the manuscript, and improved this book beyond all measure. Noelle Holten, Kim Nash, Peta Nightingale, Alex Holmes, Lauren Finger and Alex Crowe have also provided invaluable support behind the scenes on publicity, production and promotion. Lisa Horton came up with a totally on-point cover design and the marvellous Rhian McKay did a blinding job on the copy-edit as always. Thank you all.

I am also so grateful for the unstinting support of Alice Saunders of the Soho Agency. Her kindness, astuteness, wisdom and humour make her everything an author could dream of in an agent. Thank you, Alice.

I'm ashamed to say that when I am writing, I am the moaniest cow who ever moaned. Fortunately, I'm able to spread my neediness and self-doubt around a bit, with my amazing friends, my darling partner Hopi and even the cats all getting a chance to roll their eyes and say, 'Oh God, here she goes again.' Thank you for putting up with me – I love you all.

Acknowledgements

When Nat made her first appearance, as a minor character in *Just Saying*, I remember hesitating for a second as I wrote Archie's words about her. 'She's a...' A what? What career should I give this woman, who would surely only be mentioned once or twice and then fade back into her obscure place in the world I was creating?

A physiotherapist, working at a hospital – that would do.

Ooops. It turned out that Nat would grow in my imagination through *Just Saying* and *Thank You, Next*, to the point where she would need her own story to be told. And as my own experience of physiotherapists is limited to lovely Matt, who treats my never-ending catalogue of running injuries, I needed to do some homework.

Enter Sarah Hanley, who answered my questions about her work over a long Saturday morning Zoom call, revealing to me the importance of cake in hospital life, the obsession surgeons have with naming fractures after themselves and the inviolable sanctity of the stairs assessment. Thank you, Sarah.

My fellow Bookouture author Catherine Miller, a physiotherapist in her previous life, also came to my rescue when, in the later stages of writing my first draft, I realised I had a host of minor questions that needed answering, like, now.